PRAISE FOR LISA LAWRENCE'S NOVELS

BEG ME

"A strong female lead and a cracking good mystery
make *Beg Me* a solid, page-turning read."
—TheRomanceReader.com

"A great erotic thriller from a top-rate writer."
—CoffeeTimeRomance.com

STRIP POKER

"A well-written, witty and extremely erotic thriller."
—*Jade* Magazine (UK)

"Lawrence has hit one out of the park.
An erotic thriller with a mystery thread that keeps you
guessing, and a heroine who's smart, savvy, and
sexy…Naughty and entertaining."
—TheRomanceReader.com

ALSO BY LISA LAWRENCE

Strip Poker

Beg Me

SEXILE

Lisa Lawrence

DELTA TRADE PAPERBACKS

SEXILE

A Delta Trade Paperback / February 2009

Published by
Bantam Dell
A Division of Random House, Inc.
New York, New York

Library of Congress Cataloging-in-Publication Data
Lawrence, Lisa.
Sexile / Lisa Lawrence.
p. cm.
ISBN 978-0-385-34233-9 (pbk.)
1. Sex-oriented businesses—Fiction. I. Title.
PR6112.A989S49 2009
823'.92—dc22
2008037651

Printed in the United States of America
Published simultaneously in Canada

www.bantamdell.com

10 9 8 7 6 5 4 3 2 1

SEXILE

FOREPLAY: LONDON

Saturday night in the East End, and there are worse ways to kill time than watching my girlfriend dance. Especially when she happens to be a good dancer, and she's really hot. I sat watching her in one of London's secret little delights, the Smersh bar in Shoreditch (yes, named for SMERSH, the old Soviet "Death to Spies" revenge agency). Red-painted walls of a basement with Russian maps for decoration, good vodka, and rare obscure tunes. If you need a fix of Norwegian techno, this is your place, and Kim had jumped up with a couple of friends to spur-of-the-moment shake it in the tiny space available.

Kim is five foot three, skinny, with small breasts and narrow hips, a face of delicate features—a little upturned nose, small mouth, and green eyes. A mane of blond curls flying as she bounced in a tight circle on the floor, her mouth opening in a brilliant smile of laugh-out-loud joy at being alive and the thrill of moving.

Tonight she wore faded Levi's and a red-and-black baggy lumberjack shirt with the sleeves cut off, which only emphasized her petite ethereal body. She had a casual style all her own that I admired but wouldn't try for myself (can't even dream of pulling off the gamine-goes-tomboy look). We made quite the visually interesting couple, she and this tall African chick who has a dark brown complexion; round face, nose, and lips; and large eyes that can all be traced back to my ancestral people, the Nuba of Sudan. Of course, the way Kim was holding both hands of her fellow university student, Felicity, as they bopped to the music, you might not think she was with me at all.

I don't get jealous. Often. Much. No, not really.

Kim and Felicity, a tall brunette, floated back to where I sat with her other university friends, and with dramatic flair, my girl downed her shot in one go and slammed the glass on the table, laughing. "You all right?" she asked.

"Of course."

"We were just dancing."

"I know," I said simply.

Her nicely sculpted eyebrows narrowed, her lovely face frowning in disappointment. I hadn't reacted according to her script. Too bad. I knew this game by now and never cared for it—for one thing, the clumsy obviousness was a mild irritation. *Look at me dance and giggle with other girls, and I can upset you, can't I? Can't I?*

No.

She wanted me to feel jealous because she did. She resented the fact that I hadn't and won't cut off ties with certain male friends, a couple of whom, yes, are ex-lovers. My policy is you bring your lover to see your old friends, invite her along, and include her—then there is no threat, no paranoid questions over why you're visiting so-and-so. Everything is out in the open. This wasn't good enough for Kim.

She resented me calling myself bisexual, and her argument had a logic that was absolutely perverse to me—that I must be one thing or the other, that I was deluding myself, because I didn't declare a preference. I was somehow less committed to her because I'd slept with men in the past and liked it, and I can fancy a man as much as a woman. We never came to any resolution after the fights. We would just drift back to each other after a long cease-fire and go to bed.

It took me a couple of hours to realize what had set her off tonight—must have been my quiet reserve in the middle of the animated discussions of her mates. They were so . . . strident. They didn't like when I contradicted their analyses of postcolonial Africa—inconvenient for the student types that I'd been there and that I'm British-African. They didn't like me going against the fashion of completely demonizing the police when I said yes, much of that's true, I'll be the first to say it, but I know a couple of decent police officers who are trying to do good.

"You going to sulk all night?" Kim whispered to me.

"Who's sulking?" I asked in genuine surprise.

She leaned over and Frenched me hard. I pulled back, one hand cradling her face, telling her softly, "We're in public."

"Ugghh," she moaned. She grabbed Felicity's arm and went back to dancing in a corner.

It's come to this. I, Teresa Knight, have officially been accused of being uptight. Who would have thunk it?

Kim went to the London School of Economics. I thought I had fallen in love with her. I liked that she told me she didn't want to become a star player for the banks, and whilst she admitted she might end up in academia, she wanted to come up with a new dialectic, get all the strands of ambitious ideas in her head knitted together to take on the big challenges like poverty, Third World debt, et cetera. Have to confess that world saving is very sexy to me . . . when the opinions are *informed,* and when there's a focus behind the passion. I'm a pushover for that.

Anyone who knows me, of course, could say my own crusades have been accidental. I never go looking for them. I've done international courier work and helped with modern art appraisals in Geneva, and occasionally friends hire my talents to solve particularly sensitive problems. Like when they're robbed blind or blackmailed or when certain other people have been declared dead. I get into trouble. Deliberately. Frequently. You'd be surprised how often that entails winding up naked with interesting, less-than-reputable individuals, plus getting embroiled in debates over international oil concessions raping Third World countries and forgotten war crimes in struggling nations. I suppose you start to call a job a career after you start piling up the war stories.

Kim and I got involved not long after I returned from a case in America. In New York, I had infiltrated this BDSM cult, and tying up loose ends on that case literally meant tying up my loose ends, as in wrists and ankles, me nude, shining with sweat and getting lashed by leather whips. (I'm a fun date.)

I met someone when I was over there, someone who became very important to me very fast. I managed to leave New York with a couple of photos of her, because I never want to forget her face—or how I was responsible for what happened and why we're not still together. I don't pull out the photos as often anymore, but I'm glad I have them. I remember large brown eyes and lush eyelashes, hair in elaborate cornrows, café-au-lait skin. Special in every way—the things she said to me, the things she said she would do with me and on her own. I'll never see them happen.

Funny how you lie to yourself that it would have stayed perfect if it hadn't come to a sudden stop. But of course, it would, wouldn't it? You'd work at it, wouldn't you? You can steal and promise time to someone lost, time you stubbornly refuse to buy for that person you have right now.

"She's a lovely girl" was Helena's tepid verdict on Kim. At least she didn't quip that my lover wasn't man enough for me. When I pressed hard on what Helena really thought, I was told: "She's immature, Teresa."

"I'm immature."

"No, you're impetuous, headstrong, and sometimes a nuisance," she replied, striking a big-sister note. "But you don't have tantrums."

She nearly floored me with that one. "Kim's never made a scene when you're around."

"No. But she makes them, doesn't she?"

"How can you tell?"

Helena indulged herself in a light laugh. "Darling, you know I have to appraise beef all the time—take a measure of the men I send out. What you forget is I have to understand women, too."

Helena Willoughby. First acquaintance, then client, and now best friend. Beautiful, blond, late thirties, onetime hell-raiser with marauding Sloaneys and, if the rumors are true (which she won't confirm just to tease me), ex-lover of a certain Brit star known for period costume dramas. She can afford the mortgage on her five-bedroom house in Richmond-upon-Thames because she runs the most successful male escort agency in London. Rich women in their thirties, forties, and fifties will pay for company that not only looks good on the arm but also knows how to offer a compliment in a sincere whisper under chandelier light and, better still, how to prompt a moan and a shudder in the dark.

I helped save Helena's business many moons ago, and she was there to sweep up the pieces I was in after the devastation I suffered in New York. I like to know what she thinks. She's also one of the few people whom I want to think well of me.

"You know you rushed into this, don't you?" She tried to

sound more compassionate than challenging. "And you know why."

"She's not at all like *her*," I protested. "Not that you could know, you never met—"

"I know what you've told me, darling." Helena started ticking off fingers. "Intellectual overachiever, sweet, younger, not as experienced at life . . . Have I missed anything? And you know the resemblances are not the point. It's the differences really. You're trying so hard to bend over backwards to be compatible with this girl, to compromise, and I'm sure you two have many moments of joy together, Teresa, *but*—you are on the phone to me more often than not, sighing and wondering what to do with her."

"I know," I said glumly.

"Can you seriously tell me you're ready to have the girl move in with you?"

"I don't know."

"Then I'd say, my love, that you have your answer."

It was true. Kim and I were past the infatuation stage but somehow had taken a detour away from comfortable coasting. It was, forgive the pun, stranger than friction. I still don't know how the whole debate about her moving in with me started, and in my uglier resentful moods, I got it into my head it was her steering me towards the idea, guilt-tripping me into helping her out as a struggling student.

But that probably wasn't fair. She'd kept putting off the move, kept putting it off, and then she insisted that after all, she wasn't doing so badly with her roommates in their flat down near Elephant and Castle, though she did keep applying for the LSE students' accommodation at Grosvenor House. In our smoother, more romantic moments, she talked about packing and where this item of bric-a-brac she owned would go in my flat in Earl's Court—in our more romantic moments.

◆

According to the people who are versed in these things (and I do have a little experience with them myself), you never see the ones who shadow you if they're any good at their job.

If they do let you see them, it's because they want you to know. For a few weeks now, I'd been getting the creeps every so often that I had picked up a tail. Make that *tails*, because the smart way to do it is to have a team that laps each other, ones that fall back, ones that quickly skip over to pick you up on the next corner. Why I was getting such attention, I couldn't imagine. I wasn't working a case, and I was still living off the generous money I'd earned from the last one. No one should be interested in me at the moment.

Granted, it can get pretty dodgy near Whitechapel Tube Station, where we had to catch a train home after the Smersh bar, but I was bothered by the gray hoodie that conveniently lingered a few seconds too long, a woman's face I remembered back on the train now conveniently getting off at Earl's Court, same as us. A lot of conveniences in people hanging around lately, enough of them tonight to coin my own herd term—a "convenience" of shadows.

I was focused and therefore quiet, and Kim took this for me being cross with her and freezing her out. I didn't see the point in alarming her over what I thought was really happening, and whoever was following us kept a healthy distance. I didn't see the point in even trying to shake them—I was dealing with obvious pros, which meant they must already know where I live. If Kim weren't along, I'd probably start mischief, abandon going to my house, and lead them in circles, but I didn't feel like games tonight.

So we headed home in silence, the late October cold like a slap as we climbed the steps from Earl's Court Tube. That's weather in London for you. Bleak white canopies of cloud overcast the summer, and in autumn and winter you have the charcoal smear across the sky and the pelting bullets of rain. The cold and the dark made it easier for the tails to bundle up in heavy coats and hide in plain sight.

I drew the blinds when we came in, checked the bolted door.

Kim plonked herself down on the sofa and pulled out one of her textbooks she'd left earlier on the coffee table. I selected my own book to go read in bed. After a while, I heard her switch on the stereo (never knew how she could study with pop songs blasting), but I managed to immerse myself quite nicely in my narrative. I was just finding out from Christopher Hitchens why God is not great (he even titled his book that) when her voice called out: "You do know a lot, but you don't always have to remind them how little they know!"

Take a breath. Maybe do a slow count. I knew exactly what she was referring to. One of her friends feeling wounded because I'd shut her down quite efficiently during the political discussion. Me, gently: "How can she sit there and keep quoting *The Guardian* after I tell her, look, I've *been* to Nigeria?"

"There are other points of view!" she shot back.

I started to laugh, the book tipping back on the blanket. "Yeah, *The Telegraph*, *The Independent*, *The Times*—typical academic attitude. Cite sources like the Holy Bible. You want to buy what's said in an opinion piece instead of listening to somebody who tells you 'No, it's not like that', who got back less than a year ago and saw with her own eyes! You might as well tell me there are other points of view on gravity."

I heard the textbook thud on the coffee table. Kim said in exasperation, more to herself, "Can't believe your dad's a history professor . . ."

"My father has a healthy respect for common sense," I said, trying to find my place again in the book. "And direct experience."

Kim appeared in the doorway, arms folded. "*I* wouldn't know."

Oh, boy. Set myself up for a fall.

"Oh, you want to play that one again tonight," I muttered, finally losing my patience.

"Don't keep telling me about your family if I'm never going to meet them," she protested.

"You're not interested in meeting my family! You want me to out myself for you, hoping I piss one of them off so that I'm more 'authentic' for you. I'm not going to be rushed. There are guys I haven't brought around who I've dated for years—"

"You're such a coward on this—"

"No, I'm cautious," I cut in, trying not to raise my voice and get heard by the neighbors. "Why should I make my family know our personal business before we're stable?"

"We're not stable?" she asked softly, as if this was a shock.

"No!" I said in frustration, slapping the book in my lap. "Are you kidding? How often do we end up bickering like this? We go round and round in circles, and half the time I don't even understand what we're arguing about! I know you're under a lot of pressure, and I'm trying to be supportive, but—"

Tears glistened in her eyes, and she rushed over to sit on the edge of the bed and hold me. So help me, I sighed impatiently, knowing deep down I was being played again. I let it go, not because the tears worked on me, but it was the weekend, it was late, and I really was genuinely sick of our regular cycle of verbal combustion. Helena was a good friend in forcing me to start staring at the truth. Kim and I just weren't compatible. The only time we fit was when . . . It was when . . .

She kissed me hard, our tongues coiling together, and as my eyes shut, we went to our familiar place of exquisite perfect sync. Though it sounds like a cliché, she really did taste like strawberries. Probably those goofy liqueurs she chose to drink in between shots of vodka. Her tongue was amazing, playing with mine like she could anticipate exactly how my own would dart and tease. Warm, so warm, and I closed my eyes, and for a moment there was only this fusion, living through our mouths together. I opened my eyes to watch hers still shut, to see her completely absorbed in sensation. My fingertips unbuttoned and parted her lumberjack shirt and cupped her small breasts, kneading them, playing with them until the pink nipples, so delicate like the rest of her, were hard points. My God, she's so pale, I told myself for the umpteenth time, marveling at the ghostly whiteness of her body. I had her Levi's and panties off in seconds. The blond down of her mound fascinated me in the same way she and lovers of other ethnicities explored my tight curls.

Impatiently, she straddled me and began rubbing her vulva against my thigh, her eyes glassy and wild. I felt the heat from her core and watched the little bounce of her breasts as she arched her back and looked desperate for release. I took her face in my hands and kissed her again, making us collapse in a slow-motion fall onto the bed, and then I was placing two fingers on her lips below, already slick with her lubrication. Yes, yes, *there,* the *give,* and I was pushing gently inside her. Gloriously hot and wet with my pressure, and I watched her eyes close and her small mouth open as she received me. Loved that, loved the flutter of eyelashes and the high whimper. Head resting on my shoulder for the moment, the tickle of blond hair as I watched the feeling overwhelm her, light from the lamp making the delicate hairs of her mound glisten like a tiny wheat field. My girlie girl, stretching out to luxuriate in the sensation, perfect little pale tight tummy and small breasts in contrast to my dark skin. Sometimes I couldn't get enough of her feel and her taste, my mouth breathing hot on her stomach, moving south in a fervent caress of lips, hands squeezing her tits.

Kim's an ardent vegetarian (yet another debating point for us—I always joked go ahead and eat your vegetables, when the big one comes, we carnivores will consider you all nice and healthy snacks). Not to get crude, but it made her taste sweet, and I loved going down on her. I loved parting her legs and bringing my hot mouth to her gates, lapping her insistently to make her grab her own breasts with urgent need, sucking her clit in my mouth the way I preferred it to be done to me. I heard her mewl, a sheen of sweat glowing on her chest, and it turned me on, arousing my sweet girl like this. Her fingers ran through my hair, and I relished the taste of her, the tremble in her thigh under my palm. She never reciprocated, but she had other ways of pleasing me.

Far off in the living room, the stereo played a Sophie B. Hawkins classic, "Damn, I Wish I Was Your Lover."

She came in small yips and keening, an earthquake in her thighs, and her breasts blushed red, her neck, her face, screaming now, "Tee! . . . Tee!" She was the only person to ever call me that; started it because I used it to sign off my e-mails to her with. T. "Tee! . . . Tee!" Like a call, a question. Her orgasms always ignited this sudden urgency in her to embrace me right afterwards, hold me close like a child needing a reassuring hug.

"Come on," she whispered. I giggled as she reached under the bed and pulled out her most recent gift for me. I was laughing hard by the time she put on the ridiculous belt setup, but I stopped when the strap-on dildo nudged into my pussy. She pulled her shirt back and did up one button, always getting cold when she was above the covers. I loved the contrast of her femininity with the masculine shirt and the tool-belt dick.

I heard the slurp of the lubricant on the hard black rubber, and then I moaned, my girl with her arms locked, hands flat on either side of my head as she began to pump her hips to fuck me with the dildo. My fingers cupped the cheeks of her ghostly white ass, one hand moving to see if I could reach her clit to help get her off as well, but she mouthed something to me, something like *I'm okay, your turn,* and her blond locks brushed my shoulder and I gobbled up one of her nipples into my mouth, distracting her for a quick instant. Then I felt the overpowering sensation pooling in my core, building. She began to pump harder.

I screamed for her to give it to me. The dildo popped out a couple of times, and she had to direct it again and adjust her arms, and I opened her shirt once more to gaze at her breasts and belly, framed by the checked pattern, heightening the eroticism of her in that dildo getup. A new glow of perspiration was on her cheeks with her exertion, her pink areolae puffy and nipples jutting, her eyes wide and her mouth open in that look of arousal at her control, her power of making me come the way I enjoyed the power with my mouth on her pussy. It was different with girls, this expression—always a gape of astonished curiosity and peculiar gratitude.

I felt brilliantly, delightfully depraved, looking up at my girlfriend with her tits jiggling, the lumberjack shirttails like an iconic costume, dress-up butch, the halo of her blond hair and my girl's got a cock at the moment; my girl can't feel it but still it has that shattering intimacy, and fuck me hard, please fuck me hard and look into my eyes, look at me with blue eyes shining. A bit awkward but snuggling down to kiss me, warmth of skin and hair tickle again, and oh, in and out again, pumping harder now.

Kim was really sweaty, working for my pleasure. I came

loud and long, and as I crested the wave, she undid the belt and cast the dildo aside, hugging me tight. Then I felt her push her fingers inside me, hungry for the connection of flesh, not just emotional through the toy. I was so wet, and she had four fingers inside me and worked a rhythm to bring me up the crest again. Sometimes, as she confessed herself in her own blunt way, she was an "angry fuck." Now her rhythm increased with a vengeance, her other hand moving to strum my clit, and my head rose and hit the pillow again and again.

"Kim, Kim . . ." Our bellies slick with perspiration, my face in her hair, and I shut my eyes as her fingers worked me faster. Too much, too much, as if she had stripped me to the core, wanted somehow to punish me with pleasure after our squabble. She could get such bizarre ideas. *No, you're a dyke like me, and I'll prove it. I'll prove it by making you come louder and more times with my hand than any guy with his cock.* I never told her she didn't, that it was a futile quest, and it was just different with her. Ecstasy, yes, but different. One wasn't better than the other to me, and it was perverse to make me choose. I knew I was bisexual. I had accepted it. Eyes locked on each other as she wouldn't stop, a moan ripped from my soul.

Panting, spent . . .

Feeling her hug me tight again, lips on my cheek, sucking my earlobe. She made love to me the way she argued. Ours was an intimacy always athletic, like rolling down a mountain but not trying to stop the dooming momentum. I gripped her pale small back and tight ass, kissing her, still silently asking for a truce.

◆

The next morning, Kim was up before me and off to classes, and I woke up to the postman delivering a package. I knew what it was already, but it still felt like Christmas every time it happened. Here were six new smart author copies—the latest of the children's books I'd been writing.

I had created a little girl detective, Nura, who lived in a refugee camp of an African country I never quite identified (so I could make up customs and characteristics as I went along, instead of having to be faithfully accurate about one place). Nura had had some interesting adventures. Like me, she was never quite sure how she was going to get her next meal or whether she'd keep body and soul together. Unlike for me, I was always quite certain that things would turn out well in the end for Nura—the very, very end, after maybe five to ten books.

I'm not getting rich from these slim volumes, but it's satisfying seeing your name on a book, and it makes for nice extra money. I assure you that Julia Donaldson, the woman who wrote *The Gruffalo,* is definitely not looking over her shoulder in fear of me cutting into her children's market share. (Jeez, there's a Gruffalo soft toy, a Gruffalo song, a Gruffalo play that hit the West End, a new play for the Gruffalo sequel, and no doubt, the Gruffalo will be the featured villain in the next Daniel Craig Bond movie. Yeah, yeah, I know—have some envy with your explanation?)

Which reminded me that I really had to find a new gig to keep my cash flow healthy. I turned from my children's book to my address book.

No, they didn't want me to fill in for any teaching classes at the dojo, which would have been fun and kept me fit, and no, alas, the temping agency didn't have any gigs and let me down rather coldly with the assessment "You're always overseas, love." Couldn't dispute that. Hate reception jobs anyway. I thought it was Fate when the gallery in Geneva phoned me thirty seconds before I dialed them.

"You hunting for a new job, Teresa?" asked my contact.

"Great, what do you have?"

I heard a long, thoughtful grumbling noise working its way across the Swiss mountains, through France and over the Channel. "No, no, not what we meant. We're getting calls about you. You know we never mind you using us as a reference, but this . . ."

"I haven't given you guys out for ages," I replied. "What's going on?"

"That's what we want to know. First we were told it was Europol, and you know yourself they're not allowed to conduct any direct investigations, so we knew that was rubbish. And then we had one of the boys call The Hague. They say it's not them, not Europol, and we believe them. But somebody's checking up on your old appraisal cases. Remember Dupuis?"

"The forger."

"Right. You had him make a variation of Ingres's *Odalisque with a Slave*."

"Yeah, for my friend Helena. Harem art—she's got a perverse sense of humor. But as far as I know, Helena's still got it in the living room in Richmond. And Dupuis has been out of prison for seven years—he's served his time. Every one of his clients *knows* any paintings he sells now are copies."

"Your friend . . . she wouldn't be crazy enough to try to pass it off as an original Ingres, would she?"

"Are you *kidding*?"

"Apparently he was pretty shaken up by whoever visited him. Lots of innuendos and stares, as he put it. You know how he is. If it were the old days, he'd love suspicion like that and leading them on, but now he knows what it's like to be an innocent person and feel the heat. He's quite pissed."

"Jeez, I'm so sorry—"

"Well, don't be. Sounds like you haven't done anything, and he knows that. You introduced him to us and helped get him his appraiser gig—he thinks the world of you. Wouldn't hurt, however, to pop around to your friend's and check her décor."

Couldn't ask for work with them after that, not after my name was causing them trouble.

Nor did I see a pressing need to ring Helena or "check her décor." Helena had paid Dupuis a hefty price so that, forgery or not, the composition had been listed for her insurance. And the London Met's Art and Antiques Unit already knew Dupuis. Even if someone had walked into Helena's lounge with covetous eyes, they'd be crazy to try to steal it, then unload it. Too hot. No one could touch it.

Whatever was going on, this must be about more than a painting.

I went out to Sutton and put in an hour at the climbing gym, then swung back into central London for a light lunch. That ate up a good portion of the early afternoon, and my restless mind began to think perhaps it was better if I checked in with Helena and told her about inquiries going on in Switzerland. I sent her a text message asking if it was okay for me to come out to the house in Richmond, and I got a reply that, no, she needed an excuse to be in London, and I was it. She'd come to me. A couple more texts, and we had set the time for early evening.

No sooner was that decided than I got a fresh text from Kim: U FRGT, DDNT U? Yes. Yes, I had. Kim had wanted me to be an extra pair of hands for a friend's apartment move. I didn't know the girl, wasn't crazy about dragging my butt to Ealing to pack and lift boxes for a stranger and, after last night, I wasn't inclined to spend more time with Kim's mates. I hadn't given her a full commitment, merely saying I'd try to be there. I admit I hadn't tried very hard.

I rang Kim's cell phone and got no answer. After fifteen minutes, my text suggesting I could be out there reasonably soon got the reply: DNT BOTHR ITS OVR U SURE SHWD

ME. Here we go, I thought. I was no longer judged inconsiderate—I had graduated in her eyes to spiteful (the logic of her position was fuzzy to me, I thought we'd made up last night, so maybe she thought I was "showing" her and was cross with her friends). I was getting tired of Kim being offended by every small thing, but I also knew Kim's friends were closer to her than her family, who had not adjusted very well to her coming out. Maybe I could have made a better effort, especially with how rough things were between us lately. I picked up one of her favorite cheesecakes from the baker as a peace offering and went around to her flat.

Whatever resentment Kim had felt towards me, she had certainly got over it quick. As I stepped around the bend and walked up her street, she was finishing an open-mouthed kiss with Felicity, her fingers in the girl's hair. My girlfriend stood in her building's front doorway.

In her robe.

The two giggled at each other, Kim flashing a bit of leg, a joke about being so brazen on the doorstep, and then as they turned to see if any neighbors were paying attention they saw that they, indeed, had a witness. Me.

Kim's hand flew to her mouth in shock. I was frozen on the pavement, staring, glad that I was still yards away, too far to hear any pathetic on-the-spot excuses. Felicity regarded me without any guilt, any shame at all, her mouth a thin line and eyes that were empty of regret. What did she care for my hurt?

For a surreal five seconds, Kim stepped out of the doorway onto the front walk, her loose robe opening, the cotton belt slack, and I had a last glimpse of her exquisite small breast, her face blushing a vivid red. Then she remembered what state she was in and halted. Felicity took her by the arm and led her back inside the building.

I walked away. Numb. Dumped the cheesecake in a garbage bin.

◆

When Helena let herself into my flat, she found me with a cup of tea, curled up on the sofa and Seal's "Don't Cry" on the stereo. "Good Christ, somber in here with a capital Sob," she remarked, plonking herself down into the chair opposite me.

"Yeah, I've got a whole album of Seal to go, then I'll move on to Sade and then it's a mix of Peter Gabriel's earlier stuff and a few downbeat Sheryl Crow tunes, and when I start feeling pissed off again it'll be—"

"Please stop," she cut in. "What, you've made a sound-track for suicides? You didn't sound this down in your texts—well, not that you can ever tell too much from those."

"No, no, I didn't call you about personal business," I answered, and then I went into the whole saga of the gallery and the painting. Helena's expression was one of complete bafflement, exactly what I'd expected.

"It's still in the living room where it always is," she said, shaking her head. "Huh. I've been having odd things happen as well."

"Such as?"

She waved this away, dismissing it. "Oh, that can wait. What is this? What's up with you? Why the marathon moping?"

I briefed her. It was so implausible to me that someone can be stupid enough to be caught in the actual, *literal* act of infidelity. Like something out of the movies, I said. I guess I'd learned my lesson.

Helena listened, never interrupting, and finally let a long stream of air out of her cheeks. "Well, you know my opinion of her, darling. That's the one good thing about cheating. It defines things quite clearly. No wondering later if you made the right decision to break up."

"You've never given a lover a second chance?"

"Good lord, no! If you both go in with no strings, that's a different matter, but if there's an understanding of commit-ment . . . Teresa, this girl talked about moving in with you! Don't tell me you're going to be bloody stupid and take her back? Has she phoned?"

"No."

Helena was cynical. "Probably saving the case for the de-fense until tomorrow. After you've cooled down and started to miss her."

"I do miss her."

"No, Teresa, my love, you do not. You miss having *some-one*. It's so abundantly clear to those who love you that you went out and shopped for a person you could cherish and protect, someone like your American girl. You made do with Kim, and to be honest, we've all been quite worried about you. We understand—you were overwhelmingly grateful for not sleeping alone. That's human. But we all dreaded you might go on for years picking up shattered plates after tantrums and apologizing for her constant drama."

"When you say all, you mean . . . ?"

"I mean all."

I ducked my head a little, embarrassed. "Not my best choice, I suppose."

"Let's just say you're more fun when you're racing for a connecting flight and leaving lovers grateful but dizzy in hotel rooms."

"Maybe I need a case," I murmured.

"I need a movie," said Helena, getting up. "Go out or rent a DVD?"

"Self-pity makes me lazy," I answered. "Let's rent. There's a Blockbuster in the high street. Food?"

"Chinese?"

"Settled."

"No, no, there's the issue of drinks," Helena reminded me. With Helena there is always an issue of drinks. Positively amazing capacity to imbibe. She doesn't drink men under the table—she drinks them into the basement.

"What's a post-breakup drink that goes with Chinese food?"

Helena appeared to give this serious thought as she wandered into the kitchen and began opening cabinets. "Very good question. I want to say vodka. Let me check your storage facilities."

I was busy switching off the stereo, peeking through the windows and checking to see if it was raining again when Helena's distant voice hit a higher octave, one of sudden stress. "Darling, who is this girl?"

I went in to see who she meant. A photo on my fridge: me, Kim, a few of her friends. "*That* is Felicity Eden," I answered, my voice dead. "Kim's new slut." I yanked the photo out from its magnet, preparing to rip it up.

Helena gently put her hand over mine to stop me. She looked pale. "I think you and I have a larger problem."

"What do you mean?"

"This can't be coincidence."

"What? What is it?"

She took the picture from me, her finger pointing at Felicity. "About a month ago, this young woman called the agency, wanting an escort. First-timer, so we went through our screening process for clients as usual. Wore a thick pair of spectacles, looked a little frumpy but not too bad. Still, she's not even close to our regular client profile—way too young, too much money without a corporation or a family peerage attached, too convenient. You know the rare young ones who do come in either *reek* of confidence and think it's a big laugh, or they have too little. Now *she*"—another tap of the finger—"felt like a cop setup. I was completely baffled. I pay off all the right people."

"Maybe I should give Carl Norton a call," I offered. Carl was a friend. He was also a detective inspector, worked Homicide. He'd met Helena and a few others in her circle back during the infamous strip poker case.

"No," sighed Helena. "Don't do that. He'll think I'm trying to get special treatment, use his influence to get me out of a fix—"

"But you're not," I argued. "You just want to know if it's a police operation."

"Which in itself could be construed as a favor," said Helena. "Him tipping me off. You're the one to find out who she is, Teresa. And she's given you cause now."

"Ha! As far as I'm concerned Kim can have her! But it's not good if she comes sniffing around the agency. I have to say, darling, my problem is Carl's the first person I'd normally bother for help."

"It doesn't make sense," said Helena in exasperation. "You don't work for me, and she must have figured out by now that you're not one of my clients. What's her game in seducing your partner? I've always been very careful with my men, the books are as clean as I can make them, and I haven't had a problem since all that blackmail and murder a couple of years ago."

"Maybe it's not about you and the agency."

"That leaves you. What have you done?"

"I don't know," I said. "I think I'll ask Felicity. But first I need to find out who she is."

◆

The next day I made progress—but only in finding out who Felicity wasn't. Helena was probably right that I shouldn't bother Carl with this, at least not yet. Fortunately, I had my own reliable contact in Europol, a girlfriend who declared straight up that Kim's new lover wasn't on their agent list.

What next? Well, as Kim had so recently reminded me, my father's a professor. I don't often go running to Daddy, but he knew the right people over at the London School of Economics and within half a day I had a partial profile of Felicity Eden.

Scanning the material passed on to me at home. I noted sixteen phone messages from Kim. I took a few minutes out to listen to them all, then deleted them. My friend Steve had already come over at ten in the morning to replace the locks.

Back to the mystery of Felicity Eden. She fared well, rather too well, at her studies. One recent dark cloud was an allegation of plagiarism over a certain paper, but that went away. According to Daddy's sources, there were those in the halls of academia still wondering about that one. They were also wondering how Felicity Eden even managed to plagiarize the source at all, since it was apparently an internal economics report written by an analyst for Orpheocon. Her prof had noticed because he did occasional consulting work for the Octopus, as critics like to call the oil conglomerate (I prefer to call it the Forces of Darkness).

What the hell was going on?

Time to pay a visit to the address I had for Felicity, according to the information given to the LSE.

When I say pay a visit to the address, I meant just that. Since most people find the breaking and entering of their house traumatic, I try to be considerate and do it when they're not at home. I had no idea of her personal schedule, but I imagined that she was at least *supposed* to be at classes. I took a chance.

I anticipated a couple of obstacles. The first was that if I'd been followed the other night after Smersh, there was a good chance I'd be followed again today. And I didn't need any witnesses to what I was about to do. My tails were obviously very good—good enough to make me believe for a couple of days that I was just being paranoid—and I only thought I had a sure bead on one of them this afternoon. I needed to get down to Elephant and Castle, where Felicity's place was supposed to be (convenient proximity to Kim's flat, I thought bitterly). The quickest route was to jump on the Tube, take the District Line, and change at Embankment to the Bakerloo. I wasn't interested in the quickest route. I dragged my shadow friends on a merry chase over to Southwark.

The beauty of Southwark Station is that it's so big and shiny and relatively new. It has these wide concourses where at the right time if anybody wants to tail you they'll be quite out in the open and exposed. They're forced to fall back, which is when you duck into some nifty hiding spots (if you've planned ahead) and change direction.

This is how I amuse myself during train delays. Other people daydream, plan an evening meal, listen to their iPod, or play a game on their cell phone. Me, I figure out the best places to lose surveillance. According to Helena, this does not qualify as a "hobby."

So far, so good. It didn't take long to lose my convenience of shadows.

Free and clear, I had to meet my second obstacle. Students tend to be poor, and when you're poor, you usually live in tight spots where there's bound to be little privacy. I knew from Kim that Felicity lived alone, so I expected to find a sad bedsit on a council estate or a basement rip-off not worth its deposit. There might be older neighbors having a smoke out front and students at home in their own flats, keeping odd hours. So I'd have to work fast scrubbing the lock (yes, that's pro speak for locksmiths—and burglars). That's if I didn't want to draw attention or take too long, which would mean I'd be a memorable visitor.

Here's where it gets surreal. Felicity Eden's home address

turned out to be a doctor's clinic. No sign of any residential tenant on a higher floor or in a basement. Odder still was the fact that the clinic was shut in the middle of the week. I pulled out my cell phone and dialed the office number. No surprise I got an answering machine. All right, I thought, we'll take a quick look. If we see framed diplomas, well-trodden carpeting, and year-old issues of *Ideal Home,* we know somebody made a mix-up, likely me.

Took me thirty seconds. Hard lock. Then I was in, even more confused. No reception area, no examination rooms with any pressure cuffs, no equipment *at all*. But yeah, you could call it sterile. Not one photo of an occupant, no ash-tray, not even a dirty tea towel left in the kitchen. Dishes all neatly stacked in cabinets. I was about to switch on the computer when my phone rang. No ID offered.

"Hello?"

A male voice, very smug, enjoying himself: "At first we thought it was your romantic loss that prompted you to dig into Miss Eden's background, but I think we should give you more credit. You ditched our surveillance."

"You picked up my trail quick enough," I replied. "My obvious next step was to come here."

"True, you couldn't know we'd anticipate that."

Patronizing bugger.

"Miss Knight, you won't find anything on that computer. It has an emergency broadband connection and a program that wipes most of its hard drive clean when it shuts down."

I sighed. "Cameras watching me right now."

"Quite correct."

I walked out the door and closed it behind me. A convenience of shadows waiting.

◆

A huddle of them stood with their umbrellas open in the cold drizzle. Four men and two women in the drabbest business clothing imaginable, very tweedy, and this small phalanx would have been comical if they didn't have me bang to rights for breaking into the house.

I didn't know who to address, couldn't yet match the voice on the phone with a face, so I threw out the question to all. "Are you going to tell me now why you're harassing my friends and everyone I know?"

A man two inches shorter than me with receding hair, a weak chin, and eyes of a washed-out gray dabbed the corners of his mouth with a handkerchief. " 'Harass' is rather exaggerating it, don't you think?"

He never looked me in the eye, always at my shoes or down the road. There was a teardrop-shaped stain on his paisley tie, and I imagined it was old blood.

"No, I don't," I answered.

He made a little irritable grimace at that. I got the sense he wasn't used to people contradicting him.

"My name is Desmond Hodd," he announced, as if I ought to be impressed, which was odd considering the next thing he was about to tell me. "We're MI6."

Oddly enough, this wasn't the first time someone had tried to sell me that one. "Of course, you are," I drawled. "And I'm with Cirque du Soleil."

"You normally have this response to authority?"

"No, give me a couple of drinks, and I can manage open contempt."

"You might wish to rein in the attitude, Miss Knight, seeing as though we're a potential client."

"You're the government's cloak-and-dagger team," I said, "and *you* want to hire *me* as a detective?"

"That's right."

And so help me, I burst out laughing, long and loud, on the street. The trouble was, he was perfectly serious.

◆

I was invited to sit in Hodd's limousine. I didn't know spy-masters get limousines. Hodd booted up a computer note-book as he asked, "Have you ever heard of a man named Luis Antunes?"

"Any reason I should?"

"Not particularly. He's building a small reputation in the independent film world—to be more precise, soft-core porn. Pretensions to plot for the large-budget ones, though he doesn't bother with it for the on-line video download samples."

"What's your interest?"

"Better to show you," said Hodd, and he hit the enter key. Windows Media Player started a full-screen movie, and I got the idea quickly.

"I've seen porn, thanks," I snapped. "And if there are any children or other evils in this, please turn it off. I don't need those images in my head or—"

"No, nothing like that," he cut in.

I watched for a full two minutes and couldn't find any-thing remarkable or attention-getting. Girl-on-girl action, girl-boy-girl, two guys and a girl, some female wailing that sounded authentic, some obviously fake, many of the women not looking like they enjoyed themselves.

There was quite a rainbow of black and mixed-race girls. It was clear from the off-camera remarks in a foreign lan-guage, too far from the mic to identify, that this probably wasn't shot in London. That and the gorgeous sunshine spilling in through the windows in the background. I wor-ried for a moment that Hodd was setting me up for the shock of a genuine snuff film, but no, the video rolled on, orgasms abounded, and The End.

"Sorry, still not clued in," I said at last.

"The movies Antunes puts his name on over here are all
aboveboard, with young women—for better or for worse—
choosing to do what they do," explained Hodd. "*These*
women, the ones you just saw, well . . . We've suspected for
some time that many if not all have been forced into prostitution and into having sex on screen. He doesn't officially
import the films—we think he gets them through an underground pirate DVD network."

"Unless I'm very wrong, this looks like it wasn't shot in
the UK," I said. "And if I'm right, well, yeah, it's deplorable,
but what can you possibly do about it?"

"Trust me, we'll drop the whole weight of international
law on him if we confirm it."

I still couldn't believe what I was hearing. "I don't get
this at all. Why should MI6 care about a porn merchant?
Yes, he's an evil little shit if your allegations are true, but
this has nothing to do with espionage or foreign intelligence."

"That's not your concern."

"Everything's my concern when it comes to my clients."

"Not this."

"Then find someone else," I said, and I opened the door
and stepped out of the car.

"There is no one else," replied Hodd, clumsily following
me. An umbrella instantly came to the rescue from his entourage. Heaven forbid his wispy comb-over got damp.
"Believe it or not, we don't train operations officers for situations like this one."

"So I shouldn't believe what I see in the movies? The
scenes where they show a seductive spy nicking the micro-
film as she snogs the enemy?"

Hodd ignored my sarcasm. "Let us just say you have experience with hypersexualized scenarios. That strip poker
nonsense—you did a very neat job of keeping the high and

the mighty out of the tabloids. Of course, we've kept an eye on your old radical friend Janet Marshall for a long time, but you couldn't know that—"

"I'd hardly call Britain's High Commissioner to South Africa radical."

He sneered at that one and pressed on. "We haven't quite confirmed what the New York authorities say about you. They're a little confused themselves over the more lurid details. In any case, you handle yourself reasonably well; you think on your feet, though you can make bloody stupid mistakes like the one that cost—"

"*Don't,*" I said, my voice tight. He was hitting a nerve that I didn't want touched. I tried to stay calm. "You actually believe that because of what I did in those cases I'll walk into this porn merchant's studio and take off my clothes for Queen and country?"

"No, no," he said quickly in an astonished voice. I think he wasn't lying—maybe the suggestion really hadn't occurred to him. "We're not asking you to go undercover as one of his girls. We think he'd see through that. You're too confident, and too old."

"Really?" I said, folding my arms. This was a milestone Mum had never warned me about. *There will come a time in your life, Teresa, when you will be too old to be exploited in pornography. Sorry, darling, but there it is.*

The foot-in-mouth occurred to him on time delay. One, two . . . There it is: a hard swallow, eyes still looking away, but this time with purpose. Even spymasters know better than to wound a woman's vanity. "Now listen, I only meant these girls are often nineteen, twenty—the cutoff he has for them is usually twenty-four."

"Uh-huh. So what are you expecting me to do?"

"We want you to apply for his production crew, as a film editor. Don't worry, we'll train you on the latest computer editing systems. That means you'll see raw footage, which you can hopefully smuggle out to us if you need to, and you'll be able to move into his inner circle. Get him to trust you, get him to talk. We'll follow up on what you report to us. You've done a bit of modeling work in the past, haven't you? So one can believe you once held ambitions of being an actress, but you gave that up to work behind the cameras. We'll doctor up a diploma from one of the film colleges, make it look like you really have put in a year or two at the craft."

"How long do I actually have to learn this stuff?"

"Two weeks."

I rolled my eyes and stamped my boot heel into the pavement. Unbelievable. "This is absurd!" I protested. "You've *got* people for this, worse than this. This is what you professional paranoids *do,* isn't it? Sneak into places? Get a short guy who can disguise himself as a coffee table? And you still haven't explained why you're involved—*if* you are who you say you are—and why the police don't handle this. Then there's the Serious Organized Crime Agency. They—"

"We will pay," he started loudly, steamrolling over my complaints, "*this* authorized amount for a minimum of two months' work, direct deposit of sixty percent on signature." He dug through his jacket pockets and yanked out a stapled set of pages folded into thirds, very official-looking. He showed me the contract sum.

Whoa. That shut me up.

"We will not discuss with you why our organization is involved," said Hodd. "And you'll be bound by the Official Secrets Act. Naturally, you'll argue that in your distinguished career as a troublemaker you have sometimes begun investigating one thing and stumbled—and I'm sure that word is accurate—*stumbled* onto a larger design. We don't care. Her Majesty's Government will be your contracted employer this time, and we're not like your usual clients. We don't give carte blanche like SW madams or petty gangsters with their own fiefdoms in Bangkok. You see or hear a peculiar detail of interest, you hand it over to us. *We* take care of it."

"I see."

"Now, Miss Knight," he said with a thin smile, doing his best to appear civil, "can we count on you or not?"

I found myself glancing from him to the silent others, none of whom had spoken, none of whom had identified themselves. Yet you still felt a group pressure. I knew I shouldn't care. They could be his bodyguards—or hell, they could be tagging along to pick up his dry cleaning later.

It was a generous fee. To be honest, it was an outrageous fee. To stop the kind of creeps I enjoyed stopping.

"Miss Knight?"

"The answer's no."

"I beg your pardon!"

I took a couple of steps, preparing to walk away. "You heard me. You can make all the snide comments you like about what I do, and you can even say I'm not a trained professional at this. Which also begs the question why you want me. I occasionally help people—that's all. But when I do, I try to be thorough about my client before going in— what he or she needs, what's happened to spark a crisis. You're deliberately holding back details, and I won't go into a situation—especially undercover—with blinkers on."

"Is that all that's stopping you? That we can't tell you everything?"

"No, I also happen to think you're full of it. I don't believe you're MI6; I don't know *what* you are—unless MI6 stands for migraine in six minutes. There's also the matter of Felicity Eden."

"Because she seduced your lover. I see. If it is any consolation, I plan to reprimand her for poor judgment."

"Please," I scoffed. "If you are who you say you are, you

don't tolerate poor judgment. You had her target my partner. I'd be very interested to know why."

Hodd didn't say anything.

"And then you have the gall to try to hire my services."

He was still looking away, checking traffic. "Maybe I was
wrong that you make business decisions coolly, dispassion-
ately, and with a level head."

"You want a cool dispassionate business decision, you
don't fuck with my personal life," I said. "I'm going home
now. If your entourage here wants to follow me, I promise
not to look behind lampposts."

I thought that would be the end of it. I should have
known better.

1

I briefed Helena on how it was, indeed, me who was the target of all the snooping. A week passed in which nothing happened—well, almost nothing. Helena did get me a quick job, the ultimate private detective cliché, really: surveillance on a cheating spouse for a friend of hers. Sitting in a rented car, taking snaps with my digital camera and writing down descriptions of where the husband ate, who he met, I was excruciatingly bored to tears, and I realized how lucky I'd been up to now—few mundane gigs like this one.

When the job was done and I'd caught a guy having sex with someone other than his wife, I was a little frustrated myself—intellectually. And I enlisted a couple of Helena's escorts to look for the kind of porn Desmond Hodd had shown me on the computer notebook. Guys should know where to find that stuff, right? Not as easy as it sounds, not when there's an avalanche of porn out there in every shape and form and debased degree. I was trying to locate that rich sunshine backdrop. I was trying to find those girls of color who appeared less than thrilled on-screen—conscripted into sex instead of volunteering.

My male contacts all grimaced at me and rolled their eyes at the idea of this search. It was because of a dirty little secret—that men are cleaner than we like to believe. What I mean is this: There's obviously a demand for the product out there, but I happen to think there's a silent majority of males who are really, no lie, turned off by hard-core porn.

I've had guys confess to me that in all sincerity they just don't get it. And they don't want it. They don't see the need for the juvenile coarseness in the Web site titles, the close-ups of genitalia that depersonalize everything, and they wonder why cum shots are obligatory, since if anything, they smack of homoeroticism. The males I know, at least, like real eroticism. Feathers, not the whole chicken. Or, all right, they like seeing the chicken, but . . . Okay, the metaphor's breaking down, and maybe I just know a better class of guy. After all, several of them are Helena's escorts, guys who by definition *like* women and enjoy pleasing them.

Which brought me back to the puzzle of Luis Antunes. Hodd said that Antunes's operation in the UK was legit, and so far, I confirmed that this seemed to be true. You could walk into Blockbuster and find his movies. Past the whole shelves given over to *Spider-Man 3* and the latest Harry Potter, down on a lower rack almost hidden away, would be two rental copies of an "erotica" feature by his company, Silky Pictures. Hodd had summed it up well: "pretensions to plot." But Antunes scored high marks for at least trying to make the sex interesting, not quite Zalman King of *Red Shoe Diaries* fame but in his league.

I rented *Detective Desire,* an older Silky Pictures release and one that had actually been directed by Antunes himself. I thought I might gain insight into the man. And because it struck me as depressing to watch porn alone, I called up my friend Fitz, and we screened it at his place near Finsbury Park. The bonus was I got to watch the film horizontally.

Fitz was a gifted massage therapist, and now that he'd just opened his new center offering Swedish, shiatsu, and aromatherapy, he spent less time as one of Helena Willoughby's most sought-after escorts. His bookings for her are few and far between these days, and his price has shot way up. Lucky me, I'm a friend. I not only got to lie nude on his table with his magic fingers turning my muscles into mousse, I had this gorgeous man of nut-brown complexion with funky dreads naked and working his biceps as he worked me. Facing my head, he put his palm heels into the small of my back as I inspected his abs. *My, that's a nice body,* I thought. It had been a while. For years, Fitz and I had carried on this special relationship, drifting back to each other briefly when we were both single and needing attention, friends but something else, something more.

I raised myself on one elbow and took the crimson head of his long dick into my mouth. He was thick and firm and warm, like a chocolate about to melt in my mouth, only I certainly hoped he wouldn't. Mmmm . . . Firming up. Good. Then I felt a playful slap on my ass.

"Hey, I'm not done here!"

I let him go and said in my defense, "It's the movie. Making me horny."

"No, it's not. You're barely paying attention."

"Sure, I am. The famous international detective thinks he'll find clues in that girl's bra."

"Is that how they solve cases?" laughed Fitz. "Why are you watching this drivel? What can you learn?"

"I don't know. See how this guy thinks."

I rolled onto my side, and Fitz perched himself close to me on the massage table. We watched for a bit, idly petting each other. The silliness of the plot didn't matter anymore. We watched these ambitious shots of Lisbon or . . . somewhere, I forgot, didn't matter. Down a stone stairwell and through the bars of an iron gate, the clever detective lay back, his hands reaching up to feel the girl's breasts as she rode him, her hands in lacy gloves. In the movie, it started to rain, droplets running down her cheeks and torso, the girl licking her lips. Okay, this looks pretty hot. My fingers slid down to cup Fitz's balls, circling to grip his cock. He started to get hard.

In the movie, the couple changed positions, the girl gripping the iron bars as the guy took her from behind. They got soaked by the movie rain, which, of course, made them more beautiful, and two gentle fingers slid along the glaze of massage oil on my back. Fitz leaned in to kiss me. Light from the TV screen flashed in the darkened room as our tongues coiled, played, danced. His strong left hand slid down my slippery polished belly, rounding my thigh to grip a cheek of my ass, his thumb pressing in as his right hand covered my mound, fingers finding my clit. He did . . . something . . . to a muscle . . . when he was . . . strumming my clitoris and *oh oh oh*. Long minutes of gasping, my hands gripping the sides of the table, movie forgotten, as I suddenly, explosively came. *Come here.* Barely spoken but my mouth forming the words.

Feeling like we were suspended in space on the narrow massage table I slid off, leaving him there, making him lift one of his strong, beautifully shaped legs up. Then I was flicking my tongue underneath his balls, his musk thick in my nostrils as I lapped the delicate skin of his perineum. His cock was a steel bar, and his glazed fingers started to jerk himself. He had to. Had to touch himself. A tortured moan as he stopped, didn't want to come yet.

I got back on the table and pulled him on top of me, lifting my knees, and then the head of his cock teased the gates of my pussy, pushing gently, slipping in. Then all of him in one confident surge, his taut stomach against mine, my palms gripping his ass. A delicious oozing of the left-over massage oil, a silky feel. Silky Pictures. Mind wandering for just a second, and then we were kissing each other hard, nine steel-girder inches of him filling me, and he pumped only a little, a sweet and subtle momentum to keep me wet, keep himself hard, to build things. But we reveled more in the embrace, tightly holding each other, in a cocoon of oil and heat. I knew tonight I wanted it dirty, really dirty, wanted to let myself go and unravel him as well.

There was no more movie—we were the movie. Fitz braced himself on his straight arms, and my fingers slid down his chest, enjoying the view. He came out of me and climbed down, knowing I'd bleat a complaint but urging me to change positions, to slide down the table so that I was poised at its end, my legs open, knees up, and he stood and pushed into me, so deep I let out a grateful whimper. His palms on my kneecaps, he started ramming hard, my pussy making a rude slurp with the sudden intrusion of that long dark cock, and I felt him boring into me, until the sensation made my vaginal muscles contract and hold him fast, longing to keep him inside, a trip-hammer pulse. He shook violently, his dick impossibly lengthening as he shot and shot. *Come here*, an echo. Pulling me up so that I could clumsily wrap my arms around him, Fitz still in the shiver of orgasm. And then I felt my own sympathetic quakes. "Oh, fuck," I whispered. "Oh, fuck, that was good . . ."

He made this little-boy moan and looked into my eyes, apologizing for not taking his time. I wanted to ask: Are you kidding? That was amazing. He'd told me he'd been working like a dog, taking most of the bookings at his new center even though he had two other therapists. That meant he needed to be there for the City executives who wanted a treatment before the grind of the business day and the teachers desperate for relief after school was out. He had been there for me so many times, and I felt the stress in *his* body. "Burning both ends of the candle," he said wearily.

I kissed him and gently nibbled his bottom lip. "Hey, you want to see a real porn movie?"

Fitz laughed. "What are you talking about, babe?"

I reached for the massage oil on the little side table and gave myself a generous splash in both hands. Before he could say it wasn't necessary, I had him on the massage table the way he'd had me, one hand cupping his balls, the other slick and sliding up his dick, making him hard again. "Want to . . . want to kiss you." And he sat up, our tongues coming together even as my middle finger strayed under his balls exploring. His cock grew in my small fist, and if I do this right . . .

I was inside him.

Massaging his prostate, I never saw a cock snap to attention so fast, fill with blood and engorge, enormous. My fingers jerked his shaft, and I thought he'd come instantly, but no, his focus divided, and it was all the sweeter with the suspense, building, building as he gripped the sides of the table. His hand was suddenly on my ass, pulling me a little off balance as he cried out in pleasure and shock, ribbons of white cum slapping my breast and belly. But I wasn't done.

Just a little pressure, the slightest caress, and there was another twitch of his cock, another stream flying onto my tits. He kissed me hungrily and half-embraced me in this obscene clinch, the thick smell of oil and spunk and musk in the room, my fingers still inside him. His eyes went wide as he experienced another orgasm, a dribble of semen down the red cherry dome. I felt drunk on my sensual power, like Kim the last time we made love, relentlessly making him come. He did one last time, a very weak stream but all the rush of pleasure.

"Oh, shit, I think I needed that," said Fitz.

"We both needed tonight."

"Yeah . . . I wanted to say I'm sorry about Kim."

I shrugged, giving him a couple of quick kisses on the mouth and cheek. "It's all right. She wasn't the one, that's all."

He shrugged back. "Well, we're not the ones for each other. Think we'll ever find these people?"

"I don't know. But we have a blast together when we're not looking, don't we?"

A soft chuckle and a nod. By the time we thought to dive into the shower to clean up, the end credits rolled across the screen.

◆

So I can't say that I got much insight from one of Luis Antunes's movies. I was still trying to figure out his association with the hard-core stuff, the ones sold as pirate DVDs in the high street. No references to them on his Web site, no shared production company name. The hard-core ones had amateurish credit titles at the end: Ladrão Films; must be someone's idea of an inside joke, since a few taps at Google told me *ladrão* means thief.

And how did Hodd know that Antunes was hooked up with the nastier porn merchants, wherever they were, whether in Lisbon or here?

I still had the rental car for a few days, so I took to parking outside the office/studio of Silky Pictures near Canary Wharf. I soon learned Luis Antunes was forty-two, but could pass for his mid-thirties. I expected a Hugh Hefner–Larry Flynt clone with gold chains and a Seventies open shirt, but he was nothing of the kind. He was gangly with spectacles and a halo of black curls, most days in casual dress, wearing an open-necked shirt and Marks & Spencer trousers to the studio. You'd think he was the tech support guy who got your Outlook Mail to work. I imagined his unassuming, gentle manner probably worked wonders with him playing surrogate "older brother" to his porn stars—no creepy casting couch, no leering boss. Again, it made me wonder why Hodd wanted him investigated.

Helena would be amused to learn she was almost his neighbor. When the day ended and he pulled up in front of his mansion in nearby Twickenham, a lovely girl waited at the doorstep to throw her arms around him. She was mixed race, with light brown skin and big brown eyes, her dyed blond tresses in a Shakira style. She looked and sounded Portuguese from a distance. In his choice of partner, at least, Luis Antunes liked them young. The girl looked at best twenty-three years old.

On day three, I nearly jumped out of my skin with the knock on the passenger-side glass. "*Shit!*"

As I hit the button to slide down the window, I recognized one of the trench coat entourage from days earlier. Square face, small eyes, pasty white complexion. "Mr. Hodd is around the corner and would appreciate a word," he told me. "Let me get in so it looks like you've picked me up."

I grumbled but hit the lock. Yeah, *that* was credible. Guy was dreaming if he thought I'd ever pick him up, but there was always the chance Antunes or his girlfriend might notice my car staying too long. I drove around the corner and started to chuckle. Again with the limousine. I hope this wasn't their standard surveillance vehicle. The messenger boy opened the door for me, and I slid into the seat across from Hodd.

"So now, at your own expense and on your own time, you're conducting the same investigation we were willing to pay you to do," he remarked. The same washed-out gray eyes staring out the window again, not looking at me. I don't know why I found that so annoying but I did. "Well,

Miss Knight, since you didn't get in touch with us, we've come to you. And I'm here to renew my offer."

"I've been watching Antunes three days now," I pointed out. "So you can either deduct them from the two months you need me for, or calculate back pay in addition to the two."

"Agreed."

"Oh, and you'll add something special if you want my help."

"The amount offered is generous," he said sourly. "And final."

"No, the money's fine, thank you. I'm asking for a guarantee. I want it signed by the appropriate bodies, and you'll get one for me and a separate one for Helena Willoughby."

"What kind of guarantees?"

"Neither of us ever pays income tax again," I said.

"That's preposterous! We're MI6, not Revenue!"

"You can get it. I know you can."

Hodd muttered swearwords under his breath at my bloody gumption. Didn't bother me in the least. If he was real, I knew he'd pay my price.

"And we still have issues to settle."

At last, a direct glance. "I know. Give your car keys to James. He'll follow us."

"And where are we going?"

"Where you can verify that we are who we say we are," replied Hodd. "That is part of what's bothering you, yes?"

◆

By now you might have guessed that Desmond Hodd is *not* the real name of the MI6 guy who contacted me. Just as I'm sure the types that keep an eye out for these things will scrub clean any other references that might contravene the

Official Secrets Act (if this ever does get out at home or in America). So you just have to believe me when I tell you I can't offer details, but Hodd's way of serving up pudding for proof was a visit to Legoland, as they call it. *The* Legoland. Its address is 85 Albert Embankment, headquarters of the British Secret Intelligence Service, MI6.

Hey, everybody knows where it is. But you don't just breeze in the way you do at the National Gallery, with a couple of bored security guards checking your bag.

So. I wasn't looking at the ziggurat from Vauxhall Bridge —oh, no, Desmond Hodd's limousine took us right *past* the security checks, and then I was ushered inside. The rest was anticlimax, really, since Hodd and his minions led me into a banal conference room with a view towards Millbank. When I got around to signing the contract he put in front of me, I might as well have been opening a new account at Abbey National. But that came later. First, I was determined to settle a score.

"Why ruin things with Kim?"

Hodd was irritable. "You're back on that, are you? Look here. From what I understand, your relationship was not in the healthiest shape—"

"Still none of your business—"

"And I told you before that Miss Eden exercised poor personal judgment, for which—"

"Rubbish."

"Let's be candid, then," said Hodd. He made a steeple of his fingers, finding something fascinating in the pattern of the table's oak finish. "Once we learned of her attempts to become involved with your lover, we saw no need to put a stop to it. I noted your penchant for getting into hypersexualized scenarios—and *no,* we are not specifically recruiting for that . . . talent. But should you find yourself in such a situation, or just coping with the undercover situation per se, you'd do well to keep your focus on the task at hand."

"You prefer I have no personal distractions."

"Yes."

"You really are a bastard," I said gently.

Hodd was unruffled. "You are focusing your outrage on Miss Eden and myself, but I put it to you that it hardly matters who sent the girl or if the girl was even sent at all. Your lover still cheated on you."

But Felicity Eden hadn't fancied Kim out of the blue—he told her to do it. I was sure of it. Perhaps I'd never confirm it, but here he was with this convenient rationale to justify why it was a good thing in the end, all tied up with a bow ready for me when I challenged him. Bastard. It was on his orders.

Nothing I could do about that now.

"How did you link Luis Antunes to the prostitution and these alleged sex slaves in the DVDs?"

"That's not important," Hodd replied briskly. "What matters is for you to prove he's involved, that he's their man in London."

"Their man in London? Well, where's the stuff coming from?"

"Again, not your problem." A rising note of impatience here. "Just find a provable link. Get us proof."

I was still shaking my head, confused. "Proof . . . When have you guys ever cared about *proof*? You and your American friends told everyone there was proof of weapons of mass destruction, and we know how that turned out! Why don't you go ahead and nab Antunes and do what you want? Why don't you just—just *turn* him to catch the others you're after?"

"We have our own plans for how this will proceed," said Hodd. He spoke slowly, as if I were six years old. "For what we will pay you, we are entitled to expect you will act in accordance with our plans."

I played with the pen in my hand. The early deposit as

per my requirement was spelled out, no loopholes. One of Hodd's aides was, in fact, at a computer poised to transfer the funds as soon as ink hit paper. Two separate sheets waited, the legal immunities for Helena and myself from the clutches of Her Majesty's Revenue and Customs. So far, promises were kept.

I signed.

Hodd watched me finish writing my name and gave me an avuncular smile. Ah, there you are, that's better. He said a car would pick me up from my flat on Monday at nine sharp (*please* be ready, sigh). I would be briefed on a few protocols for my own personal safety, be provided lunch, and then be taken to a facility in the afternoon where I'd start my lessons in digital editing. He understood there was a good chance I had already blabbed to Miss Willoughby about my previous encounter with him, nothing to be done, but from here on, the Act applied in terms of confidentiality. I was not to discuss my work or the case with her.

I could explain the new tax status I'd gained for her with any cover story I liked.

He gave me a business card with a special phone number on it, and at any time, day or night, I could ring the number if I learned something important I needed to pass on.

Fifteen minutes after we were done, I was back in the car fighting London traffic and thinking it didn't seem real. But I had the documents. The tangible goods. And I was on my way to my bank to move the money, because I still couldn't shake my suspicion of Hodd. Paranoid. I kept fearing he'd drop the other shoe and say, surprise, we've taken the money back, consider your labors a service for Queen and country. But in less than an hour, the bulk of the funds—including a good portion of what I already had—was shifted into an offshore account, and no, not one in Guernsey. They couldn't touch it. They might still be able to follow the trail to where I had sent it, but too bad, it was safe. I left enough for the usual grocery runs or when I needed to hit a cash machine for an outfit I just had to buy or drinks with Helena and the boys. My rent check had already cleared and the bills had just been paid, thank God.

I can still remember signing the documents in that conference room. And every time I do, I repeat in my head: *Teresa, you bloody idiot.*

◆

I felt like celebrating. No—not exactly celebrating, but indulging myself.

I didn't want to bug Fitz again, not so soon. He sounded stressed and busy with the new center, and I actually was in the mood for novelty. And detachment, if that makes any sense. You know how after a breakup with one person, your mind snaps back and longs for the previous lover? Stupid, I know, but I felt that—well aware it was impossible, that it could never happen. I wanted release. If it couldn't be with the person I still dreamed about after all these months (she's gone, Teresa, gone forever), I didn't want involvement with anyone else. Not yet, at least, not unless he or she intrigued me. It seemed unimaginable at the moment that *that* could ever happen again.

With Fitz there was always affection, but no future. How about another escort from Helena's agency? No, that would require me to offer a minimum of attentiveness, polite curiosity, be "on" for someone else, even though the guy was supposed to be there for my sake and my needs.

I knew what would do. For the interim.

It's hard to keep track of the lingo, but the current Internet term these days was "soft swinging."

Desmond Hodd was right in that I did have experience with "hypersexualized scenarios" (what a way to put it). I'd become something of an amateur sex anthropologist—kept track of a few fads in the papers and magazines. The whole "dogging" craze in London had become so popular and gotten so much attention from the media, it was bound to decline. For one thing, there were the creepy guys who apparently wouldn't settle for just watching and broke etiquette, trying to join in or talk, and then there were the "Roys," as they were dubbed, the killjoys with the fake sirens to drive the doggers off (though you couldn't blame 'em—it's not like I wanted to see that either if I lived near a nice common or something).

So exhibitionist couples had taken the show inside. Just putting themselves on webcam wasn't enough—for them or voyeurs. They needed the thrill of having an audience right there, a few feet from their bed or sofa. Like everything else, you used the Net to trade pics and got vetted by the hot couple, and either you showed up at their home or you were invited to a certain outside spot where you got a great view of them through their parted curtains.

Tonight I was cleared for entering a home.

The couple showing off were young. Guy nearly thirty, blond, and looked like he had northern European ancestry, not especially my taste but cute in a generic sort of way, overly muscular build, like he worked at it because he liked being on display. It was the girl who had caught my fancy. Twenty years old and tiny. Big brown eyes and lush eyelashes, Asian, an endearing gap in her two front teeth, lovely curves on her, midnight hair that went down all the way to the small of her back.

A second-floor flat in Chelsea, and I laughed softly to myself, wondering why I should feel embarrassed; I'm only here to watch. They even had wine out and a few snacks in their living room, the lights dim, and the television enigmatically left on with the mute pressed. A cheerful white girl had opened the door for me, greeting me like a friend, but no one here knew the hosts or anyone else. We all just had the amiability and goodwill of strangers who answer an advert to help get petitions signed. Ridiculous. But no one wanted to leave.

Because the blond guy leaned out of the bedroom door and said, "Hey." And that was it, confirmation he and his girl were ready to start.

No self-consciousness to them at all, no attempt to "show us how it's done"—we were there for them, not the other way around. And when the girl's eyes took us in, those of us cross-legged on the bedroom floor, she looked at us as if we were all behind glass. We were the ones in the zoo, not the other way around.

She stayed dressed in a half-T and sweatpants, no bra, while he stripped down to nothing in front of us. There was a small gasp in the room, because he was hung like a horse and thick, and he went from dangling to a low angle of arousal, her tiny fingers tugging. on him and taking him between her lips. I was unimpressed at first, but the erotic charge came from her still being clothed, her small breasts dangling, and as she sucked him, he tugged her T-shirt up a little so that the bottom curves of her golden breasts were exposed, at the same time the hem of her sweatpants riding off her tight little ass. With a small hand urging him to move with her, she lay on her side on the bed, still sucking him, and he fondled her, hand playing a peep show for us with a quick flash of dark brown nipple, burrowing into the sweatpants to feel her mound. She let him go briefly to slip them off, revealing a neatly trimmed wedge of black fur. Then he lay down on the bed, and she straddled him.

You could hear those watching stir and make hard swallows as the girl took his huge cock and brushed its head against her pussy lips, and then, at last wet enough, guided him in, her eyes shutting, mouth open. Someone on the floor whispered, "Fuck," in the near-darkness. We watched her start a rhythm, but the blond guy forced his own, lifting his ass off the sheets to impale her as she hovered with her face close to his, and then she got in sync, and we heard the slaps of flesh, a long drawn-out whimper from the girl.

The etiquette for this game was you don't speak to the couple, you don't interrupt, you don't dare approach, let alone touch. If they *ask* you to join in, that's different, but an invitation was necessary. You could masturbate, but you were expected not to make a mess on the host's furnishings or bed linen. And you don't stare at another audience member when he or she masturbates. Sometimes "helping" the process for a neighbor was tolerated, but it was going too far to initiate a full-scale second show of your own. If the spark was there, the two of you were expected to leave and get it on elsewhere.

The Asian girl was riding him hard, the curtain of black hair splayed over one shoulder, her little tits quaking. It was amazing she could take all of him in.

Out of the corner of my eye, I saw a guy on my left moan and quickly unbuckle his trousers. He slipped them off and rocked in place, gripping his flushed red cock. It was clear he had no lubricant and didn't want to rub himself raw, but his dick twitched and a dribble of semen ran down the shaft. A couple, who looked like they were virgins to the whole scene, were more furtive, the guy slipping one hand underneath his partner's top and fondling one of her breasts. The girl's breathing began to get ragged.

I couldn't help myself. I lost all self-control and slipped down my own trousers and panties, started to play with myself in the dim light despite those around me. I tried to cover my moan, and I'm not sure whether it was me or something else distracting them, but the Asian girl looked up and right at me. Then the guy did, craning his head back. She bit her bottom lip, and I felt myself come, small but satisfying. I needed more. I'll be never sure, but I think it's why they decided to switch positions, him taking her from behind. A cloud of pitch black hair, so long and wild, cascading tresses of it, as he rammed her, and she fingered her clit, doing her best to prop herself up on one hand. "Aaaaa . . ." Looking *right at me* again, triggering a fresh rush of lubrication in me as she cried out enigmatically to be either saved or joined. "Aaaa . . . aaaa . . ."

The couple to my right had lost all composure, the girl's breasts exposed with her bra cups and her top pulled up, her guy squeezing a nipple between two fingers. She gripped his stubby pale cock pushing through his fly and didn't need to jerk him. He was doing his best to keep himself from letting go. He let out a grunt and took her hand away, and it was clear he was trying to calm down. But the blond guy on the bed surprised us all by calling, "Jimmy."

They knew each other. He waved to the guy to approach the bed. "Jimmy" looked back at his girlfriend. She looked reluctant, even now tugging her bra cups back down along with her top, feeling intensely self-conscious. The couple switched positions again, her lying on her back, her calves now on his shoulders, and he began to drill her almost savagely, the girl's whimpers rising in octaves, and it became clear why Jimmy was granted a small mercy to approach the bed, inches away from seeing his friends doing it. She wanted to see him lose it and shoot. It drove her wild, and I realized the rest of us were part of a stage set. This was about these four, and others, including myself, had been invited to make it safe, less personal. If Jimmy and his girlfriend were the only two watching, masks would be stripped away, no courage found. They could watch if others were watching. But now the couple wanted tribute, demanded Jimmy make his own sacrifice. And he did, his climax a sputtering geyser on the floor as the Asian girl wailed high and long. Her blond lover let out a ferocious grunt as he came inside her, pulling himself out to come some more on her stomach. I felt myself come again, watching that beautiful face with its splayed black sunburst of hair, mouth wide open in ecstasy as threads of semen splattered across her golden body. I imagined me on that bed with that cock inside me.

Next to me: "Eeeahh . . . Eeaah . . ." Jimmy's girlfriend masturbating, coming over the same tableau, but deeply troubled, and a tear glistened down her cheek. She was confused; both she and Jimmy getting more than they bargained for here. Seeing her man turned on by these friends, being turned on herself by the sight of him climaxing on someone else. And now Jimmy looked back and understood what had just been shattered, his face pale over a fragile trust of intimacy cracking, close to breaking. I wondered absently if they had a future together. You go to one of these things or some other scene, like group sex or bondage games, and it can be hard sometimes to find your way back to the pleasures of one-on-one (take my word for it). And if your second instinct after the need to get off was confusion and hurt, this game was not for you.

I fixed myself up, suddenly reminded of Kim's betrayal, and all the amusing pleasure of the scene dissipated for me. People were ready to drift out now, like those who shift gears after slowing down for a traffic accident, and I went home, feeling empty.

◆

Weeks later I was at Silky Pictures. Sitting at my computer, working through something called Adobe Production Studio, with my screen divided into multiple boxes, one called "Source," another called "Program," whilst below these was a long rectangle with lines like on a thermometer, and they marked so many frames per second of the film. Here's the fascinating thing: There were really no frames at all.

A camera guy had shot the movie in what's called hi-def,

which was video but had the quality of 35-millimeter film, and then he passed the footage on to me to download onto my hard drive. Now as my mouse clicked on the "razor blade" icon, I moved a black vertical line over a red one to make a cut. I didn't need a shot of the nipple that long because I had to insert male fingers straying down to the girl's pubic hair and then put in a new cut or maybe a dissolve. The film script would put it this way: DISSOLVE TO: CLOSE ON PENNY'S FACE. Or Mary's. Or Charlene's. Or Jasmine's. Or a dozen other girls.

This "slow dissolve" shit had been a cliché for how many decades now, and the worse part was, as the boys who were veterans would say, it "wouldn't cut." I was editing the footage to rescue it rather than making an artistic decision. I'll save you all the technical details, but at the end of the day if the director doesn't shoot things in a certain manner, the raw footage can be jarring, no matter how seamless the edits. That's because you're still stuck with the basic ingredients they've handed you.

More about the director in a minute. Oh, boy.

For the assignment, I was given a cover identity—no longer Teresa Knight, now "Teresa Lane" (I lobbied for a surname that was more interesting, maybe Sudanese, and Hodd quietly said no, we do not choose cover names for fun—and stop sulking). I was introduced to Luis Antunes briefly my first day there. He peered shyly at me through his spectacles like a grown-up Daniel Radcliffe and shook my hand, quite pleasant and professional, and then I was off to be shown the rest of the office and to get my own desk. In the first couple of weeks, I saw Luis in the hallway, and we did no more than exchange a "hi" as we passed each other. I was busy anyway getting the lay of the land.

Everyone admitted that Silky Pictures had been modeled on Vivid Entertainment, porn's reigning giant out of America's San Fernando Valley. Sex on the screen, not on show in the building. When you walked in the foyer, a receptionist greeted you, and you saw cubicles for Accounting and Marketing and could mistake the place for a bond trader's office. I had seen for myself that Luis drove home to a mansion and upper-class family bliss. Even from inside, it would be an uphill climb to find the connection MI6 wanted.

Not that the place didn't have its circus elements. You had young guys of nineteen, inarticulate, showing up in their metal band T-shirts and torn Levi's, applying to be in a Silky feature. Here for free sex and a vague yearning for infamy. It was creepy and pathetic. Every one of them was politely turned away.

And each week, a regular stream of girls, aged from about nineteen into their late twenties, visited the office with head shots and résumés and rattled off with sparkling, vacuous cheer their versatility in sex acts. Blondes from Essex, brunettes from Wapping. Maybe one black girl or mixed-race girl in weeks of arrivals. A female casting director named Roberta had a chat with each and every one, then made a girl take off her clothes and pose for a few digital shots up against a wall. Antunes was shown the head shots, digital snaps, and résumés and, like checking stocks for an investment portfolio, hand-picked girls to come back to see him.

If a girl was selected to star in a feature, she had to bring back test results giving a clean bill of health regarding venereal disease, and if that was a go, she was offered a waiver that made condom use her choice and signed a liability form that got Silky Pictures off the hook in case she or her sex partners were less than responsible—unwanted pregnancy, disease, injury. In the office, there was a veneer of professionalism, maybe even a sincere attempt at it. It was surreal, considering someone called "Action!" and a girl was to be penetrated in front of a lighting technician, a sound guy, and six other technical workers. And she had to look like she was having the shag of her life, and no one was standing around watching.

As for the scripts . . . Hodd had told me Silky Pictures had "pretensions to plot." But I never expected that the regular screenplay writer for Luis Antunes's movies would turn out to be a grandmother from Hounslow who used to write corporate biographies. Luis, if you can believe it, supposedly found her because his girlfriend read a novel she'd dashed off for a romance publisher, a competitor of Mills & Boon. He had no clue how to recruit scriptwriters in Britain, and since he hoped the movies would appeal to both men and women, he guessed that a woman would write more interesting scenarios to justify the sex content.

I was in the foyer when Judith, the writer, turned up one day to collect a check. As I shook her hand, she smiled brightly at me. "You can go ahead and look surprised. I get that a lot, dear."

She told me how oh, yes, she had written a short book for young people on the Stock Exchange and a chapter for a textbook on the EU, and Orpheocon had paid her to write a corporate biography to be sent as a gift to shareholders.

"It's all money, isn't it? It's the same thing with these movies. I just wish Luis would allow me to stretch my wings a little. It's always a girl needing help escaping her jewel thief husband or she needs to clear her name, and somehow romping in bed will help this detective *and/or* his partner find clues—so of course, they have to have a *ménage*. Why can't the girl be the adventurous plucky one, hmm?"

"I don't know why she can't," I offered.

The little woman scratched her white curls and adjusted her glasses. "I know Luis doesn't dream up these plots, but that director . . ."

"What about him?" I asked, sipping a Coke.

She leaned in and whispered to me, "He's a pig. Each and

every picture he rings me up and says, 'Judith, if you write it, Luis will accept it.'"

"Accept what?" I asked, mystified.

"He wants me to write a scene in which the girl is fucked up the ass," said the sweet grandmotherly figure. And I nearly spat a stream of Coca-Cola onto the rug.

"Oh. Uh, well—"

"I told you the man's a pig," she went on. "Luis knows it would offend our target audience, and he doesn't let him shoot it. Some of the girls have done this, of course, for other productions, and let's just say they're not very bright. So if the man says this is what we're filming today, they may well go along, the silly things. But I know Luis would have it cut out even if it's shot. Now our esteemed director's tactic is to try to persuade *me* to give it a story rationale! Nothing doing, I told him. They can shoot what they like, but I'm not writing *that*. Vulgar man! I think he's an Aussie or something. Well, they're always loud."

I didn't comment on that point. I hadn't met the director yet, and I had nothing against Aussies. I didn't know many either. But I had picked up on how the director was loathed in the office. His name was Duncan McCullough.

"In any case, good luck, my dear," said Judith pleasantly. "I hope this place gives you what you want."

I told her I just wanted a paycheck. She shrugged philosophically over that one and declared she was certain I had more depth than that. Then she said "Cheerio" in the antiquated way seniors still do on my father's street in Oxford, and she made her way to her Rover in the parking lot.

It was amusing to agree with her in my head that yes, I was more than what I did here, and that I probably knew more about the goings-on at Orpheocon than the sanitized press releases she was given as research for her corporate biography.

Most of the films were shot away from the Canary Wharf

building, because you needed homes with different décors so the movies didn't all look the same. But one large room at the office was used, redecorated with bits of furniture and a daybed. You'd stroll down to the lunchroom to make a cup of tea, and an insistent wailing could be heard from behind the door. It was mildly comical when the scene was abruptly cut—batteries low on the hi-def camera or something. The fresh cue would be given, and then with equal enthusiasm the girl would scream once more. Like kicking out the cord of your vacuum cleaner and plugging it back in again.

I wish I could tell you I got the job there because I had excelled at the two-week editing boot camp that Desmond Hodd had arranged. Truthfully? "Teresa Lane" was competent, that's all. Luis later admitted to me they had another guy in mind, but the first choice suddenly landed a fabulous gig in Leeds with the BBC. The second candidate became violently ill, and they couldn't afford to wait. I sensed Hodd's people pulling strings, and it was disturbing to say the least.

I wasn't even hired by Antunes. Instead, it was the senior video editor who was responsible, a geeky little pear of a guy named Joseph. Like Hodd, he couldn't look me in the eye. Unlike Hodd, he directed most of his remarks to my breasts. I got the distinct impression that for Joseph, this workplace involved a lot of Peeping Tom glances, but that he went home to watch Sky Sports over a couple of packets of crisps and a regimen of nightly wanking off.

As Hodd promised, my interviewer had watched an impressive mix of samples edited by others. When he was done, Joseph had coughed and tried to sound like he had to think about it. I knew he'd either choose me or he wouldn't, he didn't have to weigh anything.

"You'll do."

So a week into working for Silky Pictures, I learned that

Joseph's title meant nothing, and that I reported directly to Luis Antunes. Good for me, good for MI6, I supposed, all that infiltration-work-your-way-into-his-confidence stuff. But it looked like it was going to take a while.

Piled on my desk each morning were what they called P2 cards—which filled a slot under the eyepiece of your Panasonic HVX camera and stored the raw footage—all ready and waiting to download onto my hard drive for editing. A cartoon stork could have brought these babies in a blanket sling for all the difference it made. This or that PA just handed them over and went, "Here you go, Teresa."

Things changed with Duncan McCullough, Silky's director of all the movies.

He strolled into the editors' area one afternoon and imperiously demanded without even introducing himself, "Get these done by five, Lane. Right? Okay."

I slipped off my headphones jacked into the hard drive. Had I heard right? What the . . . ? In my peripheral vision, I saw this tall man in his early fifties with a long face and a salt-and-pepper beard storming off.

"Schedule says Thursday," I answered, holding up the notes I'd been given. These came from the production manager, who had a lot more decision-making power than McCullough did.

He halted in the doorway. Now I picked up the accent that yeah, could be taken for either an Australian or a New Zealander (turns out he was a Kiwi—guess they have rude jerks, too).

"Well, I don't give a shit what the schedule says, baby doll, I want the fucking thing by five, all right?"

I swiveled in my chair, biting down on my pen. In another time and place, I'd tell him to sod off. But I had a job to do here, and I sensed that this bully was tolerated. Hmmm, a more diplomatic approach was called for.

"You'll get the 'fucking thing' by Thursday," I told him.

My voice was very calm, the soothing tone of the nurse in the asylum.

"Now you—"

"Actually you won't get the fucking thing—James will get the fucking thing since he's the production manager. You want to see it, go see him. Thursday. Oh, by the way, my name's Teresa, and it's polite to introduce yourself before you ask for a favor. Otherwise, if you swear and call someone 'baby doll' they might be tempted to kick you in the crotch."

That's about as diplomatic as I get.

He made a small incredulous gasp, flipping his eyebrows, as if how dare I, and the other editors watched, half expecting us to pull out guns. "For your information, I'm the fucking director, *Teresa*."

"That's nice. And you work—sorry, fucking work—over there. When you do your job—*if* you can do your fucking job—my job starts. Now as far as I can see, we're two different fucking departments, so there's absolutely no fucking reason I need to have a fucking conversation with you at all. See the production manager—fuck. Good-bye."

The other editors looked *fascinated* by what they were doing.

Right, guys, only I see hands changing the volume controls to listen to us.

I saw their lips curl and twitch in grateful smiles, doing their best not to show Duncan how much they loved this confrontation. Without another word, he stomped out.

Duncan, I learned, liked terrorizing the editors. People told me he actually relished creating an atmosphere of tension on the set as well, and if there was a girl-girl scene slated to be shot he went out of his way to pay attention to one actress over the other, using their insecurities to create a little drama for his own amusement. They didn't understand why he did this, but I think I did.

The creep didn't like women. It was that simple. Since everyone knows actresses are often insecure—and who could be more insecure than a porn actress whose body is her asset—he orchestrated these cruel charades because he felt that vain, pampered porn stars should be taken down a peg. They should be humiliated.

It was suggested that it "would be a good idea" if I watched filming for a day to see how the movies were put together. I never doubted this notion originated with Duncan himself. He wanted me to visit his own personal fiefdom and pay obeisance to the king. So I watched and stayed out of the way, and the next week he was barking to have edits done, and once again I reminded him that I paid attention to the deadlines from the production manager, not him.

Funny thing was, I would end up owing the creep for bringing me into the inner circle and advancing me up the Silky Pictures hierarchy. I was called into Luis Antunes's office one afternoon.

It was appropriately large for the boss, with a framed photo hanging behind his desk, one that showed a younger Antunes crewing on the deck of a sailing ship for what looked like a big yachting race, the white and red triangles of other sails in the distance on the great sweep of blue. Huh. A competitive sailor. Interesting. Supposed to be big money and sponsorship in those things, and I imagined you had to park your egos to work as a team. No picture of his significant other on his desk, but this business still carried an unsavory taint to it, and maybe he didn't like the occasional creep or sleaze who might come in here seeing his girl. He struck me as the protective type.

As I walked in, Luis was as pleasant as ever, polishing his glasses and with his feet up on his desk. Duncan waited in a chair across from him.

"How are you, Teresa?" Luis asked politely in his accented English. He stood up like a gentleman and shook my hand, and I got the genuine impression he really enjoyed having me in, that he almost looked forward to this like a fan waiting in line for an author's book signing. He definitely had an unassuming charm.

"Fine, great."

Duncan leaned forward, lacing his fingertips, already starting on a pompous chord. "We called you in here because of your attitude."

I saw Luis shoot him an annoyed look. Duncan had made the bad mistake of trying to control the meeting, and I don't think the boss appreciated the "we" coming from his director. "Um, Teresa, you seem to fit in fine here and everyone likes you, so I don't want to blow this out of proportion. Duncan likes to see the final edits because he wants to make sure they conform to his vision, and he feels you don't show him the proper respect."

"Oh, no," I said innocently. "That's not true."

"It isn't?"

"No. I don't show him any respect."

Duncan's temper quickly got the better of him, and flecks of spit flew as he threw an arm in a wild-man gesture at Luis. "You see how this fucking cow talks to me right in front of the fucking—"

The naked assault of words had Luis sitting up in his chair, and now my boss was no longer focusing on my smart-ass remark but on this barrage. When I rattled off how I was only following company practice in submitting to the production manager first, et cetera . . . I'll cut to the chase, because suffice to say, I was believed and Duncan already had his reputation.

Oh, but that wasn't the highlight of the day. It was me pushing my luck.

"You're a shitty editor anyway," Duncan said as he began a new tantrum. Up until then, the discussion had been about office behavior. Now he had started a new thread, and he should have left well enough alone.

"The mix is only as good as the ingredients," I replied calmly.

"What the hell does that mean?" he shot back.

"It means I've edited five movies so far in my time here, and you rip off the ice cube down the breasts cliché in three of them. You lifted the striptease from *9½ Weeks* and the girls taking pics of each other from *The Unbearable Lightness of Being*, and you still blew the continuity in the mirror shots. Do you have anything original of your own?"

Luis tapped his pen on the edge of his desk. Smiling, without making it rude at all, he demanded playfully, "You think you can do better, don't you?"

"I think I have an imagination."

"Let's find out," he said. He hit a function key and called up the production schedule for the latest feature. "There's a straight vanilla sequence between Charlene and Todd on Friday. You direct it."

Duncan was on his feet. "Now wait a fucking minute, Luis!"

"Duncan, it's only one sequence," said Luis. "You can't be threatened by somebody shooting *one* sequence! And to be perfectly fair, you are getting a little burned out and repetitive. If you're going to insult the skills of somebody else in the office, then she should get her chance to prove she can do what you can. And it's probably a good thing if we train another director—we increase our productivity."

"Right, so I'll edit her shit, and we'll see how well that cuts!"

"No, no, no," Luis groaned. "I don't think Teresa here has ever sabotaged your footage. And you're not going to fuck up hers. She'll put it together, and we'll see what we have. It's an experiment. Maybe you both learn to cut each other a little slack, eh?"

Duncan stared impotently from Luis to me then headed for the door, muttering, "This is bullshit."

"Excuse me?" snapped Luis, popping out of his chair. A flicker of temper here. "I believe I made a decision in the interests of the company—an *experiment*. And you're about to get paid the same with your workload reduced for a while. Or do you want even *less* work?"

Duncan stopped in his tracks and went pale. If I understood that clearly enough, so did he.

"No, I'm . . . I'm good." He nodded and closed the door quietly.

Luis sighed and collapsed back in his seat. He looked at me and clapped his hands together, making a prayer gesture that said: Give me strength.

"Guy directs industrial training videos in Porto, back in my country, when I find him. He was cutting three-quarter-inch news footage in Malaysia before that—couldn't get a job in film in New Zealand or Australia. I get him off these nowhere gigs in Portugal, get him into the UK, and now he thinks he's Bertolucci." He pointed a finger at me and laughed. "You better come up with something marvelous, otherwise we both look stupid."

"I won't let you down," I promised.

I was beginning to like him. And I was developing a theory. Duncan clearly had a problem with strong women—hell, he seemed to have a problem with women in general. If he came to Silky Pictures via Portugal . . . Maybe this pipeline of hard-core nasty stuff didn't rely on Antunes as the connection. Maybe it was someone else.

2

The atmosphere on a porn set is a strange one. On my first day as a director, a naked girl was in the makeup area, fussing over her face, and I was doing my best to persuade her through intermediaries that *less* is more, because the big false eyelashes and the heavy violet shadow just didn't make it (in the end, my appeal to her vanity as an actress won out, because I wanted an "innocent" look for her). I was lucky, in that our star for the day was a veteran named Charlene from Essex, who had short blond hair with bangs, natural breasts for once, and ones that were B cups (a fact that made Duncan treat her with contempt: "You need big tits! Big!"), and she was sincerely enthused about working with a female director. She was twenty-five and had done countless porn features after her audition for one of those dance reality show competitions had taken her only to the second round. Charlene clasped both my hands in hers now, greeting me like an old friend, wearing a big enthusiastic smile.

"This is wonderful!" she gushed. "Just tell me what you

want, darling. It'll be *so* good to work with somebody who ain't barking at me all the bloody time. Brilliant!"

When I sketched out my idea, she bit her bottom lip, listening with this sweetly charming yet vacuous look and then pronounced: "Oh, wow."

I didn't think it merited a "wow," but hey, I'll take enthusiasm. She clapped her hands together with delight. She was easygoing, and though Duncan McCullough had reduced her to tears more than once, technicians told me she took direction well.

Male actors on a porn set are really cattle. They're not nearly as well paid as the girls, often treated politely but as talking dildos, and with very few exceptions, they never make names for themselves. It's the girls who are in demand. But Silky Pictures was trying to appeal to a broader base and get couples, so my argument to Luis was that the direction and editing had to adopt a different style, one that flattered the guy as much as the girl star. If a couple rented a Silky DVD, the girl got in the mood by looking at the male—his chest, his muscles, his face, not just his dick penetrating a vagina. Instead of tight close-ups of boobs and then a cut to a long shot of missionary or doggy-style sex (yawn), I wanted to mix things up a little. I argued we should be "more European" (I was bluffing—I didn't know what I meant by that either, but it sounded good).

When I explained to our male co-star, Todd, what I wanted to do for the sequence, I did my best to keep my eyes on his face. He was an athletic tall guy with Action Man good looks, neatly coiffed black hair, and a wide chest that he apparently waxed to keep smooth. And he was listening to me as he stood completely naked, nodding with his hands on his hips as his impressively long limp cock dangled between his legs—not a hint of self-consciousness. He liked my idea, too.

Oh, yeah, the idea. Right. Ummm, yes.

It was different from what he usually did, and after all, he didn't have to maintain an erection as long, not that this was usually any problem for him.

I felt too timid to call "Action!" It sounded so pompous in my ears, so I just said in a quiet voice, "When you're ready, guys." I had promised to give hand gestures and signals for when I wanted the actors to move, and they didn't have to go very far to hit their marks.

We had a full-length shot of Charlene as she leaned her elbows on the green blotter of a big oak desk, her breasts dangling, turning her head just a little over her shoulder, half in fear, half in expectation of pleasure. Todd's left hand ran over her back and down her ass, his fingers encased in a mink glove. The gloved hand stroked and caressed, winding its way to the inside of her thigh. And then, very sudden—

Smack. His right hand slapped an old-fashioned wooden ruler against her buttocks, leaving a red bar stripe. Charlene let out a small whimper. The interruption of sharp, stinging discipline seemed to come out of nowhere. Charlene didn't turn, didn't say a thing—because the glove of fur was making another slow journey along her thighs.

The camera picked up how Charlene's nipples were hardening, a slight rise in the small orbits of her areolae, and her girlish fingers dug into the blotter, nails going white. She licked her lips. I moved my hand in a director's cue, and time for her to look back at him. *Smack!* Another slap of the ruler against her ass. And yet another. Charlene's mouth was open in surprise, her mouth smiling *just* faintly, just enough to show she liked this . . .

This beautiful blond girl, all curves and white paleness and pink hard nipples, half turning; and now she placed one leg on the desk, sprawling her body over it, offering her vulva up to him, buttocks with three long red lines. The camera shot worked if her face was in it, looking back at him hungrily. Her vaginal lips glistened with lubrication, and she was actually getting turned on. The crew was spellbound.

I hadn't briefed the camera guys on angles or whether we had to move with the couple or not—I had merely said that I would give them gestures as well so as not to screw up the sound recording and have to redub it in studio later. Todd sank to his knees, his penis lifting at a tentative angle with his own arousal, and he licked her pussy as the ruler *smacked* into her ass cheeks once more. Mink glove caress, smack of the ruler.

The crew gaped and watched, knowing they were seeing a genuine moment of sexual heat. Actors were performing, yes, and we were witnesses to a sensuality that might have had an artificial start, but it swelled and grew with the raw carnal urges of two people. The sound guy swallowed hard, and I was feeling it, too. All of us were background furniture, forgotten. I didn't really give a damn anymore if my stars stayed "professional" and did what I told them, so long as we got great material. As it happened, Todd hesitated for all of a millisecond and then did what I wanted. Because it was natural. He flipped her around on the desk, his gloved hand swimming along the surface of flat white belly, a brief roaming of her tits, and then she was lifting her legs.

My hand was on the shoulder of the camera guy. Move in because we had this beautiful diagonal scene of her, so powerfully intimate as she stared at him with her eyes wide and her mouth open, her legs parted and her pussy on display. He shoved the head of his cock into her, and we kept both of them in a wide two-shot, which meant we were still tastefully showing them as he was inside her, poised, but not ramming in. Brilliant. He remembered what I had asked him to do. Gently, softly, he dangled the ruler and let it slide over her breasts and her stomach just before he slid all the way into her. That's it, that's it . . .

"Ahhhhh-ahhhh!" Charlene whimpered. "Te . . . Te . . . !"

Me: flashbacking to Kim calling me that pet name.

Banish that image. This is different.

But Charlene *was* calling for me.

The script made things easy by calling Todd's character, well, Todd, and everyone assumed Charlene was ad-libbing the start of his name, even though she had no line of dialogue here. I was the only one who understood. She felt stripped, intensely turned on and vulnerable, not calling out to the guy who began to pump his cock inside her. No, as her legs wrapped around the back of his thighs, the cry was a summons to me. I was the one who had dreamed up this scenario, I was the one orchestrating her pleasure. She felt a primitive urge to call out to the person responsible, and how was I doing this to her? How did I reach her core?

She kissed him hard, hands gripping his ass tight and her nails digging in so that they left tiny red marks, and when he steadied himself on his hands, I tapped the shoulder of the camera guy again, and he moved to get the two in a closer shot. It was beautiful. Todd was sweating hard now, and Charlene was flushed, her face bright pink right down to her tits as she abruptly came, and we got it all. You couldn't see his cock too well, but you saw enough of this thick rope of scarlet flesh plunging into her, a trickle of sweat from his abs oozing down to the base of his shaft, her hands straying to cup her own breasts as sensations took her away, the flash of exertion in a curve of his buttocks. I don't think they could have stopped if I'd yelled cut anyway.

Instead I made another motion to the first camera guy, and he took a wide angle on the two of them, making the eye of the audience a silent voyeur in a doorway. Charlene's legs shaking, her dainty feet seeking purchase on his thighs, on his calves as she came once more—very loud—and bit into his shoulder. It looked real. It was real. He came inside her with a bull's roar, and for a moment I thought the crew was going to blow it by relaxing and muttering, and I raised my hand to shut the hell up and—

Perfect. The two of them looking into each other's eyes. Todd, with good actor's instincts, reached for the glove again, and softly stroked her face. She closed her eyes and smiled up at him gratefully. One kiss, languorous, achingly slow, lips parting and coming together again. I made the camera hold on Todd still inside her, moving slowly, slowly, slowly . . . She lifted her head to bite his lip, let her head fall back, and moaned. I put them all out of their misery and yelled cut.

Porn stars, I'm told, can get off on working together. Many times the on-screen fucking is going through the motions, but the chemistry can be there just as it sparks with any random two people, and you can't discount regular body arousal. Duncan opined that genuine sexual chemistry was a pain in the arse, because the two stars would get it on, and they wouldn't have anything left when the time came for different shots to be taken. I thought this was rubbish. Instead of coming up with different positions—making them do it on their sides, making the guy take her from behind, now do it this way, now put a syrupy music track over it all—I felt a real moment would shine through. And after that sequence, I felt vindicated.

Charlene and Todd both looked a little embarrassed as they came back to earth. Hey, there's acting out an emotion, and then there's showing your real libido in front of strangers. They both rushed out to clean up and be ready for the next take.

A female production assistant made a quick fanning motion with her hand and whispered conspiratorially, "*That* was fucking hot! I feel like my knees are going to give out! Did you know they'd do it like that? *Where* did you come up with all this?"

I smiled, enjoying my small triumph. "Oh, I've had some interesting experiences," I laughed.

I was only supposed to direct this one sequence, scheduled for the end of the day's shoot (in case I didn't know what the hell I was doing, and we went over). So that was it. Duncan, driving back to the set with all his indignation and his jealousy, walked in as the crew gave me a standing ovation. As it died, he shouted, "Okay, playtime's over, kiddies! Tomorrow we do the dining room scene, and we get some *real* work done." Way to alienate everyone.

The most interesting feedback I got that day was when shooting was over, and Charlene was fully dressed again in a red long-sleeved top under her leather jacket and in her short leather mini. She was once more clasping my hands, thanking me. Then she moved in for a deep kiss that caught me completely off guard, her soft warm tongue coiling with mine, and as we finished, she said, "I'd really like you to teach me what else you know."

Oh. Umm. Well. I gave her an affectionate peck and said I was busy tonight, but I'd think about it. Wasn't trying to be a tease, she just threw me completely. As I helped the camera guys load up the van to go back to Canary Wharf, Todd was also looking fine in clothes, jeans and a polo shirt, telling me: "Teresa, you're a natural . . . Hey, fancy a drink?"

Oh. Umm. Well. Sorry, busy tonight, but I'd think about it.

I felt giddy as I headed for the Tube, wondering idly if the two of them would have liked to share me for the night.

Stupid. Stupid, because I felt the frantic desperation again. I could have had either Charlene or Todd, both of whom were safe, regularly tested, and God knows reliably capable and enthusiastic, but I would have to face them the next day for the shoot. Be *involved* with one or both of them, even if only for a brief tryst. Chicken. Here, chick-chick-chicken. Just not ready, even for casual fun.

And so I was back again, finding another Soft Swinging couple to watch.

As ever, the Internet had leads. I showed up outside one large picture window in Notting Hill, but the view wasn't as good as promised, the couple doing straight dull missionary, which meant they lay flat below the windowsill and were out of sight too often and for too long, and besides it was cold out there. Others shrugged and quickly abandoned the scene as well. I headed for a better prospect at a house in St. John's Wood, and photos of the host couple promised a mixed-race girl with café-au-lait skin and short hair, the guy slim and not a great physique on him but with a nice, cute face, South Asian.

Cut to half an hour later, sitting on another floor in a stranger's home, like watching an amateur theater group's script reading, and the two cast off their robes, and just as in the porn studio, I felt the corners of my mouth twitch in a nervous smile over the sudden brazen nudity two feet away. There was a space heater in the room, the radiator not doing its job properly, and the onlookers had to pile their coats in a corner, some reluctantly, as if they could hide their lust with them. Another small group of the desperately lonely and horny and merely curious, and I realized I was like a new worshipper of a depraved little church, looking forward to the dynamics of the group's response as much as the ritual of sex.

Porn has been always a bit sad to me (fun to make, I had to admit). If I picked up an erotica novel, I could lose myself in the story or identify with the heroine getting it on. But porn was functional for the faceless, and if you watched, you saw something filmed some time ago for everybody and nobody. Maybe that was why Luis and the others liked my directed scenes, because I did what got *me* hot. There was a clear personality in the direction, a presence. And here, in another soft-swinging scene, the actors knew we were there, they felt our presence, whether they acknowledged us or not. There was always suspense in this understanding.

The South Asian guy and mixed-race girl were ready to get down to business—lubes, a dildo and a couple of other toys on the bed—but the guy pulled up a chair and sat down, the girl reverse mounting him so he could reach around to fondle her breasts and clit. Interesting mix of skin tones, her lighter than him. I decided he was cuter than his photograph, his cock not terribly impressive, but he made up for it with a sensual style, kissing her like someone who wanted to love, wanted to worship. He kissed her long and slow as his brown dick impaled her inch by inch, disappearing into her shaved pussy, the girl making grateful small grunts: "Uh, uh, uh."

On the floor in the audience, there was the familiar stir from the aroused, a shifting of legs, one man leaning forward, a girl starting to rock in place. Strange to get the scent, the musk, of those you don't know, thick in this small room with the space heater. One woman watching stripped off her sweater just because of the heat, revealing a half-T, and even this casual motion was charged with eroticism. She muttered *fuck it*, and let out an embarrassed laugh, stripping off the half-T as well, topless now. Pasty white skin, moles, breasts that curved up, pale wide areolae. The guy next to her looked a little too long at her and then shyly away. This seemed to win her over, and she boldly unzipped his Levi's and pulled him out, small white fingertips stroking his cock, thin and veiny. She kissed the guy's cheek in a quick smack, a signal he should let things move naturally, turn his attention back to the couple. But she held on and petted his dick like a tiny creature. So we all watched the hungry kisses and fondling, the rapid slaps of flesh, but while I loved the mixed-race girl's body, this wasn't doing anything for me, not until the two got more acrobatic.

Despite having a luscious, curvy shape, she was quite the little gymnast, flattening her palms on the floor as her man almost stood up to ram her hard, but this only prompted more fevered panting from her. She wasn't even close to coming, though she seemed to enjoy the rude pose, her full breasts dangling, sweat now on her arms with her exertion. She looked up once at those of us on the floor and smiled mischievously. We all laughed, men and women alike taken with her. I once loved someone like this, innocent and yet powerfully sensual. I felt myself lifting my knees, exposing my white cotton knickers, at last starting to feel wet . . .

I sat next to a blond girl of twenty, cute but somewhat plain, and *contact*. I have no idea whether she was a lesbian or bi, but all at once, her two small fingers darted between my legs and pressed against my pussy through the cotton. I looked at her, frozen for an instant whether to allow her to keep touching me, but she took her hand away, mouthing the words *I'm sorry,* and confused, I tasted salt. I was barely aware a tear had rolled down my cheek—it must have prompted her apology. And when I looked back to see the couple, the mixed-race girl had popped loose from her man and had come to kneel directly in front of me. Her hand stroked my face. I pressed my head against her hand as her eyes said *you look lonely, you are in pain*. I let her, I let this girl touch me because I felt transparent, and because her body was so perfect and familiar, and while her hairstyle was different, the face and that exquisite hourglass, the big brown eyes, resurrected a ghost.

The girl gave me a look with a silent question, asking for

permission, for trust. Tantalized, I offered the faintest nod, and she pulled off my panties. I watched her snap on a latex glove and thought she was merely going to finger me, but I watched her slather her hand in lube, this nude goddess with ripe breasts and one glove on, while her boyfriend caressed her back with his cock still half at attention. My eyes widened with almost delighted shock, knowing what she intended to do, and I opened my legs. I opened my legs for everyone to see. I heard the rude slurp of my own juices, but she would need that lube. I told myself *you came here just to watch, not get involved, maybe masturbate but not to get involved.* Fingers penetrating me, two, very slick, three, four, testing with a slow rhythm and sliding out to make a duck-bill of her hand, pushing, pushing with tender, gentle pressure as the South Asian guy kept stroking her back and urged her to lift her round ass, granting him a shallow entry of his own.

The girl's other hand fondled me through my top, roaming, and another request and silent permission, then strangers' hands were stripping my top, undoing my bra, and I was leaned naked against a couple of pillows and the wall as the girl's hand slipped farther . . . in. It felt like an incredible passage of time for the progress of her hand, the girl leaning in and sucking one of my nipples, small teeth playfully nipping, tongue moving in circles. She released the slightest moan with her guy filling her slowly, intuitively knowing he should match the rhythm of her hand in me. The others were no longer watching only the couple, but the girl fisting me as she slowly got fucked. I was so turned on by my exhibitionism, by the pattern of bodies, my own hand idly cupping one of her breasts. The sensations from her hand were overwhelming, and I gave up and gave in.

Wave after wave, the slightest movement like an earthquake inside my pussy, and we locked eyes as I came, back arching, her inside me up to her wrist, and her own arousal must have climbed, her vaginal muscles tightening on her guy's dick inside her, him groaning and pulling out a little, not ready to come, trying to hang on. But with her free hand, she reached back and urged him back in. I watched her areolae puff out more, nipples hard, and she came silently with my fingertips stroking her ribs. Impulsively she kissed me, and her man started to pump faster. I rode another wave of rising pleasure and squirted over her hand. A guy watching us on his knees fell back and came all over himself . . .

When it was over and the "guests" were drifting back out to the street, the girl embraced her guy, flashing me a brilliant smile. I felt gravity pull me back down, the realization that I was something brief in their lives. Well, of course, I was. It had been powerful, yes, but time for the ship in the night to pull out of the bay. You wanted no involvement, right? Intimate touch didn't change that. Intimate touch wasn't involvement at all, certainly not without names. I left thinking I had a great scene to re-create for Silky Pictures, maybe with Charlene and Todd again, who knows. At least I got creatively inspired.

Can't keep doing this, though, I thought.

When this job is done, *then* I can afford to find somebody to date. Yeah. I'll catch my breath and assess why things went wrong with Kim, how I got to this point where I'm walking alone in the cold night, leaving someone I don't know instead of coming home to be warmed up by someone who cares.

◆

At Silky Pictures, "Teresa Lane" was accepted. I was in. I tagged along with the cast and crew on the Friday night trip to the pub, and Luis, playing the reserved but good-humored boss, included me in his turn to buy the round of drinks and introduced me to his wife. This was the young mixed-race girl with the Shakira hairstyle, who I learned wasn't from Portugal, but Brazil. She plonked herself down next to me in the booth with a shy smile but tremendous curiosity in her eyes, declaring, "Hi, I'm Helô."

"Teresa."

"Yes, I know, I know! I am told you are like a breath of fresh air! Where did you come from? Why aren't you still modeling? How did you think up that sequence? I saw it, and it was amazing. Luis is delighted to find someone of your natural talent. But if you ask me, I think you should supervise the editing of your directed movies, too. How did you think up such angles? You must tell me everything! Everything, come on—"

The others within earshot started to laugh, because this was apparently typical Helô, so many thoughts offered in a rush, a dozen questions fired off but barely a wait for the answers.

"You make me almost wish I was still in the movies."

"You're an actress?" I asked politely.

"No, no, no, no! I would hardly call what I ever did acting, and it was for others a long time ago. Disgusting things."

Her large brown eyes sought out Luis, and I sensed they always did in moments of vulnerability—more often than the usual appeal of a wife to a husband. She traded a look with him that hinted at the shared intimacy of some past disaster.

Well, maybe I was reading too much into a glance of brief seconds. I was so much on guard for anything useful I could learn. But it was odd that she used the word *disgusting* for her past work. At the table were girls who casually rattled off a résumé of double penetration, three-ways, blow jobs. The people around the table treated her with both the deference due to the boss's wife and the protective affection you gave a kid sister.

She talked about how she was going back to school next year, that she perfectly understood my switching careers to editing, and that she wanted to learn something that would always be in demand, maybe get a job as a pharmacist. Luis looked on, here and there suggesting how if she wanted to aim higher she could—she was smart and could learn anything.

"No, you think I'm smart because you love me," she laughed. And he insisted she was, and back and forth it went. "I'm not that smart . . ."

Interesting girl. Even though she lived in their big house out in Twickenham, she wanted a secure job, one that lasted, and I recognized that neuroticism. It's the desire to feel secure because once upon a time you were penniless, desperate, and you never want to feel that way again.

Helô seemed genuinely interested in me. When I mentioned to Charlene how nice she was, the actress laughed and said: "Of course, she likes you, Teresa! You stood up to Duncan. You know how rare that is? I think you really impressed her."

"Why should that impress Helô?"

"Oh . . . I heard she hasn't had a quiet life. She don't have to work with Duncan, yeah? But she comes in sometime and sees how he treats the rest of us—prick. Give her bad memories, I bet."

Hmmm . . . Something else to mull over. Bad memories of what?

As one of the editors, I had access to the raw footage files and to the production schedules, the slate for which girl was acting in what, even the scripts. But I had yet to find anything that tied Antunes to these nastier DVDs. I would soon direct my first whole feature, which meant I would be out of the office and less able to snoop around for Hodd.

Luckily, I was at the studio one afternoon to witness a strange scene.

To help me prepare for directing the picture, Luis had me learn a storyboarding program and outline some additional sequences, so that he could get more of an idea of how I would shoot. "It'll help you a lot," he advised me. "Duncan claims he's got a shoot all worked out in his head, but I know he makes it up as he goes along. Learn from his mistakes." I liked his consideration and his good common sense. So after fiddling around with the program and coming up with a few ideas, I put them on a DVD and went down the hall to hand it in to him.

There was shouting from his office. Perhaps the argument had erupted so quickly that he hadn't thought to close the door. That didn't help me much, because everyone in there spoke Portuguese.

There were two men, one a thin guy in his mid-thirties with bleached blond hair and neatly defined stubble on his chin, and another who was heavyset, with a black beard and too much gel in his hair. Both kept their raincoats on, both spoke in quiet but firm voices, while Luis—*very* irate over something—pointed towards his computer screen. I was too far away and the angle of the monitor too oblique to know what the issue was.

I didn't let them see me. The room we used as a film library was next door, so I ducked in there. I had no idea what I'd say I was looking for if Luis got suspicious or someone else walked in, and since I wasn't about to be fluent in Portuguese in the next fifteen seconds, it didn't make much sense. But hey, I'm a snoop. I'll ask you what you're reading on the train. If you let me use your bathroom, I'll check your medicine cabinet.

Luis made a heavy sigh, as if whatever they were talking about had no resolution, and then he ushered them to the foyer.

Go fast. Go very, very fast. I sneaked into his office and made a beeline for the computer. The screensaver was up, but I tapped a key, expecting to see something like a financial statement or another document. But all that was there was an e-mail in Portuguese with a jpeg photo of a young girl.

She was in her twenties, with light-brown skin and shoulder-length curly hair. Pretty—but not smiling. The casual shot looked like it was taken in another sunny exotic location, in a hotel room or something, light spilling in from a balcony. The girl was nude, kneeling on a bed, and there was nothing sensual, let alone sexual at all in her pose, her hands clasped in her lap, her eyes down. If she had been allowed to cover her breasts, I'm sure she would have.

I wasn't convinced Luis had been yelling because of this photo, but he had clearly made a reference to it with the two men.

No time to copy the jpeg or the e-mail for myself. But I could check his calendar. He didn't oblige me with a name conveniently written, but he'd scribbled down an address in Richmond. He had put it below six o'clock, suggesting that's when he'd head over there. Good, so would I. I'd made sure lately to have a new rental car, one none of the staff had seen, on the off chance I needed to tail someone (the car billed to Hodd, of course).

I ducked out and went back to my own desk just in time for Luis to pass me in the hall. I made a little idiotic wave out of nervousness and thought: smooth, girl, very smooth.

Boy, he looked preoccupied.

I wished I could have jumped in the car and followed those two guests of his, but I was supposed to be doing my "job." I gave Luis about thirty seconds, then returned to his office with my storyboard concepts.

Luis pounded the drywall as I walked in with the DVD.

"Sorry!" I turned on my heel to leave.

"Oh, Teresa, no, no," he said quickly, looking at me with a genuine apology in his eyes. "This is terrible, having a tantrum in front of an employee, Jesus, I'm—"

"It's okay, it's okay—"

"No, really—"

"Is there anything I can do to help?" I asked.

He fell into a chair and put his feet up, laughing. "Are you a spy?"

"*Excuse me?*"

"For Channel Four or the BBC," he said. "Maybe you're a producer undercover—one who will rescue me with money and send me overseas for projects."

"I don't think I'm following at all."

He clapped his thigh wearily and said, "It's okay. It's just . . . corporate stuff. The company that financed me here is starting a documentary division back home in Rio de Janeiro."

"Oh. I see." *No, you don't.*

"I don't think I was supposed to find out, but I did," Luis went on. "I get included on these group e-mails about budgets and accounting and such rubbish. When I called the bean counters, they were very bad at lying and told me what was happening. But of course, I am not deemed qualified to run this division! I have won so many festival awards for short nonfiction films, but of course, those don't count!"

"I thought you liked what you do here."

Luis looked astonished that I could be so naïve. "It's a business, Teresa. I try to bring style, I try to give these films purpose and quality, but I do not *delude* myself. Yes—yes, they pay very well, but it's not why I came to this country. I had to set up shop for, well, other reasons."

He sat brooding for a moment and then erupted again with fresh indignation. "I know why they are doing this!

Oh, I know, all right. They want to be respectable now. But they know *I* am a cash cow for them in London! So they won't have me produce real films, oh, no! It is cheaper to pay some spotty-faced student director in Rio, thrilled to have his first job, than to fully *commit* to experienced talent, to products that will compel people, that will make it onto television or into theaters!"

I wasn't quite sure how to answer this. "Right, but . . . nothing to say you can't do a documentary here, is there? Don't you have corporate authority over what features you choose to do?"

He grimaced at this, a nod of acknowledgment like a surrender. "It's complicated, Teresa. You know, if I wanted to, I could kill their first project in a heartbeat. Just stop it in its tracks by letting the right people know who they're dealing with. The porn merchants who would like to be *big* documentary makers! What a farce!"

"What is their first project?" I asked.

He laughed derisively again and waved his hand. "No, no! I shouldn't say so much. I have to remember that at least we have jobs here. If I become stupid, they might close this operation out of spite, put everyone on the street. That's no good."

"You can't give me a hint?' I laughed, trying not to make it look like I was digging.

Luis smiled. "Let us just say, it is one hundred and eighty degrees from what we do here."

That was obscure enough for me to shrug and give up for now. Whatever it was, I sensed I'd better not push. On the screen, the young nude woman was still staring out at us.

"Pretty girl."

"Oh, yes," he said absently, barely glancing at the shot. He closed the window down, and then he was asking me about the storyboards.

◆

The time in the day planner came, and I thought I was wasting my time when Luis picked up Helô—perhaps I had just stumbled onto an address for an innocent social evening with friends. But no, my instincts were right. Something else was going on. They came to the front door of a large mansion, and the man who answered didn't invite them in. What was this all about?

Sitting in the rented car as close as I dared park, I couldn't hear much, but a female voice from inside the house was crying. I caught an all too brief glimpse of curly shoulder-length hair, a face about Helô's age. Was it the girl in the jpeg from this afternoon? I couldn't see her properly. And I couldn't tell if the young woman was sobbing over Helô showing up or if she wanted something from her.

Luis wasn't upset the way he was with his two visitors. He kept talking to this man in a quiet gentle tone, and I recalled the initial tactics he had used to handle Duncan McCullough in the office. His arm restrained Helô, who wanted to reach the woman, and then the door slammed closed. The Portuguese couple got back into their BMW, headed home, and that was it.

I steered the car onto the A305. I could still hear those desperate sobs from that girl inside the house.

3

Two days later, I was out at the climbing gym in Sutton, working out this completely insane stunt I had in mind to have my stars go at it in harness twenty feet off the ground.

Mind you, I wasn't sure it was safe or would look good (it might just look comical, but that could be fun, too). Hence, me up a rope. I still had my clothes on, but the gym was due to close in fifteen minutes, and then I planned to use myself as a guinea pig to see if naked women looked good dangling against a climbing wall. I had asked Fitz—usually up for a dare—to come out with me but he turned me down, the big poop.

I was armed with one of the smaller cameras to check the logistics, since you would have three people suspended, and fortunately, my instructor didn't care if I filmed him at the moment, my left hand hanging on, my other holding the camera. That was when Hodd walked into the gym, dressed in one of his mortician suits, and called up to me.

I let myself down, astonished he took this chance of blowing my cover. Luis and other staff at Silky Pictures knew I was here. Hodd anticipated my protest and drawled: "I know what you're about to say, but we're not so stupid that we don't check the terrain before we make contact."

Fair enough. And I was, after all, right on the other side of Greater London.

"You haven't made a report in weeks," complained Hodd.

"There's been nothing *to* report. You can't really expect I'd make a breakthrough this early."

To mollify him, I described the argument I'd witnessed between Luis and his visitors, plus what he had told me.

"Interesting," Hodd muttered. "But they could have argued over where to go to lunch, for all you know. And you don't know what this documentary is about?"

"No."

"Could be nothing. Could be important."

"Want to tell me, please, what's really going on and what you're after?"

"Sorry, no."

My client still didn't trust me, and that lack of trust cut both ways. I held back describing the peculiar confrontation between Luis and Helô and the house-owner in Richmond.

Maybe it was wrong, but I was starting to feel possessive about this case. I was concerned that if I offered those details, Hodd and his team would move in to stay on top of that aspect, and the whole thing would be pulled out of my hands without my ever knowing what was going on. Screw that.

"See if you can find out more on this documentary nonsense," Hodd was saying. "Have you acclimatized?"

"You know, Hodd, you could simply ask if I'm getting on, if I fit in there now. You talk like you're a Jesuit hit man for the Inquisition."

Hodd's face lit up, and the corners of his thin mouth

twitched. I think he was about to make his very first joke. "Don't be ridiculous, Miss Knight. That presumes you'd know how to make a confession."

"Hodd, I have a rope here. Why don't you guess what I'm thinking you can do with it?"

"Just get answers, please. And soon."

◆

A week later, I was enjoying Luis and Helô's hospitality again, not in a bar this time but in their mansion in Twickenham. A party for the Silky Pictures staff.

"We work hard, we play hard, and we get men hard," said Duncan, thinking himself very clever. As if he were a third host. I watched the glazed eyes and slow drift away from him. He was a wallflower for much of the evening.

The actresses danced in the living room, and the editors and camera guys, like so many Star Trek geeks, sat around one of the house's many TV sets, picking apart the bad edits in classic porn shoots. Helô, I was told, had decorated the place, and it looked a little earnest in its middle-class touches, the safest art prints on the walls, a white couch my mother would have loved. A cheerful black Labrador panted and loped around the house, eager to be petted by each and every guest. Nice dog.

I wandered around as my head nodded to the pop tunes, the ground floor and others totally wired to carry the music. Luis kept a professional editing suite in the basement, and I was curious to see it. But first I popped into his study. I was lucky that a couple of interesting tidbits were pushed back in a drawer of his desk. Luis had been noticeably cooler to Duncan than usual, and now I got a sense of perhaps why.

He had a phone bill for Duncan's extension in the office, and our abrasive director had been racking up a number of calls to Rio de Janeiro. A note in black pen read: *Duncan, these are coming out of your pay!—L.* But Luis had done more than scribble off a complaint. He had made a photocopy for himself and circled one or two numbers, putting question marks next to them.

Luis was investigating his own employee.

If you're pissed off about long-distance calls, you go ahead and present the bill. Luis wanted to know *who* Duncan was calling and what for.

And wrapped with an elastic band, also with a Post-It note marked with an accusatory scrawl of DUNCAN, were a couple of the Ladrão DVDs.

He knows about them, I thought.

I was becoming even more convinced MI6 was after the wrong guy.

Underneath the two DVDs wrapped together was a print-out, a big blowup of a still photo, presumably from one of these two films. And it was a peculiar choice. The shot looked like an orgy scene, several white guys screwing mixed-race girls, some of the bodies still blurry, and for the briefest of instants the camera had *paused* at a sliding window door in the background.

The picture didn't look like it came from filming in a house. It was more like a boat—I could see a blue waterline beyond what seemed to be a rail. Luis had scribbled across the page a time index for this particular frame in the footage.

Why?

I'm terrible at math but for some reason I have a good memory for a sequence of digits. I made myself memorize the two film titles and the time index code, because I was pushing my luck to dig around in my handbag for a note-paper and pen. Better get out of there.

I left the study, made a big show of joining one of the conversations in the kitchen, and then, bored, went looking for this impressive, state-of-the-art editing suite. I found an extra bathroom and a guest bedroom, and then I pushed open a door, thinking this must be the place—

And gave a sharp yelp. There was Luis seated in front of the big screen monitor, watching the latest footage I'd edited, his shirt open and his trousers down around his ankles. He was panting hard, rocking a little as if unraveled by his own drives, and Helô, crouched down and just in her bra, was fondling his balls as he gripped his cock, both of them watching the playback.

Luis looked so vulnerable as he masturbated, his body pale and strangely boyish. His chest was flat and smooth, his cock a long, thin pole. His face wore an expression of desperate need to get off. Helô was powerfully erotic, her breasts swelling out of the bra cups, a tuft of stray fur, her natural brown shade, glistening in the light between her legs as she leaned in on her knees. She sucked him halfway in with a greedy gulp, letting out an "Mmmm . . ." Thoroughly enjoying going down on her man. All of this, this intensely intimate moment between husband and wife, I caught in a glimpse, and then I was shutting the door and saying excuse me, rushing away in embarrassment.

Only as I hurried off, I tripped over one of their Labrador's chew toys and fell face-first, splat onto the rug. I must have cried out in pain, because Helô was quickly beside me, asking me if I was all right. Luis knelt down as well, looking acutely embarrassed, trousers zipped up but his belt still undone, his crotch still bulging with his half-erection.

"I'm sorry, I'm really sorry—"

"No, it's okay, are you all right?"

They came out, I know, because they wanted to follow me. They wanted to include me.

I had their dog's toy in my hand, and feeling ridiculous, I made a nervous laugh and said, "Well, I must get back to the lab . . ."

My face was very close to Helô's and suddenly there was a spark, a shared thought. She stroked my hair. I reached out and felt her man's cock through the cotton barrier, my eyes on Helô, a little unsure how she'd react.

She unzipped and took him out, yanking down his underwear.

Helô's mouth covered mine, her soft tongue pushing in, a brief hesitancy then a delighted curiosity. I reached around and unclasped her bra, feeling a freed breast even as I gripped Luis's cock in my other hand. We could hear the anxious wails of the footage in the edit room, and she eased me down, still kissing me as Luis pulled off my trousers and panties. There was a group consent, the three of us retreating quickly into the guest bedroom, Helô having the presence of mind to lock the door.

It had been a long time since I'd had a ménage à trois, and I was probably the most hesitant. I felt pleasantly overwhelmed, suddenly in the middle of this embrace on the guest bed between the two of them, Helô's small hands cupping my breasts and kneading my thick nipples, thrilled with the tight curls of my pubic hair, kissing me and whispering how I smelled wonderful. Her body was the most toned I'd ever seen with a female lover. There was something about her athleticism, and the almost androgynous, underdeveloped musculature of Luis's frame that made me feel free and young, not weighed down by recent relationship failure. Luis's hands slipped from behind me to feel my tits, his mouth on my neck, kissing down my back. Feminine fingers began to work a rhythm on my clitoris, two fingers sliding inside me.

Helô pulled me on top, and we kissed and held each other, and I looked down at her, both of us staring in wonder at the beauty of each other's bodies. Helô laughed and rolled me as if we were wrestling, me on my back now, her sucking my left breast, Luis not forgotten as I reached out and gripped his penis. I looked to Helô, and there was silent permission granted. She let me go, and then I tasted Luis's mouth, his kisses urgent and hungry. I moved to take him into my mouth, sucking him hard, Luis kissing his wife above my head. He groaned, and I let him go, not wanting him to come yet, just wanting to take him to the brink. My tongue licked him up along a prominent vein, and he rolled his eyes at Helô, laughing. Then the two of them were playfully pushing me down, gripping my wrists. I felt his cock on my pussy lips, a brush with my clit. He slipped into me so easily, gasping above me as I half embraced Helô.

Him inside me, my arm still around her, kissing her deeply. For a moment I felt wrapped in a blanket of hot flesh, the two of them so close and warm, and it was liberating to be taken like this, feel her left breast pushed against me, the brush of his abs, hair and faces and eyes, my fingertips sliding on two soft backs, tracing their way to buttocks, thighs. I felt Luis filling me, and then blond curls tickled my stomach as her mouth ducked down to completely engulf my clit in her generous lips. My back arched, and I let out a wail of pleasure.

I lifted my legs high and rested my calves on his shoulders, and he was deep inside me, Helô sucking my clit fast in and out now, and I was coming, coming again. Luis held back his own orgasm, sweat polishing his face and chest. We played with patterns, Luis still inside me as Helô switched to 69, her mound in my face, my tongue lapping her, her upping the ante as she cupped his balls, sucking my clit. I thought he'd shoot into me then. But still he held back. I begged them to let me watch them together, to let me give them pleasure in return. And so I sat back and masturbated as he thrust inside her, Helô shutting her eyes tight, her own orgasm building with *"Ah, ah, ah,"* up the musical scale. I had a burst of inspiration, an instinct, remembering how they had watched the footage I directed and got turned on. I slithered up the bed close to them, and with no warning, slapped Luis's small white ass. He made a sudden thrust hard inside Helô, whose eyes widened. My nails dug into his buttock for a second, and then I kissed Helô as my fingers squeezed both her nipples. Luis let out a powerful grunt, and I knew her pussy must have tightened in response on his cock. She rolled him as she had rolled me, on top of him now and demanding I spank her ass as she rode him hard, pinch her nipples from behind.

"Slap meeeee, slap meeee!"

And so I alternated grabbing her tits and my hand swinging with a thunderclap on her bubble-round buttocks. They came together, tears running down Helô's cheeks. Breathing heavily, she collapsed onto him and then rolled off.

"Oh, my God!" She laughed. And the two of them pulled me down to lie between them on the bed.

◆

Minutes passed. I looked up and at last noticed the framed movie posters on the walls.

"So these must be your favorites," I said.

"Huh," laughed Luis, eyes still closed in afterglow. "They're supposed to inspire me, keep me motivated. Lately they just mock me."

"I thought your mainstream thing was documentaries," I asked.

Because none of the posters were documentaries. Bertolucci's *1900* and *Last Tango in Paris*, Alan Rudolph's *Choose Me* and *Mrs. Parker and the Vicious Circle*. Each one of the movies here included a lush sensuality and lyricism.

"No, I'm good at documentaries," sighed Luis. "But these films . . . ! They make you want to go out and tell a beautiful story. Not show people fucking but making love, and with a fabulous backdrop behind naked bodies." He shook his head and offered an almost embarrassed little smile. "Paint on screen."

Helô nuzzled my cheek and whispered she loved Rudolph's films. And like a wife who can finish her man's sentences and has adopted his tastes, she said brightly, "Jean Renoir."

"Yes!" said Luis, energized by the suggestion. He leaned over to kiss her thigh, and they shared a laugh.

"Sorry?" I asked.

"Jean Renoir was the painter Renoir's son," said Luis. "Didn't you know? Can you imagine what it must have been like to grow up with an Impressionist painter as your dad? And you become a filmmaker?"

Enveloped by a lushness of color, I supposed. Luis rattled off a list of shots in *1900* he admired, gorgeous cinematography. The son of a fisherman in the Algarve, Luis had been bursting with stories to tell when he got out of film school in Portugal. Then he was grateful just to be working in film at all and had moved to Brazil, thinking the job market would be better there. Then he was just grateful to be working on *any* film. Now that he had achieved a level of experience and comfort, he was wistful again, seeing what could be done, what could be shot, if one were brave enough to show something besides lust or Hollywood's insipid crude humor or car explosions.

"Film investment is so notorious in its cowardice," he, laughed, idly stroking Helô's leg. "They never get it—that if one were brave, one would make something new, and people would come to see it. People are tired of the old shit, even what we do at Silky. Ugh."

I wanted to say, Look, you're only in your thirties, you've got plenty of time to still make your mark. But he pulled Helô on top of him and said, "Listen to me, practicing to be an old man on a bench."

"Oh, yes, you're ancient," she replied. "Isn't he ancient,

Teresa?" She gripped his cock, and it sprang to hard, new life in her small hand. She passed his penis over to me and moved to cup my breast. Luis leaned in to kiss me . . .

And the party went on above our heads.

◆

We were comfortable afterwards. No awkwardness, no presumption that our being together had to "mean something" or that it suggested any involvement past friendship. Luis was a bit warmer to me in the office the next week, and when Helô stopped by to pick him up for lunch, she came to my desk and kissed me on the cheek hello. Sometimes I was invited along, other times not.

I know what you're thinking. If I was so sure Luis was innocent, shouldn't I have approached him about his own amateur investigation of his director? And if I were working for anyone else, I would have. But I was dealing with Hodd and MI6, and I could imagine the lectures, the self-righteous fury, the veritable *shit storm* that would result if I blew my cover to the target of this investigation. Hodd struck me as the type to ignore context if I told him Luis had in his possession two of the Ladrão films—he'd say there you are, he's in on it, now go home, we'll take it from here.

Got to watch for a little while longer.

I knew there was a development when Luis invited me to have a drink with him and Helô at that old Twickenham landmark, The White Swan (in their choice, these two couldn't get a more English spot). I sat down and took in the rugby gear in the display cases, and let the boss buy me a Scotch.

Luis sipped his Stella Artois, looking very pensive, and at last said, "Teresa, I think it's time I took a break, and I've always wanted to show Helô other parts of Europe. We've been thinking a lot about you."

"You've become a close friend very fast," said Helô next to me, giving me an impulsive hug.

I thanked them both, but didn't have a clue what was going on. Were they about to invite me along on their trip? A ménage à tour? It wouldn't be the first time I was offered that kind of holiday (last time, I accepted the offer, and maybe one day I'll get around to telling that juicy story).

"Teresa," Luis started again, looking vaguely uncomfortable. "Do you think . . ."

I waited.

"Do you think you could handle Duncan's job if I asked you to?"

"What?"

"Oh, not right away, not immediately! Don't worry. But perhaps in a couple of weeks or so. I'd rather not go into it, but Duncan's become, shall we say . . . unreliable. I shudder to think what chaos he could start while we're on holiday."

My mind conjured up images of those phone bills in the study. Sounded like Luis had learned what Duncan was up to and who those numbers belonged to. But it was strange the way he spoke. No anger in his voice, no sense of betrayal. He didn't even sound cheerful at the prospect of going on holiday.

"The business side, it can take care of itself pretty much," Luis went on. "Payroll, that sort of thing. I know you won't go crazy on budget, but I'll check in from to time to make sure you don't have any conflicts with the admin people."

"Where do you plan to go?" I asked politely. "Italy? France?"

"Italy, I would love Italy!" chirped Helô, clapping her hands together like a child.

So she didn't know. Yes, maybe he wanted to surprise her, but he didn't pick up on her joy in this moment at all. He didn't tease her or say "maybe" or give any clue to their itinerary. The corners of his mouth flickered in a tight smile, and I knew I was about to get a brush-off answer.

"Hey, this is a vacation. *No one* in the office will be able to reach me."

Or anyone else, I thought. People disappear when they're guilty of something. I wondered if maybe I'd been fooled all this time.

"No one able to reach you. What, you going to be on a boat?"

He looked at me with a small silent gasp, and I added, "You have a framed photo in your office of you crewing in a yacht race. Kind of a giveaway. You don't want people to guess where you're going, maybe you should take that down."

He nodded pensively and said, "You're very good at noticing details."

"Wouldn't be much good at my job if I wasn't," I said. "Directing. Editing."

"Uh-huh."

"When exactly do you plan to leave?" I asked. "I mean, I ought to know, because that's how long I have to prepare—to take over from Duncan, I mean."

"Like I said, a couple of weeks or so, but you'll do fine," said Luis. "I trust you."

"You can, you know. You can trust me."

Luis sipped his beer, leaned back and took Helô's hand. "I do. I do, because you're loyal, Teresa. I can tell. And I think you have a good heart. But you are like my wife here. You think a good heart will always win. Believe me, you have to show your teeth now and then. It's fight or flight." Another sip, and he said quickly, "I'm talking about the business world. See? I do need a vacation. I'm getting cynical."

I'll bet.

◆

The next evening I was working late at the studio. Soon I'd be a director, but until shooting started, I was pulling double duty. I had to finish editing a couple of features while hammering out the logistics for my first film. When I was done for the night, I planned to boot up a few of my colleagues' computers and see what else I could learn.

Especially Duncan's. I had spotted him earlier that afternoon swiping a whole collection of plastic sheets from the storage room to stack in the trunk of his car. It was a dead giveaway. Those plastic sheets were precut to be folded and assembled into DVD sleeves, only slightly better than the cheap, crunchy, cling-film–type sleeves most DVD pirate sellers in the high street use. I had been told that we used those plastic sleeves occasionally when we needed to dump stock—you could have remainders in porn just as with regular books and CDs. I helped put the sleeves together for a remainder shipment one afternoon, and the work was mind-numbingly repetitive and dull.

Well, well, Duncan. Aren't you an industrious boy.

Now if the plastic sleeves were for the nasty Ladrão features being sold across the UK, there was only one reason he'd swipe them: because Luis wasn't in on the deal. Maybe that was the point. What better way for this Ladrão Films to use Silky Pictures as a respectable (well, relatively respectable) front than to keep its managing director out of the loop? Maybe that was why Luis had argued with those strangers. They spoke Portuguese in Brazil, and maybe Ladrão Films was based there. It would explain the sunny backgrounds and Duncan's phone calls to Rio.

When I finished my edits, I was on my way to checking Duncan's computer. But I never got my chance.

I wasn't the only one working late that evening. A girl

named Nicole in Accounting had a desk close to the front entrance, and I strolled down the hall, shouting, "I'm ordering Chinese—want anything?"

No reply.

What she wanted was help. I found her lying on the floor near her desk, unconscious but breathing. *Holy shit.* What was going on? It looked like someone had hit her hard enough to perhaps give her a concussion. As I reached for the phone, I heard angry swearing from the opposite side of the office, then a rattle. Like something—or someone—had collided with a filing cabinet.

I did a hundred-yard sprint down the hall, only to stop myself at the last second before I catapulted into two men intimidating Duncan.

Duncan was fairly tall, but these guys were heavier, fiercer, and clearly in an ugly mood, and they had him backed up against a wall now, boxed in by the filing cabinet. One was in his twenties, with a prominent nose and bad skin. The other was the heavyset bearded guy who had visited Luis the other day. The young one pulled out a gun tucked into his belt and aimed it at me—

And that's not what freaked me out.

No, seriously.

I've faced guns before. Not fun, I don't recommend it. But what was strange was the heavyset guy touched his mate's arm and muttered something low in Portuguese. I heard the word *nêga* and then another stream of Portuguese, and popping out of that was "Knight"—not "Lane," my cover identity. And not *night,* because you'd use your own word in the language for that. He said my proper surname.

They knew me.

I wasn't to be shot. The young hoodlum tucked the gun back in his trousers, so now he was only happy to see me.

That was when I kicked him.

Hey, I could figure things out later. I had two creeps who had just knocked out the poor girl at her desk near the foyer, and as much as Duncan was a misogynistic jack-ass, they looked ready to murder him. Gun Happy went "Ooomph!" and flew back into a desk. The heavyset one picked up a three-hole punch and hurled it at me.

Ow. Big ow. Those things are large and heavy and made of metal, and I did something between a duck and a block with my forearm, and neither worked because the damn clunky thing hit me in both the wrist and the head. And Heavyset Guy wasn't done.

"A little help here!" I shouted.

But Duncan hightailed it out of there. Nice. Thanks a lot. Gun Happy shouted something in Portuguese to Heavyset, who let me sock him once in the chest and fell back. I was glad he felt the blow—the paper-punch thing hurt. I don't know whether Gun Happy was saying it's not worth it, let's get out of here, but I thought I better encourage that line of thought.

"That girl you hit near the door," I said, betting they could speak English. "She's hurting, but she's up—and she's called the police."

They both watched me. Maybe they knew it was a bluff, maybe they couldn't take the chance. The two of them backed up a couple of steps, preparing to go, and for a moment, my heart stopped because Heavyset reached into his jacket pocket . . . a change of mind about using his gun?

No, he pulled out his cell phone. Heavyset was turning his back on me, walking away, Gun Happy walking backwards, guarding their escape. Both of them were heading for the foyer. Nicole—

I followed them as they broke into a jog, but they weren't concerned with hurting the poor girl from Accounting any-more. They only wanted to leave. Just as they ran out the door, I saw Nicole stagger to her feet from behind her desk.

She had thrown up, nausea brought on by fear or the blow to her head or both, and she wiped her mouth with a couple of tissues.

"Are you okay?"

She nodded weakly. "I was going through files when somebody bashed my head in!"

"They're gone now. Call the police. They were after Duncan—I've got to go check on him."

"No, no, I can't," said Nicole, stopping me in my tracks.

"What do you mean you *can't*?"

"Luis told me a week ago we might get burgled. He said he noticed a car parked in a funny place outside our lot, two guys who didn't look like they belonged—nothing he could pin down as definite trouble, but I guess he was concerned. He said just tell him what was taken and leave the police out of it. He said cops are worthless everywhere."

I couldn't believe my ears. I'll bet she would have felt differently if she'd seen those two thugs coming.

"Nicole, are you mad? I'm sure Luis wouldn't say that if he knew what happened to you! Pick up the phone and dial." And I went running down the hall, searching for Duncan.

I found him back at his desk, loading up a set of DVDs and tossing a few keepsakes into a box. Wherever he'd once hidden the nasty videos, he'd found a good spot, but he didn't need it anymore. He must have listened for the pair leaving, and now he was in a hurry to make his own exit.

"That was some courageous running away back there. Now what the hell did they want from you?"

He went on packing. I was still an annoyance to him, not his rescuer. "They think we pay the girls cash for the shoots, so they expected to find a big deposit and thought I knew where it was."

"Bullshit."

"I don't give a toss what *you* think, baby doll—"

I pushed the box off the desk, spilling its contents all over the floor.

"Hey! You fucking bitch, what did you go and—"

"*Shut—up!*" I yelled. "Ladrão Films."

The name drop was like an anvil. He was all bark. He was also too stupid to lose the mask even after I'd witnessed him running away. The only thing I reckoned would work would be to hit him with the truth.

"Listen, you sleaze, I know all about these videos. Do you make them?"

"No!" He sounded like a snotty rebellious kid as he said it. "They're shot in Brazil. And I don't need to explain myself to some skank editor who's—"

I slapped him hard across the face.

Poor, poor stupid Duncan. He made the mistake of losing both his temper and his memory. It should have occurred to him that if I could make two thugs leave the building I could handle one tall, obnoxious man. As he got ready to hit me back, I did a little twirl around him and put him in an arm lock.

"Owwww! Fucking—"

"Keep twisting and you'll have a nasty spinal fracture," I told him. "Who makes these videos?"

"Fuck you!"

"Who makes them?"

"Silky Pictures!"

"*We're* Silky Pictures," I reminded him. "You wouldn't swipe the packaging stock if we made that filth. And the credits on these say Ladrão Films."

"Ladrão is part of Silky Pictures. Not this Silky, the head company in Brazil—ow! Come on, lemme go!"

"Explain," I said, gritting my teeth. "Luis doesn't have a clue what you're doing, does he?"

"Luis don't know shit! Ow!"

"Luis knows a few things," I insisted. "He talked to one of those men in his office."

"Course he'd talk to them—they're with the parent company! But he didn't know about the Ladrão releases. I mean he knew they were sold in the UK, yeah, but he didn't want any part of them. He figured they got somebody else bringing 'em in."

"Here's a headline for you, idiot," I said. "He's figured out it's you. He's been on to you for a while!"

"Fine, I am gone after tonight! Will you fucking let go already?"

"No," I said. And I was busy thinking: Maybe Luis had told me the truth. Maybe he *had* been arguing over a documentary division. So what were those men threatening Duncan about?

I was just about to ask him again when Nicole rushed in, still cradling her head. She looked bewildered by me physically humbling the director, his arm twisted behind his back, down on his knees. But she was frightened over something worse.

"You all right?" I asked. "What's wrong?"

"They're coming back, they're coming back!" she squealed, and then she was running to the back exit.

"Shit!" I muttered—and let go of Duncan. I took two steps to follow Nicole, wondering if she'd managed to phone the cops, and then Duncan was saying *fuck this* and pushing past me. Heading for the back exit.

Like a dummy, I stood frozen for an instant with all my questions pending, like why did the guys come back? I could chase after Duncan and might get a couple more answers, but I doubted even he knew how those two bad guys knew *my* name. I didn't feel in imminent danger because they could have shot me before and didn't. This might sound silly, but it happened in all of two seconds.

I literally turned on my heel to face whoever was storming back in, looking for a potential weapon, when a foot sliced the air and clipped me across the temple—

Boom. Purple light bursts. Red. Mauve. All the fireworks colors, Bonfire Night coming early in my head. Then a big, rude slap of floor and darkness.

◆

I woke up to the crackle of pages being flipped and flipped again, someone bored, browsing through a catalogue.

I couldn't seem to focus—or for that matter, move my head. For the moment, this was a good thing, because I was staring into two huge gray fuzzy circles, which weren't circles at all, but points.

Two hypodermic needles, connected as a pair, and for the sake of just this kind of torture.

They were shoved perilously close to my eyes, so close I could just feel the brush on my lashes as I blinked.

Oh, God.

Oh, God, oh, God, I've got *needles aimed right into my eyes.*

Sick, twisted, sadistic—

Calm. Yourself. You can still see. Not hurt yet. So think.

I realized they had stretched a length of electrician's tape across my forehead and fixed it to the wall. My wrists were taped as well to the armrests. Struggle and—

"I wouldn't move around so much," said a bored accented voice. Another flip of catalogue page. "You are liable to scratch your corneas."

Couldn't help it. Exhaled in a whimper of blind dread, panic rising. Worse, my forehead started to bead in perspiration, which loosened the tape on my forehead, but even a millimeter of shifting my skull off the drywall promised agony. Stay. *Still.* For now.

"That's smart, that's good," purred the voice.

I strained my peripheral vision and just managed to catch a faint glimpse of who was talking. I recognized the guy. One of Luis's visitors to the office during daylight hours, the one who came with Mr. Heavyset. Same bleached blond hair, same neatly sculpted stubble, as if Brazil had suddenly decided to have a Wham revival.

They had dragged me into the large spare room that Silky Pictures staff sometimes use for filming. Adrenaline made me see out of the corners of my eyes in Panavision, desperately looking for a means of escape. Bastards had jerry-rigged the needles to a lighting fixture on casters, the lock flipped down to keep the wheels in place.

Should have taped my legs, assholes.

Georgie—I dubbed him this for his fashion inspiration, since I didn't know his name—turned another page. Very smug, he announced, "We planned to use this trick on McCullough, maybe shove one of these needles up his dick, but you interfere. Why is that? Why you let him go?"

"I wasn't letting him go at all," I said. "I interrupted your goons, and you decided to interrupt me back. What do *you* want him for?"

"Listen, bitch, you're the one about to go blind. Who are you working for?"

"I work here."

"Bullshit."

"My name is Teresa Lane, and I'm an editor and director here," I said, trying not to blink so hard.

"More bullshit," said Georgie. "Your name is Teresa Knight, and you make trouble. Cunts are supposed to work in front of the camera here."

Charming.

"With that attitude towards women, you and Duncan must get along real well," I said, trying to control my breathing, stay calm. "Who are you? His partner in Ladrão Films?"

"You talk a lot, but you don't tell us anything we don't

know," said Georgie. "And you better believe you are going to make yourself useful."

Coarse laughter and giggles from Gun Happy and Heavyset. They were back as well. Then Gun Happy strolled over and pulled up my top. I was frozen there, needles in front of my eyes, as he began pawing and fondling my breasts. *So going to hurt you when the moment comes!*

He spoke in Portuguese to Georgie, a question as he reached for the button on my trousers, and Georgie answered back, something disdainful. "Naw, she can't get me hard," he said, switching back to English. "Hey, look at this—"

And Gun Happy moved away from me to look.

In my peripheral vision, I caught a bit of the catalogue as I heard Georgie tap a page and read out: "Jacobean Full Tester Bed, barley twist posts, start from six thousand, eight hundred fifty pounds."

Oh, for pity's sake. He was browsing through the Tudor House catalogue, checking out reproduction furniture. He put that one aside, and I heard another stream of quick Portuguese as he picked up a catalogue for Madura home furnishings. Throw pillows. He was showing his goons throw pillows.

"Did the whole metrosexual thing get to Brazil late or what?" I demanded.

"Cunt, you better show some—"

"I don't like that word!" I said.

That was the instant my kneecaps lifted, came together, and locked on the pole of the light fixture. Couldn't move my head—so move the needles away. I was flexible enough for the maneuver, but do it wrong, and I would be in a lot of pain.

Of course, they rushed to intercept me, Gun Happy and Heavyset. Counted on that. The pole capsized and swung clumsily to my left, and I unlocked my knees and let it fall, tripping Gun Happy as he moved too slowly. Their taped-up torture device with the needles fell, and one stabbed him right in the arm. Good. Teach you not to feel me up.

Heavyset went to punch me directly in the face, but I could move my head now, and his knuckles bit wall. Made a nice hole in the plaster, probably didn't feel very good. As he grunted over that, I tore one wrist free from the armrest and socked him one in the kidneys. Nobody recovers from that very fast.

But now Georgie saw he had to bust his arse and get out of his seat. He was more vicious than the others. I barely saw his leg do an impossible curve in the air, and even as I jumped up from the chair, clawing at the tape still binding my left arm, he booted me back into it and then kicked it over. The wooden backing and the armrest took most of the impact, but it wasn't a fun ride down. He was about to stomp on my head, but had forgotten again that no, my legs weren't tied, and I wasn't helpless.

I tripped him, and his head collided with the edge of a desk. I scrambled up and kicked him into the little cart we use for the cameras on a very short dolly track, and he rolled fast away from me.

"Now how about *you* tell *me* who you work for?" I said. "Who's behind Ladrão Films?"

Blinking fast. Couldn't help it. Needles for God's sake. Needles close to my eyes. You're fine. You are *fine*. Ugh.

Georgie boy staggered up, cradling his bleeding forehead. "There is no Ladrão Films here after tonight, bitch. We'll be long gone. You never find us."

So. They'd come tonight to pack up shop.

"Your mate Duncan is a loose end," I said. "You slapped him around to make sure he kept his mouth shut. Planned to kill him, didn't you?"

Georgie grinned. "Why pay off a loose end? He can be a dead end."

I doubted it. Duncan was running for the hills by now.

"Must have something bigger than porn movies you want to hide," I said.

Why else come in the middle of the night to get rid of Duncan and change things so there would be "no Ladrão Films after tonight"? I'd always suspected that with MI6 involved, something else was going on, and these thugs confirmed it for me.

"Come on," I taunted. "You're a big macho psychopath—you want to brag, don't you?"

There was a good ten feet between us for the moment. He'd kicked me unconscious before, but now he had a lovely red lump on his forehead from colliding with the desk, so neither of us was in fighting shape to reengage. I wasn't sure I could take him. I wasn't sure how this would end at all.

At least I got a good look at him. Like Luis, he looked to be in his late thirties, with a high forehead and aquiline nose, hazel eyes that glowered now, and teeth that were a little too perfect, perhaps all redone. All this and that ridiculous sculpted stubble beard and blond hair.

He barked something now in Portuguese at Gun Happy, still sitting on the floor. Heavyset was in a lot of pain from the kidney punch. But I don't think Georgie was telling them to get me, and they weren't ready to have another go. Gun Happy got to his feet and picked up the box of Ladrão DVDs sitting in a corner, the ones Duncan had wanted to leave with. And then he took them out of the room.

I let him. I still had Georgie standing there.

"We are leaving now," he informed me, snapping his fingers at Heavyset. Georgie pulled out a gun, and I thought I would have to dive for cover behind a stack of equipment. But just like earlier, the gun was only used to keep me from trying anything. I didn't understand these guys—Georgie would indulge his sadism to learn something, and he'd been prepared to kill Duncan, but *not* to kill me.

"You accomplish nothing," he sneered, retreating a step with the gun pointed at my head. "You learn nothing. Go tell your client how you're a useless woman."

Knew my name. And knew I at least did detective jobs. What the hell was going on? Had to learn more.

"Grew up poor, didn't you?"

That stopped him.

"What?"

He gave Heavyset a nudge to keep moving, and he holstered his automatic. I was trying to goad him into revealing something I could use, something to salvage the evening.

"You grew up poor, wherever it was, right?" I asked again. "Portugal? Brazil? It's why your taste is so stunted, so . . . ugh. Don't get me wrong, there are folks who work their way out of the slums, get rich, and they *learn*. They know what to buy that's elegant or at least decent. But there's a certain type who *never* get over it. Over having nothing. And they think this faux-Tudor rubbish and a bunch of cream accent pillows will cover the *stink* of being an upstart."

I let out a cruel giggle—I was sure he didn't let too many women laugh in his face, and I owed him plenty for the needles. Yep, he was staring at me, all right.

"I mean really! That sad shit you're checking out like you want to buy your Christmas presents early? So desperate to look rich! I'm middle-class, and even I can smell where you're from a mile away."

He was shaking now with rage, on the verge of exploding forward. Better be ready to block and counter.

"Kind of pathetic." I shrugged. "You don't honestly think that's what people with money buy, do you? But then you'll never know, because they don't—let—you—in."

He took a step, another, and then his lips flickered with the smile of a great comeback prepared. Only he didn't offer it. He merely said, "You are cooked, bitch. I don't need to give a shit about you no more."

I didn't know what he meant by that, and it struck me as a peculiar thing to say. After a few seconds, I heard the front door, and I was happy he and his mates were finally gone.

◆

Now this is where I do a stupid thing.

It was clear enough that Nicole never phoned the police, but instead of calling the cops myself, I rang the number Hodd had given me, ready to declare victory that yes, I had found the link, and yes, I had found the right distributor—not Luis Antunes at all but Duncan McCullough and these creepy guys presumably from Brazil. Plus I had a gazillion questions for him, like how they knew the real me and not my cover.

Would you believe the MI6 number bounced me to voice mail?

I left Hodd a message. I had every confidence that Duncan might elude the bad guys tonight, but that Hodd or the police could track him down. Even if Duncan got imaginative and skipped across the Channel tonight, he wouldn't get so far that he couldn't be extradited.

So I didn't call the police—I went to check the computers as I had originally planned.

Voilà—evidence on Duncan's machine. Idiot hadn't bothered to scrub his hard drive, and lucky for me, Georgie and his crew hadn't thought of it. The machine was full of the nasty hard-core files.

Law enforcement agencies in both Europe and North America have collaborated in the last couple of years to cut down on child pornography and other nasty genres. My guess was that Ladrão, this shell company for the Brazilian Silky Pictures, must have whipped the files across to

Duncan, and then he downloaded them onto DVDs for hard copy sale on the street. Cash sales rather than leaving a trail with credit card numbers.

Since Silky Pictures already dealt in porn, perhaps cops who patrolled the Net had failed to distinguish the nasties making their way through corporate e-mails to Duncan, especially if they featured adults. And when cops swooped in on street DVD sales, they usually focused on pirate editions of big Hollywood releases. So the disgusting rubbish Duncan peddled had floated on a bed of slime under the radar.

It still begged the question why Hodd needed *me* to find the proof. The fact that MI6 was after Luis had always suggested to me they already had their link—something upon which to base their suspicion. Hodd assumed Luis was the distribution brains in London. I had a feeling he'd be disappointed when I told him his target was really a dupe.

How could Georgie know who I was?

He and his thugs certainly weren't spies, that was for sure.

I went through Luis's machine as well. What Nicole said stayed with me—that he had suddenly grown worried and told her a burglary shouldn't be reported to the police, only to him. So. Luis was expecting a hostile visitor like Georgie at some point. Maybe that was why his hard drive had nothing that shed any light on the case.

Except for the jpeg of that mixed-race girl left on the desktop.

I printed off a copy and decided it was time for a candid chat with my boss. I didn't know how I would dance around the point of who I worked for, but with the ransacking of the office, plus Nicole knowing I had been there *and* Silky's film director about to disappear soon, Luis was bound to have his own questions for me the next day.

Better I ask mine first. Tonight. I got into the car and drove onto Westferry Road.

The house in Twickenham looked mostly dark, a lamp on but no one visible through the curtains, as if it had switched on with a timer as house security. Another welcoming bulb hung over the front door. But there was no answer to the bell or my loud knocking. Hmmm. They're both out. I tried calling Luis's cell, but I got a message that the customer was unavailable.

I stood there a long moment, debating whether Luis was in any imminent danger. But the thugs had come after Duncan, not him. I also thought if Luis could yell at one of them in his office and could advise his staff to calmly, quietly ignore after-hour burglaries at his place of business, then he should be reasonably safe until I could talk to him. Georgie and company must have thought that Luis didn't have a clue.

I decided the best thing to do was to crash at Helena's. I'd drive over first thing in the morning to hit Luis with all this before he left for the office.

◆

Helena was in a cheerful mood as I came through the door. She was wearing a black cocktail dress and stiletto heels, having just returned from a no-less-exciting evening. "It's fun catering an orgy."

"I thought we had an understanding," I said.

"We do, darling, we do! I said come out to the Lotus Eaters Club. I told you! What did I say? That we'd be having a bunch of American guests—"

"American guests, right. And you told me—you used one of their colloquialisms—'We're having a big spread.' I thought you meant food."

Helena laughed. "There *was* food! There's always food at an orgy, darling."

"Big spread," I muttered. I kept up the act that I was peeved.

"If it makes you feel any better, you probably missed an awkward moment."

"What do you mean?"

She poured us a couple of Scotches and fell onto the sofa. "Tonight was a kind of orgy-bachelor party for ol' Westlake. Remember him? He's getting married."

"Oh."

I did remember who she was talking about—an older, divorced businessman, handsome with silvering hair, a touching shyness to him at times. I was never involved with him, but there was an interesting sexual tension between us when I worked the strip poker case. Helena's gossip left me feeling hollow. Yes, it was good news he had found someone to make him happy.

I, on the other hand, was recovering from a breakup and getting hit on the head with office supplies.

"Nice woman?" I asked. "The bride-to-be?"

Helena flipped her eyebrows. "Nice *girl*."

"Oh. Black?"

"Ah, you remember his tastes. You know, she even looks a bit like you. You're the one that got away."

"Don't tell me things like that." I laughed. "Not when you've got a full liquor cabinet."

Early the next morning, I was very pleased with myself, thinking I was close to wrapping up the case as I plunged my fork into Helena's yummy omelette and sipped her gourmet coffee. We sat on stools at her kitchen island as the news mumbled away on the TV on the counter, and I confided to her how I was going to miss my work colleagues at Silky Pictures.

"You don't have to end this line of work, darling," said

Helena, and I sensed mischief. "Wouldn't it be great if my escorts had promotional videos?"

"Oh, here we go," I laughed.

"A commercial for the Web site? Please!"

"*Whoa*," I said.

Because a photo of Luis Antunes flashed on the screen.

As I told Helena to turn it up, we heard: ". . . was thrown off a balcony of an upmarket Docklands hotel that caters to visiting business executives. Police say Antunes was a Portuguese national who ran a production studio that specializes in pornographic films. They're releasing few details, citing it could compromise their investigation, but say they believe he was murdered by a suspected Muslim terrorist, who killed—"

I stared at the TV. "Oh my God."

"What, what?" asked Helena. She wanted to know what was going on, but I was already busy with another shock coming.

"—Antunes as a statement on morality. The suspect's name has not been released, but early this morning officers of the Anti-Terrorist Branch raided this flat in Earl's Court and are seeking its occupants."

Helena and I stared at the police in helmets bursting through the front door of my building, their dark figures in silhouette through the lace curtains of my ground-floor home.

Police in my home. Looking for me.

"Jesus Christ!" said Helena. "This is insane. They're calling you a Muslim terrorist!"

And still it got worse. Because the first thing I did was run to my handbag and scoop out my cell phone, dialing the number Desmond Hodd had given me on a card. No more voice mail, not this time. I got a single tone over the line. The number had been disconnected.

4

ight, I knew Hodd was for real. He had taken me the direct way into MI6 headquarters. He had to know what was going on, but he had left me out in the cold. I was in big trouble. I had maybe fifteen minutes to pack up and get the hell out of Helena's house.

She still insisted at the door that I must be mad, that if I just turned myself in, the authorities would see how ridiculous this all was. I knew I certainly couldn't hide at her place in Richmond. Anyone who knew me knew of my friendship with her. I briefed Helena as quickly as I could about Hodd, about Kim's spy girlfriend, Felicity, and about my bizarre assignment to investigate Luis Antunes. To Helena's credit, she simply whispered, "My God," and then: "You'll need money."

I stared at her like an idiot.

Her voice was amazingly patient. In my panic, I really was being a simpleton. "If you want to hide out for a while, you'll need cash. They're busting into your home—they're sure to cut off your cards."

That meant ditch the rented car, too. They'd be looking for it.

"How much do you have on you now?"

"Thirty quid."

Helena went to her desk, opened a small box, and pulled out two hundred pounds. "I'll drive you into the high street here. We'll stop at a cash machine and get some more."

"No, no," I said. "I won't drag you into this—"

"Don't be stupid; you're my friend, Teresa—"

"If things get bad, and I need more, I'll contact you," I said. "What I really need is for you to pass on information when you get it. The police are bound to come round to question you. Maybe Fitz, too, maybe—oh, I don't know who else. I'll call you."

"Teresa. Are you sure this is the best way?"

I had only a few seconds to think about it.

I said: "If this were a 'normal' murder—whatever that is—I'd call Carl at Scotland Yard and go quietly, yes. But Helena, MI6 paid me a *huge* amount of money to investigate Luis Antunes, and now he's dead. And they're not taking my calls! I don't know if they're behind the frame job but there's more going on here than what's on the news, and I can't find out what from a jail cell. If I even survive that long in one. And who will believe me when I tell them who my client was or what they wanted?"

"I do," said Helena. "But . . . I know how strange your life gets."

I had to smile at that one. I hugged her, checked outside the window, and then hurried out the door. Of course, it started to rain thirty seconds after I left the house. Small miracle they hadn't come knocking at Helena's already, and my heart was in my mouth as I walked the Richmond streets, fearing a police car might pull over at any second to arrest me.

With a bit of luck, I'd reach the Tube, and since my travel card was still good, I could go almost anywhere. And then . . . ? I didn't know what to do then or where to go. But as I hurried down to the platform, instinctively boarding the Upminster train, I remembered that while the phone line Hodd gave me no longer worked, I might have another way to learn what was going on with MI6 and why I had suddenly been cut adrift.

◆

I was disgustingly cheerful as the door opened to the flat near Elephant and Castle. "Duplicity! How are you?"

The tall brunette stared at me, mouth open like it was on a hinge, and I sort of pushed my way into the flat. Kim appeared in the kitchen doorway, her blond hair up, wearing a heavy cable-knit sweater and black sweatpants.

"Are you insane?" she demanded. "I have nothing to say to you! It's all over the news!"

"I didn't come to see you," I told her.

Kim poked her tiny finger at me, tears in her eyes. "Oh, right! Of course, you blame *her*! I'm calling the police!"

"It's your house, go ahead."

"Kim, *don't,*" said Felicity, freezing her on the spot. She didn't take her eyes off me, and now Kim was well aware that something was going on, but she didn't know what.

"What do you mean, don't?" Kim was back to me now: "That's why you were always out of town, right? Always taking off! I knew there was a reason I couldn't love you. I knew there must be a reason why you couldn't call yourself a les—"

I said to Felicity in a quiet voice: "We don't have time for this. The whole lipstick thespian thing." That is, drama queen.

"Kim, please," said Felicity, taking her by the shoulders and marching her to the bedroom. "Will you just give us a minute?"

"She's dangerous! She killed that man—"

"*Kim.*"

Like a child hearing the familiar tone that's utterly final, my ex looked at Felicity, completely dumbfounded. Looked at me, looked at her new partner yet again, and then without a word retreated into her bedroom, shutting the door.

"That will only work for two minutes," said Felicity.

"Plenty of time," I replied, "for you to tell me why your boss isn't at his number anymore."

She didn't say anything. Biting her lip.

She doesn't know, I thought.

I showed her the business card Hodd had given me with the special number.

"Yes, this is one of them," said Felicity. "New numbers come out every three months and are rotated for any call by an operative to reach his or her Control, but . . . but this should still be good. The rotation isn't due yet."

"Then he disconnected it on purpose," I answered. "Give me a different number for him."

Her face was panicked now. "I can't! You ought to know I can't possibly do that! For Christ's sake, it's a complete breach of our protocols for—"

"*I—don't—care.*"

She backed away a couple of steps, folding her arms, her thin mouth set in a determined line.

"I don't know a thing about your operation, Teresa. I am not part of it. If you were sent to kill this Antunes bloke on Hodd's orders, I was never briefed, and maybe he expected you to—"

"I didn't kill Antunes!" I yelled.

The door to the bedroom opened a crack. Felicity stomped over and irritably pulled it shut again. "I want to thank you so much for showing up here and destroying my cover!"

"Not at all. I never thanked you for taking Kim off my hands."

She sighed and sat down on an ottoman. "I suppose I had that coming. Don't you worry—I'll think of something to tell her."

"No doubt."

"Teresa, you listen to me. I know nothing about what Hodd assigned you to do. I watch certain students, I'm involved sometimes in recruiting, and Hodd put me on a temporary assignment to observe you. After he brought you in, I went back to my old duties."

"And stayed with Kim."

"And stayed with Kim, yes," she snapped. "I still don't know your business."

"You could contact your people," I said.

Her answer was immediate and brutal. "I won't do that— don't ask me again. I don't know you. I don't know what you've done, and frankly I don't care. I won't risk my cover, and there's the safety of others involved."

"Her," I said softly, looking at the closed door for a moment. "You're trying to protect her."

She didn't respond to that one.

"Hope she loves you back," I said, unable to keep the bitterness out of my voice. "She's difficult."

"I don't find her so hard," she answered with a faint smile.

It had never occurred to me that some truth might lie between my suspicions and what Hodd had claimed. I still believed he had sent Felicity Eden to seduce Kim, but the feeling there expressed . . . Protective, indulgent, quick to Kim's defense. She loved her in a way I never did or could. You're damn right it hurt.

Sirens—distant but approaching. Felicity and I looked at

each other, and I read the genuine surprise in her eyes. She muttered *shit* under her breath and motioned for me to come with her. Through the kitchen and back garden, I had a chance to slip away. This much she would do for me.

That was the last time I saw Kim. Her walking into the bedroom and staying quiet while I spoke to her new lover, secretly dialing the police to come get me. That hurt, too. I don't know why it cut me deeper than when I had caught her cheating, but it did—her believing that I was capable of such things as terrorism and murder.

And the most twisted part was how Felicity rationalized her own survival. Turning me in would complicate things for her. Helping me would also complicate things for her. So she would do nothing. She would just watch. I bet she made a great spy. And in these small, disturbing failures of conviction, I got a clue as to how her bosses suffered larger ones.

I was running again—hoping they hadn't anticipated that I would try to escape on the Tube. Lucky, Teresa. Plain stupid luck, and how long could it hold? I hadn't even checked to see what train I was on. At Stockwell, I changed lines. I couldn't keep this up forever.

I got out at Oxford Circus and rang Helena to see if she had learned anything. I could hear the strain in her voice as she told me: "They sent Inspector Norton to my doorstep."

I wasn't sure how to feel about that news. Carl Norton was a friend—I even introduced him to his wife. He might give me the benefit of the doubt, but if he thought I was guilty, London wasn't big enough to hide in. I was being labeled a terrorist, which meant a large part of the investigation was probably out of his hands.

"Now they're saying more happened to Luis Antunes than being tossed off a balcony. They say he was beaten to death in the hotel room first—a real frenzy attack, vicious."

The boys from Brazil. Perhaps Georgie boy had more

friends—ones at this hotel to murder Luis. Meanwhile, they went to the studio to take care of Duncan. Or maybe Georgie and his mates had killed Luis before visiting the studio.

"Where was his wife?" I asked Helena. "Luis had a wife. Helô."

"Yes, you mentioned—and I did ask, darling. Dinner with friends, solid alibi. And the good inspector says she's too small a woman to have done the amount of damage, let alone thrown him off a balcony. When he didn't come home, she called the police." Helena sighed. "Teresa, it's bad. They say they found a Qur'an in your flat and blueprints for how to make bombs—"

"Ugh! I don't own a Qur'an! Right, me with a Qur'an! Sure!"

"I know, I know, darling. And they're making a big deal out of the fact that you're a third-degree black belt. They've put some hard questions to a friend of yours, a man named Tanaka?"

"Jiro." I groaned. "Jiro Tanaka."

Jiro was a friend at the dojo where I trained. He was also my go-to guy in terms of IT and everything high-tech. He had helped me before on cases. I imagined he'd also tell Carl and his officers, his Japanese features scowling (but his Liverpool accent a bit disconcerting) to kindly get stuffed. He'd say for the record that people who train in karate are looking for a way to *avoid* getting into confrontations, that learning how to punch and kick doesn't make you violent, it paradoxically makes you less aggressive. Jiro would tell them I'm the last person who would deliberately try to kill someone using what I had learned in my training.

And how many Islamic fundamentalist agents go out and murder a target with martial arts techniques? Trouble was, the world had gotten more bizarre lately, and London was known as a place for over-the-top right-out-of-the-movies assassinations. During the time all this was happening to me, there were new developments out of the blue over the murder of former spy Alexander Litvinenko with a radioactive isotope. My alleged methods, I suppose, were considered far less exotic. And planting bomb blueprints was obviously to have it both ways—I killed men barehanded but also wanted to blow people up, too.

"Someone's given careful thought to setting you up," remarked Helena. "What are you going to do?"

"Catch them."

It was a weak joke meant to break the tension, but in the pause before Helena responded, I knew it *was* what I had to do.

"You do have certain disadvantages, darling—like being hunted by the police." Perhaps she thought I needed the banter for my spirits. "There's something else that's peculiar."

"What?"

"I don't mean to be morbid, but they haven't released your name or plastered your photo everywhere. They keep showing your front door getting busted in on the news, but that's all."

"Believe me, that's enough."

"What do you mean?"

I didn't want to go into the business of Kim making her phone call and sirens wailing as I raced out of her flat.

"Never mind," I said. "But you're right, that is peculiar. I don't see why they shouldn't release my name, but maybe it buys me a bit of time."

"Precious little. Please be careful, Teresa."

"I'll be in touch. Wish me luck."

As I rang off, I never expected to be tailed. Apprehended, maybe. Tailed, no.

Like I said before, knowing it's happening to you becomes more instinct than something you can prove. (It's not like you can say: See that bloke? Yes, the one with the sandwich board for the Chinese food buffet special? Well, he's ten blocks away now from his restaurant.)

I had noticed the same green raincoat on a woman passing me at New Bond Street, and now here she was crossing a block ahead of me as I approached Regent Street. The man in the reflection of a picture window wore a different jacket, and he wore spectacles, but he made the mistake of coming too close when I turned. He had used a rolled-up *Daily Mail* as a prop earlier, and I saw smudges of newsprint still on his right hand. Gotcha.

Okay, I was being tailed, but I wasn't being intercepted. If it was the police that found me, all they had to do was to coordinate their surveillance through the vast network of CCTV cameras covering London, and they could have officers catch me at every possible corner I turned.

Why, yes, Teresa, you might think, but maybe they want you to lead them to the lair of your nefarious terrorist cell. Clever you. It was possible. It was just as possible they could drag me to an interrogation room and be less than polite when they asked.

Not the boys from Brazil. They hadn't wanted me when they had their chance in Canary Wharf. And they hadn't shown me they could be subtle.

So. Someone else was on my tail. What was baffling was that my only candidate was Hodd's operation—but it was Hodd who had had me checked out thoroughly before he made me sign his contract, and MI6 knew I wasn't a murderer and terrorist. They wouldn't have hired me in the first place if my name had a question mark next to it.

Yet Hodd's contact line was now dead, and I couldn't ask him what the hell was going on. Was it possible he and his people actually believed I had killed Luis? If so, why not just grab me? They'd had no problem finding me before. It made no sense, because Hodd could have taken my call or had Felicity Eden say by all means, Teresa, I'll escort you back to our offices.

I doubled back and went into HMV—not that I would lose them in here, since you have to exit the same way you come in, but now they had to figure out how to regroup their coverage. On the escalator I had all of three seconds to decide where to go, and I briskly made my way upstairs to the movie DVDs. Damn it. What now? I couldn't afford to confront whoever this was, not with the cops breaking through my flat door, and me as a murder suspect. I had to find a sanctuary where I could stop and assess and figure out a way to clear my—

"Teresa!"

Todd. Action Man from the porn shoot, the one we did with Charlene. In a polo shirt and jeans again, dark jacket, every strand of black hair neatly brushed in place. Smiling at me in delightful surprise, carrying a couple of Jason Statham movies on sale.

"How are you?"

"I'm . . . I'm fine, Todd. Hey, still fancy that drink?"

"Uh, yeah, sure. When?"

"How about now?" I asked, giving him my best come-hither smile. "As a matter of fact, why don't we forget the drink altogether?"

"What did you have in mind?"

I know, I know. I shouldn't have used him like that. He'd spotted me, and all kinds of thoughts rushed through my head. Yes, I could walk right out with him, but whoever followed might make trouble for Todd after we parted, the same way my other friends were getting harassed. And Todd was the kind of bloke who would be curious enough to catch up if I just rudely cut him dead or made a sudden good-bye.

My tails hadn't come up the escalator yet, so I pulled on Todd's arm, and we made our way towards the rear of the

SEXILE · 123

shop floor. There are no public restrooms in HMV, of course, but there had to be a stockroom or something. There was. And thank God, it was empty for the moment.

I pushed him inside and behind some shelves, and I didn't even give a damn if one of the store staff found us. Maybe the best thing in the world would be if security led us out. My tails wouldn't interfere with him then, not with a big scene on the street. If I were really lucky, they'd be baffled, wondering where I had disappeared to and run back out of the store and down Oxford Street.

Todd was laughing, almost gasping for breath at my brazenness. I yanked his shirt out of his trousers and undid his belt, quickly getting myself half undressed as well. "I want you to fuck me hard right here, right *now*," I said.

We kissed in an animal fever, and he wasn't that great a kisser, too slobbery, too aggressive with his tongue, but when his trousers unzipped, I was presented with eleven inches of engorged pink penis. God, he'd split me. He was a talker as well, whispering useless inanities like, "You want me to fuck you? You want me to fuck you?" Me gasping enthusiastic yeses.

But in spite of all this, I felt myself getting aroused by the threat of discovery, by the danger that the tails might change their minds and move in. Hunted, scared, and God, just give me quick pleasure if I can't get myself out of this jam. So help me, I wanted him to make me come. Definitely had the build for arm candy, prime porn beef. Strong arms lifted me, and then I was impaled, my hands reaching up to grip a metal shelf rail and help him with my weight. Oh, shit, he was enormous inside me.

Chanting now as he jackhammered inside me, "You want me to fuck you now? You want me to . . ." I tuned him out and concentrated on the shadows of abs under his pushed-up shirt, the muscles of his thighs, and his thick cock as it slid out of my pussy, disappearing again within me. No caressing arms and no tender kisses, just organs fused together, body hunger. I saw beads of perspiration on his forehead. He was a construction worker, hard at his labors, willing me to come as if his professional pride depended on it. Keep drilling, baby.

I thought of faking it for him, but I never do that, not fair to me or any guy involved, and something clicked between the vision of his half-revealed chest, the sight of his hips, and the view of his cock ramming into me. Genuine pleasure took over, and I let go of the rail, arms flinging themselves around his neck. He was deep inside me, arm around my waist and hand cupping my ass to support my weight. I sensed he was ready to burst, about to come inside me.

"What the bloody hell you think you're doing?"

Yes. I did move fast. And you never saw a penis lose its erection so quickly.

I started apologizing, looking embarrassed (and it wasn't hard, trust me), and poor Todd—maybe because he didn't get his orgasm—did the exact opposite of what he should have done. He actually got *offended* that we were interrupted. "Hey! There's no need for that!"

"Todd," I said gently. "We're the ones who aren't supposed to be here."

"Got that right," said the angry clerk. "I'm calling security, you degenerate—"

"That's no way to talk to us!" Todd barked back. And in all this commotion, I pulled on Todd's arm, telling him let's go, and the clerk must have already rung for security, because as we walked out of the stockroom a guy in uniform stepped towards us. What seems to be the problem here, sir, the clerk getting more agitated, and Todd no longer even paid attention to me. I made a little wave and a timid goodbye, and ducked behind a display stand as the surveillance operatives were distracted.

If I get through this, I'll do something for him, I told myself. I won't make it up to him with my body, but Helena knows actors and directors. Maybe she could get him a bit part on *EastEnders* or something.

As I darted away and made for the escalator, I looked back and saw he was still at it. I hoped he would give up in a second. I didn't want to see him get banned from the shop.

Not my finest hour.

◆

Out on Oxford Street again. They had lost me for a moment, but they weren't stupid.

Now if you're in my situation, possibly being followed by one of the most experienced and sophisticated espionage organizations in the world (and believe me, it is *not* flattering), at this moment you need to worry about your cell phone. After all, each and every one of us carrying one is walking around with a transmitter that shouts HERE I AM and offers your GPS coordinates.

Don't kid yourself. Just because you turn it off doesn't necessarily mean you can't still be found. Credit where credit is due: I picked up this little gem from a novel by a real former American spy, Robert Baer. Sometimes I read what my friends recommend, and Jiro had liked this one— but then he loves techie stuff.

"Of course, you can be found," Jiro explained to me one day. "If you know what you're doing, you can hide a capacitor in somebody's cell phone." And for those of us who don't do DIY and fool around with the wiring in the house, a capacitor is an energy storing device—keeps energy in the electrical field between two conductive plates. "So yeah, if you've still got power—and with the capacitor, you do— you can send a signal."

It's the kind of sneaky trick Hodd's boys would have

pulled, and perhaps I should have thought of it an hour ago, but even if I managed to take my own mobile apart and remove the right thingy (probably with Jiro on a landline guiding me, but hey, good luck finding a handy public phone on the street these days), they would just put in a fresh one when they had the chance. Ugh.

As I fled HMV, I pulled out my SIM card and tossed the phone in a rubbish bin.

Along Gower Street is a row of cheap one-star hotels where they take cash. I always carry my passport, and I took a chance that the police hadn't changed their minds and released my name. I didn't have much choice. I had been running around since I'd left Helena's that morning, and I was sick of the October rain, exhausted, and cold.

For fifty pounds a night you get a room with a bed and a television bolted to a shelf, one that has no satellite and fuzzy channels, and your toilet and stand-up shower are communal ones down the hall. The wallpaper is hideous and the curtains are depressing, and even more ominous is the free English breakfast in the morning that promises flaccid bacon strips and runny eggs. The place is Spartan but clean, and you're not expected to spend hours in the gloom wondering what happened to your life. But I did.

I risked going outside later to get something to eat. Pub food—Thai. I ate alone, and still I couldn't escape my own mind. I tried to think of mistakes I had made to bring this on myself. I gave myself grief over the fact that I had chosen this weird part-time career, and how I used to congratulate myself for getting into trouble and escaping unscathed. Until now. I started to cry as I finished my meal.

Some fool whispered to his mate at the next table, "Food's not that bad."

His friend gave him a sour look of disapproval, and then he asked me if I was all right. Yes, I was fine. I had to be fine and not draw attention to myself. Then I walked back to my hotel, careful to be sure the surveillance hadn't returned. I went numb, watching a movie on Channel Four, unable to summon any answers. Tomorrow, I told myself, wiping my eyes. Tomorrow I'll get my life back.

5

I didn't. But I learned things that would help that evening. I waited until nightfall to slip across town, back towards Richmond—no, not back towards Helena. I headed for Twickenham. I had to pay someone else a visit, and this time it was better I break my way in than knock on the front door.

Helô was in a half-T and Levi's, watching TV, as I appeared in the doorway of the living room. Her eyes looked bloodshot, the effects of sleeplessness and crying, her expression vacant, numb. I knew what grief looked like and what it felt like. Hers was genuine. She wasn't involved in what had happened.

"Helô."

She instantly jumped and shrank with fear in a corner of the sofa. "You! What are you doing here? The police came. They say you killed Luis! You lost your mind and killed him in a rage!"

"I didn't." As I stepped in, she shrank a little more, not believing me at all.

"Helô, they're saying I beat him to death, and that I'm an

Islamic terrorist. Do I look like I could beat anyone to death?"

"They say you're not Teresa Lane. Your name is Teresa Knight, and you're a martial arts expert."

"There's no such thing," I said absently. "But my real name is Teresa Knight."

Martial arts expert. Whoever had spoken to her, whether police or Hodd's people, had laid it on thick.

"I have a few skills, that's all, Helô. And I've never killed anyone in my life. And why would an Islamic terrorist kill a Portuguese porn producer?"

She didn't answer that one, and I saw she'd already been wondering. But most people wouldn't accept anything a fugitive told them; they'd just dial the police.

"I did lie to you and Luis, Helô—but *only* about my last name and what I was doing at the studio. I was hired to investigate Silky Pictures."

"By who?" she asked, still bewildered.

"I'll get to that, it's a long story . . . You know something, don't you?" I knew I'd better tread soft.

"May . . . Maybe . . ."

"Maybe what?"

"The documentary," she whispered.

"The documentary," I said, nodding. "But Luis wasn't even working on that. He was here, and it was being produced in Brazil."

She nodded with a wet sniff, grabbing tissues from a box on the coffee table. "He was disgusted they should launch this division without him being involved."

"I know. But why would anyone kill him over that?"

"I . . . I don't know. But . . . But he told me the documentary was supposed to be about Islam in Brazil."

No wonder she was afraid of me. All she had was her murdered husband's indignation over a documentary on Muslims, and then a crazy chick turns up who the police say *is* a Muslim extremist, the one who killed him. Barely a connection; jagged pieces that didn't fit but also didn't feel like they had shattered and fallen out of coincidence.

I couldn't fathom it. Why would a porn studio make a documentary on Muslims in Brazil?

"Luis had an old friend who works as an editor at Silky Pictures back home," said Helô. "The main headquarters in Rio. Luis asked him to send footage of the documentary."

"You have it?" I asked, amazed. I nearly blurted out that I had checked Luis's computer at work and found nothing, but I doubt she would have taken that well.

"It was sent to his machine at home. He suspected there were spies for the Rio headquarters at the London office."

Maybe he was already suspicious of Duncan by then.

"Can I see it, please?"

"I don't know what you will learn from it, but okay."

She turned on the computer and, after a couple of minutes of looking for the file, she opened Windows Media Player, and I watched. She was right. There was not much I did learn. It looked like any raw footage for a documentary, with establishing shots of mosques and ambient sound of nearby streets, rough cuts of interviews with imams, sometimes in Portuguese, sometimes in Arabic. When I asked Helô if the imams said anything significant, she shrugged. "They talk about Islam, the Qur'an . . . One talks about coming to Brazil from Lebanon. There's nothing here, Teresa."

I couldn't do a proper assessment. I didn't know Portuguese or Arabic, and I certainly didn't know if I was looking at anything significant. The camera work was quite thorough in capturing beautiful shots of the mosques, some as banal in appearance as any modern, boxy Christian church, but several had traditional architecture. The cameraman made a point of panning from a dome or minaret to the contrast of a Brazilian landscape, making a visual statement on how the country was changing. After fifteen minutes, I was ready to chase another angle.

"Helô. Luis had an argument with two men who came to the office. I don't know what it was about because they spoke in Portuguese. One had his hair dyed blond and a stubble beard. I had a rather ugly run-in with him at the studio the night that Luis was murdered."

She looked at me warily, not sure if she should explain.

"Helô, *please*."

"That sounds like Henrique Marinho. Oh, God . . . This is Marinho. Was this him?"

She quickly brought up the Portuguese home page for Silky Pictures in Rio. And there under the "About" link, with all the usual entries for corporate bios, was a photo and brief blurb about Silky's managing director. Georgie. That bleached blond sadist was Henrique Marinho. Well, I'll be damned. Something very big must be going on to prompt the head of the sleaze to fly over himself.

"Two days ago," Helô told me, "Luis was very upset—I could see it. But all he said was that he had to stop the Rio operation from going ahead."

"With this documentary project?"

She let her head fall into her hands, close to exhaustion from grief. "I'm not sure. When I challenged him, he would not tell me more details. He said it is safer that I don't know. Then he talked about us going away on holiday, and I could tell he was afraid for us."

He'd learned something recently, something damaging. He had a piece of it. Or he had figured out Marinho's entire scheme.

Damn. The trouble with people thinking you're safer not knowing is that when there's genuine danger, they can wind up killed and you're left in total ignorance. My mind raced, wondering if maybe there was nothing to the documentary after all except Luis's professional envy. Perhaps this was about something else. I had another lead to try.

"Listen to me, Helô. Luis had a picture of a girl on his computer at work, and I think she may be important." I fished the printout of the jpeg out of my handbag. "This girl."

Her eyes glistened with fresh tears. "I know her. I think . . ." She sniffed wetly, reached for another tissue. "Maybe Luis is dead because of me."

"I don't understand."

Helô passed me back the photo. "The girl's name is Matilde. I recognized her from back home." She scooped up the remote and switched off the television. "I grew up in Rocinha. I suppose you do not know where that is."

"A town in Brazil?" I asked politely.

"It's a rubbish bin," she scoffed, laughing with no humor as she wiped her eyes. "It's a *favela* in the South Zone of Rio de Janeiro."

The only thing I knew about favelas was from my brother, Isaac, who had visited Brazil. He told me they were shantytowns.

"Rocinha is a better favela than many of them," Helô went on. "It's been promoted to a slum. We have banks, TV, drugstores—but believe me, it's still a favela. Matilde and I used to play as children near the same piles of trash. Then at thirteen, I was scouted one day for modeling. My 'audition' was to be raped behind a mechanic's shed."

My God.

"Three years later," she went on, "I met Luis when he came to Brazil. He was still building his career, making his first feature for Henrique Marinho at Silky Pictures, and he expected girls to be willing participants just as they are here. It took him a while to wake up and realize that Marinho not only makes porn, he runs prostitutes, he's a gangster . . . Luis saw how young I was, and he rescued me. He refused to film girls in debt slavery and only worked with 'professional' actresses, not the prostitutes Marinho collected. Out of his own pocket he paid me to be his assistant instead of lying on my back."

I sat down opposite her on the sofa. She looked at me as if I were an alien, a visitor beyond her whole scope of reference. Our lovemaking with her husband seemed an unreliable memory now. She needed the older, more cherished memories with Luis to keep herself from breaking apart.

"There are those who think Luis is . . . was . . . some kind of pervert. A Daddy figure taking me out of the game, saving me for himself."

"I don't think that at all," I put in. "Maybe your relationship started with him more as a . . . mentor for you. You initiated things sexually, didn't you?"

She nodded. "I loved him. And he married me. He took me from all the ugliness. I teased him about how he tore me away from the sun, how little sunshine this place gets, but it is no lie, he made me so happy here. There are stupid girls who sometimes try to seduce him, but they know nothing about real love, real commitment. It is probably why we both found you so exciting. You weren't one of these silly girls who thought he could be a stepping stone in their career. You understand sensuality."

"I liked him, Helô. I did. I wouldn't hurt him. Listen. About Matilde . . ."

"You must understand, Teresa, in some ways Luis could be so naïve. He thought he could walk with the devil for a while and then say good-bye. He heard the rumors of these nasty DVDs made by this Ladrão Films, and he knew Silky was a front for it in Rio, for Marinho. But he said, 'If I do not mix what we do here with that, it will be all right. We will make enough that we buy our way out.' You remember a shoot Duncan had with Victoria a couple of weeks ago?'

"Vaguely," I said. "Redhead, right? Didn't she cancel?"

"Yes. She did cancel. Luis e-mailed Rio and mentioned in passing how production on one feature was a day behind schedule, and the other girls were booked up. The word came back there was a girl available locally who could fill in."

"Matilde."

"I happened to see the picture of her and recognized her," explained Helô. "So Luis said why don't we go see her personally, since she lives in Richmond and she's an old acquaintance of yours? It's close by, and we were both curious about how she had got out of the favela."

That must have been the night I tailed them and saw the commotion at the mansion's front door.

"I was wondering if she lived with a new husband or something," Helô went on. "We were horrified by what we saw. Matilde is working as a domestic in the house, and she's beaten and not allowed to leave. She's nanny to the children, mistress for the husband, and he and the wife both beat her—he struck her right in front of us! It was because Matilde let out a cry when she saw me. She said she was kept in a basement. The husband put his hand out, telling Luis you want to use her, you pay me. Luis wrote an e-mail to Henrique Marinho that night, saying he was cutting off all ties with them and would buy out their share in the London operation. I don't know what Marinho's answer was, but it was just after that when Luis became very afraid, when he talked about going to France and Italy for a while."

"What about Matilde?"

"I do not know," said Helô. "Luis said we couldn't do anything right that minute. I was so cross with him, but he explained later that if I showed my outrage, he couldn't get her out. He wanted to play along and then phone the police, and when they came to the house in Richmond, the family would be caught red-handed and not be—how you say? Tipped off? Yes, tipped off to move Matilde elsewhere for a while. What? Why do you frown like that?"

"Because," I said, knowing that I shouldn't upset her further, but that I had already shown what I was thinking, "it doesn't add up. They wouldn't kill Luis over one girl smuggled into Britain as a slave. And not because he threatened to buy them out of the corporate arrangement."

There was more going on here than either of us knew.

Helô shook her head at me and said, "I see now you didn't kill Luis. You couldn't . . . But you must give yourself up, Teresa. Or run. I am sorry, but it is over for you."

Like hell, I thought.

"What happened to Matilde?" I asked.

"I don't know. I think Luis made the phone call to the police, but after his e-mail to Rio, perhaps the couple knew they'd be in trouble and hid Matilde away for a while. For all I know, she's still working at that house."

"Give me the address in Richmond."

"You should be thinking of yourself! They are looking for you."

"I'll be fine," I told her. "If I can get her, Helô, I'm going to bring her here, all right? She can stay with you a couple of days. A good friend of mine—a woman called Helena Willoughby—will contact a solicitor. With luck, the police won't add to the girl's trauma by deporting her straightaway."

"Teresa, I think you are a friend. And I am saying you have no time for this!"

"I'm not in prison yet," I said. "That girl is."

"What if this married couple come looking for her here? If they bought Matilde from Marinho's gangsters in Brazil, then—"

"Don't worry about that couple, I'll take care of them. Listen, Helô. Isn't Matilde your friend? You can't just leave it at one phone call by Luis and hope for the best! He rescued you, now it's your turn to rescue someone else."

She offered a little-girl nod. "You make me ashamed."

"I don't want you ashamed," I said. "I want you useful. This husband and wife don't know me from Adam, so they'll have no reason to think I brought Matilde here. And my guess is these gangsters will cut them loose and let them fend for themselves."

She couldn't help a laugh, incredulous at my reasoning. "What do you know of such criminals?"

"I know they cheat to win." I started heading for the door. "So do I."

◆

With a little coaxing, Helô loaned me her car. I broke into the house in Richmond as easily as the Antunes mansion in Twickenham (it's surprising how often the rich don't invest in proper locks). What I saw there made me sick.

Electronic lock on the basement door—on the *outside*, to keep somebody in. I found the fuse box and switched the breaker for it. I didn't switch all the breakers because I needed the element of surprise. When the lights go out, the first thing you do is check your power, right? So I hit the single one and snuck downstairs. And discovered Helô was right.

"Are you Matilde?" I asked.

Eyes wide, small mouth open in astonishment. Up close, she looked a couple of years younger than Helô. I don't know if she understood English, but she could understand her own name, slowly nodding an affirmative. Shivering under a blanket. It was clearly uninsulated and unfinished down here. She was in a corner past tools and dusty wood shelves, and had been provided with only a space heater. Unbelievable.

I took her hand, trying to make her understand that I was taking her away from this place, and she rose nude, with just a pair of tatty panties on. I guessed they took away her clothes at night, perhaps to inhibit her from sneaking out a window or something. When she turned, I saw her back and buttocks were a canvas of welts and bruises. There are organizations in Sudan trying to eradicate slavery, and here it was within reach of the District Line.

She was indeed, I learned later, expected to be nanny and mistress on twenty-four-hour call. Even with the baby requiring attention at night, the couple didn't deem her worthy of having a bed in the nursery. Instead, they had the electronic door wired so the lazy creeps only had to roll over and hit a button. Matilde was then freed and expected to come upstairs, feed the child, and, once the baby was settled, return to this fucking *cot* in the damp, dark bowels of the house.

I led the girl up into the kitchen and fetched a butcher's knife. It didn't take impressive miming skills for *stay put* and *use this if you need it*. I doubted the girl had many belongings here but she would need her clothes. We both nearly jumped out of our skins as we heard—

"Who the hell are you?" demanded the husband. It was natural he was angry. I had invaded his home.

Unfortunately for him, I was far more pissed off. It was the first time I think I'd ever hit somebody first. I sent a side-thrust kick into his gut, and he collapsed into a fetal position, wind knocked out of him, scared to death.

"I'm here to collect Matilde."

"Who?" he coughed.

"This girl!" I said. "This girl you keep in your basement!"

"We don't call her that. She's Dora."

"*Really?* You *renamed* her? Like a *dog.*" I kicked him again. Hard.

"Who the hell are you?" More whimper than bark now. "We'll call her what we like! She works for us!"

"You don't pay her. That's not a good thing."

"What is this?" he asked, his own outrage returning despite his pain. "What the fuck do you care?"

"Unbelievable," I muttered.

It took all of my self-control not to mark him some way with the knife, to leave him a shaming scar. I mimed to Matilde for her to show me the phone. She may not have been allowed to use it, but she would at least know where it was. I dialed the Antunes house. I was informing Helô that her friend was safe and I'd be back with her in fifteen minutes when the creep's wife picked up the line.

"Who is this? Jonathan? Jonathan!"

"Come down and say hello," I told her sweetly. Then I ripped the line out of the wall. That was more to inspire her to come downstairs than because of any concern about the police. I really wanted the cops to get a good look at the dungeon this pair had rigged up.

I kicked the husband before he could cry out to warn his wife, and her footsteps went *boom-boom-boom-boom* down the stairs as she flew into the room with an imperious rage. "Jonathan, what is going on? You don't bother to tell me someone's here, and now the phone line's gone dead and—"

I held out my hand politely, throwing her off guard. Her own lifted in automatic reflex to shake it in greeting, and that's when I put a joint lock on it that sent her to her knees.

"Hello. Don't worry, I won't stay long."

"You're . . . you're *hurting me*!"

"A lot?"

"Ye . . . yes!"

"*Good*. I'm glad. You two like cages, don't you? Lucky

you, you'll get to be inside one! Oh, not like Matilde's here—your experience will come with an arrest and a trial. Now stay still—I want to tie you up nice and tight so the blood gets cut off at your wrists."

◆

I drove Matilde back to the Antunes house. I considered ringing Helena to get her help right away, perhaps have her drive out, but no. I was really paranoid by now, and between the spies and getting followed on the street, it occurred to me her phone might be tapped just in case I did call. Better that Helô contact her the next day.

There was an hour of bittersweet girlfriend chatter, Helô explaining that Luis had been murdered, Matilde crying several times and kissing both our hands that she was saved, and Helô fed her a meal, ran her a bath, and put the exhausted girl to bed. I worried she might need a doctor, but she probably needed a good night's sleep in a real bed first.

When Helô came back downstairs, she embraced me like a sister. "I'm sorry I ever thought . . ."

"It's okay."

"You must understand. It's not only what the police said. A woman did try to kill Luis once."

"*What*? Why? When?"

"Back in Brazil," said Helô. "He told me about it. He made a big joke out of it at the time, but I think it shook him up, and maybe it's one of the reasons why he wanted us to come to London. She used a sniper rifle from a rooftop. Luis said she nearly shot him because he was walking with Henrique Marinho that day."

"Who was she?"

"Luis said—well, he was told—that her name is Beatriz. Marinho claimed she was crazy, a bitch—all kinds of wild things, that she is angry over a contract dispute. Luis suspected there was more to it. He suspected her life in these movies had been like mine, maybe worse. That was when he started to see them for what they were. He wanted to disentangle us from them and move far away, take what he could from them and escape."

"You say he started to see them for what they were. What were they?"

"I told you: gangsters. I grew up in Rocinha. They plucked me like a cherry to use in their films. There are thousands of girls like Matilde and me in the favelas. The gangs run things there. They are the parallel power."

"I know how men can seem to have a lot of power—"

"Teresa, you do not listen. We call them this. The 'parallel power.' They are criminals who are in groups so organized, you would not believe. They control whole favelas. The Comando Verhelmo, the Terceiro Comando, Amigos dos Amigos. The Primeiro Comando da Capital in São Paulo. I told you: Luis thought he could walk with the devil and say good-bye. After he sent his e-mail to Henrique Marinho over Matilde, he called up people working for a man named José Ferreira. He was trying to play one devil against the other."

"What do you mean?"

"Ferreira runs one of the biggest gangs in Rio."

Good God, I thought.

"This is mad," I said after a moment. "You're saying Silky Pictures is run by a favela crime lord, and Luis and you moved to London to get away from him. But then he makes an appeal to another gangster in Brazil *to ask for help*?" I shook my head in disbelief. "And we've got, of all things, a documentary on Muslims . . ."

"Who knows if this documentary has anything to do with it?" said Helô. "I don't know anything anymore. I only know Marinho and his bastards killed my man. They must have! And you cannot fight them, Teresa. They are based way over there in Brazil, and their empires are like nothing you can imagine. No one here will believe their reach can be so far—and no one will believe me. A former whore and trophy wife of a porn merchant."

I'll make them believe you, I thought.

"Helô, I'm afraid we need to take a look at some porn."

I hadn't forgotten about the two Ladrão DVDs Luis had zeroed in on, but I had needed to rescue Matilde first *and* gain Helô's trust before I told her, oh, by the way, the night we all made love? I was rifling through your husband's desk. She was ready now to accept that I was an investigator on her side. We took the DVDs into Luis's editing suite, and I said, "He must have had a reason for keeping these."

"He didn't tell me," she protested gently.

"I know, Helô, but there must be something important on them."

I zipped through to the time index code Luis had scribbled down, but there was nothing that jumped out. The film was crude—mostly hand-held video footage that bordered on amateur, no attempt at any story, just shots of an apparent orgy on a yacht. The guys were all in their mid-thirties, most of them pasty pale, a couple with red hair, and I heard a Midlands accent and then a Newcastle one in the vulgar comments between the girls' moans. British. And the girls were Brazilian. The life jacket in the background was stamped *Eurydice*—the name of the yacht. Somebody's pretentious, I grumbled to myself. The camera panned across the display of writhing bodies, and I saw a couple of ghostly reflections in the glass. Could that be it? What made him mark the time index? Too quick.

"Do you recognize the people there?"

Helô shook her head.

I zipped back over the footage. A millisecond to glimpse,

and when I freeze-framed the shot, it wasn't enough. Useless unless Helô knew anyone. Maybe Luis had. Or—

Maybe I was on the wrong track completely.

"Luis sailed. In fact, he sailed competitively. He'd know ships, boats."

"He loved to sail," said Helô, her voice breaking.

I put my arm around her shoulder to comfort her. I hated making her view this ugly footage in the midst of her grief, but I needed her eyes, her memory.

If it wasn't the people on the boat, maybe it was the *boat itself*. But I could see nothing in the time code that was important about the yacht.

So why had he cared enough to scribble down this point on the footage?

For editing purposes, you make notes of time codes when you need to make a cut. But Luis wouldn't need to edit this footage, so—

Alteration. Special effects. That was another reason why you mark a time code. So that you can play with the shot. Change the light in it, use a filtering effect like a red or a blue tint for atmosphere, blow up a detail.

Luis had wanted to check something. He had wanted to be *sure*.

"Do you mind if I take these DVDs with me?" I asked.

"Go ahead," she muttered. "I want this awful shit out of the house. I don't want to think about this kind of stuff ever again."

I pulled the DVD out of the drive.

My next step was to trawl the Internet, and with Helô translating the Portuguese pages, I got more of an idea who I was dealing with, that catalogue-browsing blond creep Marinho and this gang leader José Ferreira, who at the moment was, it seemed, in prison.

It was easy to see how they could loathe each other and

be rivals. José Ferreira, according to one news report, had been a Jekyll who had devolved into a Hyde. He came from a middle-class background and had graduated as an engineer, specializing in hydraulics. He was no fool. He had worked at Brazil's massive Itaipu Dam and gone to Syria as a consultant on a hydroelectric plant. But then he had gotten stupid and greedy and had experimented with a different kind of piping.

The general assumption was that he had made his criminal contacts during his engineering work in the Middle East. The heroin he smuggled came out of Afghanistan, and after it made its way through Lagos, Nigeria, where security was lax (something I can tell you myself), Ferreira arranged for it to be packed in shipments of industrial equipment. He was the acknowledged ringleader, but the evidence could only put him away for five years, which would soon be over. He was no model inmate either.

This accomplished engineer apparently discovered a taste for violence. No one could prove he shanked a rival in the prison exercise yard in broad daylight, nor would the guard he allegedly raped testify against him—the man resigned and moved to the distant city of Salvador. It was as if Ferreira's conviction and imprisonment had revealed what he truly was, and under his intelligence was a beast of raw appetites and cunning.

The expansion of his empire, directed from behind bars, had run smack into the advancement of Henrique Marinho. According to Helô, the head of Silky Pictures in Brazil had charted a course in reverse. No wonder Marinho was quick to boil over from my taunting—I was right that he had come up from the streets. No university degree, limited education, and he had bought his way into fine restaurants and exclusive nightclubs, doing his best to hide that he was a predator. I imagined he had a degree of charm that

ensnared naïve individuals like Luis, ones who didn't realize who they'd gotten into bed with until it was too late.

Helô couldn't tell me what else Marinho was into—she
knew only of his prostitution and porn empire. And she
wasn't sure how those interests conflicted with Ferreira's. It
was just common knowledge that these men hated each
other.

So Ferreira had either turned Luis down or had failed to
come to his aid. As much power as he wielded, there were
still things he couldn't or wouldn't do. Plus the guy was in
a prison cell for the time being.

Henrique Marinho, I guessed, must be one dangerous
pimp. Maybe that was why Desmond Hodd had kept me in
the dark. It was beginning to look like I had been sent to investigate Luis to find the goods on Marinho.

But if that was so, I had done my job, and my client
ought to have a good explanation for why I was being
hunted all over the city. *You're cooked*, Marinho had
laughed, knowing I was to be framed. And Hodd was letting
it happen. Or he was in on it.

And I kept wondering why.

◆

"You're mad," I heard Fitz say on the line.

I had hugged Helô and Matilde good-bye, leaving the
house in Twickenham early in the morning, then wandered
the streets of London, not knowing where to go but doing
my best to be inconspicuous. Too early to book into another cheap hotel. Staying at the same one after two nights
was risky, and it wasn't fair to have Helô or any friend har-
bor a fugitive.

So by the afternoon, I had rung Fitz's cell phone to find
out what he had learned. I gave him a loud hint to run from

his massage clinic to the café next door to use their phone—I would ring him back there. He was telling me at the moment that I not only couldn't get out of the UK, but I was insane to try.

"You do know we live on an island, yeah?"

"People get smuggled in, there must be ways to smuggle yourself out. What did the police ask you?"

"Shit! 'Did she ever talk politics or complain about how Muslims were treated here? Did she ever introduce you to new friends?' Rubbish. Your inspector mate, Carl, just hangs back in a corner and listens, barely says a word."

Maybe that's a good thing, I thought. Or maybe he feels very betrayed.

"I'm all right, babe, don't worry about me," said Fitz. "It's Helena they're putting the screws on."

"What do you mean?"

"They haven't charged her with anything, mind you, but they're poring over her books and shining lamps in everyone's faces—me, the other escorts, her *clients*. It's getting bad, Teresa."

"Carl knows her! He knows she has nothing to do with this or any of my cases! And he knows me!"

"I don't think he's running the show. Yes, he knows you, so they're using him to catch you. Listen, I told him it's ridiculous. He brought up New York . . ."

I sighed into the phone.

"Teresa, you were in a state after you got back from there . . ." He did his best to sound reasonable and not upset me. "I told him come on, that's not fair, and he said well, what if she got turned? Indoctrinated? She gets into these strange scenes—"

"I'm not in a strange scene. I've been editing porn movies out in Canary Wharf!"

"Yeah, they confirmed that, but they think your 'cover' or whatever it's called was to work for this extremist organization. Ugh! Look, it sounds crazy to my ears, too! But Norton says they tracked down this girl who works there. She saw you having a fight with their director—"

"Duncan."

Jeez. That one I had brought on myself.

"Right, this Duncan McCullough. He's going away for a long time. Distributing these nasty rape videos. They found a stash of them in his flat."

"Okay, so Duncan must have confirmed there were three guys there who broke in."

"Carl didn't mention *that*. The story is you were beating up this director creep, and then you decided to pay a little hurt to Luis Antunes. The nasty porn thing was your motive—that and just sending a message about Western decadence."

"I don't believe this."

"I'm not sure the good inspector does either, Teresa, but he's coming after you just the same. Maybe you better go peaceful-like, babe."

Can't, I thought.

I had nothing to fear over Nicole witnessing my fight with Duncan. She had been hit over the head, and she damn well knew *I* hadn't done that and neither had our director. She also heard me insist she phone the police, and that didn't sound like a woman about to murder Luis in a fit of outrage. But someone was keeping her from telling the whole story. Maybe the same ones who planted a Qur'an and bomb blueprints in my flat. Sad enough that having a Qur'an should even be thought incriminating.

As for Duncan, he might be afraid of giving up Marinho and his thugs—if they were organized crime, they could perhaps get to him in jail. A little proper interrogation; and he would tell all. But I had a sinking sensation that Inspector Carl Norton was being handed his marching orders and not given the opportunity to question Duncan or Nicole.

It was this whole perverse "me as an Islamic terrorist" that really kept me from turning myself in. It was so . . . calculated in its evil. I could have been framed without it and left to rot in a cell until the killer was safely away. But no, Marinho and whoever else was involved in this chose to use the ultimate label, and I could think of no other reason except they wanted me shot down in the street or quietly disposed of once I was locked up.

But I was exhausted. Maybe I wasn't thinking straight.

"Teresa."

"Can't," I told Fitz. "Tell Helena . . . I don't know. Tell her I'm so sorry."

"She doesn't blame you, Teresa. I know she doesn't."

"But it's my fault anyway. I'll get it sorted, trust me, I will."

"What can you do?"

"I'm going to make trouble."

"Well, you are good at that."

Fitz was an old friend, and I took a few seconds to tell him how much I cared for him. He told me I had just ended up on a high note, sounding strong, and now my words sounded like I was dictating a eulogy. "Go kick ass, girl."

I made a sound of something between crying and a laugh, and then I let him go back to work. God, I was tired. I was sick of washing my few items of clothing in hotel sinks, checking my wallet for the ever-decreasing bank notes, feeling terrified to duck into a drugstore because I needed toothpaste.

I dropped a couple of pound coins into the pay phone slot and dialed a different friend—one I was sure the police had forgotten I knew, and who could help me vanish like a magic act.

6

I have no idea how he came up with the rendezvous point, but I have to admit that Edgeware ranked low for me in terms of both convenience and what comes to mind for secret meetings. I had to lift one of those rattling aluminum security doors—it made a noise that played hell with my nerves—and then my old contact Dupuis waved me into a shop with all kinds of tool and dye machinery.

I didn't have a clue what was made there, but it was oily and dirty and none of it mattered. By this time of night, I was oily and dirty and wondering where I'd stay this evening.

"Teresa! *Bon*. Come in, come in."

Dupuis was a funny little man who looked like someone had shrunk a slightly older Nicolas Sarkozy down to four foot five. Same square face, and the brown hair had salt and pepper in it with age. The smoky eyes and Gallic nose were still quite handsome. But Jeez, he was tiny.

He was also self-effacing, painfully shy about everything except his craft. He told me once he had realized quite soon in his fine arts career that he was a technician, no lightning spark of creativity in him, and when he accepted that sad truth, forging Jackson Pollack or Matisse was the natural way to go.

"You must never listen to the French when it comes to art," he laughed. "We can hang it, but we really must learn to shut up about it! You lose such respect for people's intelligence when they stand in front of *your* Cézanne and declare how it lifts their souls."

I always thought there was something profoundly sad about his cynicism and the revelation he would never be a gallery star in his own right. I couldn't feel too sad for him, though. Before Dupuis went away to prison, he did a brilliant job of hiding his money. I didn't get him his authenticator gig in Switzerland because he needed the cash—he needed to finally take a straight job because every European police force knew his brushstrokes. That didn't enter into my recommendation—he was the best choice for that job because he had an eye like nobody else.

Sitting at a workbench was his friend, who he introduced as Alain. A fleeting smile, and then Alain returned to peering through one of those magnifying glasses on a swing arm in front of a row of open passports.

I have this theory. We know that geeks in America and the UK become the science-fiction writers, astronomers, and physicists of tomorrow. In France, maybe disaffected pimply youths at school grow up to become the criminal elite: forging paintings, figuring out the laser beam patterns over big diamonds in glass cases, writing vicious restaurant reviews for the Michelin guides . . .

It's just a theory.

Alain, Dupuis explained, was the man to make me into someone else.

"A new passport," I said.

"Not just one, three to be on the safe side," he answered. "Say, for instance, it is reported on the evening news that

Miss Knight is traveling on a Dutch passport, and there you are, stuck. So we give you three possible identities. You will keep your own support network to alert you, yes?"

"Yes," I said, not having a clue how I'd do that without putting my friends at more risk.

"So how much will this cost?"

"Cost?" Dupuis sounded offended. "It will cost you nothing. Don't be ridiculous, my dear. You are my friend! And I owe you so much."

I impulsively hugged him, which baffled Dupuis and embarrassed me. But I had been up for hours, on the run, and even the smallest kindness at this point stripped my composure. "*D'accord*," he muttered in the awkward pause as I pulled my arms away.

"Our biggest enemy is time," he announced. "They are not stupid, those who run security at airports and train stations. I am sure that when I came in on the Eurostar, they realized it was no coincidence I arrive just as you are in trouble."

"So they might guess why I need you," I said, my heart sinking.

Dupuis was stoical. "It makes no difference. If you decide to flee, you need documents. If you need documents, they need to be forged. What is good for us is that your face is not all over television—why, I cannot understand! Now, border security being what it is—rushed, in a hurry—attention is paid to spotting a forged passport but even more to how the person *behaves*. If he does stupid, nervous, guilty things. This is good for us. And you are not stupid or guilty. So. Please work on being less nervous."

"Okay." I took a deep breath and asked how good the documents would be.

"The best!" He laughed.

"Come on . . ."

"No, no, I am quite serious." He warmed to his subject,

pointing at Alain's array of passports—Greek, Polish, German, and more. "The smart way is to steal an existing blank. Now a few years ago, Belgium obliged everybody in this because of the utter stupidity and peculiarity of its municipal politics. Mayors—can you imagine!—*mayors* had the right to distribute passports, and so you had maybe six hundred of them stored at the town hall behind a simple lock. Can you believe it? Alain will tell you personally how in Tongeren, they left the key to the safe right in the desk drawer! Alas, the Americans, of course, put pressure on the Belgians, and the fun ended. *But*—"

He went to Alain's counter and picked up a handful of the tiny thin books. I didn't have a clue why he zeroed in on these particular ones.

"Occasionally, you get lucky. Stolen blanks from a diplomatic pouch. And Swiss. A gold mine! Many countries are slow to report stolen blanks. It's a good thing we're in Europe. You could never get away with this in America."

"Why not?"

His eyes widened, and he blew air from his cheeks. "Oh, the Americans, they don't fool around. They had fewer than fifty blanks stolen for years—even before 9/11! Our biggest obstacle is the biometric chip."

"Which you won't have on the passport you use to leave," piped up Alain, staring through the magnifying glass.

He could see the question forming on my lips, so he switched to rapid, easier French, and Dupuis translated.

"Yes, he's right. He says the beauty of what we're doing is that you are *leaving* the UK—you are not trying to get in. Many times security checks are only too happy to have one leave and are less on their guard! After all, you will be someone else's problem." He allowed himself a chuckle at his witticism. "We are also limited by your race, whether you know other languages—in other words, what else you can be."

That makes sense, I thought.

"Our best course is to make you a citizen of one of the smaller African countries," Dupuis went on. "There are certain ones we must forget. I know you have been to Nigeria, but they have improved their passports. South Africa is also a bad option for similar reasons. Hmm . . . Botswana. Chances are the guard will know next to nothing about that country. True, they're clever at tripping people up by asking who's the prime minister of such and such a place, but they often don't know the answers themselves! Do a little homework, look bored and tired like everyone else when you get to a checkpoint, and you should be fine."

"I'm not sure if I can masquerade as someone from Botswana for the rest of my life," I argued. "There are places I have to go after Paris that—"

Dupuis clucked his tongue, once, twice, three times very fast, scolding me. "Oh, ye of little faith! Did I not say we would give you three passports, Teresa? Fortunately for you, we have found a way to *transfer* the biometric chip from your current passport onto two of the blanks."

"You're kidding!"

Now he and Alain were both laughing, enjoying their cleverness. "Oh, no, we're not. You see, the British passports of the past couple of years or so only use digital imaging, they don't have fingerprints or anything else included. If it were fingerprints, there'd be a problem, and we'd have to get someone else's, and ugh! Many headaches."

I was flabbergasted. "How can you do that?"

Alain answered again rapidly in French, and Dupuis was getting tired of playing translator. "It's all quite technical, and of course, it's the young people who know the computer tricks, so Alain brought one in. He says it has to do with something called RFID—Radio Frequency Identification technology and using transponders to switch things around. On a slightly older passport like yours, the information wasn't encrypted, so we got it easily and can copy it twice onto your two extras. Better not risk playing games with British security when you try to exit. With the Botswana one, it has nothing—they'll look at it, and it's a judgment call, but again, you're leaving. It's in their interests to keep the queue moving, to let you go. So we use the biometric chips for when you're outside Britain, traveling elsewhere."

He tapped the counter where Alain's first masterpiece was almost finished. "Ha! If we were in America, you couldn't get away with this. They encrypt the biometrics, and they're putting very fine mesh shields on the passport covers to try to block the chips from being scanned at a distance by forgers. Then we get around that, and on and on it goes."

"You're scaring me that it won't work," I said.

Dupuis patted my shoulder. "Not to worry. Take it from an old liar with a paintbrush, my dear. A passport is a small bedtime story, and we are telling each child what he wants to hear."

◆

The Eurostar was a study in dread. Show my fear, and I would be done, game over. Alain had chosen a name I wasn't even sure how to pronounce on first reading, but he and Dupuis were right. It was a long and busy queue for the train, and when the moment of truth came, the security guard barely glanced at the passport. No biometric chip to read, one less thing they could use to verify me, so I got a polite nod. On your way, love.

I had a new, disturbingly authentic-looking British passport. (If I had one this good, I thought to myself, what do the bad guys have?) I could use it practically anywhere, and given that the UK was known for its stringent controls, I should probably flash this one in Europe.

"Forgers like to pick on Belgian ones, Portugal, Poland,

the eastern EU," Dupuis had informed me. "Those they'll study closer because of their history as forgers' targets."

My third forgery was a blue Canadian passport. The logic was that if my British cover was blown, very few nations had a problem with Canadians as visitors or tourists. My British accent wouldn't raise a flag, as many Brits immigrated to Canada, and just to make it even more plausible, it claimed I was married and lived in Winnipeg. I told Dupuis I sounded incredibly dull. He said that was the point.

His other parting gifts included a laptop and a disposable cell phone with prepaid units. I waited until we were across the Channel, and then *ring, ring:* time to enlist Jiro Tanaka, the only person even mad enough for the scheme I had in mind. Hopefully, he wasn't pissed at me for the cops giving him the third degree.

I called him at the dojo, not a location the police would likely choose to eavesdrop, and so far, so good, he took my call and told me no sweat, he was outraged at them, not me. But as I sketched out my idea, I heard a long sobering silence. Maybe I gave him too much credit for recklessness.

"Teresa," he said quietly. "You really take the . . . What you're asking for is bloody well next to impossible." He sighed in exasperation and then said, "Umm, right, how did you get out of the country?"

"I had a little problem with documents so I got help."

"Forgery?" he whispered in amazement.

"Umm . . . Yeah."

"*Cool!* How did they get around the RFID?"

I should have known my favorite tech geek would be hungry for trade secrets. "Jiro, please, later? The task at hand?"

I finished explaining what I needed and asked, "Can it be done?"

"If it's on a computer, it can be done. But if it can be done, it won't be by me."

"Jirooooh," I whined.

I heard a long groan from London. "I can hook you up with a bloke who *lives* for this kind of shit. But I have to tell you, love, that if you do this—"

"They'll what? Launch a manhunt for me? Charge me with something else completely bogus? Someone went to a lot of trouble to ruin my name and drop a big steaming pile of law enforcement on me. First step is to confront their lies."

"Teresa, it's insane," he said calmly.

"No, it's brilliant!" I insisted. "Look, they've labeled me a terrorist. So they'll use the Counter-Terrorism team at Forensic Services, right? And *they*, according to the police department's own Web site, handle evidence from retrieval right up to analysis. They do it all. They're unique."

"I follow the logic," he said irritably. "You're expecting they'll dump it all in one big place. Okay, say my mate hacks in. What do you hope to gain?"

"You're the one who keeps reminding me everything's digital," I argued. "I bet you anything their crime scene photos will be jpegs or PDFs. I want to see them."

Jiro failed to see the beauty of my grand plan. "You're do-ing all this to see photos of this guy, this Luis—"

"Luis Antunes, right."

"This Luis Antunes battered and bruised."

"Exactly."

"I don't get it."

"You don't have to," I assured him. "With luck, those photos will clear me."

"Won't you have to come home to use 'em?"

"The job's only half done with the photos," I said. "It's not enough to prove I didn't do it. I better serve up who did kill Luis Antunes and why."

"How are you going to do *that*?"

"I don't know. I need to mull that one over."

I was famous for my mulling. *Let me mull,* I told friends during a crisis. Which was my code for I'd probably be making it up as I went along. This situation really required it.

I gave Jiro a new e-mail address to send along the goods, and then he rang off. He wanted to get back to class in the dojo. It was *kumite* night, and Jiro loves sparring. I asked him once why I never saw him hit the wooden post, the *makiwara,* and he grinned and said, "Oh, I like to hit bodies."

God, I missed my friends. I thought of Helena—wondered how she was coping. My fault.

Sitting on the Eurostar speeding its way to Paris, I put the Botswana passport away for safekeeping and pulled out my "new" British one. For now, I was Susan Braithewaite, two years shaved off my actual age, and my birthday moved to August. I lived in Shepherd's Bush, my job neatly handwritten in the space provided as library technician (as if). I wondered just how long I would have to be Susan Braithewaite.

What really made me stare was that the name written down as my emergency contact didn't exist, completely made up. There would be no emergency contact. If I needed something done at home, I could call Jiro or Fitz, possibly Helena if she survived the ordeal they were putting her through. But if something happened to me out here in the void, I was on my own. After I got out of Europe—and I *did* have to get out of Europe—no one could run to the rescue of little Teresa Knight, because Teresa was off the map.

I had never felt so alone in my life.

◆

Paris. Romantic. Poetic. Artistic. Seine place, Seine story. But not for me, not this time. No big deal. I've done the touristy things, the shopping trips, the gastronomic pilgrimages, and I was really here to mark time before I fled to a new hiding spot.

Dupuis had booked me a one-week stay at an apartment-hotel where I was sure to be invisible: Clichy-sous-Bois, one of the most infamous of the *banlieues,* the suburbs of Paris. It was a district where North Africans, immigrants from other parts of the world, and the poorest of the French working class managed to find a place to live. Big ugly Sixties blocks turned into flats turned into tenements. The awning markets with produce and wares, *halal* meat shops, avenues and boulevards that looked like parts of Hackney or Lewisham, only instead of English mixed with the Arabic you had French.

The riots had been bad here a couple of years ago, and all the burning cars and bottle-throwing against the helmeted police with their shields had stirred up again during the presidential elections.

My room was all right, clean and functional without an ounce of charm. There was a bed, thankfully my own bath this time, and a dark wood wardrobe that you seem to get in every French hotel room of two stars or less. Basic terrestrial French TV, and I ended up after a quick dinner out the first night watching *House* dubbed in French. Surreal. Well, it was surreal watching *House* in English anyway, with star Hugh Laurie from my own childhood stomping grounds of Oxford doing his American accent. Fitz and I once had a joke of a game, listing our favorite TV stars we'd like to sleep with, and I shocked Fitz by saying I wanted a three-way with the blond Aussie guy on the show and Omar Epps, who plays the black doctor.

A happier moment. Before someone took my life away.

Halfway through the episode, my mind said: *Violet.* I wondered if she had ever watched the show. With the way her mind worked and how she loved science, I knew she would have loved it.

I summoned her to me in my imagination. Large brown eyes with exquisite, generous eyelashes set in a long face,

hair in elaborate cornrows, still all of nineteen with baby fat
around her belly and hips. I remembered the way she used
to suck my nipples, coming up to kiss me, our tongues so
perfectly in tune with each other as they coiled.

She was in lace tonight in my head, so beautiful, eyes
shining, and we were on a hilltop in summer looking up at
the stars, somewhere very far away from the inner grotty
streets of London, though she'd never seen London in her
life. We were away from the dirge of garbage trucks making
pickups beyond my window. She was miraculously, merci-
fully here with me, her sweet fingers dipping into my
vagina, already wet and granting her entry, and I heard the
words she said to me when we slept together the first time.
If you're loud, bite me when you come, bite me here. On the
breast. I cupped my own breast and played with my clitoris,
and I could almost smell park grass, the scent of her. The
image melded with the girl who fisted me in the apartment
in St. John's Wood, her hand now, yes, Violet's hand . . .

Then she was wearing a strap-on like Kim had used with
me, but it was so much better with her holding me tight,
the black dildo plunging into me, and the images blurred
again, and Luis was penetrating me. I could feel that his
cock was a hard living organ, Helô nude and beautiful with
her mouth open in wonder just before her mouth ducked
down to suck my clitoris. But I banished the picture, a re-
minder of my current troubles, and my old lover, Violet,
returned. The old familiar guilt welled up, but I needed
the comfort of her affection far more. And I knew she had
loved me.

Outside the room's window, on the lonely Paris street below, I heard Alicia Keys's new single playing loudly on the
stereo of an idling car. Alicia was singing how no one could
get in the way of what she felt, no one. The tune sounded
confident and yet somehow so very sad, a tragic hymn. Or
was it just me? Because I once believed the sentiment of

those lyrics? Violet . . . I had no right to feel confident about anything anymore.

Don't cry, baby. See the stars?

I felt the brush of her dangling breasts as she thrust the dildo into me, I felt her kiss me and stroke my cheek again and again in long, soothing strokes, my hands on her generous but tight ass. Twin pillows of full lips were on my cheek, my hand holding her breast, playing with her nipple, and the dildo was all the way in again as she kissed me, her tongue warm and soft and exploring. I felt the points of her shoulder blades, two hemispheres of buttock, and I even imagined the delicate lace and the rougher texture of the dildo strap. But most of all, I imagined her features set in a lovely oval, the adoration in those trusting eyes. *I miss you so much* . . .

Like a tape rewinding, my mind brought the two of us back to me undressing her, a new fantasy started. We were in my flat, Violet sitting against a wall, as I had sat for those swinging scenes, her beautiful shapely legs stretched out, and I tickled her exquisite bare foot to make her giggle and then lifted one full breast out from its lacy folds, exposing her, massaging her breast on display, kneading it and watching her mouth open, her small white teeth bite down on her bottom lip. She was completely real to me in my imagination, and I could see her dark erect nipple, I could *feel* the warmth of her thigh under my fingertips, and I saw the glistening of lubrication on her pussy lips. She was here and wanting me, because she had always wanted me, we belonged together, and if I concentrated hard enough I could make her come, I would hear her . . .

A fire was burning, and I heard someone behind me use the poker to stir it. Strangers were watching us. It was our time to perform on the soft-swinging circuit, and I imagined myself stripping naked in front of these people, Violet encouraging me. I became so wet at the thought. I imagined myself mounting her, now her in the dildo harness again, my pussy on show with the black dick filling me, hugging my girl tight. Making love to her and letting the world know we were together, something that only a few close friends ever learned. I let her fuck me with the dildo, and I could taste her breast (*bite me here*), smell her perfume, hear her tell me not to cry because she was impossibly wiser in this fantasy, knowing everything, understanding everything, still loving me.

I shook with my orgasm in that lonely, shabby little hotel room, and then I felt the fall. I was still alone. I had always been alone. She had never been here, and she would never be with me in that park. I made a loud wet sniff and rubbed my eyes, thinking: My friends will never meet you, darling. Ever. They'll never know how good you were for me. And I realized what a sham my relationship with Kim had truly been, because I had never told her about the cases, all about what was involved in what I do, and I knew that instead of confiding in a partner, needing his or her sympathy, I wanted someone who understood this life from the inside. No explanations necessary. I couldn't have had that with Violet, but for her, I would have given up the travel, the insanity, for domestic bliss with my sweet young stargazer.

Look at what this life has cost you.

Look at where you are.

The room felt so small. When I sat up and checked the window, I could hardly see a damn thing. The song was over, the car's driver pulling out from the curb after getting takeout. I couldn't see the stars at all, only smears of grime.

◆

Dupuis and Alain had left a message with the hotel desk, letting me know they had safely made it out of the UK after me, and before returning to Geneva they were at a friend's in Neuilly, in case I needed them. I was certain now I would. I had one last favor to ask of them before I left France.

Meanwhile, Jiro was true to his word. His contact (and I wondered honestly if it weren't Jiro himself) dumped the Forensic Service's Counter-Terrorism unit's entire case file into my e-mail account. As a matter of fact, one e-mail came with a PDF of the written police report, and a second e-mail had what I really wanted, the crime scene photos. I guessed Jiro, or his contact, wasn't taking any chances. Better for their own security that they break the stuff up and send it from two different e-mail addresses.

The photos were the key.

I downloaded everything to the laptop, and then I took a deep breath before opening the pictures. Hard seeing Luis like this—this man who had become a friend, who with his wife had shared something special with me. I owed it to him to catch his killer as much as I owed it to myself to clear my name.

Go to work, Teresa.

I studied the photos carefully. You're probably telling yourself, hey, she's not a medical examiner—what does she know? And you're right. I'm not. Fortunately, I didn't have to be. Experience and common sense were needed here. The fall from that hotel balcony had severed Luis's spinal cord and smashed the back of his skull, but it wasn't enough to obscure or alter the injuries from his beating. Those were where the truth lay.

Luis had several bruises to his face. There was one just under the nose (the "sweet spot" as karate practitioners sometimes call it, because you punch there, and not only does it hurt like hell, you can't roll your head with the blow *at all*). He also had a rather odd bruise, shaped in a weird el-lipse, which covered much of the temple area up to his right eyebrow. No way the heel, knuckles, or palm of a hand could make that blow—no part could leave that mark, so the killer either used a tool or the edge of his foot.

But if he had used his foot, he must have been floating *Matrix*-style in the air when he struck Luis, the bruise impression was so bizarre. What wild technique had the killer used for *that*?

Lucky for me, there were also two defined sets of knuckle impressions from punches to Luis's chest. I'll get to those. Be patient.

Luis had two broken ribs from kicks to his side, and the report said his spleen had been ruptured before he was tossed off the balcony.

But the clinchers for the theory I was slowly developing were his hands. Luis's hands were perfectly normal. Not a scratch on them, no knuckle abrasions, no cuts.

The photos took me part of the way to exonerating myself, but I needed to rope in another expert. This is why I wasn't yet finished with Dupuis.

He was a man who understood forgeries, which meant he understood art supplies, which meant he also knew people who did sculpture. What I needed was a friend of his who could make plaster casts.

For the first time in days, I began to feel better about my future and getting my life back, and I rang the dojo that evening to thank the resourceful Monsieur Tanaka. Jiro's voice sounded strange on the line.

"What's the matter?" I asked him. "Are you in trouble? Did the cops find out you did it?"

"No, no, I'm fine, Teresa, that's the thing, I didn't do it, well, I mean *my mate* didn't do it—not all of it."

I told him I didn't understand.

"We could only crack one part of the database. We sent you the police report to keep you happy until we could figure out the rest. Teresa . . . We didn't send you any crime scene photos!"

◆

It would take a couple of days for the plaster casts to be finished, and Dupuis promised they would be delivered to my hotel in Clichy-sous-Bois by someone we could trust.

In the meantime, I went to an Internet café and replied to my mysterious helper. There were ways, I was sure, the photos could have been placed in Jiro's hands with him never knowing he was helped. But I think my benefactor wanted me to notice him. And I had a pretty good idea who it was.

I wrote: THANKS. ARE YOU OK? HOW DID YOU GET THEM? No sooner had I hit "Send" than the computer offered a chirpy bell, inviting me to use the Windows Live Messenger. No on-line display picture, certainly no webcam image. My ally called himself *Sibar Sexy*.

He did it, no doubt, not only to tip me off to who he was, but to wind me up a little. Jeez, Simon, you never change, I thought.

Simon Highsmith. We had once made love during the Sibar festival in the Nuba Mountains of Sudan. The word *Sibar* was sufficiently obscure that unless you knew that part of Africa you'd never guess the reference. He was already answering my questions:

I'M FINE, NOT THE PRIORITY. NEVER MIND HOW GOT IT, YOU NEED IT.

Fair enough. I'm sure he had his own friend who handled tech stuff the way I consulted Jiro.

IN MAJOR, MAJOR SHIT, YES?

This, too, was a reference to a time we once had together. Simon had playfully asked me if I would rescue him if he were in trouble, as in "major, major shit." I never gave him a serious response, but the truth was that I knew I would come running, just as he would for me. I'm not sure I'll ever understand the peculiar bond between us—not lovers that last, always friends out of touch, but strangers that can and will fight side by side. Maybe he understood it better. I had asked over a breakfast ages ago: *Why should I come racing to the rescue?*

And he had replied: *You think about it.*

Maybe because in the end, we both fight for the same things, and one of them was Africa. Well, I was nowhere near Africa now, but he was still in my corner.

I typed back: YES. IN MAJOR, MAJOR SHIT. THINK H BETRAYED ME.

After a few seconds (and God only knew where he was), his reply came back: WHICH H? *Which H?* There was another one besides Hodd?

My fingers were scrambling over the keys. WHICH H DO YOU KNOW?

Another long pause in which the tiny lettering across the bottom of the window told me: "*Sibar Sexy is writing a message.*" I hate those prompts because inevitably the message coming your way after the long pause is some brief, anticlimactic reply. And it was:

NOT SAFE TO SAY THIS VENUE.

That also bothered me. It suggested two things: that Simon wasn't as "fine" as he claimed, since he couldn't send information openly, and there might be another player in this game I didn't know about. But then again, I had no way of knowing how familiar Simon was with the case. He obviously was aware I'd been framed, since he sent along material to exonerate me, but—

Another message. THIS IS BIGGER THAN SAMBA.

That was clear enough. He knew the trail led to Brazil, and probably guessed it was where I would go. But the ramifications went beyond a porn merchant and a couple of big-league gangsters in the favelas of Rio de Janeiro. If I asked, he'd probably write that it wasn't safe to discuss them here either.

To hell with it, I asked anyway. HOW BIG?

I pictured him somewhere, brushing a comma of his blond hair away from his forehead, always his preliminary gesture before he put his hand on his chin, his ice-chip blue eyes staring at the screen, figuring out the safest way to tell me something. Simon liked to play mysterious at times, but that was when he was at cross-purposes to my solving a case, and lately we had worked together well, our cards on the table. He didn't play games when it counted. He knew the major shit I was in, and since he'd gone underground, far away from his old spy clients, I was fairly sure he was in trouble himself.

BIG ENOUGH TO BURN ME HERE. TRIED TO WARN H.

"Great!" I muttered, annoyed. "But *which* H?"

Perhaps sensing my impatience, new lines formed on the screen: WILL BE IN TOUCH AND TRY TO HELP WHEN I CAN. BUT FIRE'S BIG THIS END. YOU KNOW I'D PREFER BEING WITH YOU, ALWAYS MORE FUN.

I thought he might disconnect in a second, so I typed quickly: WHEN DONE WHERE GO TO HOOK UP? HINT. In other words, give me a code for a rendezvous point after I wrapped up the case. It seemed I would rush to his rescue after all.

Sibar Sexy is writing a message . . .

Ten seconds, fifteen. Then: WE DON'T.

What?

YOU'LL DESERVE VACATION WHEN SHIT IS OVER. I'LL TAKE CARE OF IT SOLO.

I got the message Sibar Sexy had gone offline, and that was it. For now.

"Good luck," I whispered to the computer screen. I grabbed my handbag, paid for my time at the counter, and then walked back to my hotel.

◆

A day later, I sat calmly at a café table in the Marais district as the swarthy, stocky guy, somehow always with a six o'clock stubble, lumbered in, coat draped over his arm. The black eyebrows furrowed, and the mouth was a grim line. He'd been annoyed with me before, but this was Inspector Carl Norton of the London Met simmering, boiling, without equivocation *pissed* at me. I had, no doubt, made him look bad at home.

At least he'd taken my call and made the trip. And I had to admire his self-restraint as he ordered an espresso and plonked himself down at my table.

"Give me," he growled, "one good reason—actually you better make it *five*—why I don't whip out my cell phone and call the locals to have you carted home on the next Eurostar."

"One, by the time you explain who and what I supposedly am, I'll be out the door and vanished just as I had to do in London. Two, I know you're doing your job, but if you did as I asked and *did* come here alone, you'll probably give me the benefit of the doubt now."

"Don't count on my loyalty, Teres—"

"Three, I think MI6 can claim they've never heard of me and that all the paperwork I got from them is bogus, but I bet they forgot about the police CCTV footage from cameras that cover the Albert Embankment on this date—" I slipped him a set of notes across the table. "Pick up footage of my rented car at the intersections near Waterloo Station and then work back. You'll have my face through the windshield—you know it's me. Look where I was driving my car from, where I had my appointment. I was set up, Carl."

His voice was deadpan. "That'll be inconclusive."

"Release the footage to the media," I suggested. "See who runs for cover. It'll get really embarrassing. I may stay a murder suspect, but they'll have to take me off the list of Islamic terrorists. You think anyone will believe it after I'm seen leaving the spy clubhouse?"

Poker face. No sign he bought this argument.

"Fourth," I continued. "I'm handing over to you now a set of plaster casts."

"Of what?"

"My knuckles, my whole hands, sides of my hands, my feet, edges of my feet—"

"Lovely souvenirs," said Carl. "What do you think they prove?"

"Compare the casts against the size of the knuckle bruises and the spaces between the knuckles in your forensic photos—"

"Which you've somehow magically been able to see," said Carl, muttering a curse under his breath. "Fucking hell! They will *not* be happy you got that material. Teresa—"

"This is my life, Carl. I'm not letting anyone strip it to pieces. Let me finish answering your question."

"Your casts won't hold up!" he protested. "I don't know how you got the bloody things done, and I don't care. They won't be allowed as evidence because we have no idea who made them, what methods, the fact they're coming from no recognized authority—"

"But they'll become part of the record," I cut in. "The minute you show them to your people, I know the whole case against me will crumble apart. Because if I ever am brought back or return voluntarily, I will *demand* new casts be made. And the measurements won't change, Carl. The size of my feet and hands won't change. But to set your mind at rest, I've included photos of my hands and feet filling each cast. They fit. And the spaces between the knuckles on Luis Antunes's bruises confirm a *guy* beat him to death— the hands are too large for any woman, let alone me."

He didn't say anything to this.

"The killer hit him with shock blows," I pressed on. "One powerful concussive blow hits, and you should go down. Everything else is theater. I knew it the minute I saw the photos of the body. A rage attack? Impossible. They would never have that degree of accuracy. And Luis's hands and knuckles had nothing on them, no breaks in the skin, not one defensive cut. Don't you see? The killer hit him—and hit him again for *show*. How cold is that? To make it look exactly like a martial artist had beaten him to death. But he enjoyed his work too much."

"What do you mean?" asked Carl, now intrigued in spite of his reservations.

"There was a kick to Luis's head," I explained. "You'll see it's the blade edge of the foot, made with a sneaker. You've got no distinctive shoe tread or heel edge to work with, and unfortunately, you'll just have to believe me on this, because I can't prove it. But the blow when it hit him was *inverted*. The foot that kicked him was swinging counter-clockwise and upside down."

"What are you saying? How the hell can you even do that?"

"The killer was proficient in capoeira. It's a Brazilian fighting art—uses a lot of cartwheel maneuvers and high kicking. I did a little checking on the Web, and as far as I can tell, the killer used a move that was either an *aú aberto* or an *aú batido,* not that I'd really know the difference. But the good ones can literally stand on one hand, twist their hips and swivel, sending their legs around. I've had to go up against people using gung fu, aikido, boxing . . . That inverted foot blow bothered me. So I did my research and figured it out."

"And I suppose you know who this killer is?" he asked dryly.

"Not sure yet, but I have a suspect."

I thought of Marinho whipping me upside the head. I

hadn't gotten a chance to see his full range of techniques that night, but I certainly remembered how he dropped me on the spot.

"What's his name?" asked Carl.

"Marinho, but I'll bet he's flown back to Brazil by now. It's where I'm going."

He grimaced. He didn't want to know where I was going. "What's reason number five?"

I smiled. "Don't have one, really. Except you know me, you know I didn't do it."

"If you have any sense at all, you'll come back with me to London and surrender yourself to the patrols at St. Pancras International."

"Can't do it, Carl. Are you going to try to stop me?"

Carl groaned, scratching the stubble on his large square jaw. "You know you really piss me off, Teresa!"

"I know I probably made you look bad, Carl, but—"

"No," he growled. "*No*. That's not it. You call me a friend, but when it came down to it, you didn't trust me. Teresa Knight, troublemaker and amateur sleuth, and your big ego got in the way. Well, this is what I do for a living. *I'm* the professional. And you didn't give me the benefit of the doubt to clear you."

"You saying you can find evidence with all the political games going on? I know someone powerful is hindering the investi—"

"I have," he snapped.

"What?"

"I said I have, Teresa. You ever hear of this soft-swinging fad? Part of it is couples having sex in front of people in their homes or leaving their window curtains open. Came out of that nasty dogging—"

"I'm familiar with it," I said, wanting to move things along.

He rolled his eyes at me as if to say, yes, of course, *you* would be. "Luis Antunes was beaten and tossed off a balcony. As impressive as your plaster casts are and your deductions, what's the one thing, Miss Sleuth, you can't do from your position that I can?"

"I don't know," I groaned tiredly.

"Interview potential *witnesses*," said Carl. "On the night of his murder, two balconies above him, a couple was putting on a show. I've managed to track down two tenants in the apartment across from his who saw men on the balcony, *no women*, certainly not a woman who's black and fitting your description."

I'll be damned. The whole phenomenon I'd been exploring lately turned out to actually help in clearing my name.

"Don't get too excited yet," said Carl. "I'll put that detail into the case file when the time is right. Not even these tenants' names are in my notebook for now. By themselves, their statements that they didn't see a woman won't be conclusive, but maybe with your casts and the CCTV footage—"

"What do you mean when the time is right, Carl?" I demanded. Then it sank in. My friends had been correct. "Someone high up is screwing with evidence, interfering with the investigation, aren't they? That's why you're not putting them in the file. Who is it, Carl? MI6?"

He paused, choosing his words carefully. "I don't know. It might be—I get my marching orders through chain of command. We're told to disregard this or that, and then a day later, some new directive is passed along that contradicts the old one."

"Like a power struggle going on somewhere," I muttered.

Carl looked grim. "Yeah, maybe. Look, Teresa, you can't stay on the run. We can get it all sorted. If you come back with me—"

"Can't do it, Carl. Not yet."

He saw how serious I was.

"And if I do make a call right now? You've got your escape route all planned out, haven't you?"

I know he didn't expect an answer.

"How does it go, Teresa? You have a couple of mates watching the front and rear exits of this place, maybe one farther up the boulevard?"

My turn to play sphinx. As much as I'd hurt him over my supposed lack of trust, I *had* come alone.

Carl tapped the set of plaster casts in their packaging. "Right. I got a mysterious call to come to Paris, where I obviously have no jurisdiction. This was left for me. A waiter in the café says a black woman fitting your description left this at the front counter, and you tipped him generously—"

"I would."

"Don't interrupt. Fifteen minutes after I thoroughly checked to see you weren't watching me from outside, I rang the French police, who did their best to keep an eye out for you at the train stations. Knowing you, of course, you were already in a rented car, making your way to the border or something. By the way, your fifteen minutes starts now."

"I'm sorry it has to be this way, Carl. Thank you. And give my best to—"

"Don't push it, time's wasting," he snapped. As I grabbed my handbag, he added, "Teresa."

"Yes."

"Luck."

I nodded and made for the door. Fifteen minutes, no more and no less.

7

I didn't take a rented car as my friend said. I was booked on a flight that afternoon out of de Gaulle for Frankfurt, where I'd catch a direct flight on Lufthansa for Rio.

Double-digit hours on a plane are never my favorite, especially when I'm traveling under a fake passport and hoping like hell I made no slip-ups through security. It's a post-9/11 world, one that increasingly questions your very right to see another part of it. I was no tourist. This was exile, a mission of mercy for my own good name. And for the long flight to Brazil, I had packed questions along with my new summer clothes bought in the department stores in the Opéra district.

Everything pointed to Brazil: the mysterious documentary project, Luis's uneasy relations with Marinho and his creepy Ladrão Films division, the nasty porn I'd confirmed was being filmed and produced over there, even Luis's hope of bringing in a rival gangster, José Ferreira.

I kept circling back to mull over another question. Why would Henrique Marinho, who did porn and prostitutes, decide to make a documentary on Brazilian Muslims? It didn't fit. And yet I had seen actual raw footage for it.

It made me wonder again if this wasn't the real reason Desmond Hodd had aimed me at Luis to investigate his movies.

Which brought me to still another question. I had found the way to clear myself, but I didn't have the reason why I was set up in the first place. Hodd and MI6 had left me out in the cold, and I was righteously, justifiably outraged about that. But now in the sheer boredom of coach and with the insipid in-flight movie being washed out on the screen (because there's *always* an idiot who has to leave his window shutter up to ruin things for the rest of us), I was having my doubts that Hodd was the one involved with Marinho behind the frame. It didn't make sense to approach me and say, hi, we're a bunch of spies, here, have some money—a *big* chunk of money—if I was about to be set up for a fall.

I also couldn't forget what Helô had told me about the woman who had tried to kill Luis—actually, she had suggested that perhaps the woman was trying to kill Marinho. Luis might have simply been caught in the crossfire. Right. Then what was she trying to kill them for? Did she have any connection with Marinho's rival, the engineer-turned-prison-gang-leader José Ferreira?

Her name was Beatriz. No last name offered to Luis.

Questions and more questions. But I at least had names, people to track down—Marinho, José Ferreira, and a mysterious woman named Beatriz.

◆

Rio de Janeiro. Hot and humid, tall and tanned. Tall as in hills, the famous *morros,* tanned as in check out legendary Ipanema Beach, where bikinis are about the size of male good intentions to "just be friends." Rio: land of contradictions, happy and hedonistic and constantly horny.

I entered Brazil on the fake British passport—UK citizens don't need an entry visa. Got to hand it to Alain and Dupuis—they'd done an admirable job forging credit cards for Susan Braithewaite that could draw on my offshore accounts.

So I'm walking out of Galeão Airport, completely disoriented, nearly knocking over a poor British Airways flight attendant, and I'm looking for a cab to take me into the city when I get a vibe. Soon to be upgraded to The Vibe. More stares as I entered the Hotel Glória on the Rua do Russel. It was only when the credit card authorization went through that the front desk clerk dropped the attitude. I kept wondering: What the hell's going on?

Later, I learned the explanation for all this: I'm black. Simple as that in their world. What was a black woman doing checking into an upmarket hotel in a better district of Rio? I must be a criminal. I must be a whore. The only third plausible explanation was that I was from elsewhere. I was a "gringa"—a foreign woman. Give me strength. Or a cricket bat.

My hotel was in a good location, close to Guanabara Bay and Flamengo Park, and the windows had a view of the famous Sugarloaf Mountain. I took a couple of days to decompress, lying on Ipanema Beach, checking out the view under the outstretched arms of Cristo Rendentor at the top of the Corcovado mountain, taking in the other sights. I was on what I promised myself was my last day of goofing around when I walked out of the hotel and there he was. Standing before me in sandals, white linen trousers, and a white shirt of Egyptian cotton, a young black man more or less wearing my face. His cheeks were cut by a wide grin of brilliant white teeth, and he waved and waited for me to rush into his arms. Isaac. My older brother.

"How are you, Tig?" he asked gently.

Since we were little, I was Tig for him and only him. I don't remember this, but apparently I insisted on being called Tig for a full week after seeing a Winnie-the-Pooh cartoon. Teresa, to my childish logic, had too many syllables. I think I began calling my brother "Roo" as a put-down because I needed a corresponding nickname for him, and again with childish logic, Roo was a mama's boy. Hey, he lived in Kanga's pouch—you can't get more mama's boy than that.

"Oh, my God! *How* did you find me?"

He looked shocked that I could be so dim. "Don't you remember who introduced you to Dupuis? Silly girl!"

We went to the Ateliê Culinário in the Leblon district, and Isaac ordered a couple of cold drinks. His Portuguese sounded impressively fluent, but he assured me he'd just learned a few choice phrases to get by when he came here.

"Must have been a marathon for you coming from the Middle East," I said.

"Especially when you can't go through Heathrow or Gatwick," he replied tartly.

"Oh, like you never get into trouble."

He shook his head in melodramatic woe. "I always thought I'd be the one, Sis, to land in it because of doing business with the Arabs. So there I am, sipping Scotch with the boy prince in his limo, or rather his daddy's limo, since it's *his* emirate, and we're watching news on the portable. Gee, that looks like my sister's flat. They were pretty understanding about my having to get away." He started laughing. "They said to me, 'Oh, yes, we get yanked off as terrorists all the time, go, go, go!'"

"I'm glad somebody can take it in their stride."

"You should be pissed. I'm pissed for you, Tig. You know who I keep on retainer—about time they earned their keep—"

"I don't need solicitors, Roo. They won't make a difference when I'm up against MI6 as well as the police. But I've
given Carl Norton a set of plaster casts that should clear
me . . . . Look, I'll call Daddy soon. How's he holding up?"

He took his time to answer. He knew I worried over what
our father must be going through.

"He's better than you might expect," Isaac claimed, lifting his drink as if to toast our father.

"What do you mean?"

He chuckled into his glass. "He's giving them hell,
Teresa. You'd laugh yourself silly if the stakes weren't so
high. You know how he is: He loves a good fight, and you
should see the expression on the faces of the cops when
they come to the door. They *know* how much verbal, legal,
and all-around *shit* he'll put them through! Not that it does
him much good—they always take what they come for. But
there's nothing in the house, nothing incriminating at all,
so both sides are baffled. They look like they get orders to
go back and dig around, they know not for what, and he's
indignant all over again. I think he's secretly having a wonderful time."

"Uh-huh."

"He's all right, Tig. I've got Walter and Allen checking in
on him every other day." Trusted friends. "Have to advise
you to wait a little before calling him."

"They've tapped his phone." I didn't need to make it a
question.

He nodded.

"Bastards."

"Right," he said as he put down his drink. "Where do we
start?"

"*We* don't."

He smiled patiently at me. Distance and time don't erode
the family shorthand—not if you're close, and we are. You
can have an entire heated argument in silence, trade points

and anticipate what each other will say, all in a few seconds. The obvious didn't need to be said: that I'd want to work the case alone. Yes, but he knew the country better than I did, he could muddle through better in Portuguese and he *was here* after all. And I would counter that it was my mess to clean up. Our parents used to say I was more stubborn than Isaac. They were right.

A final plea, the protective-brother argument all packed into my name: "Teresa . . ."

"Hey," I said. Not very logical but equally concise.

"You'll need me."

"I need you to pull strings for me in London," I argued. "Listen, I distinctly remember you having those psycho ivory poachers after you five years ago. When I offered to fly in, you said stay put, didn't you? And what about when you and Dupuis nearly got shot in Slovakia? And whoever heard of a Slovakian transsexual assassin anyway?"

"Well, Dupuis always surrounds himself with colorful people," Isaac pointed out. "I think we stayed alive just out of sheer dread of how the obituary might read."

I should mention my brother solves problems for people, too, sometimes. When he's not trying to start restaurant chains, found magazines, or deal in large foreign exchange trades. He always seems to hold on to his fees longer than I do, but Isaac was always smarter with money. He's either very rich for a long while or suddenly skint, needing to go out and drive a cab or unlock a few investments.

But I never worry about my brother. To me, he's invincible. I think of the way he greeted me in Brazil, casual yet stylish, ready for war but not stepping into it without looking *damn* good, fully briefed and yet cocky as hell because I was the innocent, and no one should mess with us and so of course, we'd win. I'd win.

But I needed him in the other hemisphere.

"After you've conquered the forces of evil," he said, waving the bartender to bring another round, "how about back to Geneva? For a vacation? At least we both have friends there."

I couldn't think that far ahead.

"I don't like leaving you like this, Tig."

"You're not. I'm shooing you off."

We downed our drinks and hugged good-bye.

"Well, I'm going to waste some of the prince's money on a flight to New York," he informed me. "I don't think it's wise to stray *too* far while all this is happening to you. Anything you want while I'm there?"

I thought about it. "No, I don't think so. But go and check out the new planetarium for me."

"Since when do you like astronomy?"

"For a while," I answered. "Someone got me interested in it the last time I was there."

Watching him go was one of the hardest things I'd ever had to do in my life. Still. My brother did business here occasionally. He had friends here. I suspected I was about to enter a shadow world, what with Henrique Marinho's operation and José Ferreira's operation, and even though my brother is probably my most trusted ally, fully capable of taking care of himself, I'd put him and perhaps his network of beloved friends and associates at risk.

Our father already had one child drop off the radar. It was unfair to risk us both.

◆

The problem never was tracking down the enemy in Brazil. Silky Pictures had its corporate headquarters right in Rio's Western Zone, and as Helô had shown me, Henrique Marinho was in a staff photo on the company's Web site as if he had no shame to feel. I was sure he didn't. I saw this young business type in his open-necked shirt and jacket, this grinning jackal who thought the world was a dim sum cart wheeled around for his personal appetites. And I remembered Matilde.

Watching him through a high-powered lens, I studied how Marinho dealt with people as a managing director, his disguise for being a thug. I saw that the tumblers were always clicking, Marinho folding his arms when he listened, unfolding them, fidgeting, and though I couldn't hear what was said, I watched the pauses after he gave a reply, or what body language seemed to indicate was a decision. That was when he finally stood still. And whoever he was with froze in place, too.

Because of something Marinho said.

The threats that curdle your bowels come in quiet whispers, very gentle, very soft. Those who know what they can do don't need to yell.

Henrique Marinho was scary to me because he didn't even seem to enjoy their fear. He just clearly wanted the job done, and then he moved on to intimidate someone else. I remembered that quiet, almost toneless voice demanding information when the needles were close to my eyes. As if life as a street criminal had bled almost all emotion out of him except for his precious furniture catalogues and pleasure of acquisition. When he touched a woman here on his home ground, two fingers slightly lifted her chin or rested on the small of her back, and the woman always stiffened. She went mannequin still, as if knowing from experience not to flinch or shudder.

Someone who *didn't* flinch was the peculiar visitor Marinho welcomed to his house.

This was a couple of days after I'd begun watching him. By then I already knew Marinho lived in Barra da Tijuca, one of the priciest and most sought-after upper- and middle-class neighborhoods. His mansion was a sprawling two-floor beast, with as many bodyguards as his fleet of cars, plus a canopied pool. And he had dogs. Dobermans.

I know I shouldn't generalize, but invariably the choice dog breed of your hard-core creep, asshole, wanker—take your pick—is a Doberman. Or another dog that can be bred and trained to be vicious. I don't get this and never have, the whole mean-dog thing as male status symbol. But then I also can't imagine walking around with a phalanx of guys who look like they walked off the set of *300* to put on shirts and ties.

Marinho was well protected, well insulated. Probably thought he was invincible.

He wasn't—that's what I wish I could tell you. That I already had a well-considered plan for how to get past his thugs and that I would break in on Marinho with more than harsh language. The truth was, I had no idea how to bring him down, especially since it was growing clear that in this country I would have zero credibility with any authorities.

I know, I know. How on earth could I think of running to the authorities now?

The visitor. Right. Back to the visitor. He arrived one afternoon, emerging from a chauffeured limousine, and I saw him gasp at the heat after coming out of his nice air-conditioned car. He and Marinho shook hands, but there were no smiles, no warmth. Business was done between the two, but it looked like they preferred to keep their distance.

The stranger looked to be in his mid-fifties, with a paunch, and he was much taller than Marinho. He had a hawk nose, his black hair was in a severe widow's peak, and his complexion was far too pasty to be Brazilian. European perhaps? Wearing a dark suit that was wrong for the weather and paying for it, his face shining with perspiration.

He and Marinho strolled the grounds of the mansion in pensive circles, yet the man refused to take off his jacket, collecting gin and tonics from a servant's tray like he was being handed communiqués. Marinho got visibly annoyed at whatever he was being told.

The man was good with the dogs. He knelt and petted them, and they didn't dare growl at *him*.

I took out my digital camera, which had a decent zoom, and snapped away.

The visitor only stayed for an hour, and then he gestured to his driver—who never got out of the car—to start the engine. Marinho leaned on the open door as the older man got back inside, making what looked like a final grumbling complaint. Then the car pulled out and drove off for the comforting parks and neat avenues in the rest of Barra da Tijuca.

Interesting. Marinho didn't fear his visitor, that much was clear. His body language, his temper, were kept under control in front of his dour guest the way he dealt with people in his office. All this suggested to me he was one taut watch spring. Henrique Marinho didn't like chaos. True, he didn't follow routines, never arrived or left his office at set times like other obsessives, but he clearly liked things in their place. He liked people not to disappoint him. He liked order. This gave me a vague idea of an approach.

Marinho sold sex slaves. To be a slave is to live in constant fear. I wanted to teach Marinho what real fear was. I wanted to lure him out of his nice safe house and then harass him, annoy him and eventually terrorize him, right to the point where he would think of running back to his bunker, believing he was safe. And then he'd discover he wasn't.

◆

First step: Learn more. I had no other starting point, really, except for my enemy's base camp, the office. That would be tricky. I couldn't just walk into Silky Pictures here and apply for an editing job as I had done in London. The boys from Brazil had known who I was. Suicide to just walk through the door, even pretending to be Susan Braithewaite.

Good thing I have a talent for burglary.

Mum tried to teach me to sew and eventually gave up, and my brother Isaac's a better cook than I am. I disappointed our father because of dropping out of university. But hey, if you forget your keys and lock yourself out of the house, I'm your gal.

Like many newer design blocks, the Silky office in Rio boasted these long picture windows that were absolutely perfect for me to look in. Took me a whole day and a half to find vantage points from every direction, but I was able to narrow down the closed-circuit security cameras inside.

There were a couple that checked the foyer by the receptionist's desk, keeping tabs on who bothered to visit them. There was another set near the modest locker area just outside the actors' changing rooms, probably to discourage petty theft. And there was a third camera that watched the parking lot just below a fire escape exit from Marinho's private office. He must have recognized it as a potential weak spot, where maybe José Ferreira and his men could drive up, climb the fire escape, and shoot holes in him unless he had men watching his back.

I wouldn't try to disable the cameras—well, not most of them. Not necessary. Yeah, I had to take out one or two, because I didn't want Marinho and his thugs to be sure of exactly why I'd come here. But it wouldn't bother me that he knew I'd broken in. What could he do? Call the cops? I wanted my visit to disturb him. I wanted him rattled.

I timed my entrance to coincide with the security guard's patrol outside the building. He was overweight, lazy, and his idea of a perimeter check was a fifteen-minute cigarette break. Good for me, because I didn't expect to take longer than fifteen minutes.

The front and parking lot entrances had doors with electronic keypad locks. That was fine, because the building also had a basement with a window around the side, with only a wire mesh grille in front of it. I was there with a waistband money belt holding wire cutters, a small battery-operated screwdriver, and my lockpicks.

I had eyeballed it correctly. I was small enough to crawl through the window, especially since it was so warm that I wore only a bikini-style top, shorts and sneakers, so no clothing to catch on loose bits. The window frame gave my back a nasty scrape, but no blood lost. Then the challenge of the door leading upstairs.

It would be locked, but I anticipated that. They kept nothing down here except broken lights and their older videotape products, now all transferred to DVD. So this lock wouldn't need any keypad, it was a regular Chubb with pins, and I had my trusty set of lockpicks.

The guard would be on his second cigarette now.

From all that staring through windows, I had worked out a rough layout of the building and its offices. The pecking order always has your pawns near the front, your big important types deeper in. I walked briskly through the hall, not in a rush but with purpose, and I noticed an overhead camera where it was inconvenient.

Men's shaving gel. Big and blue and gloppy. Can't see anything through it. I got on a chair and sprayed it all over the lens.

Then I sat down at the administrative assistant's computer. I used hers because Marinho no doubt had all kinds of protection and security on his, but people are less scrupulous with the underlings. You're right that I could be taking a bungee jump with my huge assumptions, and if the bungee snapped . . . But I was sure I understood the way this creep thought.

He guarded his cash, not his product, not here on his home turf where no one cared about the next missing Matilde. His enemies would kill him for revenge or for his money in a safe, not for DVDs that still needed to be sold to make a profit. Hence all the thugs loitering by his pool. That's where the bank was, I'd bet.

I tapped away, fingers making the keys mumble in soft plastic crunches. Come on, come on, come on—

This was another moment when I wished I had taken up Isaac's offer to stay and help. I had gotten a couple of tips from Jiro on cracking in and getting by passwords, since programming code is reasonably universal and, thanks to economics, tends to be done in English, but once I was in, I was back to *Você fala Inglês?* All their invoices, their banking, their shooting schedules, everything was in Portuguese.

Fortunately, I had brought along a USB flash drive with sixty-four gigabytes of storage, my little lorry to dump all this stuff into and examine later. When it was done—and it worked pretty fast—I did my best to figure out what I got out of a straightforward keyword search of files. The Portuguese word for Muslim was easy enough: *Muçulmano*.

But I let out a groan as I discovered the same raw footage I had screened on the computer at Helô's house in Twickenham. The lovely camera shots panning from the mosque minarets to the modern and secular Brazilian landscapes, the same interviews with imams . . . There was nothing new for me to learn here. I tried documents, and what *wasn't* there was more enlightening.

No shooting schedules for any documentary on Muçulmanos.

No Arabic-sounding names listed in interview transcriptions, no production notes or research details on Muslims or Islam at all.

But here was the footage.

My time with Luis had demonstrated one thing to me. You make any kind of film, and you are an old-fashioned baggage caravan on an exodus. You must organize. You must include camera people, technicians, assistants, and drivers. You must keep records.

Suppose there is *no* documentary, I thought. Suppose there never was.

But if I was right and there wasn't, why create the outlandish fiction—highly improbable for a porn manufacturer—that one was planned? And why get footage and interviews?

While I was mulling on that, I got on-line and checked a Portuguese phrase for what it meant in English. Thank you, Babel Fish Web site. When I opened another document and tried to copy a paragraph to check, I read: *File is read only, file in use, STN 5.* Of course. I was on the assistant's computer, which was networked.

And if the file was in use then someone else was here. *Shit.*

A moment of panic, and then my brain woke up, and I realized this stranger wasn't supposed to be here either. Could be someone working late, but I doubted it, not *this* late. Whoever it was, this person could screw up my escape.

I had gone to a lot of trouble to time all this, and when the guard came back to his desk and noticed the fogged-up camera looking over the admin assistant's workspace, he'd probably check the wiring first. By the time he got off his arse to come down and take a look, I was supposed to be heading out the way I'd come, through the side basement window. This second intruder could draw the guard's attention, and the guard could wind up finding me instead. Thanks for landing me in it. Cheers, mate.

Smart of the admin assistant to keep an office diagram with each terminal numbered. This "Station Five" was down another hallway. If the guard took that route, he would cut off my escape.

I had to get to the intruder first.

It occurred to me the admin assistant might get a closed circuit feed of the security cameras, and sure enough, she kept it as an icon on her bottom task bar. I brought it up.

I don't believe it, I thought. The guard was still in the parking lot with a taxi driver, obviously an acquaintance, both of them sharing a bottle and chatting away, killing their break together. Maybe that would buy me another two minutes.

Move, Teresa.

I found the intruder in one of the combination studio and editing rooms, the kind Luis had back in London. There was no security camera watching him here, but no matter which hall he took to leave, he would pass a camera.

I paused to watch him for a few seconds, seeing what he was up to. Tall guy with his back to me. He had a shaved head and mahogany skin, a black shirt and gray trousers, and was rummaging through DVD cases and playing one of the features on the monitor.

"Policía!" I barked.

His body was racked by a shudder of panic, but as he turned, brown eyes glaring, he tilted his head at a weary-wise angle. "Oh, please! Unless the Rio police wear bikini tops and white shorts, I don't think so."

British. Fairly posh accent, like he went to the right universities.

"Eu não entendo," I said, trying to keep up the bluff. *"Você poderia par favor—"*

"Give it up, darling," he said, smiling. "Your accent's wrong for one thing. Like Berlitz for a weekend in Lisbon."

Oh, well.

The face was bright with amusement, all large brown eyes and white teeth, a merry expression at how ridiculous the situation was. The high cheekbones seemed to go with the high mahogany forehead, the nose wide but not too wide, the lips full, still curling with this amused expression that had a bit of charm and a lot of nerve.

I should have dropped the act, because neither of us had the time, but it irked me how sure he was that I didn't belong here.

"I think I'll call the cops anyway. And then I'll call my boss to tell him you broke in here—"

"Go ahead," he dared me. "I've figured out everyone who works in this place, and that doesn't include you. Oh, and I don't think your 'boss' has an amicable relationship with the *policía*."

I folded my arms, tapped my sneaker against the linoleum. "So we've both been naughty. How did you get in?"

He smiled. "You first."

There was no reason to hold back. "I came in through the basement window. It's small, but I managed to squeeze through. You?"

He fished a digital camera out of his pocket and began playing a movie. It looked like he'd shot it from across the street on a balcony somewhere, zooming in right at the proper moment when one of Marinho's men tapped the keypad combination for the door. I rolled my eyes. I should have thought of that.

"Clever. What are you doing here?"

He grimaced in embarrassment, hand running over his bald head, but as he struggled to find the delicate words to explain, there were suddenly grunts and keening moans that did it for him. I took a step to the side. He stepped with me to block my view. I took another step, and he moved with me, until I did a basketball maneuver around him to see the computer monitor.

He had found the right DVD all right. There was a dark brown ass in the foreground (very nice and tight, by the way) while a mixed-race girl looked up at her anonymous lover with clear admiration at his prowess, his head out of shot and, fortunately, his willy too, for the moment, the girl's full breasts jiggling with his thrusts.

"Okay, I was very drunk and we smoked a lot of weed that night," he explained, "and *she* had the idea. I thought I was with friends. I don't even know this Marinho who runs this sleaze operation. His people could have put me on a dozen DVDs—"

"I get the picture," I said, raising a hand for him to stop. "Is there only one session they filmed?"

"You mean have I done this kind of fool thing before?" he asked defensively. "No, thank you very much! And that's not very nice. Are you saying you've never done any stupid compromising thing of a sexual nature?"

"Me? I give nuns an inferiority complex."

He gave me a crooked smile that said aren't you cheeky and turned back to the computer. He tapped away at the keys, doing a file search. "Fortunately, they seem pretty good at organizing and naming the files, so yes, thank God, I seem to be on just one of them."

"Well, you might want to erase the hard drive just in case."

He nodded. "I was about to."

"How could you even know where this footage was going or where they would keep it?"

He looked at me hard and raised his eyebrows. "When I rang up the girl again just to see her, she told me she did this and started trying to recruit me for their films, saying they could pay me big money. She gave me the name of the company, how their films were supposed to be good quality, all this other rubbish. Then when I got pissed off, she said fine, if you don't want to get paid, they could use the film anyway, tough luck, and they'd make plenty off just the one. Wasn't hard to track their office down."

I watched him erase the hard drive, and then he turned to me and asked, "Shall we look for your video now?"

"Sorry to disappoint. Never been a star."

"Then what are you here for?"

Hmmm . . . Hadn't expected to meet and greet tonight so no time to prepare a cover story. Things had gone really pear-shaped with him turning up—I couldn't go digging around with an audience. I wasn't sure what I was looking for anyway. Time to improvise, and I was fairly good at it. Whenever Isaac and I got into trouble together as kids, he left it to me to spin a plausible excuse or fanciful story for our parents. *You're just so much more credible, Tig.*

Finally, inspiration.

"Henrique Marinho's people ripped me off. I did some video editing for them, even directed a couple of their features. I was supposed to get paid. I didn't."

"Bet you don't tell the nuns that."

"I'm not the one who had his boom mic in the shot."

"Touché," he laughed. "At least you didn't get to see my boom mic."

"Well, your girlfriend looked like she died and went to heaven."

"She's a wonderful actress."

"Such modesty," I said. "Come on, let's get out of here. You do know there are cameras watching the halls?"

"Better they have me taped in a hall with my clothes on than naked in a hotel room." He put a hand gently on my arm. "Wait a minute. You said why you're here, but what did you come for? I doubt they keep a safe with any petty cash. Were you going to trash the joint?"

"No, I was looking to rob the place, but I think you're right. Doesn't look like they're stupid enough to keep any cash here."

"I wouldn't try it anyway," he warned. "It's one thing to sneak in and reclaim an amateur porn session. But I've heard this Marinho is involved with some deadly customers. He'd probably take it as a personal affront if you swiped his money."

"I'll think it over," I said. "I can always come back. Let me see your camera again?" I wanted the keypad code.

"Oh, no, you don't. I just told you I've heard this guy is mixed up with dangerous—"

"I already have an older brother, thanks," I cut in. "And all right, I'll just break in my own way."

We heard a voice in rapid Portuguese. The security guard. Break time with the taxi driver was over.

My partner in crime muttered *shit* and yanked out the computer's power cord, the quickest way to silence the audio and picture. But it was too late. We could hear the guard walking down the hall. Must have heard something.

"I don't see any closets," I said, frantically looking for a hiding place.

"Follow my lead."

He switched on one of the big white lamps, and we were suddenly awash in light, his hand hitting the record button on a hi-def camera. Before I could protest, he yanked down one cup of my bikini top and pulled me into a clinch, one hand massaging my bare right breast, his mouth coming down to suck in my nipple. I felt shock, then the sudden sharp tingle of pleasure. Just to get him back, I tugged on his pants button, had them open and down in seconds. I'd be damned if I were the only one exposed as the guard walked in.

Which he did. *"Opa! Merda!"*

My accomplice barked in outraged Portuguese at him,

and the guard meekly backed out, our little act working, and as he yanked up his trousers, I saw he was already at full attention. The red head of his cock poked over the hem before he fixed himself. Certainly well equipped for our ruse.

"Best we go out the front door," he whispered to me.

"You could have warned me."

"I thought you caught on when I switched on the lights!"

I went over to the camera to make sure the hi-def *hadn't* been recording us. It caught maybe five seconds, and I deleted its memory.

"You can forget about coming back here through the window."

"Why?"

"That guard is sure to tell this story to his mates tomorrow—or maybe even the receptionist," he said. "As word gets around, someone will know there was nothing scheduled for after hours. We'd better get out of here."

We strolled out hand in hand, the brazen couple.

8

After a couple of minutes, we were safe and dry, away from the Silky Pictures building, but he still held my hand. I let him.

"Now that we've survived, mind if I ask your name?"

"Jeez, you were already copping a feel and having a taste!" I laughed. "I wondered if you'd bother!"

"Oh, come on, that's not fair. You've got the wrong impression of me—and you weren't so meek and shy in there either. So what is it? Your name."

I began to stammer, then thought to hell with it. "Teresa." I didn't want to give him the cover name. I was using that one at the hotel, and I wasn't sure I wanted to know him past this evening. "And you are . . . ?"

"Thirsty. Why don't we get a drink at the Scenarium?"

"You move right along, don't you?"

"Look," he said, sounding sincere. "I want to celebrate my little victory, and I can at least buy you a drink for not achieving yours. And I owe you, don't I? The guard could have walked in on me alone. I don't think I'd convince him just sitting there and playing with myself."

"You're right, you do owe me."

"Graham. It's Graham."

"Okay. You owe me, Graham."

"From the south, eh?" he asked, his eyes narrowing.

"Very good. Grew up in Oxford. London these days. What about you?"

"I hardly know what London looks like anymore. I only go back once in a while. Can't say I miss it too much. Business keeps me here, *and* it's so beautiful. I have a boat, and I take tourists out for a sail, a bit of diving. I do all right for myself."

"I can see," I teased him.

I was poking fun at his car, which turned out to be a pale blue Volkswagen Beetle convertible. Not the new yuppie model but the old-fashioned classic, with one door covered in livid red rust. It even had the antique dashboard, which he told me was the kind they used for the models manufactured in Mexico. He had arranged for it to be driven all the way down from Mexico City.

"It's indestructible, this car!" he boasted. "It's *perfect*. I buy a Beamer or some flash thing, it'll be gone in a day. Paid next to nothing for this wreck. Nobody ever wants to steal it." Graham stood six foot two, so he was not your usual candidate for a vintage Bug. Funny to see him with his knees close to his elbows.

"The people's car!" He made a point of going down an alley and sideswiping a row of rubbish cans and then a phone pole on the driver's side. As I yelped, he laughed. "See? Indestructible! And if we do smash a wing, who cares?"

"Can we not smash one tonight?"

"I found our escape a little too anticlimactic, so I thought I'd give you your money's worth."

"Let's get that drink, and we'll be fine," I urged him.

I thought I heard him faintly humming "The Self Preservation Society" just to wind me up.

"If you want to do that," I said, "you need a Mini."

Why is it every British male knows *The Italian Job*? The original, not the Mark Wahlberg version, which guys like Fitz and my brother Isaac deemed sacrilege.

We were in the Lapa district soon enough. I had walked its streets when I first came here, checking out the Belle Époque colonial buildings renovated for antique dealers and clubs. I had sat in a café and watched a lazy afternoon turn to night, the gathering swarm of party enthusiasts taking over. But in those visits I was detached, apart and alone. Getting constant sleazy come-ons can be annoying whether you speak the language or not. Tonight, however, I had a guide from back home, a man who obviously relished getting into occasional trouble as much as I did.

I felt a crackle of sensual energy ripple through the crowds and sneak up my spine, teasing me with vague yet beguiling promises. Graham smiled at me as if he perfectly understood. We could be in the spectacle but not of it, take from it what we pleased. Boy, I liked that smile.

Rio Scenarium, I learned, is something of a landmark in the Lapa's Rua do Lavradio. People hang out, leaning on the balconies of the three floors that look down on the stage, and it's usually jazz-edged samba playing. It was packed this evening, and Graham fetched us a couple of *caipirosca*—vodka with crushed lime, sugar and ice. At Scenarium, there are countless rooms with antiques and small paintings, little nooks you can meander into and keep yourself visually amused. And we did. Later we squeezed in to share a table with a Brazilian couple, and Graham kept a running dialogue with the cheerful boy who, like his girlfriend, looked only nineteen. Then Graham was pulling me to the dance floor.

"Don't worry about the acrobatics," he said, big mischievous grin of white teeth. He must have guessed I was more or less a samba virgin. "All that fancy stuff is just for competitions on TV."

"Couldn't pull that stuff off if I tried," I said.

"Oh, I think you're being modest," he said, swinging me around. "What does the girl say? Hips don't lie . . ."

"This is Brazil. She's Colombian."

He twirled me, laughing. "I don't care!"

My hips said *move*. For me, there's a perfect density to the dance floor, when it's full enough that you can still turn and strut your stuff but you feel the encroaching heat of strangers. Your eyes take in the panorama of faces and sweaty limbs, of skirts fanning with a breeze of body twirls, hips shaking, and faces glistening with sweat. The energy drives the band, and the band reciprocates. And something both primeval and sophisticated takes over, a sensuality that's lush and quickens the heart, gets the brain racing with anticipation. I saw open joy on Graham's face, the joy of being alive and the two of us shaking it. Our ordeal, no matter how dangerous or ludicrous, was over and dispensed with, and he was right, it was good to celebrate.

Our hips flowed through the haze of the dance floor to almost collide, then parted, then approached again, his fingertips briefly, tantalizingly on my bare waist, my back, and I turned and danced into him, hearing him laugh with delight over the noise. He was a good dancer. Not conceited and needing to impress with peacock moves. Confident, assured, his fingers gently steering me, always knowing where I'd go and where I'd be. The crowd hemmed us in a little closer. I leaned in and kissed him.

His mouth let my tongue duck in, and his was soft, allowing me to explore.

As our mouths parted, he sent me in a fresh twirl. Minutes passed, and I felt drenched in perspiration, the crowd around us too thick now, the heat of moving limbs almost perceptible in fantasy steam currents, but it was only a haze of smoke. We were pushed together, making me bold and outrageous, and my palm cupped against his

crotch. His lips brushed close to my ear. Dancing, dancing . . . He tugged my hand for us to escape the floor, the
same way we had confidently walked out of the film building. I knew exactly what we were going to do, both of us
hungry but not wanting to break the spell and say it as we
ran upstairs.

We only needed a hidden spot.

Up to the third floor, in one of the little side rooms of
paintings, he took a handkerchief and unscrewed the bulb
so we were in the dark. Then he pounced on me, a half embrace, a half-lifting maneuver to sit me on a table. I heard
the band start a fast number, the rapid drums a perfect ac-
companiment for lust. I was undoing his trousers, and he
was pushing up the cups of my top, sucking my tits again in
greedy mouthfuls. I thought *fuck this* and didn't care anymore, tearing his shirt open, and then he was on display for
me, mahogany washboard leading down to tight black
curls, and his long brown cock with its angry red dome was
already pointing north, insistent. I caught sight of two
brown buttocks in a mirror on the opposite wall, and he
hardly needed to yank down my shorts, taking my underwear with them—I was helping him.

We heard packs of men and women circulate through
the nearby halls and rooms. Something from these shadows
warned them to peek but not enter. I grew aroused beyond
all self-control, my mind playing back images of strangers'
apartments in London, my fantasy of stripping naked in
front of an audience at home, but here would do, and I undid my top and let it fall, now completely nude for him, my
juices flowing over the perverse desire to be intruded on,
watched. But no one dared come and interrupt, not yet. I
had been too caught up in my escape to feel this way with
Todd in HMV, but I wanted to live out the fantasy of exposure now. I hadn't let myself go like this since . . . Well,
since the case in New York. Graham and I kissed in raw

urgency, our mouths slurping, tongues playing, our person-alities almost gone with basic body hunger, and two meaty hands pulled my legs to slide my ass along the table. We stared into each other's eyes as he shoved his way into me up to the hilt.

I made a whimper with the sudden pleasurable fullness of him, so thick, and my hands grabbed his ass to keep him in as his own braced on the table. No, don't start pumping, not yet, not yet, not yet, teeth sinking into his bottom lip, *stay in*. Let me savor this. Sucking in his lip as his eyelashes fluttered on my cheek like tiny butterfly wings, and the mu-sic, the darkness all conspired to unravel me.

His cock seemed to ooze out of me in a languorous re-treat and then *uhh*, abruptly, rudely pushed back in. Fingers against his cheek, feeling the tiny hairs on his shaved head as he kissed my neck, my shoulder, one hand still on his ass, squeezing his buttock like a melon. His right hand came up to cup my tit, my nipple between two fingers as he started his rhythm, out so slowly and mmm, yes, back in . . . Two girls wandered in and stood spellbound for an instant, watching. Yes, go ahead and watch. Graham didn't notice, and I didn't look at them, afraid my stare would drive them away. Watch us. Watch us now. My mind flashed an image of Todd and Charlene screwing for a scene back in London, and I knew the secret no one had ex-pressed from the ranks of the crew and staff. How editors, cameramen, script girls all wanted to be that free, how they all secretly wanted to exhibit themselves, and I was even wetter with the girls watching at a distance, I was that free now, here. I played voyeur to myself, too, looking beyond his shoulder to the mirror, delighting in the quiver of his buttocks as he kept thrusting. Graham was pumping me hard, his engine of ass and hips rushing like a locomotive towards an inevitable conclusion, and as he groaned and I heard my own squealing cries of pleasure, the two girls fled as if this was too truthful for them.

Animals, the two of us, and I didn't even notice the glass on the table that fell off and shattered, the two of us clinging to each other as if welding in hot combustion. Horns and drums covered my scream of orgasm as I felt his broad back and ass, and I felt the welded metal stretch and thicken inside me, the flood of him as he came . . .

I opened my eyes, looked into his. We shared a gasp of revelation. *That* . . . That was powerful. Neither of us expected something so raw, so urgent, to be so good. Right-to-the-core good. We held each other tight, and beyond probability in this noisy, bustling club, we had privacy of time suspended for another minute. Naked in his arms like that, and he was still thick and hard inside me, arms wrapped around my back and waist as I rested precariously on the edge of the table. If he hadn't let go, muttering about how we ought not to push our luck, I think I would have clung to him for even longer.

◆

In the Beetle again.

"I'll drive you back to your hotel."

"This is good, this is it," I said. We were at a red light in the Flamengo district. I'd have a brief ride on the Metro or maybe I'd catch a taxi.

"This isn't your hotel."

"How would you know?"

He offered me a patient smile. "I know we moved pretty fast tonight, and I'm hoping you don't think it's a mistake. I'm a nice guy—honest."

"Who says I want a nice guy?"

"Uh-huh. Ohhhhhh-kay! I want to see you again, Teresa.

If you let me drive you to your hotel, I promise not to stalk you."

I told him I was at the Glória, and he knew it, steering the old Volkswagen through the winding avenues. Every so often we caught a glimpse of Guanabara Bay in the distance.

"Where do you live?" I asked.

"I rent one of those hotel apartments in Botafogo. Let me give you my cell number."

I fished a pen out of my handbag and scribbled it into a notepad I always keep with me.

"What are you doing tomorrow night?" he asked.

"Can't."

"Night after that?"

"Mmm, still can't promise." His disappointment was so sudden and like a boy's that I quickly added, "It's not you, I've got to go out of town for a bit."

"What, another film producer ripped you off?"

"No, no. But it's . . . business of a kind."

"Want company? You sound like a girl who gets into trouble a lot."

I laughed. If you only knew, boy.

"Don't you have a boat to run, Cap'n?"

"Hey, I set my own hours, and I'm doing well enough I can take a couple of days off."

"Tempting," I said. "Let's just see each other when I get back. I'll give you a call."

He groaned, and I shut him up with a long kiss. Things were heating up all over again in the car, but I finally pulled free—reluctantly. I would have asked him up, but I could see a lazy morning turning into a lovemaking session lasting into the afternoon, and it would be even harder banishing him so I could get some work done.

"I *will* call," I promised.

"You'd better!"

◆

If you do happen to go to Brazil, let me confide that I do not recommend the prisons. Between Rio and São Paulo is a lovely city called Taubaté, a nice university town, and I didn't get to see any of it because I was steering a rented car up to the gates of a penitentiary. Big granite walls. Chain-link fences. Towers. Jumpsuits. Echoes of shouts and the smell of strong bleach.

That's not what gets to you. What's disturbing is the look combined with those walls, the look in the eyes of trapped men who have become feral with the slow agony of time dripping out, a puddle of time that has the stench of urine in an alley. Their eyes inspect you and imagine every inch of your body with more than lust, with this creepy canni-balistic rage, eyes that want to hurt you and cut you and don't care who and what you are. Eyes without pity, and what good is remorse in a place like this anyway? It wouldn't even come into their line of sight.

Forget about empathy with the trapped. There is no em-pathy here. You're quite sure the walls are holding you in with them, no matter how temporary that is. You don't see this longhaired thug with his leg chains rattling and con-sider what it would be like for you to be sentenced. No, you thank God you *get to go out and never see him again.*

Bad riots had happened here recently, just as they'd ig-nited at other prisons in São Paulo state. This was the birth-place of Primeiro Comando da Capital, or First Capital Command, one of the strongest and nastiest of the Brazilian prison gangs. And if it wasn't the birthplace, it had at least played midwife to the creation of the gang run by José Ferreira. Now here I was, signing in under one of my aliases, going behind the electronic locked doors and the thick bars to visit Ferreira himself.

You're right. I must be completely mad.

Helô had told me so. It was when I asked her back in London to translate a couple of Googled Rio newspaper pages mentioning Ferreira's gang. My logic was that the quickest way to get to Ferreira was through his lawyer. Every underworld figure's got one, right? José Ferreira's particular weasel was a man named Andrade. A little more homework told me the lawyer was fluent in English, having taught seminars in Miami on banking law in South America. His receptionist was less than fluent, but she was smart enough to put me through when I dropped the name of Luis Antunes.

"Excuse me, Miss Knight, but I have no idea why you are calling me," said Andrade. "You have quite the nerve after murdering our friend Luis."

"You don't have to pretend," I said tightly. "I think you know very well who had Luis killed."

"Yes. And *you* followed Henrique Marinho's orders to do it."

"Rubbish. If you don't believe me, maybe your boss will when I tell him to his face."

The lawyer thought that was rich. "You really want to go tell Mr. Ferreira in person? I would like to see that very much."

"I'll give you the chance."

"Maybe José Ferreira does not want to see you. From what I hear, you are on the run, Miss Knight. It's quite foolish for you to wander close to a prison."

"I came to Brazil to take down Henrique Marinho," I said. "I think your boss will be interested, and maybe he can offer me information that will help that."

Andrade was really laughing now. "You will take down Henrique Marinho all by yourself? Yes! Oh, yes, I think Mr. Ferreira will find you very amusing!"

And so I was here.

I was led by guards through the labyrinth of thick concrete walls painted a hideous green, and then into a peculiar visiting area. Not what you would expect—there was no glass barrier with telephones on either side, and it wasn't a regular cell either. It was a large open room divided by a barred gate, and perhaps it was used for a waiting area or delousing or something.

Andrade had already arrived. Solicitors always announce themselves through their suits and attitudes, and his suit was a surprisingly loud powder blue, his foxlike head with tiny eyes accentuated by his goatee and spectacles. He sat in a corner on a folding metal chair, his briefcase by his side, going through papers. To him, I was an inconvenience his client would quickly dismiss.

Ferreira wasn't so much led in as the guards followed him like an entourage. He wore no handcuffs, no leg chains, and except for the orange jumpsuit, you might have thought he ran the place. I'm sure in many ways he did. From what I had read and understood from Helô, to be a guard in a Brazilian prison was a grim probation itself, with inmates like Ferreira quite willing to have you shanked if you treated them disrespectfully. There was a concession that as a guard, yes, you had a job to do, but never forget you must feed the lions.

Ferreira's physique had an aura of menace. He was an animal—not a stolid bull or a wild boar, not a sleek deadly creature like a jaguar or a snake, but something that implied stealth and strategy. Hard to believe he had ever been this unassuming, clever engineer. I bet he was a crude, vulgar Leviathan when he stomped and punched and raped, a being of flesh pounded by a meat tenderizer instead of sculpted by any weight-lifting regimen in the prison yard. If he was ever good-looking, it had been beaten out of him in his youth. His nose had been broken more than once, and he had a scar on his throat that had a paleness to it. You'd think his large head had been sewn back onto his body. Best bet was that whoever gave him that scar got a deeper, lethal one.

Ferreira looked over his shoulder to his lawyer. The drunken lout in a pub on comedy night, looking forward to the opening act. He spoke in quick Portuguese: "*Se você soubesse quem eu sou, você nem sonhava em entrar na minha casa. Você é muito magrinha pra mim. Eu espero que você seja divertida como Andrade disse que você é.*"

Andrade translated. "He says, 'If you had any idea who I am, you wouldn't dream of coming to my house. And you are a little too skinny for me, so I hope you are as amusing as Andrade tells me.'"

"I didn't come here to entertain you," I snapped.

"*Você veio vender alguma coisa, e se não é seu rabo preto, então pra que perder meu tempo com você?*"

Andrade translated again. "'You came to sell something, and if it's not your black ass then what do I waste my time with you for?'"

What a way to look at the world: every woman a potential whore.

"I would think," I said, trying to be patient and choosing my words carefully, "you would willingly arm an enemy of Henrique Marinho with information."

"That is, if you are not working for him," said Andrade. It was the lawyer talking, not Ferreira. He cocked his head, explaining to his client what he had just said, and Ferreira gave a faint nod.

"I'm not with Marinho. I've never been with Marinho, and I didn't kill Luis Antunes. Your enemy did a very good job of framing me. Luis was murdered by someone who knows capoeira, and then his body was thrown off a balcony."

"'Capoeira is for tourists who like to see the pretty dances in the streets,'" said Ferreira through the lawyer. "'When Brazilians murder, it is not pretty.'"

"Yes," I agreed. "When *you* kill. But I'm the one who was implicated—so Marinho made it look 'pretty.' Does it make sense to you that he'd use a gringa to kill Antunes? It's clear what you think of women. Would you use one as an assassin? Would Marinho?"

Andrade translated all this, and almost a full minute went by as they debated my point. I sat down in the metal chair left in front of the barred gate. I could tell I had opened their eyes to something they hadn't noticed for themselves.

And to wake them up once and for all, I added: "I wasn't framed to fool *you*. I was framed to fool *someone else*. You didn't enter into the equation."

The dark feral eyes studied me hard. " 'Why not?' " Andrade translated.

"Because you know who benefits," I replied. "Marinho needed Luis out of the way because he was about to rip the lid off his slave girl operation in Britain."

Okay, I didn't know if Marinho had a slave girl operation in London—Luis discovered he'd sold one girl, Matilde. But I had to sound to these guys like I knew what I was talking about.

"I think there's another reason Marinho wanted him killed," I went on. "I think you two know what it is. You guessed right away that Henrique Marinho was behind the murder, so who cares who did the actual killing? You didn't need to concern yourself whether I'm innocent or not."

Ferreira laughed cruelly. " 'I still need not concern myself,' " the lawyer translated.

"Except if I can be useful in harming your enemy."

Another look between client and lawyer. Andrade folded his legs in an almost effeminate manner, lacing his fingers behind his head. "He says, 'Antunes was soft. He takes a wife from a favela, he gets stupid ideas that women can think.' "

"Yeah, we're real stupid. I'm not the one in a cell. When they hunted me, I got away."

Andrade stiffened. No one talked to his boss like this.

The dark eyes narrowed, and a hand with thick sausage fingers and blackened nails rubbed the bulbous chin. *"Tem uma diferença entre você ter culhao e pensar que tem porque, na verdade, o que você teve foi sorte."*

"Mr. Ferreira says: 'There is a difference between having balls, and thinking that you have them just because you got some luck.' "

And then Ferreira's hand reached out—

And yanked back the barred gate—

Open. Open all this time. Oh. My. God.

Yes, he had enough power in here through bribes and intimidation to arrange this. He offered me a lewd twisted grin of uneven teeth, framed by sweat beads. I jumped out of my foldout chair and backed away. He didn't move to follow. He didn't have to. There was no point in shouting for the guards, in calling for any help at all. I would leave when he said so. When he was done with me.

Unless I took him down. It was starting to look like I would have to.

Oh, yeah, Teresa? And what then? You're in a *prison*.

He wanted to play, but he was intrigued enough by the points I had made. There was the possibility I might be useful for something besides being a rape victim.

"What did Luis Antunes learn that Marinho needed to kill him for?"

I backed up a couple of steps. Granite walls, locked door. I felt like muttering *nice doggy*.

"He says this is bullshit, that your job is to find out what he knows so you can take it back to Marinho. And then Marinho's spies in here will make their attempt. An assassination."

"Marinho did *not* send me here!"

Show your panic, and you're dead.

He began to unzip the orange jumpsuit and reveal his naked torso. He had a barrel-shaped chest, the pecs defined, but no six-pack. There were grim black tattoos on his biceps, ugly and repulsive in their vulgar style, the ink dull with age.

"What are you doing?"

And now Ferreira was pulling off the brightly colored outfit, along with his underwear. Showing me his tree trunk legs, two columns simply designed to hold this tank of a human being.

I've seen lust. I've seen passion and tenderness. We're told that rape is a crime that's not about sex, that it's about rage and power. I still don't understand it, and I don't want to. I can tell you this was the first time I had ever seen a man's erection prompted by a desire to hurt. And to hurt me. It made me almost physically sick, even as it prompted the base instinct to smash his face in. Here was this bastard taking a step forward with a glowering red, rude hard-on.

"*Nêga é de quem pegar primeiro!*" He laughed.

And the lawyer cackled like a chattering mascot gargoyle and translated for me. "He quotes a saying we have here. It goes: 'A black woman belongs to the first one to put his hands on her.'"

Charming.

"We have a saying where I come from, too," I replied. "The Brazilian walks funny because he didn't keep his hands to himself."

"That's not a saying," sneered the lawyer.

"No, it's a billboard. Take the hint. If I have to yank something hard to throw him on this cement, three guesses what I'll pick. And I haven't clipped my nails."

"What did you come here for, bitch?" It was the lawyer

asking, not Ferreira, and the phrasing sounds harsher than the way he put it. He sounded almost bored, using *bitch* the same way Marinho did, as if it were an afterthought of salutation picked up from American gangster movies. A punctuation mark.

"Why would Luis Antunes need your help to stop a documentary about Islam? Especially when there *is* no documentary on Islam?"

Ferreira got a look in his eye like a confused wolfhound, its prey not tracking where it expected. I didn't like the fact that his penis was still hard. He said several fast things in Portuguese.

"He calls you a pizza girl," translated the lawyer. "Now say what you really came to say."

It took me a couple of seconds to decode the reference. Pizza, delivery . . . Okay.

"No, I'm not a messenger for anyone."

"*Bullshit.*" This time the lawyer barely waited for Ferreira's answer. "Go ask Marinho why he wanted Luis Antunes killed. And you may tell him we will skin his ass when we catch up to him."

Then Ferreira added a comment in English. He was even more disturbing when he tried to speak my language. Looking at me with his dead eyes, he told me in his thick accent: "The British always fools."

Now what the hell did that mean?

More Portuguese. From what I could tell, the lawyer began to suspect I was telling the truth. Ferreira was less sure.

Finally the lawyer said in a bored voice, "If you really are this ignorant, you have no part in this. Go home. We will take care of a bastard like Marinho."

Ferreira offered me a good-bye leer. "I see you again," he laughed in his halting English.

Andrade breathed on his spectacles and wiped them with

a handkerchief. "Did you know that Mr. Ferreira is due for release in three days? You better fly home, gringa. You stick around, and the next time he sees you . . . Let us say the locks out there are even easier than the ones in here."

I went to leave, inwardly grateful that a couple of guards had arrived to escort me to the gate.

"Andrade. You tell your boss that works both ways. He comes for me, he's going to wish there were still iron bars between us."

Tough girl. Yeah, right. I held it together until I reached the rental car. Then my body shook in terrified spasms, and it was five minutes before I could even grip the key to turn in the ignition.

◆

I had walked out of the prison with more questions than answers. Ferreira seemed to know why Marinho had had Luis murdered, but he didn't trust me enough to give me the reason. And what did he mean that the British are "always fools"? Could he possibly know I was hired by MI6 to look into the porn makers?

Okay. Desmond Hodd had sent me to investigate Luis which meant he was really investigating Marinho. And MI6 didn't care about internal criminal feuds—like every other Western espionage group these days, it cared about terrorism.

But how can there be a terrorist threat with a gang feud, porn DVDs, and Brazilian slaves?

Damn it. I had to find someone I could trust who understood I was a conscript in this war, not a volunteer.

And I had to find out how a porn merchant and master of a sex slavery empire could possibly pose an international threat in, of all places, Brazil.

◆

That morning I'd sent a jpeg of Henrique Marinho walking around his mansion with his strange guest—the man with the widow's peak who got along with Marinho's Dobermans—into the great beyond. By the time I was back from Taubaté and checking my e-mail in the hotel's Net café, there was a response from "Sibar Sexy." With no hello or good-bye, Simon had typed in caps: I SPY. I SPY BIG.

Shit. Easy enough to decode. Marinho's mate was MI6, someone way up there from Legoland.

I signed in to Instant Messenger and typed in: ARE YOU THERE?

The response was instant: YES.

I typed back quickly: THX FOR LEGO PIECE BUT NEED MORE.

Sibar Sexy is writing a message . . .

THERE IS NO MORE.

There had to be, I thought. I was in the biggest Catholic nation in the world, but somehow there was an international threat tied to Islam being hatched here, which involved sex slaves and British intelligence. He had already told me it was bigger than Brazil.

I was about to whine and plead for him to tell me more when a new line flashed on the screen: THEY WILL USE SAMBA AS TEST CASE.

I couldn't understand this at all. *Who* will use *what* as a test case? Then another line: FOZ.

What was Foz? An acronym? I sent a one-symbol question:

?

He must have typed so fast he completely ignored punctuation: YOU MUST STOP IT CAN'T SAY MORE BIG EARS LISTENING I HAVE FAITH IN YOU.

I typed back quickly: NEED TO HOOK UP WHEN DONE.

HINT. Pretty much the same thing I asked him in Paris. Where do I meet you? How do I find you?

And an answer just like the last one came back: SOLO RUN ON THIS ONE. Five seconds, ten . . . A FAR, FAR BETTER THING, ETC. LOL.

Oh, oh, The Simon Highsmith bravado. Just enough self-promotion to remind me he was trying to stay on the side of the angels. He was definitely in trouble, and on past cases, he would tease me or goad me, want to get involved in my business or have me ride along. But wherever he was, he wanted me to keep out this time, thinking of my safety. I offered, and he shot me down. Even though our cases, by his own admission, were somehow connected.

Mine was a "test case," and he was somewhere with the bigger piece, hunted by the bigger sharks.

And there wasn't a damn thing I could do at the moment to help him.

9

The next morning I made my eyes bloodshot combing through the spoils of the USB flash drive, the one downloaded with all the goodies from the administrative assistant's computer. I learned nothing from the shooting schedules or the payroll accounts, and I certainly didn't learn anything from the paid invoices for the bottled water delivered to the Silky Pictures building in Rio. The assistant had everything, and I do mean *everything*. Ecch. Financial stuff puts me into a coma.

Helena once passed along a great saying she got from a banker: "Big money has no shame." In other words, I didn't need to play accountant, because often you can ignore the more intricate, buried figures. If the profit is big enough, the bad guys inevitably have to park it out in the open, hoping no one pays attention. This time the saying was right.

Literally hundreds of thousands had been transferred as payments from Silky Pictures to a company called Lemos. I smelled another inside joke. Just as *ladrão* meant thief, Lemos was the name of the Portuguese explorer who first came to Brazil. The Lemos Company might be a dead end, only existing so that Marinho could launder his profits, but I thought I better check it out anyway.

It took another hour to track down the Brazilian equivalent of Companies House in London—a government office here that could tell me where Lemos was headquartered, who ran it, and what the business was actually about, whether it made anything or did anything or was just part of the Marinho Monopoly board. Of course, this office had to be in the capital of Brasilia, and I was told it would take a day or two for the information to be dug out of the record archives and sent to me.

Great. More waiting.

I returned to watching Henrique Marinho's house in Barra da Tijuca. He sat by the pool in shorts and a shirt buttoned only halfway up, reading his beloved furniture catalogues. Guy had a serious fetish for acquiring stuff. His gang friends swam and splashed away, and his guards glowered, and I knew Marinho would have to leave his enclave sooner or later.

I didn't have long to wait. After a couple of hours, Marinho went into his house and changed, and came out jangling a set of car keys, two bodyguards ready to come with. I went for my car. Marinho drove for about forty-five minutes and then parked his car at a sensible distance from the edge of the morros. I did the same.

This is where the favelas are, the shantytowns that are infamous blights on the glamour of Rio, São Paolo, and other cities, yet now are paradoxically also tourist attractions in the safer quarters. Can you think of anything more repulsive than "slumming it" through an actual slum on a bus tour, as if the residents there are animals in a zoo?

I couldn't tell which favela he and his mates were venturing into, but I didn't hesitate to tail him into the winding streets. Hey, I'd made my way out of tough spots in

Sudan, Thailand, Nigeria. I thought I could handle myself here, especially since I was dressed in a casual top and shorts, wearing my "tailing work" sneakers. Plus there were enough black and mixed-race people here that my color made me blend in. Or so I thought.

I was hopelessly naïve.

I barely knew more than two words of Portuguese, but they didn't have to hear an accent. It was in the way I walked, the way I moved past the homes made out of bricks and aluminum sheds and sometimes even garbage. My confidence in assuming I had a right to go where I wanted to was a dead giveaway to these people. *You* don't belong.

Never mind my confident stride. Most favelas don't have running water, and my clothes were *clean,* not ones worn for days. And not clean as washed in a bucket but machine-washed clean. Marinho could come and go as he pleased, because he packed a gun. They feared him. I was an alien here, a gringa looking for trouble and about to get it.

Teresa, you idiot.

Men on the steep hill of the street were looking down in disbelief that I should be so stupid, and Marinho eventually looked back. He remembered me, oh yes. Then he was on his cell phone. I was too far away to hear and couldn't understand anyway, but the rising pitch of his native language and the hand gestures tipped me off that he was just as amazed as the favela residents. His two guys stayed with him, but within seconds a new gang of thugs jogged around the corner and down the hill. Marinho pulled out a large black and silver gun.

The worst of it was, just as in London, I knew he only drew it to stop me. If he planned to kill me on the spot, he wouldn't need his pals. Oh, yeah, he had other plans for me. Marinho would want to know why I'd followed him back here after the frame job and what else I knew and who I'd told. Then his creeps would have fun with me.

Needles right close to my eyes. Won't allow another sadistic stunt like that. Ugh.

I could run.

Yeah, right. This was where drugs and gang warfare thrived. They would know exactly where to get ahead of me and cut me off. The people who sat in front of their shacks and sheds wore glum passive expressions. These people would not interfere. Why should they? They'd watch with their stoic blankness. The ad hoc life in these ad hoc streets would go on after my blood was washed away by the rain.

I ran anyway.

I heard the *crack* of the automatic behind me, a millisecond later the metallic *pang* of the bullet smacking into an aluminum panel. Then two more, *pang, pang,* a spiteful child drumming a stick along its side, gunfire to scare the shit out of me and make me stop. I've been shot at before, but let me go on the record as saying it's far preferable if you know where you're going as you flee in terror. The squeals sound more heroic.

But I didn't. I ran into a labyrinth of broken, winding streets so narrow and cracked you couldn't even navigate a motorcycle within them. As I ran, I heard heavy footsteps above me. Marinho's boys were *above my head,* jumping from corrugated aluminum roof to brick and garbage surface, easily following me with their bird's-eye perspective.

Along the rooftops—none at a horizontal angle or at the same level—women hung washlines, kids pedaled their tricycles to nowhere, and a couple of them dared to play soccer. You even heard the hiss and pop of barbecue meat from the two-stories as I looked for which way to go. Marinho's thugs chased me *tramp tramp tramp* on rusting metal. They waved their guns to scare the favela residents out of their way but didn't fire at me. I was right: They wanted to take me alive.

Can't keep this up forever. I'm good for a short sprint, but no, I'm not the girl who jogs at five in the morning, hate those cheerful, oh-so-tireless people. I've told friends that if you have to run, it had better be away from something or towards a buffet table. And I sure wasn't a woman who *glowed*. I was drenched now, my lungs burning, and the favela went on and on. If I climbed up to see ahead, I might run to a roof edge where I couldn't get down. The same could happen to them, but they had their mates at street level to intercept me as they doubled back.

"Damn it!" I snapped, finally losing my temper and feeling the chill through the fear sweat. I got out of London—*London,* the city with the most CCTV in the world and big efficient police forces that can calmly, nonchalantly scoop you up like a bug in a pair of tweezers. I made it out of Paris. Only to—what? Get captured by these sociopaths after a stupid reckless mistake? *No.*

Fail, and something bad happens here in this country. You know it. Simon warned you as much.

So don't fail.

If you can't run, you fight, I told myself.

Um, yes, that's all fine, very plucky, darling, but you *do* remember they have guns, right?

I was hoping not to concentrate on the negative.

Fight anyway. Use what's available for weapons.

I turned a corner and spotted a worn but thick rope tied to a pair of oversized, literally gigantic alligator clips. Must be large for the sake of some industrial machinery purpose, "borrowed" from a factory or construction site so the resident could climb up the wall. No one around to object to my taking it. Good for me.

Then I doubled back through the honeycomb of zigzagging streets, which forced the gang to split up. I had no idea if the guys on the ground were closing in, but I had to deal with the ones above first. As one ran along a slanted corrugated roof, I hopped up on a set of crates. *Pang, pang, pang,* and here he comes, hope this works—

I swung the rope up in my best lasso fashion, and it was the weight of the big iron clips that completed the arc. The cord wrapped around his legs, but the iron clips flew into his crotch. He yelled out in pain. Hitting him there wasn't the idea, but a nice added benefit. I don't know whether he slipped, or if my pull really did yank him off his feet. But he slid off the ramp of the metal roof and landed hard on the pavement.

"*Merda!*"

One of the guys on the opposite rooftop saw what happened. He half climbed, half jumped his way down.

The first guy was out of it. I unwound the rope as quickly as I could, and as the second thug ran up, his gun was out of his belt. I swung the rope, and the big iron clips hit him like a wrecking ball. *Smack.* You don't get up from that, any more than you pop back up after falling off a roof.

Run, Teresa.

I dropped the rope, too cumbersome to take with me, scurrying through the streets again—but these all went up into the hills, and I couldn't find a down route. I heard more shots behind me, but only when I turned a corner did I realize someone was *shooting back.*

Cops? No. The police made raids on the favelas, but couldn't venture too deeply in, and I would spot them in big numbers, wouldn't I? This sounded like a single automatic rifle.

As I ran down another ripped and scarred avenue, small fingers yanked me hard around my biceps. As soon as I let out a yelp, a hand covered my mouth, and then I looked into the large dark eyes of a peculiar girl.

She was a head shorter than me, with a round face and café-au-lait skin, with large full lips and a slightly hooked nose, her curly hair in a wild black cloud. She wore a man's white cotton shirt with the sleeves rolled up and Levi's torn at the knees, with one tear suggestively under the curve of a buttock. Her shoes were sensible but expensive-looking. She may have been petite, but like many Brazilian girls, her face and body were an exotic ripe blend, so much sensuality packed into her curves that no way could the shirt hide it, two undone buttons showed the divide of her breasts.

I'm describing her now, but truthfully, what caught my attention right away was the rifle she was holding. From barrel end to stock, it was as tall as she was.

"Gringa," she whispered with immediate disgust in heavily accented English. "You are an idiot."

"Thank you," I whispered back. "Call me anything you like while you shoot those guys, just get us out of here."

She hefted the rifle with impressive skill and sniper-fired at a guy on a rooftop. There was a *crack* that made me cover my ears, and the thug dropped.

"I have work to do," said the girl. "You fuck that up."

"Fine! You give me cover fire to the nearest way out of here, and I'll be on my way!"

The girl fired again, missing Marinho as he ducked behind another tumbledown structure, hitting one of his goons in the neck. This wasn't the movies. The goon didn't fly backwards as if a cannon had hit him. His legs gave out, the bullet short-circuiting the cables to his feet. He fell on his back, making a hideous, haunting wet gurgle, one hand to his throat.

None of his friends did anything.

Except Marinho, who shoved out his arm and fired off several loud rounds. I heard a piercing cry above our heads.

One of the bullets had struck a child, a girl who looked about nine.

Oh, sweet Jesus.

She'd been ducking for cover with her older brother, who now called hysterically to someone in the house. I heard a horrible scream and the wail of the girl's mother—

"Oh, my God!" I blurted out. Horrible. I wasn't paying attention to Marinho and his thugs any longer. I was taking a step out to see the mother frantically sobbing for help. Oh, God, the child—the bastard fired wildly hoping luck would find the target, and the little girl—

"Get back, fool!" barked the girl with the rifle. "We can do nothing for them!"

This was a nightmare, a South American West Bank, and *don't* tell me I can't do anything. "We have to get her to a hospital!" I said.

"You don't know what goes on here, gringa. I have big fish to—"

"I don't give a shit!" I yelled. "We are not running out on a wounded child because these bloody maniacs tried to hit me!"

She stared at me a moment, and it felt longer than it really was. There was time enough for Marinho to squeeze off a couple more shots that ripped away the bricks above our heads.

"What's your name?"

"Teresa."

"I am Beatriz," said the girl.

Well, well. Small favela.

I have no idea where she pulled out the 9mm automatic from, but she held it out to me, a big ugly black and silver gun.

"Do you know how to use?" she asked.

Yeah, I'd held guns before. Don't like them. And I wouldn't even try after that lunatic's indiscriminate fire.

"No thanks," I said. "But I'll be grateful if you'll keep them from shooting me . . ."

"You crazy woman! Get back here!"

Too late. Ran for an alley about twenty yards away, Beatriz popping off round after round to hold Marinho back. My rationale was that the poor mother would be stranded up there, unable to run a gauntlet of thugs to reach help or to take her daughter out. Hell, they'd probably charge her for the privilege of leaving her own district. And no ambulance or doctor would come in here.

I went into billy goat mode. I sized up the hand and footholds I had available in the amateur brickwork and scaffolding, but I was terrified of a bullet slamming into my spine and dropping me on the spot. Beatriz switched her rifle to full automatic fire. A steady, cacophonous barrage as I climbed the accordion folds of the hanging metal. I hoped, in my selfish survival frame of mind, that the goons didn't take her out either. If they did . . .

The mother waved her arms, still hysterical, enraged at me on the one hand for being the cause of it all, but making an equally raw appeal to help her. My nerves shot, I started to make my own complaints in English, ripping a blouse off a clothesline and saying, "At least have the bloody sense to apply pressure!"

I put the blouse on the girl's stomach—it was soaked in blood within seconds. I motioned to the little boy to bring more clothes off the line, and he went robotically to help, his eyes saucer-wide with the trauma of seeing this. The mother screamed over the side of the roof. It wasn't hard to get the gist: *You shot my child. Let me take her to get help.*

Not allowed.

I crept behind some cover and yelled out: "Marinho! Listen to me, you bastard! The little girl's in trouble!"

"Too fucking bad!" he laughed. "Come down, Miss Knight, and maybe I will let them go."

Beatriz let out a long burst of automatic fire—yeah, it summed up my reply.

"We are leaving," I announced, and I carried the little girl in my arms down the stairs to the interior of the house. I had to prop her head on my shoulder as if she had fallen asleep in my arms. Poor little kid. Thirty seconds more, and she would have made it to the stairs with her brother. I couldn't imagine living like this, but I was getting a good idea.

A desperate run from the front door with the girl in my arms, mother and son in tow. Beatriz sent a hail of bullets to cover us.

Don't ask me how we got out of there. Lady Rambo would say "This way" or tell me "Go here," and I barely kept track. The mother was sobbing and praying, and it was the little boy with the instincts of a small fleeing animal who consulted back and forth with Beatriz in Portuguese and enlisted a couple of trusted friends to let us cut through their homes. His family was known here. Beatriz was known here. I was a stranger.

At the bottom of the hill was a large van, and Beatriz lost all her composure now. She tossed me the keys to unlock the door and yelled *go, go, go,* get in. As if we really needed coaxing. We jumped in while she swung the heavy rifle left to right, not knowing if Georgie and his pack were hard on our heels.

"Beatriz!" The little girl couldn't wait.

I held her in my arms as my new cranky best friend gunned the engine and drove us out of there, the little boy chattering, the mother still crying, but now in low and mournful sobs. Beatriz said something to her over her shoulder. It could have been *It's going to be all right,* but it might just as well have been *Be quiet, trying to concentrate here.* The tone was even, not quite brusque, but there was an edge to it. She was what an American friend called a hard broad.

After fifteen excruciating minutes, she pulled the van into the drive with the bright sign for PRONTO SOCORRO,

and then I handed the little girl over to her mother at the
hospital's sliding entrance doors. The little boy looked up at
me, his dark eyes very sad, as he said: "*Obrigado e desculpa . . .*"

I understood him thanking me. But *desculpa*? Telling me
he's sorry?

It was surreal and grotesque. As if Beatriz and I were a cal-
lous Thelma and Louise pair belonging to another criminal
faction—as if our brutal intrusion into their lives had to be
interpreted as *their* fault, for form's sake. Lest we come back.
Lest we punish them. I found myself kneeling in front of
the little boy.

The mother called for him to hurry to her side, and I
kissed the boy's forehead and told him: "No, no! *Desculpa,
desculpa.*" Trying to make him understand—I wasn't part of
the factions in the favela.

He ran to his mother, and Beatriz yelled at me to get back
in the van. "Okay, we go! She get cared for at this place,
okay? We can't stay here!"

I'll probably never know if the girl lives, I thought. I
hoped she would. Let her survive this and be whole.

I was quiet for a few minutes, barely noticing that Beatriz
was driving back to the favela.

"Hey, whoa! What's going on? Where are we going? You
can drop me off here, and I can—"

"You will be dead the minute you step foot in your hotel
room," she snapped. "Listen, *honey*—"

Why did the folks with guns have to talk like a bad
Hollywood movie?

"It's great you kill Luis Antunes, but you are . . . What is
word? . . . Amateur. They know you, and they will wait for
you at your hotel."

I wasn't convinced of that, or at least I didn't want to be.
I had checked in as Susan Braithewaite. "I'll be fine."

"Do you joke?" she sneered. "You are black!"

"I'm *African*," I said. "And so what?"

"I see no one explain you the facts of life."

Getting tired of this. I fell back on sarcasm. "I thought Brazil's supposed to be this big happy ethnic mix!"

Beatriz scowled. "You try marry a white man or get a good job, gringa! I don't care you change name when you check in at your hotel—they don't see many confident black chicks from Britain. Try. They know where you stay."

She had a point. I watched the morros getting closer. She couldn't drive the van into the narrow favela streets, so if I needed to bolt and part company, I'd have my chance. But Helô said this Beatriz had her own reasons to try to kill Marinho, and if I could avoid getting my head blown off, it might be worthwhile finding out her story.

So these were the "facts of life" according to Beatriz—or at least the facts of the favelas. Most of the blacks of Rio and São Paulo lived in them. There was, according to her, no black middle class to speak of, and in fact, the old "lighter you go, the better things are" rubbish went on here. In the country that has the largest population of African origin outside Africa itself, black pride fought a war for hearts and minds with the adoption of "white culture" and trying to jettison your heritage. Race was Brazil's dirty little secret. The multihued citizens may always smile on the beach in travelogue television, but miscegenation had originally been a tactic practiced with a vengeance to divide African slaves.

This was the last country in the Western hemisphere to abolish slavery and when it did, there wasn't even "forty acres and a mule" for those freed. With no legal and financial access to land, black people drifted to the cities and built their houses in the morros: the favelas. "In Brazil, we don't even have racism as a criminal charge that deny bail until 1988," said Beatriz. "No one think it a big enough problem."

So never apartheid here and no *Whites Only* bathrooms, but there was no need. "Society can take care of it with a word," my guide informed me, cranking the steering wheel hard. People could—and still did—put you in your place. I got the idea. Poverty, the average white Brazilian would say, is the big social problem. Then you looked hard to see who lived in the favelas, which literally rested across the street from upmarket luxury homes. Beatriz drove the van past the invisible boundary, an uncanny juxtaposition. You didn't even need to throw a stone. My God, the big rich houses sat *a few feet away* from the slums.

Later, much later, I clicked on the BBC news site, which informed me that Rio alone has 752 favelas, with more than eighteen percent of the population living in them. Incredible.

Up in the honeycomb of brick and metal shacks, the crime barons and parallel powers ruled. "The gangs have weapons the army don't even have!" And teaching them how to use those weapons were refugees from the civil war in Angola. "How you think *I* learn?" Even before I tipped off Marinho by drawing attention to myself, Beatriz said, one of his lookouts probably flew a kite to warn the gang. It was the tactic used when the police came to make a raid.

"So where are we going?"

"The other side of the favela where we'll both be safe, and things calm down," said Beatriz, staring darkly at the shanty town. "Tonight you stay with us. Tomorrow you can help me with a chore I have to do with my boyfriend."

"What's his name?"

"He's British like you. His name is Graham Bailey."

◆

She didn't notice how quiet I got, sitting next to her as she drove along. For a long while, I couldn't listen to her steady monologue, too busy feeling hurt, thinking what a fool I was to be inspired by the instant attraction, the sudden connection I had with Graham. *He has a girlfriend.* Damn it. Well, we'd have much to discuss next time we met.

Finally I pulled my head out of the dark thunderclouds and tuned in to Beatriz, who was rolling out some of the details of her life. She'd come to this particular slum, known as the "Favela do Buraco," as a naïve, insipid girl from the country, manipulated into a life of prostitution by a *cafetão*, a pimp. He told her she owed him a large financial "debt" for letting her stay with him—then raped her and turned her into a whore.

But Beatriz's life was, relatively speaking, better than that of other girls forced out on the street. Her beauty was worth call-girl customers, rich ones. She actually took lessons in English to help her to communicate with johns. Then her luck got worse. Her *cafetão* "sold her debt"—in effect, sold *her*—to Henrique Marinho.

"Marinho always a pimp!" declared Beatriz, spitting out the window. "You know why he go into porn? Math."

"*Math?*"

"Marinho wish to be respected. To be a *cafetão,* no matter how big his house, how many fancy chair and sofa he buy, he cannot do that. So he look at math. I hear him say this in front of friends one day. Girls who sell themselves on the street still need to eat at least once a day, must look pretty, can complain and whine and like that, okay? But a few girls—told how to behave, who only have to fuck now and then—they can bring in thousands, no, *millions* from fools who watch them and jerk off. Then he say: 'Fuck it, we do both.' "

A cold bastard, yeah. Definitely sounded like him.

"That's when you escaped, isn't it?"

She parked the van and switched off the engine. "He's a monster."

"Luis Antunes wasn't. When he learned about the girls being used in movies he fled to Britain."

"Don't be stupid. He go there to make more money— money for him and Marinho."

"Listen to me, Beatriz. I was hired to investigate him, and I found out the truth. He didn't use sex slaves in his movies there. If anything, you lost an ally in London, not an enemy."

I rolled out the whole saga, and to her credit, she sat and listened without interrupting. She had never heard of Helô, but she remembered Antunes had married a young girl from Rocinha. When I told her how Luis and Helô had tried to rescue Matilde, how I had brought the poor girl out of a dungeon back to her friend, Beatriz swore under her breath in Portuguese, her face going pale.

"I almost killed him."

"Yes, I know," I said tartly. "You can't go in guns blazing to every situation. You don't know who'll get hit . . ." I started to think about that little girl. *Please be okay.*

"Oh, yes?" said Beatriz, lifting her chin defiantly. "So you say I can't go bang-bang against a pig like Marinho?"

"I'm not saying don't go bang-bang, I'm saying find out first who's caught in your crosshairs."

She didn't understand the reference to *crosshairs,* and I pointed to the rifle scope. She laughed and chattered something fast in Portuguese. Eureka. "Oh, I see, I see." With perfect timing for gallows humor, she added, "You not worry. I make very sure to kill the right man who drive this truck."

Lovely.

She drove us to her safe house on one of the fallen-soufflé mounds of the favela. As the van rolled up, I heard the rattle of at least a dozen unseen rifles being lifted and taken off semiautomatic fire to full auto. *Click. Click, click, click, click, click.* Jeez, I had trouble keeping the emotional pieces together after only weeks of looking over my shoulder—couldn't imagine a permanent life of bunker mentality and paranoia.

Beatriz jumped out and offered a hug to a scruffy-looking guy playing guard, then a girl, and she rattled off a set of quick introductions. I instantly forgot all their names, too many to keep track. Her men were ex–drug addicts and petty thieves. Some had escaped the ranches where there was debt slavery. Most of the women were once prostitutes indebted to Marinho or some other gang. Rescued and recruited. I soon picked up how Beatriz played mother or big sister to all of them.

In a ramshackle house, much like the one belonging to the family of the little girl who had been shot, Beatriz supervised cooking of a communal meal. Black beans, rice, vegetables, smoked sausage and salt pork . . . I watched her dart back and forth from counter to sink, passing utensils and bowls, all while making suggestions (giving orders?) in Portuguese to her brood and then switching back to her stream-of-consciousness lecture for me.

"Cooking for family is like cooking for army," laughed Beatriz. And I thought: Yeah, and you have both. "You wonder why we all together, why we don't go back to our homes, back to the countryside. What would we do there? Work jobs for shit? And then types like Marinho put us back in debt? What, make babies?"

"Have a normal life," I offered with a shrug, "instead of playing Robin Hood."

"Robin . . . ?" She didn't get that one either. One of the men did, miming a bow and arrow, and there were peals of laughter in the kitchen. Instead of reading a criticism into it, they took the reference for a compliment. Of course. How could working a pitiful plot of land or raising children compare with this amateur revolutionary life? It was one where they each finally got a say, had a measure of control.

And getting shot at brings its own rush. But you can't run on the fuel of adrenaline constantly.

I noticed after a while that many of her followers had drifted out of the kitchen and even out of the living room beyond. I looked to Beatriz questioningly.

"Oh, they've gone to pray," she said absently.

Hey, this *is* one of the most Catholic nations in the world, I reminded myself.

"What, is this a holiday or something?"

Not that I know much about Catholics, but they had seemed to all go together. Beatriz shook her head no.

"*You* don't need to pray?"

"I go later," she said, stirring rice. "They don't like to wait for me, because I take so long."

"You have a lot to ask God?"

"Other way around," she replied, and she enjoyed my reaction.

"For the longest time I was an atheist." She laughed. She said it like a young woman recalling her childhood, as if telling me that for the longest time she collected Barbies. "It make no sense to me in holy texts how women are treated—we are stupid, we are second, we must be told what we do."

"But now you believe in God again," I prompted gently.

She paused a moment from the cooking and said, "God make no sense without war—without war for what is right. We here to struggle, you see? Every animal, every tree, earn its place. And if you must earn your place—it is natural, yes? You can only earn it by doing what is right, and then God save you. They dump my ass at thirteen in a lorry and take me to fuck how many guys a day. Because I was stupid and let them take me. Years! Years of that life until I shove a corkscrew in the chest of one guy to run away from Marinho. I tell myself: *Now* you are strong enough. Now you smarten up. We give birth because we women are strong enough. We raise children because we are secretly the stronger. But we must stop being stupid. We must lead the war for what is right, the war to take down bastards like Marinho . . ."

I stopped paying close attention. I'd heard some of this before, the masochistic notion that we are only given the burdens we can handle. Maybe she needed the world to make sense this way, this weird mix of "evolve or die" with the line that God really loves you after all, baby, you just have to try harder. Yeah, right. She saw the skepticism in my face.

"You think I am peasant."

"I don't think anything of the kind."

But I was lying. I did feel a twinge of condescending superiority, doubting she'd ever had a chance to be properly schooled. The old liberal conceit: People will surely believe what you do if they learn more.

"I read," snapped Beatriz. "I read plenty when I learn English. I read about Joan of Arc, about Russian women—Stalingrad—fierce soldiers. I see the movie about it on DVD. I read about God to see if I'm wrong."

"I'm not saying you're wrong," I answered. "I'm saying I don't know. That's all I can ever say. I think that's all any of us can say if we're completely honest."

She was dismissive. "Oof! People who say they don't know—they just don't like churches and temples."

"I like churches and temples fine. My experience is: you know the people who admit they don't know? They tend to *not* like guns. Yeah, I'm in their camp. Both feet."

Religious arguments were always a waste of time. I already knew how volatile she was, and since I was a houseguest for the evening, it would be stupid to offend her. Had to admit she was casually fascinating, this hyperactive bandit and rape survivor, and it was easy to see the charisma that influenced the others.

Her followers drifted back, and we ate our meal, washed up, and then Beatriz surprised me by saying her group wanted to check out a *baile funk* (a funk party, as the locals call it). It was being held on the edge of the favela in safe territory for her people. It struck me as strange, like a group of students wanting to see a live band, but I thought, okay, they can't be bandits twenty-four hours a day with this Marinho vendetta, raiding brothels and robbing gangster businesses. They all lived together, and if individual hopes and dreams were abandoned long ago, there must still be a communal urge to seek some normalcy. Have a beer. Listen to some music.

Funk carioca. Brazilian funk. (Hey, don't ask me how to categorize it, I heard heart-attack thumping dance music, and some people compare it loosely to Miami Bass, but that's way oversimplified for me.) It pounded out of enormous speakers in the bare-bones shed of a venue. Beatriz explained how the *bailes* had started in the middle-class districts of Rio thirty years earlier and had slowly migrated to the favelas, so that now you found the parties all over the place.

Like everything else in music, it seemed to be constantly changing, getting an edge like *proibidão,* the hard-core stuff that slammed the cops, or the newer funk that had explicit sexual lyrics, and on it goes. Maybe this had started as Brazilian black culture, but everyone was welcome now, white middle-class kids dancing away with young people of every brown hue. No one gave a damn what you were here.

I watched the members of her little army shake it and dance, and I weighed the idea of slipping away and trying to get back to my hotel to confirm if Marinho's creeps were really waiting for me, or if I could at least sneak in to collect my belongings and check into another spot. Probably

232 · LISA LAWRENCE

wouldn't go down well with my hostess, and to take down
Marinho, I needed all the friends I could get. Well, perhaps
I could suggest a couple of her people come with me for the
task. I found Beatriz out back, finishing up some sort of
meeting with a guy in an open-necked white dress shirt and
beige slacks who did his best to stay in the shadows.

I got a reasonably good look at him—prominent nose,
deep-set eyes, and a thick mustache. He looked vaguely
Turkish or Arabic, and he glanced once in my direction
with a look that said I wasn't welcome. He made a curt nod
to Beatriz before he turned to go.

"So you didn't just come here for the music," I com-
mented.

"Oh, I like the music," she replied evenly, about to float
back to her friends.

"Who was that?"

She paused a second, as if measuring whether I would let
it go. I wouldn't. "His name is Qabbani. He's our gunrunner, our weapons man. We can't kill Marinho with bad language."

"I've seen your stash of guns. You've got enough for an
army."

Beatriz smiled as if it were a big joke. "We need more.
Qabbani's professional, and he is reliable. We do favors for
each other, and now I've said enough."

"Favors like what?" I asked.

The little bandit queen blew air from her cheeks and said
irritably, "Like we test Qabbani's weapons on somebody
Qabbani don't like! If a favela gangster rip him off for payment, he would like very much that creep to be dead! Oof,
you ask so many questions, gringa. This is *our* world, and
you cannot learn it in a day."

I didn't bother to tell her I'm a quick study.

More dancing, more partying, and when we got back to
the house, the party atmosphere continued for a little

while, with Beatriz's people sitting around and drinking in the glow of candlelight. I plonked down on the uneven floor and took in the bits of sad furniture, the low, chipped table and wicker chairs with ratty holes in them, guessing that no one bothered to fix the place up since it might have to be abandoned at a moment's notice if they were attacked—whether by the Brazilian cops, Marinho's people, or another enemy. Then Beatriz showed me where I would sleep for the night: a nearby room with a modest futon mattress laid on the floor of rough unfinished plywood boards. I've slept on worse, but I felt like a child abruptly sent off to bed. Part of me wanted to surrender to oblivion, collapse right there after the long day, but I heard sounds and murmurs from back in the lounge area.

I tiptoed up to take a look from the hall.

A young boy with fuzz on his upper lip pretending it could be a mustache and a black girl with freckles, people who didn't betray knowing each other *at all* earlier in the day, were passionately making out on a futon couch. They were like small animals, clinging to each other and wild in their petting, the girl already topless, holding her man tight, rocking back and forth as they seemed to devour each other. But more interesting was the scene in front of them. Beatriz knelt on the floor before the couple, and for a moment it looked like she was doing yoga or something. She stretched and offered her arms forward, and one of the other men gripped her by the wrists. Beatriz barked something in a whisper, a single word that I could only assume meant *tighter.*

Suddenly, she broke from his grasp, her arms flailing as if she were on fire, eaten by mosquitoes, something that drove her to strip off her shirt and all but tear off her bra. Her full breasts spilling out with large and dark areolae, thick erect nipples, breasts like overripe fruit. She bleated a command to have her arms gripped again, and a muscular guy behind her yanked off her trousers and panties. Beatriz never looked back at him, looking down once at the floor, up again hungrily at the couple as the guy behind her opened his trousers and guided his uncircumcised cock into her pussy.

Amazing. The soft-swinging phenomenon had been around since we discovered sex was fun in caves, just went by a new name with the Internet, and here out of sexual frustration or maybe boredom, Beatriz and her followers had created their own incestuous little club. The guy fucked her. There was no other word for it. She wanted to be roughly taken, and in the candlelight flicker, the shadows on her muscles changed with each pounding thrust, lit up his six-pack and his pecs, defined his hip bone . . . and made me wet my lips. It seemed he fucked her for his own pleasure rather than hers, but I would be proved wrong soon. When at last he came, he pulled out of her and let his spunk fly along her back. This only made her tug harder on the arms gripping her. A second guy, skinny with six o'clock shadow, took himself out as well and penetrated her—with a quick rude jab of his stubby cock. He rammed her as if to inflict hurt, and while Beatriz gritted her teeth, her eyes widened, and only now did I see any betrayal of mounting arousal. But the guy inside her . . . fucking her, but taking no joy in it. He pulled out and a spatter of semen struck Beatriz's calves.

On the futon the boy with the peach fuzz had graduated to missionary position inside the black girl, her knees up and one arm holding her breasts from jiggling uncomfortably with his momentum. Beatriz watched them, and a third guy knelt in front of her, took out his dick and pushed it into her face. She went through a kind of ritual of refusal before she gobbled him into her mouth to suck him, her lips slurping and urgently tonguing his shaft, all as a fourth guy took his turn with her from behind, his curved dick eliciting a groan. When the guy in her mouth let out a cry, she let him go, and he, too, ejaculated on her back.

It was only when the fourth guy inside her bellowed with his own orgasm and pulled out that she made a kind of wail of half protest, half pleasure. And the men . . . The men who had taken her and spilled themselves on her, they looked smaller for it. As if this gang-bang demeaned them, not her. One of them grabbed a towel and wiped off her back, but the game wasn't over. She rose from the floor, stagger-stepping until she yanked the boy rudely off the black girl and sloppily kissed him, pushing him down. She was short but overpoweringly voluptuous, mounting him quickly and taking his hands to squeeze her large breasts.

She rode him hard, slapping his chest, and crying out with her teeth gritted, the left-behind spunk smeared on her back drying, but now fresh beads of perspiration between her tits and down her belly, her pussy fur matted with it. She exorcised her demons in a swirling storm that sucked the others into it. It captivated the room. And me. No tenderness, beyond even personality, just blind will to reach release and use this boy like a tool. I've seen women have sex in front of others before. I've seen women try to fuck to demonstrate how good they are, and I've seen them act on their own lust. I've seen women come from being whipped and love every second of it. It wasn't how she was taken or how many partners that struck me as aberrant (and I've seen so much, I don't know what you call aberrant anymore). No, this was different because it was the first time I had ever seen a woman fuck somebody as if she needed to burn rage like gasoline.

She came with her nails digging into the boy's chest, her neck arched back and her mouth open in a silent cry, a grunt like a man's. She slipped off him and, completely nude, walked out of the house into the wretched little gravel yard. There was a half-moon that painted her sticky and exhausted body white, and for a second I recognized the emotion that shuddered through her, that made her touch her breasts and caress her own belly. I had felt it back in those strange apartments, watching just as I watched tonight, felt it when the girl had her fingers inside me and when I was naked in the upstairs of the Scenarium with Graham. It was the first time I think I understood anything about Beatriz. It was the desire for oblivion, to extinguish yourself through exposure and complete vulnerability, no longer caring who saw you, forcing the world to see you in all your rawness. A kind of freedom, but a kind of death, too. I wondered which one she wanted.

◆

The next morning I woke to toddlers screaming outside from nearby households, playing naked and barefoot while banging tin. The favela was a parody of a city block, looking like a giant had stepped on its lumpy tiers, and from up here, the sound of Rio's traffic was a distant growl. I bathed with cold water out of a bucket. Not fun, but at least I was clean again. In the primitive house, no indoor plumbing yet Beatriz's gang had a television with an aerial, and she even had a laptop. I wolfed down a quick breakfast, grateful once again that they shared their food with me, and Beatriz and her followers behaved like nothing had happened last night. For them, maybe the sex games were not important.

I asked my hostess, "You have a modem?"

As she blinked at me, I added quickly, "Internet. Can you get Internet?"

"Yes, yes—of course, help yourself."

I checked the special e-mail address I'd set up, and the government authority in Brasilia that oversaw corporations had gotten back to me on the tie between the Lemos Company and Silky Pictures. They sent PDF copies of the signed legal documents, including the list of the senior corporate officers. The managing director, the chief financial officer . . .

Oh, no. *No, no, no.*

No wonder. And now I had a picture to prove the revelation in these documents.

Jiro's techie geeks had helped me with a freeze-frame blowup of a shot of film—one from the orgy yacht DVD. When I brought it up, I saw what had frightened Luis Antunes and what made him want to run away to Europe with Helô.

Reflected in the glass window of the door on the yacht—one of the party revelers looking on while the wild sex continued on the deck—was Andrade.

Ferreira's lawyer.

Luis had recognized him in that briefest glimpse, had wanted to go over the time index frame to be absolutely sure. I could imagine his blood going cold, realizing that Andrade could only be on that ship because Ferreira and Marinho were working together.

The PDF documents showed that the managing director of the Lemos Company was José Ferreira. *Marinho was actually working for him,* funneling profits from the porn empire into the gangster's company.

Luis. Poor Luis. When he first imagined the scope of whatever was going on, he had gone to Ferreira to enlist his help. And had given himself away to the enemy, shown his hand. By the time he noticed Andrade on the DVD and realized his fatal error, it was too late.

Beatriz came up behind me and looked over my shoulder. "I know him. He is that pig lawyer, Andrade."

"On a yacht at a party held by Henrique Marinho," I said, and I told her quickly what I uncovered.

She looked at me in astonishment. "But Marinho and Ferreira are enemies!"

"Look at the corporate documents," I insisted. "I can show you the money transfers. There is no gang war between the two of them. There never was."

"But that—that doesn't make sense—"

"It makes perfect sense," I argued. "There are all kinds of prison gangs and favela crime lords out there, right? If Ferreira and Marinho pretend to be enemies, each operation can report back to each other on who might make a move. Maybe someone comes to Marinho and wants help so he can attack Ferreira. Great, Marinho tips Ferreira off—Ferreira gets an early warning. And the pipeline works the other way. Someone comes to Ferreira and says, 'Help me get rid of Marinho'—so Ferreira picks up a phone, and Marinho finds out who's after him. A secret alliance. It got Luis Antunes murdered. He was looking for help from the same people who wanted him dead."

"With his reputation, I always think Ferreira worth killing," snapped Beatriz. "Now he give me good reason—working with that slime Marinho. I swear I'll kill them both."

Ferreira was the real big fish. And what a good laugh he must have had with his lawyer, Andrade, when I came to visit him in prison. What a wonderful performance he put on, with me stupidly trying to enlist his help. I was in the dark, just as Luis had been. Clever. Clever, clever bastard. He might be the smartest and most dangerous enemy I had faced. After all, he'd seen me coming from an ocean away.

Oh, but we're not done yet, you and I, I thought to myself.

The trouble was that by now Ferreira had been released, probably already back in town and out on the streets of Rio. A free man. I was going after him on his home turf, and I still hadn't figured out his spy connection or what he was truly after.

◆

In the afternoon, Beatriz and I piled back into the van, and she drove us to another obscure corner of the favela. I had no idea where I was again, even as we scrambled up one of the cracked streets. When she led me to a storage shed, I understood she hadn't shot one of the gang just to steal the van.

But we didn't need the goon's keys for the shed. Someone else was already using bolt cutters to haul out the chain and quickly push up the door. As it slid up, light shone in, and the stench of thirty, perhaps even forty girls trapped inside hit us in a wave. They had barely been able to breathe. They couldn't wash, and they'd been given a couple of buckets for toilets. Their eyes were blinded by the sunlight, and only a couple were able to stand. These were the ones, I was told, who would have been shipped overseas like Matilde. Marinho liked to stash them in a shed to break their will and their spirits first.

Oh, I wanted that son of a bitch to feel fear.

Graham helped the first one out as Beatriz called his name.

She rushed over to throw her arms around him and kiss him. Notice I wrote: She threw her arms around *him*. I watched as he yanked her hands off his neck and, to my astonishment, pushed her back. There were a few sharp exchanges in Portuguese, and it sounded like she was either apologizing or expecting a warmer reception. He was having none of it—quite angry with her, in fact.

With a huff, Beatriz went into the shed to help bring more girls out.

I walked over, and as he noticed me his face fell. "Teresa . . ."

"Way to go, poker face," I told him, folding my arms. "I could have believed you were her boyfriend—"

"I am *not* her boyfriend," he snapped. "Crazy bitch nearly got me killed once and—"

"*And* I could have believed you're just doing the right thing, showing up to help these women."

"But it's too big a coincidence, isn't it?"

"Yep."

Better believe it. Right after I meet him breaking into Marinho's production company? He was here freeing the girls, so I knew he wasn't with that creep or Ferreira, which meant he could only be working for one other outfit.

"Doesn't matter," said Graham. "We need to talk anyway. By the way, you made MI6 look very foolish slipping out like that."

"So I guess you'll be the class favorite if you bring me in. I thought you were a nice guy."

"I thought you were going to call me."

His eyes strayed to Marinho's victims, many of them barely able to walk unassisted to Beatriz's van. We both had other priorities for the moment.

10

We couldn't help forty women escape in a single lorry, of course. Graham got on his mobile to a taxi company and soon had two more vehicles pulling up to drive the girls away. The young women all needed medical attention, but Beatriz—now exhausted with explaining everything to me in English and reverting to Portuguese to Graham—said it would be wiser to have a nurse or doctor tag along and move the girls out to a suburban clinic. From there, aid organizations could relocate some of the girls and help others return to their villages and towns.

Beatriz agreed to follow up with the shed girls and meet with us later. I think she meant just Graham, but he was the one who said she'll meet *us*. Whatever was between them, he wanted it over. He led me down to his rusting Beetle, and I have no idea what made me go with him—he worked for the cloak-and-dagger types eager to put me in a cell. On the other hand, he had absolutely no jurisdiction here, and the Brazilian authorities would be just as chuffed to deport a foreign agent as to hold a suspected Islamic terrorist.

We rode in silence for a couple of minutes. Then I announced: "I need to get my things out of my hotel somehow. According to Beatriz, the bad guys will find out about it soon—if they're not already there."

Graham nodded. "I don't know if you trust me enough to stay with me—but that is the safest place for you."

"Oh, really?" I laughed.

"It is, Teresa."

"I wonder how that will go down with Beatriz."

"I don't give a damn."

"What's the deal with you two? You slept with her, didn't you?"

"Hey, shall I ask about Luis Antunes?" he shot back. "And his wife?"

I looked at him, not so much taken aback by this point but by the fact that he was so well informed. Huh. Maybe Helô had been forced to admit our dalliance to the cops or to MI6.

I suppose he did have a point. It's not like he'd led me on—I had just seen for myself moments ago that he and Beatriz were not together, at least not anymore.

"So that video of you with the girl? The one you had to retrieve from Silky Pictures? I suppose that was for my benefit."

Graham kept his eyes on the road. "It was." I could see he wasn't proud of his on-camera performance. "We're not involved in any way. She's an operative who usually works out of Lisbon. She—"

"I get it. I know how MI6 brings loving couples together."

He didn't reply to that. I guess he knew about Kim, too.

"Teresa, we needed a plausible scenario for how I could run into you. Here I am in this city, British, same as you, but before the high season starts and right after you escape trouble. We thought it would look a bit suspicious if I was on the prowl in a nightclub or walked up to you on the beach."

"But we ended up in a nightclub just the same."

"That wasn't the job, that was us. I like you. We shared something special—at least it was special to me."

"Was it? Special?"

"*Yes*. Hell, yes!"

"Because MI6 knows an awful lot about my sexual history," I said. "Maybe you were curious and wanted to confirm a few intimate details for them."

He looked hard at me, willing me to recognize the sincerity in those large brown eyes. "Hey, that's unfair. And think it through, Miss Detective. We arrange for you to accidentally walk in and see a sex tape of *me*. That doesn't make me look very good, especially if my plan is to seduce you."

It had been a special night.

But I wasn't about to turn off my brain simply because I liked the guy. "I'd like to know how you could be so bloody sure I would come down the hall in that office to check you out! I mean you go to all that trouble, you have footage actually filmed of you having sex, you break into the office and plant yourself in that very spot—"

Graham made an embarrassed little wince that turned into a mischievous smile. "Well, er . . . We didn't have to count on luck as much as you think."

"Sorry?"

"The girl you saw on my sex movie—you didn't recognize her, which is a good thing. The same girl was in a British Airways flight attendant uniform when you deplaned in Rio. She jostled you for all of two seconds when you went to Customs."

"And?"

"She planted a tiny Radio Frequency Identification tag on your handbag strap."

"*What?*"

244 · LISA LAWRENCE

"Well, come on, a spy's got to have a few gadgets," he laughed. "What bothers you more? The tag or that you finally ran into somebody good at tailing and surveillance?"

"This isn't funny! Where the hell is the thing? Where is it?" I started frantically searching my handbag, inspecting every mark, checking for tiny foreign objects.

"Teresa, calm down," said Graham. "I'll show you where it is later—"

"Let me guess. And plant a new one."

He groaned and made an appealing look to the heavens. "Teresa! It was my assignment to track you. My job. I wasn't sure what scenario to use with the sex tape, but because it didn't make me look very good, we decided it was believable. When you went on your little excursion, I saw my chance and took it—got ahead of you and broke into the office first. I had a feeling you wouldn't be able to resist finding out who else was in there. You're a detective. Much better that you think you discovered *me* than me coming along and bursting in on *you*."

That smarted—him anticipating my moves. And his girl operative planting that device! Errgggh.

"Well, this tag didn't help you very much to protect your cover," I said. "If you've been tracking me, why didn't you know I'd turn up at the storage shed with Beatriz?"

"It's *Radio* Frequency Identification," he reminded me. "I get a fantastic range on the thing, but it was never meant to deal with the obstacle course of the favelas. Once you went in there your signal went dead—like trying to pick up music on an AM frequency under a bridge. You get nothing in that honeycomb. You know the movies where the good guy taps away at a laptop, and some big satellite above pinpoints your movements? Yeah, we got stuff like that, but as notorious as you are, babe, they don't deem you worthy for the major hardware. And I do work on a budget."

I watched the road, and after a moment, he offered, "Yes, it's a shitty thing to do, tracking you with the RFID. It was necessary. I didn't know who I was dealing with."

"So I guess your bosses finally woke up and accepted my evidence," I ventured.

"Evidence?"

"The plaster casts, the inverted foot blow to Luis's head, the—"

I didn't finish because his face was blank, not at all understanding my reference to the material I had given Carl Norton.

"I don't know anything about that," said Graham.

"Then why are you . . . ?"

His ignorance completely threw me. How could he *not* know about the evidence I'd offered Carl? If our run-in at Silky Pictures in the middle of the night was just to arrange his introduction, maybe he wasn't sent to haul me back to Britain—at least not yet. Maybe he couldn't afford to at the moment.

"This is your back garden, isn't it? You're stationed here. If you move me out, it will create a fuss and bring you unwanted attention."

He watched the road, smiling as if the whole situation had collapsed into farce. "You're wrong, darling—it's a good guess, but no. I've been to Brazil a few times, but I hardly know it better than you. I *was* sent here to track you and eventually take you back to London—I got this errand because of my language skills. I trained for Angola, never learned Portuguese for here. I'm a Deputy Chief of Operations for West and Southern Africa."

"West *and* Southern Africa? Pretty large brief."

"You know how it is—it's Africa. We're never a priority until the next time someone has a crisis over oil, diamonds, Coltan. Lately it's chocolate. Now suddenly people care about child slaves used to get the cocoa. Well, better late than never, I suppose. Here in Brazil it's all debt slavery on ranches, or Marinho's girls used in brothels and porn."

"Right," I said. "You found me quick enough, but you haven't tried to put me on a plane."

"Yet."

"You obviously don't want to. Why the delay?"

"You *are* trouble," he laughed.

"Come on. Why the delay?"

"Did anyone ever mention you're persistent?"

"No, they say relentless. Give."

"But it's more fun this way, making you guess."

"It's childish," I sang, looking out my window.

The beach and the sparkling water beyond were, as ever, beautiful. He finally relented, laughing because I was clearly stubborn and didn't want to play his game. "Okay, okay . . ."

He shook his head slightly, trying to choose his words. He looked vaguely troubled.

"Listen. With all the satellite and thermal-imaging software, the pin bugs for surveillance and other hi-tech rubbish, this job still comes down to human judgment." He took a deep breath and added, "You saved that girl in Richmond-upon-Thames. What was her name?"

"Matilde. So? I fled. They still had their bogus evidence against me."

"But you *saved* her," he said, his voice growing intense, as if I were missing a crucial point, something very precious to him. "I asked for and got the interrogation notes for Helô Antunes—relax, they can't touch her, she's done nothing wrong. They'll probably grant Matilde a stay on humanitarian grounds. Anyway, I read the accounts. My superiors at MI6 are so convinced you're an Islamic extremist—an assassin. And yet you rush off and save this girl kept in a basement while the police are hunting for you."

"I couldn't just leave her there."

"No, you couldn't. A fanatic would. Somebody who really does have bomb blueprints in their flat would."

"So you know those were planted. Who did it? Marinho and his thugs?"

"I can't be sure, not yet," he said, watching the road. "They're not the subtle types."

As he felt my eyes weigh on him, he added, "I honestly don't know, Teresa. I'm telling you all of this didn't track. I certainly didn't like the fact that my higher-ups refused to share the news about Matilde with Scotland Yard's Homicide detectives."

Whoa. I sat there, astonished. It never occurred to me to mention saving Matilde to Carl Norton when I saw him in Paris. After all, it wasn't relevant to the evidence I'd tried to gather to clear myself. I honestly wasn't interested in how it looked, I just wanted to get the girl out of that dungeon. Carl didn't mention it either. *Because he didn't know.*

"Teresa, it doesn't take an expert in psychology to figure out you're innocent—that you couldn't murder a man in cold blood."

"Well, you could always be wrong."

"Oh, I don't think so. Beatriz was bitching and complaining for several minutes about how you insisted on taking that child to the hospital. I know her. *She* has fanatical tendencies. She's running around, trying to take potshots at Marinho. And Antunes when he was here. Yes, I got involved with her briefly. I had this stupid romantic notion I was saving her or protecting her. Sexist, I know—little girl, *big* rifle! Then when I woke up and saw she didn't need my protection, I thought, here's a smart, sassy woman I can collaborate with, who's been through the wars and can help us do some good. Now I work with her only when I have to. We're not nearly as well networked here as operations in Africa."

"What happened?"

"She's a loon!" His hands lifted briefly off the steering wheel to shake them in frustration. "Last time I was here, I tried to get to the bottom of these sinister connections we've found between South America and Africa. Nothing we can put our finger on, but I managed to hook up with these Angolan expats. Very dangerous guys tied in with the parallel powers here and hoping to stoke old political fires back home. Then Beatriz blows my cover. Not deliberately, mind you, but she comes in, guns blazing, with a few of her favela vigilante types, and she 'rescues' me in front of the villains. It's 'Hello, baby, aren't you lucky I'm here?' and I'm burned in two countries. The creeps can send an e-mail to warn their mates in Luanda."

I was incredulous. "How can you walk around Rio safely if your cover's blown?"

"Oh, I had to get out fast when it happened, believe me! But things cooled down after six months, and it's a huge city. All concerned now have bigger fish to fry than me. Everyone expects a war to start soon between Marinho and José Ferreira."

"They're wrong," I said.

"You just got here a few days ago. How can you know they're wrong?"

I went over what I'd found in the corporate documents.

"This is not good," he said grimly. "Ohhh, this is not good at all. Marinho *works for Ferreira*?"

I nodded.

"Not good," he muttered again. "Whatever's going on, we don't have a clue what's at stake. I have a terrible feeling that Beatriz walking up and blasting Marinho or Ferreira won't make it go away. I've tried before to get her off her vigilante kick, but no joy."

"I think she's in love with you," I said gently.

He shook his head, annoyed. "She's insane. I'll watch her

back if we storm through a door together, and I'll gladly free more of the sex slaves, but the personal . . . She's head-strong, reckless to the point of suicidal, and I think the only reason she keeps jumping into my arms and hoping I'll take her back is . . ."

He didn't finish the thought. So I offered to end it.

"You're a lifeline to the outside world for her. Even if she met a regular guy from a nice neighborhood in Rio, there'd be class and baggage and other nonsense. You come and go, Graham, and she hopes one day you'll take her with you."

I paused before I added, "But you know all this. You feel guilty about it. It's why you do still come charging in to help her, isn't it?"

He nodded, checked the traffic. He was quiet for a long moment, and I thought maybe I had embarrassed him. I could imagine his position. Whatever he had needed from Beatriz, he probably hadn't promised her tomorrow, but his very presence, everything he was, suggested to this woman who lived day by day that there could be hope. With him.

All this sunshine, and yet the mood had gotten pretty dark in the car.

"Umm, I know I've crashed the party in terms of all this intrigue and gang stuff," I said. "You don't begrudge me making Ferreira or Marinho's life uncomfortable, do you?"

"Oh, these guys are maggots!" he sneered. "As soon as I learned about the storage shed, I was on my way. Marinho already knows who I am—which means Ferreira does, too."

"If that's your position, let's have some fun."

"What's the idea?"

I had him find me a public telephone. I rang Henrique Marinho's house, asked for him by name and listened as a servant brought the cordless receiver out to the boss. A splash told me he was still in the pool.

"*Olá.*"

"Marinho. Can you guess who this is?"

There was a slight pause, and I knew he was shocked I had the nerve to call him directly.

Then the low voice became calm, doing its best not to give anything away. "Gringa. You are such a fool to come here—a clown bumbling into the furniture. You got out of England, woman, and you should have found yourself a comfortable spot to pass your years in exile."

I kept my tone breezy and taunting. "Oh, but all the fun's here! By the way, Beatriz and I just emancipated some of your victims from their garage hotel. It's a small start, but I'm sure I can dream up more headaches for you."

"You . . . ? You . . ."

"Marinho? Hello? I'm sorry—did you swallow some pool water? I didn't catch that."

Another pause of one, two seconds, as he understood that yes, I had seen his home, I had been watching him.

"You little *cunt*!" he barked. For the first time, losing his temper in front of me, the ice cracking. "Okay. Okay, you cost me money. Well done. But Brazil is full of tight, young pussy waiting to be turned out—I'll make it all back. And I'll make some more off your ass! When I catch you, bitch, I will have a line around the block and my camera crews ready! You better run."

"Marinho, I don't think you fully get the picture. Is your boss there?"

"I don't have a boss, you stupid cow."

"Oh, we both know better, don't we?"

Long pause.

He pulled the receiver away from his mouth, but I could still hear exchanges of rapid Portuguese, a small group deciding what to do. After a second, I heard a deep growl on the line: "Ferreira."

There was the telltale *click* of someone picking up an extension—Andrade coming on to help translate.

"So, Miss Knight, we are supposed to congratulate you

on being so clever? To us, it seems it took you a long time to know anything useful."

"Oh, it takes me a while, but I do get to the truth. You don't have to come after me, boys. The way I see it, I owe you *big* for killing a friend of mine and framing me for his murder. I'm not running anymore. I'm going to do a little hunting of my own. And Ferreira, guess who plays the scared little bunny?"

"If you're so clever you know who my friends are, gringa. I am untouchable."

I Spy, Simon had typed on the Instant Messaging. *I Spy Big.* I still had that piece of the puzzle to figure out.

"Oh, Ferreira," I said with the pitiful tone you give the village idiot. "Just remember: If they couldn't stop me getting out of England . . ."

Andrade translated, his voice impatient now: "Yes—yes, yes."

"What makes you think they can possibly stop me when I put a gun barrel to your head? *Tchau.*"

I hung up.

Graham had leaned against the phone booth, covering his mouth when he had to laugh. Now he was throwing his head back and guffawing openly. "Oooooh, very *Underworld* Kate Beckinsale!"

"Seems to be the only thing these sexist Neanderthals understand. And stop grinning at me—I'm still cross with you."

"No, you're not," he said, and waved to the Beetle.

He was right. I wasn't. Damn. He shouldn't know me so quickly after so little time.

He gunned the engine and said we ought to hit the shops to buy me a couple more outfits to wear.

◆

MI6 does not keep active operations staff full-time in Brazil. Their operatives are based in another country in South America, and no, I can't tell you, but take a look at the headlines and you can guess where. As a result, all Graham had to work with in Rio was a few sleeper agents (Jeez, and they actually call them that) and informants.

He hadn't lied to me about the hotel apartment he rented in Botafogo, about the size of my flat far away in Earl's Court. He said his employers selected the spot for agents because it had a little-known service lift perfect for quick escapes. But he loved the district for its cafés and cinemas, its touches of 1940s architecture.

I was glad he had injected a bit of personality into his temporary home. The spotlessly clean but sterile décor was heavy on brown and red pillow accents, with a banal framed watercolor of Ipanema Beach. But on a glass coffee table, Graham kept what he called his "airport art"—really the term they used for the kitschier trinkets you buy at the Futungo Market south of Luanda. Wherever he traveled, he spread these out in a convenient spot in the room. Hung on the wall was an unrolled print, its corners trying to lift like shirt collar wings after so many rumpled journeys. It was a print of a beautiful abstract called *Ritual* by the South African artist Lucky Sibiya. Man had taste.

He mixed a couple of *caipirosca*. "Here you are."

"Thanks. We're drinking a bit early, aren't we?"

"After that little misadventure, you bet," he said, raising his own glass. He sipped and put it down, declaring, "I am going for a shower. See you in a couple of minutes, make yourself at home—"

"Oh, no, you don't! Don't you have a sister?"

"I have three."

"Then you know to let girls go first. I've been running like mad through the favela, and I'm a mess!"

"I'm the host, I have to be presentable." He started walking in the direction of the bathroom.

I grabbed his arm. "You're the host, so you're supposed to offer."

"Want to share it?"

"Presumptuous."

"Oh, no," he said innocently. "Practical, ever practical." And he leaned in to kiss me.

I met his tongue with mine, and then he was gathering me into his arms, hopefully not suspecting I had steered our bodies in a semicircle. "Oh, no, you don't!" he laughed, as our mouths parted for a second, and I let out a happy squeal as he held me fast around the small of my back. I jumped into his arms, locking my legs around his back, and he grunted as if I were too heavy. That got him a playful slap on the back of the head. He offered a deep kiss apology, and I slid down.

"Guest!" I said, scampering to the bathroom.

"Host!"

But I made it there first. I could see he hadn't been back long. The maid had left a bundle of paper-wrapped soaps in a dish and, thankfully, there was a shower cap. I was humming and lathering away when I heard the door open, and he walked in naked, not taking no for an answer.

He got in, and I began soaping his broad chest, losing track of what I was doing while he was kissing me, but the cascade of water was heaven. Pretty much done, I washed his back and enjoyed the delicious sight of his muscles flexing as he pushed his face into the spray, arms coming up in a beautiful pose to rub his eyes and blink away the water. Tall nude black man, soaking and looking like a waterfall had carved him out of its droplets. He cupped my breasts in his large hands, and his cock was half erect the whole time, pointing up accusingly as if I'd been neglectful. Well, we'd do something about that. We toweled off, and I knew where we were going.

Scenarium had been a passionate rush, now it was time for exploration. For minutes on end, we just lay on the bed, his face in my hands as we kissed, his fingers playing with my nipples, working the orbits of my areolae in slow, massaging circles. Kissing him with my neck back, him cradling me from behind in his arms. His mouth fluttering down my spine as his thumbs pushed into my buttocks, his right hand doing something . . . Oh, God, I thought only Fitz knew that trick. His lips making a butterfly capricious trip to my hip, sliding up to kiss me as he lay on his side. Feeling somehow torn from gravity as three cupped fingers, four, were inside my vagina, finding my spot . . . finding my spot, and kiss me, kiss me please as shudders racked me now, Graham patiently, so expertly using his hand, my nails digging a little into his back.

"*Aaaaaahhhhhhh!*" I felt the quake, unendurable, still screaming as he relaxed his hand to withdraw, and I squirted in a lewd stream over his hand and thigh. I had to lie there, panting for a long moment, and then excused myself to duck into the bathroom again.

When I came out, I was ready to devour him. I know what happens to me after I have an orgasm like that—the match is lit, and my body is in almost a blind frenzy for sex. I jumped on the bed laughing, pinning down his wrists. I slithered down to tease him, working my tongue around the base of his cock, driving him wild because I refused to lick upwards to the tip, at last my lips parting to take him in, sucking him and feeling him swell in my mouth. I had tricks of my own. Finding a rhythm to drive him wild, coming up to suck his nipple into my mouth as he easily slipped into me.

I gasped with the sudden fullness of him all at once, and then I was grinding my hips, wanting to take my vengeance on him with pleasure. We were so in tune, easily shifting from the languorous exploration and tenderness to this gymnastic expression of want. He rolled me so that I was still half on top of him, half falling onto the bed, and it allowed him to sink even deeper inside me from underneath. We kissed for what felt like minutes on end as he thrust away. I recognized how much I missed making love with a man. Yes, there had been Luis recently, but I had shared him with Helô, and his body had been boyish, a delicate fragility to his limbs so that I couldn't even imagine him holding me without her embrace. There had been Todd, but he was jackhammer fucking, a dildo with abs. Fitz was technique, prowess, the two of us always in a dance of passion, but trying too often to impress each other with our moves. Graham made love. He took me with a quiet masculine dominance that didn't come from muscles but assured style, and appreciation of my body and how his should fit with mine. And he had every confidence from the beginning that we fit perfectly.

He wanted to be on top. Draped in his body, my arms flung around his back and squeezing his ass, the two of us both in a sweat now, and he gently bent my legs and put my ankles on his shoulders. I watched his long brown penis slowly sink into my pussy, until I felt the tickle of black curly pubic hair, the gratifying touch of flesh at his base. *Just stay in for a moment,* I whispered. Just stay *right* there. He did. Kissed me deeply, the way he had in the club when we were shamelessly naked, broken glass at our feet and me perched on the table. I felt prowess, I felt curiosity and desire and every damn inch of hard cock. I felt enveloped in strong arms, under the gentle weight of a wide chest. I smelled him and drank him in, relished the sweet pressure of thighs and the tiniest pulse of his rod. *Oh, baby, just stay in.*

I felt a small distant orgasm, and as I looked into his eyes, he withdrew a little to start a rhythm. A slow rhythm that took me up until I came once more with tears in my eyes, me whispering *I want you to come*. Hearing myself chant it, *I want you to come,* as he withdrew and eased back in, still kissing me, my pussy muscles tightening their hold on his cock, a caress of his fingers along the back of my thigh, almost tickling me with my ankles still on his shoulders. Building, and a little faster, a little faster, and *I want you to come,* I want to feel the flood of you as your arms brace, and your torso rears up, cock so deep, and now baby, now, and as he pumped me with a fury and at last grunted and shook, the whole damn bed scraped an inch on the floor with our momentum. He shot and shot and shot, my nails digging into his ass.

◆

Beatriz sent a text to Graham's cell phone that she had to talk to him. We finally got out of bed, had a meal, and drove over to see her in the Laranjeiras district.

We met her at Casa Rosa—the "Pink Room"—a hot spot, I was told, that used to be one of Rio's famous brothels. As we sat down at a table at the large outdoor patio, Graham wasn't perturbed at all by the men and women glowering our way. They wanted us to know who they were and that they were watching.

"Beatriz's people," he whispered to me. "They're more dangerous because they're *not* professionals."

"God, I keep wondering why they don't want a quiet life after all they've been through," I whispered back.

"I know," he said. "I don't like the number she does on them. If you want to rescue somebody, you don't treat 'em as a potential convert to your politics. Well, maybe 'politics' is being too generous. Her vigilante band or—"

He stopped because Beatriz glided up to our table, wearing a brown leather jacket zipped all the way up and dark trousers, looking oddly severe. Her curt nod told me everything she felt, all her resentment towards me. She had let me go away with Graham, perhaps hoping he would put me on a plane and get rid of me. The gringa who was inconvenient—for Marinho, for Ferreira, for her. Well, I was still here. Too bad.

"I thought you cared for me," she said, her tone intimate as if I weren't there at all. "I call you, and you say yes, you'll come—you help free those girls."

Graham was incredulous. "I helped free those women because they needed freeing."

"I see," said Beatriz, dropping her eyes to the table. "This helps decide things. I knew tonight would. You've brought *her,* so I guess my people were right. It's time I opened my eyes."

"And just why did you bring *them* along?" he asked. Under the table he reached for my hand. I don't know if he needed the strength of contact or thought I did.

"They are here to watch me," Beatriz answered. "They're here to witness me tell you something. You need to go away, Graham. Take her with you. We have operations planned, and you make things complicated with your presence. This is not your country or your struggle."

"Beatriz, do you even know why you do what you do anymore? You showed up late for your own rescue mission. You were too busy blasting holes in Marinho's men in the favela."

"If I hadn't gone into the favela, your new girlfriend wouldn't be with you tonight."

I knew better than to open my mouth this time. In this, she was correct.

I listened to them, and at first I thought this had the sound of two exes squabbling, but as they argued, I saw how Graham had been accurate about their relationship.

Maybe I had doubted him because I was looking for a flaw, having too good a time with him to believe he was real. Talking to Beatriz, he kept his voice soft and his words were reasonable. But hers were growing sharper, more defensive.

"Those women in that storage shed—"

"Could *wait*," snapped Beatriz.

Whoa.

"Maybe they have time to think how stupid they are to get trapped like that! Don't give me such a look—I know I was stupid, too, once. This whole country teaches women they have to be whores and it tells men to treat them with no respect! A nation of hypocrites! And you're no different. I open my legs for you and think it's a way to express gratitude. Me, a fool again! And you sit there now and ask do we know why? Believe me, we are quite tired of cleaning up, here, there, wherever—shooting down one of Marinho's men when we get a chance. Some ways, okay—you think how can you blame him? He sees the fool, he take advantage. He looks out on the beach, and he see a free meal—the sheep can't wait to be sheared." Flecks of spit flew from her mouth, and she pointed at two of her group at a far table. "But I still owe them vengeance! I owe them!"

Graham looked mildly bewildered. "What the hell are you talking about?" he asked gently.

I couldn't blame him. Disconnected thoughts and free-floating anger. She stood up, and her seat tipped back and clattered to the ground.

"I am saying go home, Graham! Go save Africa or Britain or somewhere else and take her with you. I am saying I forgive you that you make me a fool—"

"I did *not* lead you on," he cut in.

"But I cannot do my work running into you in the favelas or the city."

"You called me today, remember?"

"Well, no more."

Graham flipped his eyebrows with a shrug that said fair enough, downed his drink, and gave me a look. Time to go. Boy, was I ready. I wasn't sure what had happened here, but I understood even more now why he considered her a liability.

But what was also disturbing was the behavior of her followers. They didn't appear ruffled at all by her outburst. Maybe they had been questioning her judgment—and they had wanted her to demonstrate she could tell him off. Or maybe they were simply used to her volatile nature. Me, I thought it wasn't the kind of emotional display that inspires the troops.

And I wondered how long you could run on the fuel of outrage over your trauma. I suppose if anyone questions the inflexibility of your resolve, your eyes would darken and burn with the intent to shame—just as hers had tried with Graham. To his credit, he wasn't buying it.

◆

In bed. Later. Lying beside each other.

"How does a guy like you wind up a spy?"

"I can't be a spy?" he demanded playfully.

"Okay, you can be a spy, Mr. Macho. It's just . . . I don't know. You don't seem emotionally scarred with a need to flee home, or politically driven to strike fear into the hearts of evildoers. You don't seem bored with comfortable middle-class life and looking for kicks. And yeah, okay, I haven't seen you too much in action, but you don't strike me as the ruthless type who gets off on liquefying people."

"You mean liquidate, don't you?"

"Liquidating people, right—"

"Liquefying!" He laughed.

"Okay, okay, slip of the tongue."

"You have some funny ideas. It's like any job and can be just as dull."

I doubted that.

There were familiar themes in our backgrounds: middle-class parents with high expectations of their children, siblings who were best friends—in his case, his sisters. He was the only son. But the differences were intriguing as well. My father had instilled in us a pride in our direct African lineage. For the Baileys, family pride was in the survivors' tales of overcoming slavery by fighting on the side of the Loyalists in the American Revolutionary War. "I've got some long-lost ancestors here in Brazil too," he told me.

His father, he said, was an economist for one of the banks and had wanted him to go into law. Graham had other ideas. He studied languages and got his M.A. in International Studies at Cambridge. (I could hear Daddy now: "Oh, you mean *he* finished his degree?") Rather than jump through the hoops of applications to think tanks and aid agencies, he drove a cab like my brother for a while, saved up, and took himself off to Africa. "When you're right there, on the spot, they grab you and say he'll do." He worked on pioneer microbanking investment projects in Kenya, bummed around South Africa for a bit, and found himself recruited in late 2000 into helping British forces in the Sierra Leone Civil War.

"Fighting the West End boys was the worst," remembered Graham. "Psychos all in one splinter faction. That movie *Blood Diamond* doesn't even come close! You are in the bush, watching children made to torture their own parents, and you actually have to *wait* until everyone's in position while some poor bastard gets his arm chopped off. You could jump the gun and save him, but then half your unit would get blown away."

In recent days he'd flitted across Africa—from Abidjan, a

city he fell in love with before its recent violence, to Johannesburg, to Dar es Salaam, to others. We compared notes on Lagos and the craziness of the Balogun Market.

In a strange way his work paralleled mine, hopscotch flights to foreign locations and putting together mysterious political jigsaws (though I suppose he worked for one "client," and I think he was more entitled to call what he did a career). I imagined him unpacking his collection of "airport art" at each new destination and hanging his print, and I wondered if he ever honestly looked for love or just arms that offered temporary comfort.

"You love your work, don't you?" I asked.

"On good days. Don't you? I'm surprised they never tried to recruit you before."

"My language skills aren't even close to yours."

"Oh, you can learn. You'd be a natural at fieldwork."

"I'd rather play detective."

"Yeah, I guessed as much," he said. "When I—no." He broke off abruptly, and I nudged him with my hand to say what he was going to say. "Not sure you'll like it."

"What is it?"

"I sort of met you already in a way—I don't mean for this op of bringing you in. They sent me your kids' books to analyze. Keep in mind, we're dealing with paranoid types, and since you were zipping around the Sudan and other places, they looked for hidden messages in innocuous publications."

"You're joking!"

I couldn't believe it. They pegged me as a security risk because I wrote about little Nura in a fictional African village?

"That's insane."

"You'd be surprised at what's used to pass ciphers or what-have-you. I know, I know. Ridiculous. Anyway, I reported that no, these are books for kids, you're a bunch of nutters in your asylum on the Albert Embankment, please go away. Then I bought a couple of your books to give as birthday presents to my niece and nephew."

"Excellent. I made a sale."

"Good, now since I have the author, come on—spill. Tell me where Nura is supposed to be. The books never say. Where's her village?"

I laughed. "It's not a secret, Graham! I didn't pin it down so I wouldn't have to stick to details of one place."

"Yeah, but you must have had one place in mind when you started, yes? Is it Sudan? It's Sudan, isn't it?"

He just wouldn't take yes for an answer. "Trade secrets, my son. Can't tell you."

"We have ways of making you talk."

"Show me . . ."

11

L isten," said Graham the next morning as we ate breakfast together. "Do you trust me?"

I trusted his eggs. Fluffy and with the right amount of basil, and I can't cook eggs to save my life.

I let him steal my toast and said, "Hell of a time to ask. What do you want to know?"

"I only have bits and pieces, and I'm guessing you have a few more. It's time we put them together. The bad guys started to make some fool documentary on Islam here, right? I saw a bit of the footage before you and I met."

"Yes, but I don't think it's real," I said. "I saw that footage, too, but . . . it's strange. There were no production schedules or notes or any paperwork on their computers. I think it's a smokescreen for something else. Have you ever heard of an organization or something that goes by the acronym F-O-Z? Foz or something? Why the frown?"

"Teresa, how much of Brazil have you seen?"

"Just here. And a brief trip to a prison I'd rather forget."

"Foz isn't an acronym," explained Graham. "Foz is for Foz do Iguaçu! It's the fourth-largest city in the Paraná state, and it's got one of the largest Muslim populations in Brazil. Sits right on the borders with Paraguay and Argentina. What's supposed to happen there?"

"I don't know. My source wouldn't—or couldn't—give me any more."

"Who tipped you off?"

I hesitated. But Simon was evading Graham's bosses anyway, and it looked like Graham was quietly defying his orders. I decided the risk in telling the truth was minimal.

"Teresa?"

"Simon Highsmith," I answered, and took a long sip of my coffee. "He's a friend. Of sorts."

"Simon," he echoed, his voice gathering both the syllables into an impressive groan, his features settling on a scowl.

"I take it you two know each other?"

"He used to be a friend," replied Graham. "Of sorts. Let's just say we had a falling-out, and I disapprove of his methods. If he's mixed up in all this . . ."

"I don't always approve of his methods either, but he hasn't lied to me, and he came through when I needed help clearing myself. If he says the key is this Foz place, I'm inclined to believe him."

Graham didn't speak for a long moment. I had a burst of telepathy. "He's never lied to you either."

"No . . . no, he hasn't. I'll give him that much."

He cleared our plates, rinsed them, and stacked them in the small dishwasher. He poured us some more coffee as I waited in the silence, wondering how big a grudge had been left between these guys.

"Teresa, can you get in touch with him again? Have him cough up more details?"

"Uh-uh. I think he's got his own problems, wherever he is. It's up to us. That's why I blundered into Favela do

Buraco. I wanted to tail Marinho, hoping he'd lead me to a few answers."

"You're gutsy, babe, I'll give you that."

"Why didn't you ever nab him off the street before?"

He looked mildly embarrassed. "My last operations here, I didn't have nearly as much discretionary freedom. I was sent to check out the Angolans here and their political connections to Africa. Marinho and Ferreira weren't even on my radar until Beatriz came along. First she wanted one gang to help against Marinho, and when they didn't oblige, she pretty much declared war on all of them. I told you the rest of that mess." He was quiet a moment, then said, "It keeps coming back to an Islamic connection. Simon telling you about Foz do Iguaçu, the documentary on Muslims in Brazil . . . And why does a porn maker do a documentary on Muslims anyway?"

"I keep asking myself the same question," I said. I went and fetched the USB flash drive from my bag. "Maybe we're looking at things the wrong way."

He followed me to the computer. "What do you mean?"

"I don't know. I've watched the footage a couple of times, still can't see what it could be for. And I went combing through this drive, but there's a ton of stuff on here."

He tapped me to get up and give him the chair in front of the monitor. "Well, let me look—a fresh pair of eyes."

I said I'd make us some fresh coffee and was happy to leave him to it. I plonked myself down and sipped my coffee, staring out the window and wondering how Helena and the others were doing back in London. Only days since I'd left, but it felt like a lifetime. I barely noticed any passage of time until I heard Graham grunt, peering somberly at the computer screen.

"What?" I asked.

"Did you check out the other video files on here?"

"No," I answered with a shrug. "I focused on the financial stuff. I just assumed they were more porn—or the same mosque footage we've seen. Why?"

Another troubled grunt. "Remember when I said we got cool stuff like satellite surveillance, but they didn't deem you worthy for the major hardware?"

"Yeah."

"Remember how I said I work on a budget?"

"Yeah."

"*Somebody* has decided a certain other lady is worth the dosh."

He had me on my feet now, and I rested my hand on his shoulder as I peered at the screen. "That looks like . . ."

"It *is*," said Graham.

"Oh, my God."

We were staring at satellite footage files of the safe house, the one in the favela for Beatriz and her vigilante pals. Marinho, and therefore Ferreira, could pull up a satellite link anytime they liked to keep tabs on her and her small army.

"If they've got these images . . ."

"They got them with intelligence network uplinks," he said, his finger pointing along the bottom of the image. "See these scrolling numbers? That's encryption coding descrambled. This is really bad—letting these maniacs have access to the most sophisticated technology of . . . The most bloody stupid irresponsible thing I've ever seen! How could any intelligence outfit do it?"

"We've got another pressing question to worry about," I said.

"What?"

"Isn't it obvious?" I asked. "We both know Beatriz wants to kill Marinho—and now Ferreira, too—first chance she gets. Marinho turned her into a whore, and she hates Ferreira as the big boss of everything. She'll blow either of them away on sight. *So why are they allowing her to stay alive?* They know exactly where she hides out. They can pinpoint her from space, for God's sake! Maybe they can't watch her every minute of the day, but they can move in anytime they like with their firepower to massacre her and her mates."

Graham wrinkled his brow, nodding slowly. "There's only one reason in their world you leave an enemy alive."

"Because she's useful in some way."

He nodded. "Exactly. But what use can Beatriz possibly still be to Ferreira? Or even Marinho?"

I tapped the screen. "Go back for a second."

He ran it back for me. As good as the footage from space was, we were still looking down on people's heads, kind of difficult at times to tell who was who. "Wish there was a zoom on this thing."

"Just so happens I have one," said Graham. He flipped to the desktop and tapped an icon, and suddenly a new program started. He typed so quickly, I could barely follow, but within seconds, we were seeing a blown-up image of the shot.

"Hey, how did you do that?"

"Trade secrets, my dear," he laughed, and I swatted him.

"This software must cost a lot," I said. "Thought you worked on a budget." But before he could reply, I was pointing at the screen again. "There! I've seen this guy."

Deep-set eyes, mustache, Turkish or Arabic—Beatriz's contact from the baile funk. "She said his name is Qabbani. Says he's her gunrunner."

"Gunrunner hardly covers it!" replied Graham. "That's Bassam Qabbani. He's Syrian, known to British intelligence. He's not your small-time thug selling rifles out of a garage. He deals in Semtex, missiles—you're shopping for a tank, you go see this guy."

"Beatriz said they do favors for each other."

"What the hell is going on?" murmured Graham, sitting back.

"Whatever it is, Ferreira and Marinho must already know. They've got this footage—they're two steps ahead. Let's go ask our nice pimp."

"Teresa, we've got to be very careful with Marinho."

"Oh?"

"I know he looks ridiculous, but he's a killing machine. People think the martial art of capoeira is pretty, but it's lethal if done right."

"Yeah, I got a quick sample in London. He's the one who beat Luis to death, isn't he?"

"I don't know what happened to your friend, but I'd lay odds . . ." Graham sucked air in a hiss through his teeth, nodding his head. He believed it, too.

"Whether Marinho killed him or not, he had a part in the murder. And I owe him for a couple of very scary minutes in my life. I definitely want another face-to-face with him."

◆

More like a foot-to-face. And if I were still editing movies—I mean something other than porn—there would be a fast cut to the nice African girl getting another boot to the head. Okay, I'll back up and explain.

Short version is that Graham knew where Marinho's girlfriend lived, at a small luxury suite in Copacabana, and MI6 kept a safe house in the same district where we could stash him once he was subdued. We were lucky—he stopped in to see the girl, settling in right where we needed him to be. His familiar routine made him careless. No bodyguards in the building foyer—they were sitting bored in a car, which we easily slipped by. Once upstairs, Graham listened by the door. He whispered to me that he could hear our prey inside, and now came the hard part, the actual subduing.

I was better with locks, so as we heard muffled chatter and a loud stereo, I got the door open. I was thinking how Graham and I made a good team as we rushed in, his 9mm Glock raised—then everything went pear-shaped. Marinho was on a couch, literally pulling on his socks, his expression dumbfounded. Good, good. Then his girl screamed from another room and launched herself at Graham with an expandable baton. Maybe Marinho had given it to her to protect herself.

"Watch out!" I yelled.

The baton swung down towards his head. Graham spun out of the way, but now he was close to Marinho. The socks were dropped and the gangster's feet were airborne. Oh, oh.

He clipped the gun from Graham's hands as the girl rushed forward to hammer him with the baton. I watched my man do a little sidestep, grab her wrist, and use an aikido throw that catapulted her into the kitchen—*boom*.

Marinho's feet were deadly. Like a child's spinning top, his head went south, his heels in the air arcing around to slap him in the jaw. Capoeira.

All at once I was facing Marinho on my own.

"You killed Luis Antunes personally, didn't you?" I asked. "Killed him before you went after Duncan at the studio."

He grinned as if I'd just told him a marvelous joke. "Yes. And it was *easy*."

That's all I needed. I launched a side-thrust kick.

Bad move. Capoeira stylists are good at sinking to the ground and getting out of the way, and my heel bit air. He did a jack-in-the-box spring upwards and clocked me right to the temple with his heel. Heavy foot calluses. *Ow*. The kind of blow that dropped me unconscious the first time I ran into him.

Be. Careful.

I *hate* guys who know capoeira.

My peripheral vision caught the girl vertical again and collecting her baton. She vented pure fury at Graham, letting Marinho have his fun with me. Graham did another spin around her and put her in a quick sleeper hold, and I heard metal clatter on kitchen tiles. I knew he'd be with me in two seconds, but I didn't have two seconds—Marinho might end this in one. Unless I took him out with something inspired.

Marinho sank again, his leg swinging to clothesline me and drop me on my ass, but I made a little hop and then stomped down in a move right out of a Shotokan *kata*, Tekki Shodan. If he hadn't pulled away, I would have broken his leg.

"Chivalry time?" asked Graham.

"Not yet, darling," I said, as Marinho nearly took my head off.

Got to fight your own duels, girl. But I loved the fact that he *asked*—he didn't jump in to take over.

Inspiration came. These guys like spinning arcs, I thought. Fine. I was sure Marinho could use his hands, but I bet he relied too much on his spectacular feet. I also knew my karate kicks were no match here, so I backed up, backed up, and the blond grinning psycho chased me. Good.

He saw Graham wasn't going to interfere. If he'd let a logical thought enter that macho cranium, he might have remembered my partner simply had to pick up his gun.

Graham knew I wanted this moment.

Marinho followed me into a bedroom. Excellent. And as he sank down again for another spinning kick, it hit him too late he didn't have the room for it. His calf smashed into a mirror above an end table, and I booted him in the gut. He did a handstand, trying another kick, but the range and the confines were cramping his style, easy to tag him with a punch to his upside-down belly. He recovered well, decided to fall back on punches.

I was right. Fists weren't nearly as quick as his feet. Odds were evened now.

"You murdered somebody I liked," I said, and I deflected his punch with an inside block. Counter flashing in a second curve—

He screamed and dropped to the floor—I had broken his elbow joint. No more handstands to launch those high kicks. I backed away, because while it's one thing to practice this stuff in the dojo, it's another to let instincts take over and actually maim somebody.

I got over it. He had killed Luis.

Marinho passed out from the agony.

Graham whistled a Brazilian pop tune as he walked in, casually putting away his Glock. "I get so much more done when you're with me."

"Some men don't like it when you show up where they work."

"Oh, not me," he said. "Here, kiss me in front of the bad guys."

◆

The girl we left behind. And Marinho learned the trunk of the Volkswagen Beetle is surprisingly spacious. By the time we hustled him into the safe house ten minutes away, he was awake but swearing over the pain of his broken arm.

He had lost his fighting spirit but none of his bad attitude, especially handcuffed to a radiator in the bathroom.

"We want to talk to you about Beatriz," said Graham.

"That little whore?" sneered Marinho. "Only one piece of her was ever any good, and even that was—"

"We *get* the idea," interrupted Graham. "How about you

tell us why you've got state-of-the-art satellite surveillance on her group?"

"Or why British intelligence gave it to you?" I added.

Graham shot me a look.

"Yes, I figured it out," I told him. "It's fairly obvious. For one thing, you were so disturbed by seeing the technology in the office—because you knew where it came from. You probably even recognized those encryption codes. And who do you think hired me to investigate Silky Pictures in the first place?"

Now Graham was really shocked. "I thought . . . I assumed Luis Antunes brought you in himself! To track down who was putting out the nasty hard-core DVDs."

I shook my head. "You assumed. You never asked. If you don't believe me, I can describe the foyer of Legoland."

"I believe you, I believe you. Shit, what a mess. We've got to talk later."

"The British are always so foolish," laughed Marinho.

"Right, that's the second time I've heard that," I snapped. "First Ferreira, now you—you're both awfully smug."

"Look at you!" cackled Marinho. "You don't even know each other's secrets. You think you can know ours? Big spy! Big detective! Your own superiors will let it happen. And they left you two in the dark."

"Let *what* happen?" I demanded.

"What the hell are you talking about?" asked Graham. "Why are you watching Beatriz and her group? What's so important about Foz do Iguaçu?"

Marinho tried to cradle his broken arm. We had cuffed his good one to the radiator. I had to give him credit for keeping up his defiance.

He made a wheezy laugh like a cartoon hyena. Whatever was so funny, he thought it was outright hilarious. "Hey, calm down, gringo. You can't stop it anymore. And when it's over, your superiors will let me go, Shit-for-brains."

Graham and I stared at each other. I had the same taste of bile in my throat, the flavor of dread.

Graham yanked Marinho hard by his hair, lifting him inches off the floor.

"What the hell are you saying? We can't stop *what* anymore? Are you saying you guys watch Beatriz because she'll make an attack . . . ? There's a terrorist attack planned there, and you bastards will let it happen?"

Beatriz meeting the arms dealer that night at the baile funk.

The Syrian, Bassam Qabbani. She must have been finalizing arrangements to get what she needed.

We thought . . . at least *I* thought Qabbani had sold weapons to Beatriz simply for her vendetta.

He was selling her weapons for a major attack.

"*I* don't live in Foz do Iguaçu," Marinho laughed. "I don't give a shit!"

"Where will it happen?" asked Graham.

Marinho glowered at him. However he came by the information, he wasn't ready to give that up—yet. "I wonder if she'll face east before she sets it off."

Graham kicked him in the face. A sudden explosive whip of his foot directly into the thug's nose, and there was a geyser of ugly dark blood.

"What's the target?"

Marinho spat blood on the floor. "Fuck you."

"*What's* the *target*?"

I pulled gently on Graham's arm, drawing him out of the bathroom. "Look, maybe there's a faster way," I whispered. "You've got ways of contacting Beatriz—call her right now. Tell her to call it off, whatever it is. They've been watching her all this time, and they *want* this attack to happen. She hates these guys. She'd be damned if she went ahead with anything that makes them happy."

"We don't know what her purpose is," said Graham. "Or

her target. We tip our hand, she might push up her schedule."

"Do you really think we have much choice?"

He saw my point and pulled out his phone. Beatriz
wasn't picking up, so he tried one of her lieutenants,
quickly asking where she was, telling him it was an emergency. "Damn it, yes, I know we're on an open cell-phone
frequency, just spill it! Where's she gone?"

I listened to the pauses, saw the growing shock on his
face.

"Don't you dare try to justify it!" he yelled into the phone.
"I swear to God if—" But he didn't get to finish his threat because Beatriz's man hung up.

"What's happening?" I asked. "Where is she?"

"He won't tell me," said Graham quietly. "But he did tell
me what she's doing. She got a lead on Ferreira's where-
abouts. She's gone to assassinate him. With a *bomb*."

Wonderful. Beatriz had already shown she didn't care
about who else got hurt in her struggle. Graham and I went
back into the bathroom, and I watched him yank hard
again on Marinho's hair.

"You better tell us where your boss is or he's going to get
blown to bits."

"The stupid whore," muttered Marinho.

"Where is Ferreira?"

"So he is blown to bits." Marinho shrugged. "The prick
never appreciate me. Every time he buy a new place, I always send him a housewarming gift. Sent him an antique
globe only last week—you think the son of a bitch thank
me? They can watch the bits come down on the beach. Way
I see it, I will get a promotion."

"Your loyalty is inspiring," replied Graham.

I was a beat behind. "The beach . . ."

Now Graham focused. The beach—that meant Ipanema.
Too late, Marinho recognized his slip.

"Narrow it down!" roared Graham.

Marinho said nothing.

Graham's foot blurred up from the floor tiles to kick him cruelly in the face.

"Narrow it down!"

"*Merda,* I don't know his every step! He's supposed to have dinner at Satyricon in—"

"Rua Barão da Torre, I know it, everyone knows it," said Graham. To me, he added, "It's one of the best seafood restaurants here. Very upmarket, the kind of place Madonna goes to when she's in town." He pushed Marinho's shoulder hard with his foot. "Fine, he eats. Then where does he go?"

"I don't know!" answered Marinho. "He likes the spots around Bar 20 and on the Rua Visconde de Pirajá. If I can't get him on his cell phone, he makes me track him down."

"Marvelous." I sighed. "So that's our job now. You might as well tell us the rest. What's the target in Foz do Iguaçu? And when?"

Marinho grinned, blood running from his nose and lining his teeth, making for a demented rictus of spite. "I don't know that . . . You want to go save Ferreira? You want to save the whore? That's fine by me! Maybe you two blow up when you arrive, and I get lucky."

He watched Graham, expecting another kick in the face. It didn't come.

Graham planted his knuckles on his hips, eyes turning to me. We would have to move fast in a moment, get down to Ipanema as quickly as possible. I confiscated Marinho's cell phone, but just calling Ferreira—even if he listened to us—didn't guarantee the safety of thousands.

"We've got to call the police," I whispered.

"And tell them what?" replied Graham, walking out of the bathroom. "A description of a black woman in the center of Rio? Dressed in what? Carrying what? You've seen

Beatriz in action now. She sees cops coming, and she'll set the thing off early. If I get there—"

"That's insane!" I said, following him out. "You're betting she'll relent because she doesn't want to kill you."

"She tried to get me to leave—and take you with me, remember?"

"If she's going through with this, she's past caring! Unrequited love only lasts so long, Graham. Plus, do you know anything about dismantling explosives?"

I watched him go to the desk in the apartment and pull out a drawer. He lifted out a small cotton money belt with a shoulder strap and undid his shirt to slip it on. I heard a rattle that didn't sound like coins. It reminded me of the noise my lock picks make.

"If she's planning a suicide run, she'll use a detonator," said Graham. "I'll have to shoot her down."

"You think you can do it?" I asked gently.

"It's one thing for her to play sniper in the favelas, taking out members of the gangs," he answered. "There is *no way* I will allow her to pull a 7/7 in the heart of Rio de Janeiro."

◆

Ipanema was at least a twenty-minute drive away, and Graham sped like a madman.

He had mentioned the July 7, 2005, attacks in London, and I remembered that day too well. Of course, I was in town. I was at home that morning. I remember watching the horrible scenes on TV, the cell-phone networks completely jammed as Helena phoned to check that I was nowhere near, everyone phoning everyone else in the Greater London area. My friend Jiro works close to Tavistock Square—he saw in person the sheared-off roof and hulk of twisted metal that was the bombed double-decker bus, barely five minutes after it happened. Horrible.

And then a fortnight later: four more bombers trying it again, thankfully failing.

And only months before my flight to Rio, the discovery of the car bombs in central London, and the flaming Jeep Cherokee in Glasgow. Horrible.

We were driving into a blast zone before the explosion was to go off, knowing it could go off, and the only thing more horrible than that sickening apprehension would be to actually see it, to have sobbing and bleeding victims in debris and aftermath ruins. *No*. Can't allow it.

As Graham made the Beetle hug corners and run lights, appearing only slightly more insane than the average Brazilian (or French) motorist, I thought about Beatriz. Graham's hands tightened on the steering wheel, his mind in denial.

"She's *not* an Islamic terrorist," he announced, probably more to convince himself than me. "Consider the source. That bastard is full of it."

"Why can't she be?" I asked. "Just because you've never seen her face Mecca or wear a *hijab*? You work in Africa, Graham! You know wearing a veil depends on what brand of Islam you want to practice."

Hey, if you're a fanatic group in Brazil trying to cause mayhem, you *don't* put your girl in Islamic clothing. If anything, a hijab would instantly identify her. There are some African-American women who are Muslims who won't wear a *hijab* to work, because they think if they do, they won't advance in their careers.

The Qur'an called for modesty, and modesty is relative.

"Beatriz an Islamic terrorist," Graham muttered, shaking his head. He was still reeling from the idea.

The conversion of our madwoman of Favela do Buraco was perfectly plausible to me. Beatriz had endured sexual and physical abuse, poverty and racism and sporadic violence on the streets where she lived. No, she wouldn't look to the more traditional Muslim community, but to the first Islamic group that accepted her with all her personality excesses.

Right in front of me, and I didn't see it. *Oh, they've gone to pray . . .* Her followers. Me, assuming they were Catholic.

Once treated as a sexual commodity, she must have felt an awakening in a faith that had sharply different attitudes to women from what she'd endured in her life experience— even if you want to debate those attitudes as sexist. Only her vision of that faith was warped through a prism of vengeance and trauma.

God make no sense without war—without war for what is right.

Holy war.

Every day, the world had told Beatriz she was small—a bug. In her reckless raids in the favelas, there was something of the doomed warrior about her, desperate for life's meaning.

We are stronger than the men . . . We must lead the war for what is right . . .

Graham found a place to park, the Volkswagen so reliable in fitting almost everywhere, and then we ran to check Satyricon and Barão da Torre. We weren't properly dressed for the restaurant and we didn't care. We barreled past the doorman and through what looked like a hotel foyer. I nearly capsized a seafood platter and felt sorry for the waitress. A bodyguard for a pop star jumped to his feet, fearing Graham had raced in here for his client's sake. But no, we went past, checking tables, checking corners . . .

"He's not here," I said. "Neither is Beatriz. How could she even know where to find Ferreira?"

"You let her know that Ferreira and Marinho were in cahoots," answered Graham. "My guess is she kept watch on Marinho's house, the same way you did. Waited for him or one of his men to lead her to Ferreira. We should be able to spot him if he's in the district." He stomped his foot in frustration. "Damn it! A bomb—she's never used bombs before. Maybe this is her 'closure' before whatever happens in Foz do Iguaçu."

I pulled his arm. "Come on! We can't have much time!"

We were out on the pavement again. Ipanema's streets are in a grid, but I hadn't a clue where I was or where to go.

We hit the peculiar Rua Visconde de Pirajá, where not one green and yellow streetlamp stood straight, every one of them at a leaning angle. Shops and more shops. We flew by them, growing more agitated in our search.

We reached Bar 20, the improbable square right next to the Leblon district, and stood on the yellow rubber transfers on asphalt. There was a big honking streetlamp, twenty yards high, in the middle of this banana-colored space, and maybe if we didn't get blown up I could ask Graham what the Obelisk was for.

But not now. There they were—Ferreira, Andrade, and an entourage of thug bodyguards passing in front of Sorveteria Itália, the city's ice-cream landmark, as we stood right in the open.

Ferreira saw us. Absolutely no cover to dive behind. His men drew their guns—

"Beatriz!"

—And didn't pay attention to her. Beatriz appeared out of the crowd behind Ferreira and hooked something quickly to his belt. I felt my spine freeze. *Oh, my God.* I know a rock-climbing carabiner when I see one. She just snapped the spring ring onto his belt.

A small tag dangled from the ring, and now Ferreira's stocky frame was tethered on a black cord to another carabiner on a gym bag. Beatriz fired her pistol at the only bodyguard trying to take her out. Point-blank range, *crack,* perfect shot to his heart, and he was dead as he hit the ground.

"*Ferreira!*"

The other bodyguards fired blind at Beatriz, who ran into the street, the two of us in the square forgotten, but Graham was desperately trying to get Ferreira to stop doing the natural thing: trying to release the carabiner on his belt, sawing at it with a pocketknife. Andrade, ever the sycophant, was holding the cord, making a big show of helping.

"It's a bomb!" shouted Graham in English. Shout it in Portuguese, and we'd have a panic stampede of pedestrians. "It's on a proximity detonator!"

Which meant we were really in trouble. There could be only one reason she had hooked it to Ferreira's belt and left him with the obvious means to cut the cord. Because that tag dangling from the carabiner had a radio device in it. Tamper with it—break a certain distance from the bag—the bomb instantly goes off.

She had armed the bomb before she saw us. It didn't matter anymore whether Graham was here or not.

"What the hell do we do?" I yelled.

"Go after her!" said Graham, not hesitating at all. He shoved his automatic into my hand, and then, spur of the moment, handed me the car keys, too, in case I needed them. "I've got this! Don't let her get away!"

A millisecond to hesitate.

"*Go!*"

So help me, I ran.

Gun weighed like a brick in my hand, nowhere to put it, dressed in just shorts and a tank top. And left Graham with a bomb that could take out the most famous district in Rio de Janeiro.

I ran as if it was nothing to leave him there, the shops and restaurants blurring in my eyes, half of me waiting for the deafening roar, a shock wave that even this far away would knock me and everyone else to the ground.

He had sent me, the choice made, and I had to go.

Beatriz was our one lead to the horrible action planned for Foz do Iguaçu, and if Ferreira's hotheads shot her down first . . . More death. I imagined bloody faces with hands to eyes, others struggling in a daze to walk, others who would never get up. I saw Tavistock Square in news reports. Sick of it, we're all sick of it. Don't you maniacs understand? It doesn't change minds, it doesn't prove anything, and *we're sick of it!*

I ran.

Does he even know what he's doing? Does he know how to defuse a bomb? With what?

I had no idea where I was anymore. First I was chasing one of Ferreira's men after her, and then I could see Beatriz yards ahead. Another bodyguard was farther along, trying to aim, but she zigzagged—she must have known they were close behind. As I closed the distance with the nearest guy, I gave him a hard shove, and the extra momentum pitched him forward off balance. He catapulted hard into a stone wall. I saw a spatter of blood. I couldn't stop.

Can't fire. Barely know what to do with a gun in my hand, and not at this distance.

Beatriz suddenly stumbled, and as she hit the ground and rolled, the guy on her tail slowed his pace. He wanted to take her alive, haul her back to Ferreira and—too late, he realized it was a feint. She was a small target there on the ground, aiming up in one quick decisive stretch of her arm and *bang*. A cluster of pedestrians gasped in shock, one woman screamed, and as Beatriz jumped to her feet, she saw me coming.

"Why?"

She still had her arm straight, the gun aimed point-blank at me.

I will never forget that face.

Glassy eyes washed in waves of stunned curiosity at my being here. Then irritation, for I was the intruder into her

282 · LISA LAWRENCE

hell, an inconvenience, and perhaps she still saw me as a rival for Graham's affections.

Aiming the gun—

And still more conflicted emotions making her lip quiver, her eyes moist and angry and deluded and frightened. The agony of a suicide just before the blade cuts vein. Rage turned inside out.

Aiming the gun at me—

I asked her why. I got my answer in a tortured sob, wrung out of her in a teeth-gnashing wail. It said: *Don't ask about my whys, my whys are pain and pain and pain, and you can have all of it.*

She pulled the trigger, the gun shaking so badly in her grip the shot was wild.

It did succeed in scaring the shit out of me.

People ducked down on the street and, thank God, the bullet slammed into an empty parked car.

"Beatriz!"

People behind her. I couldn't shoot. People too close who might be hit, and I was not Henrique Marinho who could fire a gun and not care where the bullet went, even if it went into a little girl.

If Beatriz gets away . . .

Shots behind me, multiple *cracks* and *pops,* and I dived behind a parked car, losing sight of her as two more bodyguards in a Porsche roared up to us, the one on the passenger side firing like a madman out the window. Beatriz fired back once, twice—practically emptied her magazine into the windshield of the Porsche, and with a squeal of tires, it jumped the curb onto the pavement and slammed into the patio furniture of a bar. A snap of giant matchsticks, and the car folded like a tin accordion into the concrete wall and the picture window.

A curtain of fleeing pedestrians ran from the steel jugger-

naut, and the driver lay dead on his horn, honking contin-
uously for the wall to get out of his way.

Car and smashed chairs and tables, fallen awnings—all
of this between me and Beatriz, a crowd in front of me, and
by the time I was on my feet getting around the debris, I
had lost precious seconds.

"God damn you, Beatriz!" I screamed, knowing more people would die because I had failed.

At least five different streets she could escape into.

Gone. No point and not enough time to even fetch
the car.

Graham.

I ran back, blessed that Ipanema was in a grid, and I
could find my way to Bar 20. But another shock was coming. From yards away, I watched as a kneeling Graham did
something with the apparatus in the gym bag, his back ob-
scuring my view of his hands. He was working with the
tools from the little kit he had brought along. Then he
slumped and sat down on the street, chest heaving a re-
lieved sigh. And dropped his guard.

Ferreira was on his cell phone.

A car pulled up, and Ferreira kicked Graham in the face.

"No!" I was too far away to stop him.

Ferreira moved forward quickly on his short tree-trunk
legs to kick him again in the stomach.

He had the black tether cable wrapped around Graham's
neck now, but it was more to subdue him than kill him.

A man got out of the car, and together, he and Ferreira
shoved my lover into the backseat, Andrade scooping up
the defused bomb bag to take with them. Ferreira barked in
Portuguese the equivalent of *go go go*.

The car roared to life again and tore down Rua Visconde
de Pirajá.

I had lost Beatriz. I had lost Graham.

◆

Minutes later, the cell I had taken from Marinho chirped away. I had brought it along when we drove into Ipanema.

"You still want to be clever, gringa?"

Andrade. He didn't bother to check who answered—he and Ferreira had either learned from Graham we'd captured his mate or they had figured it out. There was no reason for him to call—except that I had Marinho as a bargaining chip.

"A swap," I said tightly into the phone.

"Very good," Andrade answered. "Meet us in the Buraco in two hours at—"

"Wait a minute," I broke in. "There's no bloody way I'm going into the favela where you can—"

"You don't have a choice, bitch."

"Such a pity we couldn't dump you and Ferreira in the Atlantic with that bomb. I'm told water doesn't stop that kind of explosive from going off."

I heard Ferreira's growling laugh in the background then a stream of Portuguese. "*Talvez a gente amarre ele nisso, e vamos ver se ele é rápido sem seu alicatizinho de bolso.*"

"Oh, we still have it," said Andrade. "Mr. Ferreira says to tell you, 'Maybe we'll strap your man to it, and we'll see how fast he is without his pocket pliers.' Two hours—Buraco. I will post directions and a sketch map in the personals 'men for women' section on Rio's Craigslist. Watch for it and then move your ass."

I heard the click, and they were gone.

◆

At the safe house in Copacabana, Marinho was where we'd left him, miserable and still moaning in pain, dried blood from his nose caked on his upper lip.

"Two go out, one comes back," he observed.

"He's buying me flowers. Tell me how you guys know Beatriz is an Islamic terrorist."

If I had to release him back to Ferreira, I'd better learn as much as I could before letting him go.

"I think you are in trouble, gringa," chuckled Marinho. "I don't think I have to tell you anything."

"You want to have two broken arms?"

He panted a little at the thought, knowing I could do it. Then: "No . . . If I tell you, Ferreira will do worse to me before he kills me."

"You know Bailey can get you out of the country."

"You're a fool, woman."

Players so big they scared the assassin. And I was back on my own, with not a clue what was going on and running out of time.

I could waste more time doing a half-assed amateur interrogation, or I could check Craigslist on the apartment computer. I considered going to the rendezvous point early, but reconnaissance wouldn't help. No way to learn the terrain better than the local thugs in less than an hour, and I had no backup. I just had Marinho and Graham's Glock pistol. Might as well drive to the Buraco.

Marinho needed persuading for his second ride in the trunk, and I heard muffled epithets for five minutes as I navigated the Rio streets. The favela loomed in the windshield, taunting me with more humiliation.

Ferreira had chosen a spot on the edge of the Buraco where I thought I had an escape route for the Beetle, a narrow road leading down to a main thoroughfare. But then six of his men popped out of the honeycomb of shacks, one with a machine gun. He didn't need to have me surrounded—the machine gun would cut me in two before I could get back into the car and drive out. A new red Porsche drove up, and Ferreira was all smugness and smiles, Andrade in tow.

And there was Bassam Qabbani in the rear seat. I watched for a brief moment while Qabbani stared at me, quite chagrined. Andrade seemed to chastise Qabbani, looking back and forth between the Syrian and me. As if Qabbani should have reported sooner spotting me with Beatriz.

The Syrian with Ferreira. Of course. How else could Ferreira possibly know in advance precisely where Beatriz and her group would strike in Foz do Iguaçu? Her words came back to me from the Baile Funk. *We do favors for each other. Like we test Qabbani's weapons on somebody Qabbani don't like. If a favela gangster rip him off for payment, he would like very much that creep to be dead.*

I remembered reading up on Ferreira in London, how he was once an engineer who helped build a hydroelectric plant in Syria. He could have met the arms dealer there.

We do favors for each other . . .

It was Ferreira who had chosen the target in Foz do Iguaçu. And his man Qabbani had demanded that Beatriz and her group attack it, either as another "favor" or as payment for the weapons. Beatriz wasn't only being watched— she'd never stopped working for the men she hated the most in the world.

Ferreira, waiting for me now.

I opened the Volkswagen trunk and yanked Marinho out like a bag of garden soil.

"Show me Graham Bailey," I demanded.

"We'll get to that," said Andrade.

"Where is he?"

But Ferreira ignored the question, and before I could react, he raised his gun. I jumped for cover behind the Beetle, but he wasn't firing at me.

A red splotch bloomed in the middle of Marinho's forehead, and he fell down dead. My bargaining chip gone.

"*No!*" I yelled. I had nothing now, nothing. And I stared at Andrade and Ferreira in my stupid shock.

"*O Ferreira diz que o Marinho é um babaca incompetente.*"

"Mr. Ferreira says Marinho was an incompetent jackass," offered Andrade. And with the slightest smile, he added for explanation: "He was in charge of Mr. Ferreira's security after his release from prison."

Ferreira was laughing. Laughing at me. "*Aqui tá seu homen, pelo menos um pedaço dele.*"

" 'Here is your man for you,' " translated Andrade. " 'At least a piece of him.' "

Ferreira tossed me a small white box with a pink bow, the kind you'd use to gift-wrap a watch. Coordination took over as my hand reached out and caught it.

"Go ahead, open it."

He wasn't about to shoot me. None of his men would shoot me. They wanted to enjoy this.

My mind flashed back to a horrible day at a special location in New York, a place I doubt I could ever bring myself to visit again. Someone had defeated me there too. *No, please, not again, don't let me lose again to a sociopath who's—*

I opened it. I had to.

And then I threw up beside the car.

" 'I thought you would like to have them as keepsakes,' " Andrade translated. " 'Personally, I believe yours were always bigger than his.' "

I wiped my mouth, and Ferreira could read what was in my eyes, his gun lifting again, every gun aimed and ready to fire in case I moved out from behind the Beetle.

"You know I wanted you dead, Knight, but this is so much better."

"I *am* going to kill you," I said. "That's a promise."

Ferreira made a duckbill of his hand, flapping it to tell me I was all talk. In English, he said, "I—am busy—bitch."

He stepped backwards one, two, three steps, before turning his back and heading for the Porsche. His bodyguards knew better than to show me the same contempt.

But they were safe enough as long as I was near the favela. Our final showdown had to be someplace to my advantage, and the only thing going for me so far was this cretin still couldn't respect a woman as an opponent.

If I made him change his mind in the last five seconds of his life, that would be long enough for me.

◆

I was inconsolable, eyes brimming with tears, only half bothering to check whether I had tails following me. It didn't hit me for twenty minutes that I had been played. *Graham was still alive.*

There were two reasons for thinking this. First, I don't want to get gross here, but as much as a severed body part looks different from attached and alive, I'd been intimate with Graham, and those things in the box didn't belong to him. Shock had blinded me to the obvious for a couple of minutes. And there was another reason, one I couldn't be sure of, but it was enough for me to hope.

Don't get me wrong. I didn't doubt Ferreira wanted Graham dead. He wanted me dead, too—he'd just said it. And he could have killed me minutes ago, as easily as he'd executed Marinho. He wasn't the type to leave enemies alive. But I suspected the gangster couldn't indulge himself yet.

Why not? Well, I realized we'd proved only this afternoon that Ferreira was working with somebody inside MI6. The satellite footage of Beatriz's safe house confirmed it. And I hadn't forgotten Mr. Widow's Peak, the Big Spy—the creep I took pictures of with my digital camera. He was somebody important, someone Marinho—and therefore

Ferreira—had wanted to stay on good terms with. My guess was Big Spy wouldn't look too kindly on Ferreira killing a British agent, even one like Graham who was not supposed to know what was really going on. That might make life inconvenient and raise alarms back in London.

Ferreira could have shot Graham right in front of me in Ipanema. He could have gotten the same reaction from me as when he tossed me his sick "gift." He didn't.

So a poor anonymous victim had been castrated for the sake of a diversion.

Ferreira wanted me grieving and scheming revenge, but temporarily out of his way as plans went ahead over Foz do Iguaçu—the terrible something that he would allow to happen, that Beatriz would help set in motion.

If I was right, Graham still didn't have long to live in Ferreira's clutches. I steered my way back to the safe house in Copacabana because I had nowhere else to go. I needed to mull.

I unlocked the door and nearly jumped out of my skin. A familiar and condescending voice ordered, "Be sure to lock it, please."

Desmond Hodd sat on the sofa, his agent minions checking Graham's computer. "It's time we had another chat, Miss Knight."

12

I stayed by the door.

"I don't have time for this bullshit," I said. "You sent your man to fetch me, and he's in trouble. He's the only decent man in this whole mess, and how he can work for you psychopathic corrupt bastards is beyond me. Now if you don't mind, I need to find him before José Ferreira puts a bullet in his head."

One of the silent members of the entourage took a step forward. I think he was ready to slam the door shut as I went to reopen it.

I looked at him, my voice adopting a tone I had never used anywhere before, but it was heartfelt and genuine and so help me, I meant it. "Your boss here only wants to detain me. That means you won't use lethal force. But I'm not bothered at all about killing *you* if you get in my *fucking* way! Now is he paying you enough to risk your throat crushed? Just because I want to open a door?"

Guy didn't move, eyes appealing to Hodd.

"Miss Knight," sighed the man on the sofa. "I didn't send Graham Bailey after you."

That got my attention.

I saw text script on an Instant Messenger in my head, a warning from Simon. *Think H Betrayed Me*. I had asked which H, never sure who he meant, but Hodd had topped my list. Until recently.

I pulled out my digital camera and flipped through the camera images. I stopped at one of Mr. Widow's Peak.

"He's yours, isn't he?" I asked.

Hodd sighed and looked to his agents.

"Hodd. Damn it, I am running out of time for Bailey."

"Bailey will be fine," he answered and, knowing I would push, he added: "We know the place he'll be taken to. My men are nearly there and about to reacquire him."

"Fine, give me the location, and I'll say good-bye—"

"Don't be ridiculous, young lady. You want to know more, and now is the moment—we'll never get a better one. And trust me, you need to know more right away. All of it this time, I promise."

I held up the camera image of Widow's Peak. "Start with him. He's MI6."

Hodd offered one of his infinitesimal nods, resigned that I had "stumbled," as he would put it, onto the truth. "I take it you didn't get this information from Graham Bailey but from another source you trust."

"One I trust more than you," I snapped. "Who is this guy?"

"His name is Cameron Haskell. Yes, he's one of ours—in fact, his position is on a par with mine."

"Something tells me that's being somewhat generous to yourself."

"Very well," replied Hodd irritably. "In the greater hierarchy, yes, he's superior to me, and that's how all the trouble started. Ferreira is Haskell's creature. In situations where we seek out and groom an ally in a field of operations, there is always the risk that we've backed the wrong horse. That they will tell us whatever we want to hear and line their own pockets."

"I've read John Le Carré and Graham Greene, thanks. Get to the point. Are you saying Luis Antunes was Haskell's man in London?"

"No, he wasn't," said Hodd. "You don't understand. That stubborn bastard Haskell wouldn't listen to the intelligence reports. We knew José Ferreira wasn't a common malleable thug like ordinary informants in Brazil—he'd built a huge drug empire and then merged his operation with Marinho's sex-slavery ring. The only way to end the farce would be irrefutable proof that the hard-core sex videos had found their way to the streets of Manchester and Newcastle."

The pieces started to fit. "You came to me because you couldn't get one of your own camp into Antunes's operation. Not without tipping your rival off. You wanted me to get proof of the hard-core nasty stuff coming in so you could take it to your superiors. Show them the whole thing was a cock-up."

"Correct," said Hodd.

"That's why you never tried to turn Luis," I went on. "You *couldn't*. If Luis is Henrique Marinho's man and Marinho is supposed to be already working with Ferreira and Haskell, what would be the point of approaching Luis? He could tip off Ferreira and Haskell."

"Essentially correct, yes," said Hodd. "I promise you: You were not framed by us. Not by the people *I* count on. Ferreira is politically sophisticated. He knows there are divisions in the ranks of MI6. And he knows Haskell sees Muslim terrorists hiding under every bed. Haskell believes fundamentalists in Africa and the Middle East are now working with ones in Brazil. When you happened along, Ferreira saw a golden opportunity."

"I don't follow."

"Don't you see? If one's an enemy of Marinho and

Ferreira, well, one must be an enemy of Britain! That's the twisted logic for intelligence people who use the Ferreiras of the world for allies. You've caused trouble in Sudan and Nigeria, you're big on letting Africans decide what's best for Africa. Forty years ago, they'd brand you a Communist—now the bogeyman label is Islamic fundamentalist. Haskell was quite ready to believe an agent of terrorism was assigned to fight back on the Silky Pictures front. Haskell will believe whatever Ferreira tells him."

Hodd let out another exasperated sigh. "I made a terrible mistake. I never considered the possibility that Antunes might be clean. As you discovered, Luis Antunes was trying to break free. Ferreira and Marinho decided he could be useful in one last way. They eliminate him while accusing you. Haskell learns about your politics, and he sees what he wants to see. It comes down to Haskell needing Ferreira and Marinho for something—something big, we don't know what yet. And Ferreira told Haskell that you were in the way."

"Who planted the bomb blueprints and the Qur'an in my flat?" I asked.

"Haskell's people, Marinho's thugs—it hardly matters. These things might not have been planted at all. An agent could have simply written in his report that blueprints were found, and it's suddenly 'true.' He wants to keep his boss happy. He knows how to play to the biases of his superior. They listened to Ferreira and Marinho and needed it to be true—so they made it true. Your friends were told blueprints were found when they were questioned, but I doubt any one of them was ever shown these items as proof."

"Oh, wonderful, like weapons of mass destruction." I had to sit down. "Oh, my God. My whole *life* got ripped apart because of your fucking bureaucratic infighting?"

"Miss Knight, listen to me," said Hodd. There was a note of defensive irritation in his voice but shame there, too.

This time he glanced away because he had good reason not to look me in the face. "The stakes are *larger:* How do we fight our enemies? Who can we count on and who should we recruit to help us?"

"You idiots never learn!" I said, shaking my head in despair. "Divide and conquer, and you prop up dictators and gangsters and then wonder why it all comes back and bites you in the ass! There are reasons why nobody picks on Sweden or—"

"Try telling that to people in *Bali,*" snapped Hodd. "Remember their terrorist attack? They were minding their own business, weren't they?"

I didn't have an argument for that one.

The surveillance team on me in the streets of London. It wasn't Hodd's people at all. It was Haskell's team—buying this fantasy that I was a terrorist and could lead them to my evil network of accomplices. Then they were the ones who kept Nicole at Silky Pictures from talking to the police—they couldn't afford to have Marinho's presence discovered, or for that matter, the knowledge that he was the real murderer.

Hodd paused a moment to brush his comb-over and said more gently, "You are preaching to the choir, Miss Knight. I didn't want any of this. And by the way, my people intervened at risk to their own careers to let you skip out of France. When you foolishly rendezvoused with Inspector Norton in Paris, it didn't take much to cross-reference black women who took the Eurostar out of London with those flying to Brazil out of Europe."

No wonder Graham's female operative could plant her tracking device on me at the Rio airport. Everybody and his brother could find out when I was getting in. I just happened to catch a break because Haskell had assigned my capture to Graham, a guy with a conscience.

"I didn't rendezvous with Carl Norton, I merely left him a package at the café's front—"

"Oh, please," Hodd interjected. "You've worked as a courier—you know you wouldn't have to leave it for him there. I am quite sure you have the connections for someone to hand-deliver your plaster casts and such right to his office at the police station. You saw him in person. You needn't worry—no disciplinary action has been taken against him, and right now the wheels are turning to introduce that evidence and clear your name."

"You wave your magic wand and 'all better'?"

"I deeply regret what has happened," said Hodd. "Your name was never released to the public. We prevented that much. Two of your neighbors tried to sell it to the papers, but we slapped them down hard and fast with the Official Secrets Act."

"You could have taken my calls," I pointed out.

"There is absolutely *no way* I could speak to you or deal with you directly while Haskell lowered the boom. The frame was well staged, and if I had come out and declared you as a freelance contractor, Haskell would simply turn that around and destroy the credibility of our operation."

"You mean *your* credibility. You cut me loose."

"No," insisted Hodd. "This is a business that requires vast amounts of patience."

"Let's tear your life apart and see how patient you stay!"

"We did what we could to help you leave Britain. We distracted Haskell's agents with decoys at Heathrow and on the Eurostar. You got most of your funds out of the UK, and any sane person would have fled to where there's no threat of extradition." He stood up, nervously pacing the small room. "Haskell sent the orders down for Bailey to bring you back. The rumor mill says he was furious his team lost you in London. I flew into Rio not even knowing you were here! I wanted to persuade Bailey to take down Ferreira instead. I guess you convinced him in better ways than I could."

I rolled my eyes. I wasn't in the mood for innuendo.

"Hold on," I said. "Graham didn't know that Henrique Marinho was secretly working for Ferreira. But you did."

"I was wondering myself, Miss Knight, how *you* figured out the connection," replied Hodd.

I explained about going through the corporate documents for Lemos and Silky Pictures. Then I remembered I'd left the DVD of the yacht orgy here in the safe house, and now I slipped it into the drive of Graham's computer. "Luis Antunes came across the footage from one of the hard-core videos. It frightened him badly. It took me a while to capture what he saw in the frame, but I finally got it. He recognized Ferreira's lawyer, Andrade, on that ship. And he knew right then that Marinho and Ferreira were working together. I think Luis knew more, but I haven't been able to figure out how."

"It's on this footage, right out in the open," said Hodd.

"What do you mean?"

"Did Antunes ever mention sailing?" asked Hodd. "He apparently liked to sail."

"Yes—yes, he did," I said. "He also said he was the son of a fisherman back in the Algarve."

"Then I suspect he might have taken the initiative to check a few records just like you, such as who's the registered owner in Brazil for that yacht. See the name? How's your knowledge of Greek mythology?"

Eurydice. The yacht was called the *Eurydice*.

"I'm sure you're going to delight in telling me, Hodd, no matter how obscure this reference is."

"Eurydice was the wife of Orpheus."

Ladrão Films, *ladrão* meaning thief. Lemos, a reference to an explorer. And Eurydice, wife of Orpheus. Everyone just had to be clever with the names.

"Orpheocon," I said. "Damn it! The bloody boat belongs to Orpheocon!"

Orpheocon. The octopus. The conglomerate that's pil-

298 · LISA LAWRENCE

laged my ancestral home of Sudan. The company that was a leader in oil spills off the coasts of Nigeria, and yes, the firm that liked to employ ruthless mercenaries and even gave them their own corporate division. I had history with these bastards. And I kept running into their dirty little ventures.

"Correct," said Hodd. "You must have noticed all the girls are mixed race, all look Brazilian. All of their clients are white males—"

"And a couple of northern and Midland accents on the audio," I said.

"Every single one of those men is either a British or white South African operative for Orpheocon's black ops division," explained Hodd. "I recognize at least five myself there, and I'm sure we could identify most of the others after a while. The yacht is one of the company's treasures, just like its corporate luxury suites in Mayfair. I guess Orpheocon decided to treat its agents to a party. Marinho supplied the entertainment—and decided to maximize this meeting of worlds by taping his girls' customers."

And Luis Antunes found out who owned the yacht and realized something terrible was going on, bigger than even crime lords in Rio.

"This is not just bureaucratic infighting, Miss Knight. I told you the stakes are larger, and I am fighting in my own quiet, low-key way for the ideological soul of the British intelligence community."

"What the hell does that mean?" I asked. It seemed a reasonable question.

"It means this goes beyond Brazil," he answered. "Haskell has pushed some very good people out of MI6. He's going for the top job of running things, and heaven help us, he's four years away if he keeps advancing up the rungs. I grew alarmed when I noticed how many missions he arranged to be handled as private contracts for Orpheocon and its private mercenaries—as if the interests of British intelligence are one and the same with those of the octopus. He also personally authorized Simon Highsmith to be assassinated, apparently upon request by the company. Simon has made as much trouble for them as you have. They tried to kill him in Nairobi, and as I suspect you already know, he's gone to ground. Since Highsmith is now freelance, he's not under any official protection of Her Majesty's Government."

"Where is Simon now?"

"We don't know. We assume he's still in Africa."

"Oh, that's just . . . wonderful." And I wondered something else. "How did the bad guys figure out Teresa Lane was Teresa Knight? When Marinho went after Duncan McCullough, he knew exactly who I was."

Hodd groaned and collapsed back into a chair. "You, young lady, were too good at your job. Marinho and Ferreira are sexist, macho types. Word spread through the corporate grapevine at Silky Pictures of a talented new *female* director for Luis Antunes, and Marinho naturally grew curious. He never believed in a convenient bit of luck, especially with talent. I sent you in to be a lowly video editor, and lo and behold, you're promoted to director. I never expected Marinho to hear of you at all, let alone fly over to Britain! I never thought he would be smart enough to use Orpheocon to check you out—and discover there was no Teresa Lane. I underestimated him. And Ferreira. God . . . This is a huge mess."

"It's worse than you think," I said. I briefed him on Beatriz. How she was unknowingly about to commit a terrorist attack that for some reason, Ferreira, Haskell, and Orpheocon wanted to let happen.

They all stared at me, Hodd and his agents.

"My God, this is . . ."

"What?"

Hodd completely lost his temper. *"The stupid bastard!"*

He got up and went to the window, staring out at the ocean as he struggled for self-control.

One of the agents, a young woman with thick black hair and black eyebrows, perhaps of Middle Eastern heritage, spoke in a low voice to her colleagues. She had a Yorkshire accent. "It's contemptible. Either he's allowing himself to be played or he's letting it happen."

"Haskell," I prompted.

She turned to me, her eyes down as if she knew it was unprofessional to speak her mind. But she couldn't help herself. "Yes. After 7/7, after 9/11—it's unthinkable to let this happen to a friendly nation."

"I suggest," I said coolly, "all of you, when you have the time, take a nice long look at what Orpheocon has done in Africa for the last couple of decades."

We heard the cell in the woman's handbag—the ring tone was a Beyoncé tune, and it sounded inappropriate and ridiculous in this grim moment.

Hodd walked back from the balcony as she answered her phone. "Your point is well taken, but let's debate corporate colonialism another day."

"And Graham?" I asked.

Hodd was out of patience. "Don't second-guess me, Miss Knight. I know mistakes have been made, but I told you my operatives are moving in. They're fetching him now—"

"No, they aren't," said the young woman on the phone, looking mildly terrified as the bearer of bad news. "They've raided the location, but . . . No Ferreira. And no Bailey."

"What?" barked Hodd. "I was told—"

"It doesn't matter what you were told," I snapped. "You were told wrong! Where else could Ferreira hold him?"

"We thought of that, so I sent operatives to watch six

other houses we know Ferreira owns. Bailey won't be at any of them."

I headed for the door. "Hodd. What about Marinho's house in Barra da Tijuca?"

"Abandoned after Ferreira shot Marinho. Bailey isn't there. My men have it secured."

"Good. I'll go over there now."

"I just told you it's been abandoned," grumbled Hodd. "What do you want to go there for?"

"To check a hunch."

I was already halfway out of the apartment as Hodd told one of his agents to go with me. Then the agent and I were running downstairs, out the exit, and to a BMW parked across the street.

◆

The catalogues. Those silly furniture catalogues Marinho always flipped through, picking out shopping items. We betray ourselves in our obsessions, and in handcuffs and with an arm broken Marinho had said: *The prick never appreciate me. Every time he buy a new place, I always send him a housewarming gift.*

Marinho had known where Ferreira's properties were.

Yes, it was slim, but I was hoping that a delivery invoice would turn up among Marinho's things, something that left a trail. *Sent him an antique globe only last week.* Maybe, just maybe, it got sent to a house that Hodd's people hadn't discovered yet, the spot where Graham was actually being held.

Marinho's interior décor was as hideous as you'd expect. A clash of styles with his greedy selection of items, no thought given to how they'd go together. Not that I bothered to really look around. The agent with me, a guy named

Sims, got us through the door past Hodd's men guarding the place, and then I rushed for the catalogues. Wasted ten precious minutes, flipping and stopping at pieces circled with red felt marker, and then one of the agents found Marinho's receipts in a kitchen drawer. One was for the globe.

"This place," I told Sims. "Did Hodd's people check this place?"

A house blocks away in Barra da Tijuca.

No.

"Then let's get the hell over there!"

A five-minute drive. Sims, me, and another agent from Marinho's house tagging along for backup, since Hodd and additional men would take half an hour to join us. Sims pulled the BMW up a good two blocks away from the new location, so as not to spook anyone inside. Then things got bizarre. As we approached, we spotted a couple of Ferreira's men leaving from the back door of the house. In a hurry.

Sims kicked the door in, getting the drop on one of Ferreira's men, and I shouted, "Graham? Graham!"

"Teresa . . ." Weak, distant, from a basement.

"Miss Knight!" Sims called out in a panic. He had his knee in the back of Ferreira's man on the rug, couldn't chase after me. I was being stupid—rushing farther into the house without checking to see if there were more bad guys.

But there were none. Strange that two of Ferreira's men took off with just one left alone to guard Graham. Surely Ferreira knew one wasn't enough, considering that Graham was a trained intelligence officer.

Found him, slumped in a chair, but already disentangling himself from ropes. Tall man with deep mahogany brown skin and a shaved head, a bruise formed on his chin and another above his eye, but not too worse for wear. My gorgeous man.

I threw my arms around him.

"Are you all right?" I asked, but I don't think I gave him

a moment to answer, hugging him and kissing him hard. "How did you untie yourself?"

"Haven't. Just used some isometrics and yoga to loosen the ropes," he said weakly. "Took me bloody forever to get to this point. Next time Ferreira's hooked to a bomb, let's dump him in the ocean."

I laughed. Great minds think alike, I thought, but I didn't say it. I was busy laughing and wiping the tears from my eyes, kissing him again and holding him tight. "You're all right," I muttered. "You're all right . . ."

"We're both all right . . ." He shushed me gently like a child and kissed me, and we rocked in each other's arms.

◆

Sims said he and the other agent would keep the house secure, and he passed me the keys to the BMW to get Graham out of there. Sims had already phoned Hodd to let him know Graham was safe, and he had even found Graham's gun on a table in the lounge. As Graham holstered it, he made a weak joke about how Hodd better not want paperwork, and he swayed a little, still weak from his beating. I put an arm around his waist to steady him as we headed out the door.

We were a block away from the BMW when we heard the limousine. I thought: You've got to be kidding with the limousine again. But Hodd couldn't have gotten here that fast.

No. Not Hodd. A power window rolled down, and we heard a deep voice call out, "Bailey."

Graham and I both froze. Graham pulled the Glock out of its holster.

"There's no need for that." The voice sounded vaguely offended by his caution. The car door opened.

I recognized the figure emerging, the hawk nose and the black hair in a severe widow's peak, the pasty complexion.

He practically loomed over Graham, and I guessed he stood six foot five. Gaunt in his charcoal suit, looking like he'd just sold an insurance policy to Death. If I haven't made it clear already, the guy gave me the creeps.

"Haskell." Graham muttered the syllables of his name like a curse.

13

The MI6 man raised his palm towards us in a calming gesture, the blue eyes wide in disbelief. "Would you care to explain what you think you're doing, Bailey? Have you gone mad? I send you here for a simple extraction, and you become a wandering case of paranoia, hunting down our cutouts—"

"Cutouts?" I asked, tugging on my lover's hand.

Graham sounded bored. "Fancy word for go-betweens and couriers." He looked crossly towards Haskell. "And he's using it inaccurately, since we know José Ferreira is more than a courier, he's a player."

"Bailey," sighed Haskell. "Graham. I can ignore the insubordination, especially given what you've just been through. And God knows Hodd has fooled people before. If you want to know what is truly going on, let's go for a drink, and we'll discuss it. We'll drop Miss Knight off at your apartment in Botafogo."

"Cameron," said Graham, lifting the Glock and aiming it at his head. "That wasn't even very subtle, mate. Pretty obvious we'll both be dead the minute we get inside the car."

306 · LISA LAWRENCE

"No, not you, just me," I corrected him. And as both men looked at me in surprise, I explained, "That's why Ferreira's men were heading out just as we arrived—with one guy left to guard you. He was supposed to hand you over to Stretch here. Haskell needs you for something, Graham. *He's* what kept Ferreira from killing you."

Stuck here on the street, the two of us, Sims and the other agent back at the house.

"That does make sense," said Graham, and he shook his gun at Haskell and ordered, "Tell your agents in the limo to drive off. They can pick you up here in five minutes."

"You kill me, Bailey, they'll drop you on the spot. And Miss Knight."

"Oh, I reckon they won't, Cam. You see, if you're dead, your toadying protégés sort of become masterless samurai, don't they? Not worth it to kill us and piss off Hodd. He wouldn't forgive them and take them back after that. You don't think he would hunt them down over us? Hold them accountable for this little rogue show you're putting on? Orpheocon's hiring, true—but your men won't be useful if they have death squads after them."

"London will consider the results—*then* it will judge who's gone rogue."

"Waiting, Cam. Waiting and running out of patience. If it helps, I promise I won't kill you."

Haskell smiled at this innocent request for trust. He looked towards the limousine and gave the driver a nod. The car pulled away from the curb. "Right. What do you want?"

"Just like that," sneered Graham. "Buy us off."

"Yes, just like that," replied Haskell. "You've had people kidnap you, try to kill you—I would think you would appreciate the novelty of another approach."

"You want to brief me, so go ahead. Why allow the terrorist attack?"

The giant glanced at his shoes, all the way down there, and looked up with a triumphant smile. "Ah, I see. You know nothing. And therefore Hodd knows nothing. That changes things. It does actually help you, in fact. I can offer you a financial incentive as well as guarantee your safe passage out of Brazil. You can leave tonight."

"That's it," I said gently, interrupting.

Graham relaxed the Glock only a little. "What, babe?"

"The Grinch who stole Christmas. The cartoon—not the crappy movie. He looks just like the Grinch."

He made a point of studying Haskell with a pensive frown. "Yeah, at first you spot it around the eyes, then you realize it's mostly the evil."

"That's not very fair," I said. "I mean to the cartoon."

"Sorry, you're right."

"I don't find either of you amusing," said Haskell. "I thought we'd have a productive five minutes, Bailey, and set a price."

"In the future," I pointed out, "you might want to consider the bribe *before* you frame someone and order them killed. It's a credibility issue."

Haskell laughed. "What makes you think you're included, Miss Knight? Any arrangement here is with Bailey alone. You've made yourself such a headache to certain people they're well past the idea of corrupting *you*. I suppose in a perverse way you might consider that flattering."

"Coming from an egomaniac whose best friend is a drug lord, I suppose I have to," I said.

Haskell glowered at me. He loomed. In the middle of the Brazilian night, despite the palm trees and architecture, he demanded we pay him more awe than this place, a force unto himself. I'm sure the bastard thought he was.

"No, Miss Knight, what is truly egotistical—and arrogant—is this idea of the individual. The notion that *you* are important. You and that man there walking his dog across the street and those stupid, illiterate bumpkin girls you liberated. I don't pity those women. I don't pity the veal I order at dinner. Your father is a professor of history at Oxford, and I am astonished he never taught you an important lesson: Every populist movement bestowing power upon the ignorant—power at the expense of the trained elite—has been an unmitigated disaster, from the French Revolution to the psychopathic Khmers to the Taliban."

"I see. We little people should know our place."

"In a word, yes," said Haskell. "The community to which I belong and in which Bailey here plays a role no longer guards antiquated nation-states. We are the real economists. We always have been. And you, Miss Knight, are a dilettante. You run around and play detective and, true, you've caused us a few setbacks, but we carry on. Bailey has been trained, and we've invested in his skills. There is room for promotion for him—advancement. Which is why I want to remind you now, Graham, that one woman is as good as another." A wolfish chuckle here. "And you do so enjoy variety, don't you?"

The tactic didn't work. I didn't feel threatened by Graham's past—I couldn't. And he wasn't by mine. We were past that. Graham kept the Glock aimed at Haskell, keeping his eyes fixed on him.

"You're making me wait again, Cam. I don't like waiting."

"And what are you waiting for, young man?"

"*Waiting* for you to explain." There was more hidden anger in that tone than what had exploded with Marinho cuffed to the radiator.

"Go ahead. Explain it to us. It's so big you still want to recruit me for it. Teresa's right. It's the only reason Ferreira didn't kill me at the house, right? You stopped him. You just hate throwing away a tool—one that's stupid and useful. Whatever it is, it's that big, and you need me for it. But the job is elsewhere, not in South America."

"Very clever—you're right. Call Brazil a 'rehearsal' if you like, though I suppose that's not precisely accurate. The big show will be in Africa. Simon Highsmith has tried to stop it, but we've made him run with his tail between his legs—for the moment. Maybe you'd like to kill him for us?"

"If I ever kill Simon, it will be for my own reasons. Will the operation go forward if I kill you, Cam?"

"Yes, it will. And you won't kill me, Bailey. I know you won't. For one thing, you gave your word. And you're so concerned with London and what it thinks. Politically, you know it's better to have me around than to have to explain why you executed a senior Field Control supervisor."

"You're right," said Graham, and he relaxed his gun arm.

And without hesitating, shot point-blank at Haskell's knee.

"*Shit!*" I yelled. I couldn't believe it.

Haskell's face went white with shock and then agony, and he fell like a tree onto the pavement. He stared up at us, wide-eyed in disbelief, blood already soaking his hand where he grabbed his leg.

Graham leaned over and said, "Teresa Knight would make a better field agent than I could ever hope to be. But she's too good for you, you walking cadaver." He turned to me. "Let's go, babe."

He gripped my arm and steered me away. "Walk. Just keep on walking. Where's the car?"

"That one there. You promised you wouldn't shoot him."

"I promised I wouldn't *kill* him. A wounded man ties up resources, attention. Fewer guys to chase after us."

"That was a very Simon Highsmith thing to do," I remarked.

"No, Simon would have hung onto that bomb and tied it round Haskell's skinny neck."

Yes, he would. But to be fair, Simon would have dumped Haskell in the ocean too.

◆

He didn't show it—none of the stress, none of the effects of his brief ordeal—until after Hodd's debriefing and he was alone with me in the apartment hotel in Botafogo. They had hit him a couple of times, but unlike Marinho, Ferreira's other thugs weren't very skilled at throwing a punch. It was the helplessness of being tied up in a chair, the apprehension that death or some horrible torture before death was imminent, that made his body shudder all at once in a nervous spasm.

He muttered sorry to me, explaining that he'd never been taken hostage before. Yes, they tell you what to do, how to cope, he said. You get training—how to store away useful details for later debriefing and how to check opportunities for escape. But it's another thing to go through it.

"Bastard threatened to castrate me," said Graham, sitting on the couch, his hand running over his shaved head. "He's the kind to do it, too."

I'd tell him later about Ferreira's sick gift box for me. Not the time.

"Stupid—letting him take me like that."

I started to undress in front of him. He looked at me with innocent curiosity and made a nervous chuckle.

"What are you doing?"

"Make love to me."

"I want to," he said. "But . . ."

"But you've just had a knock to your confidence," I answered for him. "There's always a small part of a guy that's still a little boy in the playground. The one who hates losing to a bully. And you're kicking yourself now, because you feel like you blew it as a professional. And you didn't have time for the fear when you were in the shit, but now you can feel it, you feel how close you came to getting hurt and killed."

"I suppose I'm like glass to you," he said, dropping his eyes, embarrassed.

"Is it a bad thing that I can figure you out and know what you need?" I asked.

"No."

"Then trust me."

I led him into the bedroom. I pulled out the belts from the terry-cloth bathrobes and told him to tie me to the bars in the brass headboard. And with my wrists bound, naked and offering myself to him, I watched him kneel on the bed, his breathing becoming rapid and loud, his hands running over my belly, my breasts, my mound with a new sense of discovery. I'm sure he'd played bondage games before, but this was different, and his cock was a vivid red, pointing north with what looked like an almost painful erection. He sucked my nipples and brought his teeth down in gentle nips, felt me between my legs and let his hands roam all over my skin like a pottery artist with clay. With a groan torn from his soul, a kind of desperate anger in it, he straddled me high on the chest, careful not to bring down his weight, and I opened my mouth for his penis, anticipating what he wanted. Firm in my mouth, a twitch in reaction to my tongue, pleasure coursing through him, and if he needed to come . . . I thought he was almost there, almost there . . .

But another groan of self-restraint. He pulled himself out and down, and after a second I felt him squeeze my tits so that he could rub his cock between my breasts. Tied up like this, it was a vaguely pleasant sensation, still the anticipation he might suddenly shoot and release his spunk all over me. But after a moment, he let go of my breasts and moved to hug me in his arms, a new shudder of naked emotion racking his muscles. Outrage. Fear. Vulnerability.

"How can you . . . ?" He stared at me in grateful wonder, barely able to finish the question. How could I know this would work for him? Give him back his masculine power— *no,* let him realize that he'd never lost it, through the exhilaration of having me vulnerable for him, to be cherished or ravished as he pleased. And despite his hard-on, he slithered down the bed and parted my thighs, putting his whole mouth on my pussy. I moaned as he began to lap, drinking me in, his tongue probing my vaginal lips, pushing in as far as his tongue could go, then withdrawing and flicking up to tease my clitoris. After a while I was begging him to get inside me. But he wouldn't. His lips and tongue played with my clit until I was yanking hard on the bonds of cloth, but he had tied them good and tight. Then with a jaguar's grace, he climbed on top of me, the head of his cock nudging my pussy lips. But with a laugh, he didn't push deeper. I felt a pulse in my core.

"Fuck me!" I cried. "Come on, fuck me!"

He made the shallowest penetration, prompting my desperate moans, and his control was torturous and exquisite. Only after my second orgasm did he plunge completely inside me. His teeth sank into my breast above my nipple, and I told him to leave a mark. I keened with the glorious pain and pleasure from the bite, laughed as I saw the impressions of his teeth. Now he couldn't get inside me deep enough, kneeling and lifting my ass off the bed with my ankles once more on his shoulders as his cock rammed inside me. I came with a scream, and this seemed to spur his orgasm, but as he let my ass back down on the bed and pulled out, I saw he was still hard. He thrust in again as if by instinct and shook violently, completely overwhelmed, the sensation unexpected. I felt him shoot inside me once more. And as he laid himself on top of me, his cock on my belly, he let out a high moan with yet another new gushing stream, coming all over my stomach.

My right hand nearly tore the brass bar out of the head-board, the terry-cloth bond ripping, and my hand free, I grabbed his cock and jerked him once, twice, a dribble of spunk from the crimson head as he shut his eyes tight and climaxed a final time. God, it was like holding a spear of steel flesh, my fingers slick on the great length of him.

"Uhh . . . Shit."

"Come on, baby."

Fell next to me, kissing me, both of us exhausted.

"I didn't know that was possible," he said. "Guys having multiples."

"You can," I said, panting.

"It's you that makes it possible."

"I need to clean up."

"Noooo," he sang. "I think I'll bathe you here."

"Well, that could be fun, too."

◆

We didn't stay in Graham's place in Botafogo—we couldn't, now that it was clear Haskell was still in town and posed an active threat. That meant the safe house in Copacabana was also blown, since Haskell, as an MI6 big shot, would know it. We were left with the Control base apartment Hodd had personally set up in Greater Rio, a spacious penthouse in São Cristóvão, out near the zoo and the Maracanã Football Stadium.

Good news was that London believed Hodd's reports, and it didn't like how chummy Haskell was with José Ferreira, nor that Haskell had never bothered to share his grand scheme with the Foreign Office or his superiors on the Albert Embankment. London certainly didn't enjoy informing the Brazilian Federal Police that there was a major threat involving Islamic terrorists, organized crime, and a multinational conglomerate (only it didn't have useful details, and no, it couldn't explain how it got confirmation).

Hodd was positively beaming at the news that Graham had shot Haskell in the leg.

We spent a day cooling our heels, and I thought about my time with Luis and Helô. I thought about the whole case. Editing the movies, watching houses from a parked hired car. I wondered what Ferreira and Haskell were arranging for their shadow masters, the vampires at Orpheocon. And my tired mind flashed back to images of the soft-swinging couples, desperate fucking in front of an audience in a stranger's bedroom, bodies entwined—

"Voyeurism," I said softly, more to myself than to Graham and Hodd. "Political voyeurism."

"What?" Hodd's eyes peeped over his spectacle rims. He lifted his nose out of a report.

"This whole case," I answered. "All of it, it's been about watching."

"What do you mean?" asked Graham.

"I mean my directing the porn movies, what Orpheocon and Haskell are doing with Ferreira . . ." It was difficult to explain what I felt. "It's kind of the same thing."

Hodd flipped a page and drawled, "A little overanalytical for porn, don't you think?"

"Simon told me—well, as much as he could tell me—that they would use all this, whatever their plan is, as a test case—"

Graham moaned irritably. "Yes, well, your friend Highsmith and his grand assumptions—"

"Just hear me out," I started again. "I think he was right. We know who benefits—the question is how. This terrorist attack—they'll let it happen. That's what Marinho said while he was cuffed to the radiator. The goal isn't the attack, whatever it is. It's the fallout, the reaction—political or economic. Orpheocon wants the attack to be a catalyst for something else. *That's* the test case."

"Makes sense," Hodd mumbled.

"The whole point of a terrorist attack is to terrorize, and if you want to do that, you make a big splash where you hurt and scare the most people. Now where is that?"

Graham shrugged over the obvious. "Here. Rio, of course."

"And if not Rio?"

"São Paulo," offered Hodd.

"But that's the insane thing. They plan to hit Foz do Iguaçu. So there must be something in or near that city that Haskell cares about, something important. Orpheocon wants it, whatever it is, and when Beatriz and her people make their attack, it will allow Haskell and his corporate creeps to somehow go in and take their goodies and . . . what? What's wrong?"

I stopped because Graham was staring at me.

"No, I think you're right," said Graham quietly. "Oh, God, Teresa, you're brilliant. You're brilliant, and we're stupid, and they're quite mad."

"You want to tell me what all that means?"

"Please do," urged Hodd.

Graham moved to a bookshelf and pulled out a *Times* atlas. "Haskell said it, Teresa. Remember? He bragged on the street that he was one of the real economists—the son of a bitch."

He flipped the pages of the atlas quickly to detailed views of the Paraná state. "Right, never mind the terrorism target for the moment. I think you've nailed it—the key is the reaction to the crisis. It's about what Orpheocon hopes to get for itself. It's got a private 'security' army just like Blackwater, so it has the means to take what it wants."

His finger poked a tiny circle on the map. "Here's Foz do

lguaçu. The tri-border—Brazil, Argentina, and Paraguay. There's supposed to be a secret U.S. military air base here. In Paraguay."

"There is," Hodd piped up. He came over and traced his own finger on the map. "Here. Mariscal Estigarribia. It can house up to twenty thousand soldiers. The Americans dug in to stay two years ago. They feared Islamic terrorists using the tri-border to sneak up through South America and across Mexico. Washington has always denied it's a base, claiming that their personnel are there simply for joint exercises with the Paraguayan military—Her Majesty's Government knows different. If you want to land a Hercules aircraft, this is the place to do it."

"Which the Paraguayan air force doesn't have," Graham said tartly.

"It gets worse," sighed Hodd. "The Senate of Paraguay signed a deal that grants full immunity to U.S. troops from national and International Criminal Court prosecution."

I heard myself make an incredulous sound. "Are you joking?"

"I wish we were," said Graham. "If a U.S. soldier has a go with a fool in a bar in Asunción, he can stab the guy to death and never see trial. I'm sure that extends to the security contractors. And guess who's the biggest military contractor in South America?"

"Orpheocon." I groaned. "But what are they after this time?"

Hodd was frowning, brushing his wisps of comb-over. "If they want to use a terrorist attack as a pretext for Paraguay—and/or the U.S.—to invade Brazilian territory for 'international security,' it must be big. Something that's precious like minerals or natural gas. Bolivia has that on the other side of Mariscal Estigarribia, so maybe it's—"

"*Water*," said Graham.

Hodd wasn't buying it. "Water? Oh, come on. Something bigger than that."

"It's big enough, believe me." Graham flipped the atlas page to a larger view of the continent. He rapped a knuckle on a patch of green space. "The world's freshwater reserves are decreasing. In the future, water will be the new oil. And the tri-border sits on top of the Guarani Aquifer—one of the largest underground sources of fresh water in the world. Des, the Americans have got to be in on this."

Hodd was doubtful. "Washington gets accused all the time over the tri-border, Graham. I suspect this is Orpheocon's show. I'll bet they want to raid the shop before the Americans realize what they're after. Their mercenaries can move into Brazil without a single U.S. soldier leaving that base. By the time it's done, the octopus will just say to Washington, 'Oh, but we did it for international security and *your* sake.' They'll argue they were 'protecting' an American ally, Paraguay, from terrorists by moving into Brazilian territory."

"So get on the phone and call the Americans," urged Graham, falling onto the couch.

Hodd waved that away. "Too dangerous—that could backfire horribly. Think about it. They won't hear 'Orpheocon,' they'll hear 'terrorist attack' imminent. They'll *run* to help the buggers. It's diabolical! Beatriz's attack offers the perfect excuse for Orpheocon to invade in Paraguay's name. And even if the Americans start asking hard questions, Orpheocon might say, 'We'll cut you in.' Washington won't assert Brazil's sovereignty—they'll have all that lovely water and the map swept clean of Islamic fundamentalists. Or so they'll tell themselves."

"There's got to be something you can do," I insisted. "These bastards will drink this country dry."

Simon's assessment came back to me, and I knew now it

318 · LISA LAWRENCE

was spot-on—this would, indeed, be a "test case." A corporate colonial strategy: Cause political chaos that changes the landscape in favor of your business.

And Haskell had wanted to recruit Graham for a bigger operation in Africa.

"We don't know the target of Beatriz's group, and we have one shot at stopping this," said Graham. "There's someone else we need to talk to."

I sat down next to him. "Who?"

"A contact of mine."

"I can't authorize you meeting that person!" said Hodd. "You know the official position of the British government on—"

Graham cut him off. "Des, I don't care. Yes, London has made you Control of this op now, but we've come late to the party. Forget the official position, we need all the help we can get."

I let them bicker over that for a moment. My mind was still reeling from the impending horror. Graham went into another room to place a phone call, and after a few minutes, he emerged, looking grim, and addressed Hodd.

"They're willing to talk," said Graham. "But not to you or me. It seems they've learned a few things on their own. And they'll only speak to Teresa."

"Who are we talking about here?" I asked.

"Hezbollah."

◆

That was how I found myself staring at a massive, ginormous, absolutely *huge* curtain of water: Iguaçu Falls, sitting on the border of Brazil and Argentina.

Graham's spooky *they*, Hezbollah, had left instructions that I should get there early. They had an entire route I had to follow as a tourist until they felt it safe enough to approach. ("And of course, you'll have a better time," they added, "seeing things before it gets hot and all the wildlife is gone." Cheeky buggers.)

Graham told me I should relax and keep my mind off the rendezvous, that I "might as well enjoy myself."

So I got the panoramic view of Garganta do Diablo, what they call "the Devil's Throat," and got thoroughly soaked in my summer dress on the walkways. Well, my man had warned me to dress for a dousing. Kids chattered excitedly around me, and thirty digital cameras flashed away.

The cascade makes you think Niagara is a council estate's leaky tap, and its only rival is Victoria Falls over in Zambia and Zimbabwe. I got the close-up, more intimate vision of it from the Argentine side, and after a quick bite, I went roaming in the rainforest of Iguaçu National Park.

It's one thing to see toucans in Amazon documentaries or breakfast cereal commercials, and quite another thing to have this goofy orange bill extending over a tree branch as its owner looks down at you. I burst out laughing, and it eyed me suspiciously. I spotted a couple of monkeys, and I almost forgot what I was doing there, reading the safety pamphlet about what to do if one encounters a jaguar (rare, but still possible—oh, *great*) when a voice in the trees said: "Hello, Miss Knight. It's something, isn't it?"

There was a dull crash of leaves as a man came out of the bush, smiling politely at me. He looked about thirty-five, and his coloring suggested he came from the Middle East— that and the light accent to his English. His curly black beard was full. He had sweated through his white dress shirt, and he wore beige Dockers and sensible sneakers.

No way in this dense foliage could Hodd arrange surveillance.

"So," I said in mild wonder, my nerves getting the better of me, "you're Hezbollah."

He smiled but didn't confirm it. He didn't really need to.

I was face-to-face with a guy from one of the most controversial and—depending on where you were—despised Shi'a Islamic political and paramilitary organizations. Washington hated them. To the Arab world, they were resistance fighters against Israel. And if you were in Brazil?

"You may call me Khalil," he said politely. "First, it is important for you to understand that this young woman Beatriz is *not* one of ours. She is not with us."

"I didn't think she was with anyone. I thought she was operating on her own."

"Beatriz calls her group 'True Base.' We have been watching them for some time, a terrorist group in its infancy, growing out of a gang of bandits. Did you know the Arabic word *qāidah* means 'base'? It's where Al Qaeda gets its name."

"Actually," I said in a modest voice, "I did."

"Oh, yes, of course," said Khalil. "You visited your ancestral home of Sudan, you must know a little Arabic."

Jeez, did everyone have a file on me?

"About Beatriz and her people," I prompted.

His lip curled contemptuously at the thought of them. "She has cells in other communities, not just Rio, but we haven't pinned down where yet. As far as we can tell, they have no coherent ideology at all, except as a nihilist group. And what she believes of Islam! They make it up as they go along." He made a bitter laugh, no humor in it. "She loves Allah—and hates every Muslim group but her own. Says they've always been wrong in their treatment of women."

"So far," I said, "she and her group sound like just a different brand of fundamentalist. You know the kind—people who want to force others into their own ideas of how to live."

"There is no need to antagonize me, Miss Knight," he answered calmly. "We know your . . . biases about *sharia*. You might want to remember we are the party of God in

Lebanon, and our stands on women's rights are more complex and reflective of Lebanese culture than the Western media would have you believe. Our war is with Israel—"

"At the moment, I don't give a damn about Israel, about Lebanon or Middle East politics," I said. He was right. I shouldn't have antagonized him, but I hated this mess that indicted ordinary people as culpable in foreign policy when they just wanted to get on with their lives. I was losing my patience.

"This is Brazil, right? I care about millions of innocent people *here* who have nothing to do with your struggle or this crazy girl's deluded crusade. They're the ones that will pay. You don't have to persuade me of anything, and I won't try with you. But I am *asking* you to help save lives."

He paused a moment, conceding the point. "Very well. I say again: We are not involved with this misguided woman, and we have actually worked to neutralize these fools before they cause real damage. The problem is that what they lack in intelligence acumen, they make up for in natural guerrilla tactics. I was one of the first to warn Bailey about her volatile nature."

"Hezbollah is top of the enemies list for British intelligence," I said. "Kind of bizarre that you and Graham should swap information from time to time."

He nodded sadly. "I, too, can be disillusioned by cynical politics and bloodlust, Miss Knight, and sometimes in this shadow world . . . Let me just say that one must rely on human judgment."

I heard the echo of Graham's words. I studied this stranger, this delegate, and I could only hope there were others out there like him, who at least paused to weigh their personal conscience.

"You guys have to keep ahead of Western intelligence services," I said. "Do you have any idea how Haskell or Ferreira managed to figure out that Beatriz and her people

322 · LISA LAWRENCE

were moving in this direction? I mean this whole 'terrorist group in its infancy' thing."

Khalil made a dry, humorless laugh. "It would be ridiculously easy for either Haskell or Ferreira. I am sure you are aware that Beatriz wrecked Graham Bailey's cover during one of her Don Quixote–style raids."

"Yes, he told me about that."

"Her fellow amateur jihadists are just as reckless—they don't have the first clue about internal security. Several of the women involved are ex-slaves of the porn empire . . ."

I rolled my eyes. Of course. "The gangsters traced the group through the women. Some of them had to have contacted families, old boyfriends—they worked the communication line back to the favelas."

"Correct."

"Do you have any idea what their target might be?"

He threw up his hands. "True Base could pick anything. They're delusional! You know there are Muslims all over this city who are sympathetic to Hezbollah, who, yes, send money back to Lebanon—but for the hospitals and schools we run. If these fools make an attack here, innocent Muslims will suffer in a crackdown. Listen. Can you be sure it will be in Foz do Iguaçu? That doesn't make sense. There's a larger population of Muslims in São Paulo."

I reminded him of the secret military base and briefed him on what we thought was Orpheocon's plan.

"It's barbaric," he whispered. "They will just *let* them do it? To watch and wait for carnage . . ."

"But you and I won't let that happen, will we? Do you have any idea where Beatriz is now? Could she be here?"

"I'm sorry, no. Our Rio surveillance teams lost track of her. We were caught off guard by her assassination attempt on Ferreira."

"So were we."

"Something else I don't understand," said Khalil, gesturing that we should be on our way out of the park. "Ferreira's lawyer, Andrade—he is in Foz do Iguaçu today."

"*He is?*"

"That's what we've learned. The criminal rumor mill is not quite the BBC, but it's fairly reliable. We keep our channels open."

"Do you know where he is?"

"We are trying to find out. Please. If Beatriz's attack is planned for here, why would *Andrade* come to this place?"

That puzzled me as well for a moment—but not for long.

"Ferreira must have sent him to make sure it gets pulled off without a hitch," I reasoned. "If Beatriz's group fails, there must be a second team to blow up the target and leave True Base implicated."

"Then we can't have much time. I will drive you back to the city. Our people will coordinate to try to find Beatriz and her people. If we can find Andrade's exact location, can you handle him?"

I nodded. We'd better. "Unless you find her, we'll have to hope and pray those thugs lead us to the target. We won't know what it is until then."

"Understood."

As we hurried along, I asked, "You could have discussed all this with Graham. Why did you insist on meeting me?"

The Hezbollah man offered a shy laugh. "To be honest: curiosity. You've hurt all the right people. We were impressed. And you *are* quite beautiful."

As I gave him a look, he added, "I'm a Muslim from Lebanon, Miss Knight. We admire strong beautiful women. One day you may appreciate the beauty of our faith."

"I can," I said. "And I do. Give me some credit. Come on, we'd better hurry."

14

The city of Foz do Iguaçu isn't terribly remarkable in it-self besides the attractions of the nearby falls. So the logic went that a slimy lawyer like Andrade would prob-ably prefer to live large, and there would be only a few choice places he would want to stay. Khalil rang Graham a couple of hours later, and we learned Andrade was booked into a suite on the highest floor of the Hotel Internacional. He was in the heart of the city, with a couple of Ferreira's thugs along to keep watch amid all its marble grandeur.

Why not? Cameron Haskell was sure we knew nothing. Ferreira and Andrade probably thought the same.

Hodd and London smoothed things over with the au-thorities in Brasilia, and his team coordinated with the Federal Police to watch key points of interest in the city. Left unsaid was that they should tolerate Hezbollah while it did its best to find us a lead on Beatriz.

Graham was given the "less risky" assignment of keeping an eye on Andrade. Since I wasn't about to hang around our hotel room and I'd seen the rain forest, I tagged along. Hodd sputtered a protest about my safety, how I had done enough, and Graham laughed and told him, "Des, don't you know by now you're wasting your breath?"

He put an arm around my waist, and we walked out together as if heading for a picnic.

So I was with him when he tailed Andrade's Porsche, following in the BMW borrowed from Sims. He wished we were back in the Volkswagen, he said. He trusted the Beetle. It was a scrappy old fighter of a car, and he had luck with it in Rio.

From a block down the street, we couldn't quite see what Andrade and one of the thugs loaded into the trunk of the Porsche—a large case of some kind.

And we were totally unprepared for where Andrade led us. Down one of the main thoroughfares and into a street called Rua Palestina. I saw what looked like parkland, lovely trees and grass lawns. And I started to get a bad feeling about this. Andrade stayed in the car while the thug stepped out and unloaded the trunk. We pulled the BMW up yards away, giving him a wide berth.

"Oh, my God," I said. "Get Hodd on the phone. Get him quick."

Because I saw twin white minarets in the distance.

"What? What?"

"We're here," I said. "We're at the target!"

He was dialing Hodd on his cell but looking at me, confused. "I don't understand." I heard ringing.

We hadn't realized it. We had tailed Andrade's car right to the Omar Ibn Al-Khatab mosque. It was exquisite traditional architecture, with a Brazilian-Arab school and cultural center on the same grounds. All about to be rubble.

"*That's* the target," I explained quickly, and now I opened the car door. "Hezbollah is Shi'a Islam. When it's done, they'll paint Beatriz and her gang as Sunnis or a breakaway sect or whatever. It'll bring all the Muslim-versus-Muslim conflicts and bloodshed right here to Brazil.

And we're on the border. That's how Orpheocon will justify barging in with their mercenaries! They'll claim Paraguay's security and that of the tri-border is threatened by the terrorist attack. Muslim infighting right on their border with Brazil."

"Son of a bitch," muttered Graham, getting out on his side. Into the phone he said, "Hodd? Hodd, are you there? Who's this? Well, get him!" And as he waited, I saw the question on his lips: *How?* How did I guess?

"The documentary," I said. "The footage was *reconnaissance*. The artsy pans away from the mosques? All the shots of the exteriors around them? That was to find escape routes, best ways to approach!"

Graham looked off in the direction of the beautiful white structure—and towards the thug setting up some equipment. His mouth opened in shock. "That creep has an old SACLOS."

"A what?"

He ran around to the trunk of the BMW. I watched as he pulled out the case for a sniper rifle. "He's got an antitank guided missile! Semi-Automatic Command to Line of Sight. SACLOS. Hodd? Are you there? Listen to me—"

It would take the thug longer to set up his missile launcher than Graham to assemble the rifle, but now we had another problem. Graham was still talking frantically into the cell phone.

"I think the bastard has semiactive laser homing," Graham told Hodd. "I've got nothing to jam his radio signal, Des, I've got to sniper him out—"

Much bigger problem than laser homing or whatever.

"Graham!" I shouted. I pointed to the walk leading up to the mosque.

Beatriz, already there. She wasn't veiled or wearing robes, in just a regular white blouse and shorts, carrying a backpack. By the time those inside objected, it wouldn't matter.

Oh, God. Khalil had said it. She loves Allah—and hates every Muslim group but her own. And more of her words came back to me from the favela house. *It make no sense to me in holy texts how women are treated—we are stupid, we are second, we must be told what we do.* So she was happy to do another "favor" for the Syrian Qabbani as payment for the weapons. Traditional Muslims were enemies, just as Ferreira was an enemy, Marinho had been an enemy. Just part of her personal holy war.

Walking towards the mosque.

We had two targets.

"She's closest," said Graham, taking a breath, knowing he had to do it. But the moment the bullet hit her, the guy with the missile thingy would be tipped off.

"He'll see her shot," I told him, but Graham knew that already.

"No choice," he answered. "We've got one chance—he's got an old launcher. He has to stay perfectly still and aim the thing so it can ride the beam to target. The new ones are fire and forget. It might buy us a couple of seconds. *Shit.* Shit, shit, shit! Better pray, babe."

"He'll wait for Beatriz to go in," I said. "He's the insurance, right? He'll see if she's successful before he makes his own try."

Graham's eye was at the scope now, as the tinny voice of Hodd came through the cell: "We can't be sure of that."

I could. Yes, it was instinct, but I was sure. They wanted a patsy to be implicated for the attack—Ferreira's thug would wait for Beatriz's attempt, and they'd use the missile only if they had to.

Andrade sat in the car, waiting for the man to do his chore so they could speed away. I yanked the Glock out of Graham's jacket and started running.

"Teresa!"

He couldn't shout louder or the guy at the launcher might hear. I might not reach him in time, but I had to try. Beatriz was getting closer. Graham had to trust me to do my job while he found the nerve to shoot her.

I could guess what he was feeling. Yards away, she would never know it was him, not that this would give him any comfort. Broken, deluded, pitiful girl, so warped in her thinking, walking at an unhurried pace, and it would be even more excruciating for Graham because now he had to wait for me.

If he shot Beatriz first, the guy at the launcher would see her drop and know he'd better fire quickly.

Two targets, and no time for Graham to hit both. So it was up to me to reach Ferreira's man and Andrade. Racing against her progress up to that door—

I ran. I ran so hard I imagined my lungs bleeding. I ran and stopped caring about the pain and saw the way the guy had his kit set up now, my sneakers were silent on the grass, and still there was no noise of the missile fired and no shot of the sniper rifle, and I tried to stop my noisy breathing as I reached the monster with his back to me. I saw him fiddle with a mechanism on this big ugly tube thing resting on a tripod.

"Don't!"

Not that I expected the guy to listen—just to be distracted. He started in shock and turned, his face pale with disbelief.

Beatriz a couple of yards from the mosque entrance.

I lifted the Glock and fired three shots, couldn't miss at this range. The guy's stomach ruptured in sprays of black and red, and he crumbled to the cement on his back. Andrade gunned the engine and roared off. Damn it, getting away—

As I stood there, barely believing what I had done, there

330 · LISA LAWRENCE

were two *cracks* like a couple of lazy echoes across the lawn. I didn't pay attention to the wheezing and dying thug on the ground. I was listening to the screams of the faithful near the mosque doors, the terrible panic.

Beatriz was down on the pavement. She had turned like others when she heard my shots, and that was when Graham fired. I looked across the expanse of green, but he was already gone from his spot. Dropping the rifle, running over to her. If she was still alive, conscious, and could reach her detonator—

She lay on her back, and even from here, I could hear her agonized gurgling. Graham had been quite efficient. One shot had hit the arm she needed to set off the bomb. The other had taken her down. She wouldn't live long. Lebanese-Brazilians were coming out, forming a circle, but I heard Graham shout in rapid Portuguese. There was a gasp from the crowd, and they turned around and rushed back inside the mosque.

He was alone again, crouched next to her.

I took a couple of steps back over to the thug on the ground. He was going fast, too, and his eyes as they lost their life looked so enraged. How dare this woman, this black woman, interfere and cut his life short? I watched him bleed to death, paying witness. Not for the sake of whatever humanity was left in this criminal, not even for Beatriz's sake, but for my own. I thought: *If you're going to do it, then be here for all of it. See if you can live with it.*

He died, failing to kill anybody, and I saw that I could live with it.

I don't think I lost any piece of my soul, and if anything, the world's lungs opened a little wider, breathing easier.

After a few seconds, I reached Graham. He was still kneeling over Beatriz's body. She was gone as well. He was making sure her explosive was completely deactivated.

"She told me where the True Base militants are," he said quietly. Reading my astonishment, he explained: "I . . . I had to tell her the truth, that Ferreira wanted her to go ahead and blow up the mosque. You got the guy?"

"I got him."

No Beatriz with her bomb. And no gangster thug there to blow up the mosque in case she failed.

"Oh, God," I whispered, looking down at the young woman dead at our feet. Graham understood. A terrible way to die, to realize in your final moments you were a puppet and it was all for nothing.

We heard sirens, but Hodd and his agents reached us first, all scrambling out of their cars.

Graham stood up. I saw that his hands were shaking. I reached out and grasped one of them. He said, "I reminded her about the women she saved, the ones from the storage shed. And the little girl."

"What about the little girl?"

"The one you rescued from the favela," said Graham. "I didn't get a chance to tell you before. I had Hodd check on her. She's going to be all right."

◆

Recovery. Trying to put it behind us, killing to save lives, ugly little schemes of world domination. Back in the Beetle, driving along the Serra do Espinhaço mountain range. When I asked Graham where we were going, he would only reply coyly, "Minas Gerais." Since Minas Gerais is the fourth-largest state in Brazil, that meant we could wind up anywhere. I guess my spy lover knew how to keep a secret.

He asked me if I liked hikes and history, and when I answered yes, he told me great, then you'll love this. He was taking me, he said, to a place that was personally very special to him. The trip was to be our "vacation." We lapsed into a comfortable silence, enjoying the countryside, but my nerves hadn't yet healed from the last few days.

"Still got Haskell to take care of."

"Don't worry, there's time," replied Graham. "Hodd will mount his head on a wall. All is right with the world, Teresa. No mosque attack, no invasion by Orpheocon's mercenaries, and we've got mop-up operations on the rest of the True Base—and at least Henrique Marinho is dead, the way he should be."

"Ferreira is still out there, wanting my blood."

"Let *us* take care of Ferreira," Graham urged, his hand on my shoulder. "Once you're back home—"

"He's probably got people in London he can send after me," I argued. "Hey, why are you so quick to put me on a plane?"

"I'm not!" He laughed. "Hey, would I take you to a wonderful place if I was in a hurry to see you leave?"

"We'll see how wonderful . . ."

At last he parked the Bug at the rise of a steep curve, and announced, "We're here." We had already gone through several small towns, so now I was genuinely surprised. We were in the cobblestone center of a town ringed by modern granite blocks and the ever-present tuna melt tiers of favelas in the hills. As I got out and looked at him, he smiled and explained that "here" was Ouro Prêto.

The name, he said, meant "black gold" in Portuguese, and the town was once the capital of Brazil's gold rush—black because the precious metal had been coated with iron oxide. We quickly checked in at our hotel, and then Graham led me up and down the cobbled streets, spinning tales about Galanga, an African tribal leader in the Congo sold as a slave, who became known as Chico Rei. Hiding gold flakes on his hair and body, Chico Rei bought his freedom, then his son's, and then grew rich enough to buy a mine and purchase the freedom of others. Graham took me out to the Chapel of the Third Order of Saint Francis of Assisi, where Aleijadinho, "Little Cripple," the son of a Portuguese architect and a black slave, sculpted bas-reliefs while coping with leprosy.

Here was a town where our distant brothers and sisters had worked their fingers raw and bloody but let the world know they'd been here.

"My family had a distant relative brought to Ouro Prêto in the early 1700s," said Graham. "We're pretty sure he worked in the Encardideira mine—the same one that Chico Rei eventually bought. An aunt of mine has a cameo portrait of him, so he must have made it out somehow and climbed the social ladder."

"For all you know, maybe Chico Rei helped get him out."

He smiled. "It's a nice thought. I like to believe that happened."

I threw my arms around him and kissed him hard. I was touched he wanted to share this with me, that he put the thought into bringing me here instead of just saying, hey, baby, let's hit the beach. He knew this location would resonate with me, and it did. I was grateful for this precious glimpse of a piece of our diaspora. I wondered if Isaac knew of this place. Probably, but if he didn't, I would tell him.

The next day Graham was playing mystery man again, driving us out of the Barra suburb past a university, a grim aluminum plant, and along a road that gave way to gravel. Lurching and bouncing from the bumps in the road, I started to believe the Beetle *was* indestructible. He kept laughing away. "You're trying so hard to be a good sport and not whine."

"You're right," I said.

And then he asked me if I knew how to ride a horse.

"I know a place—twenty American for a half-day."

"You're joking, cowboy. I'm a city girl."

"Well, I guess we hike the last bit."

But it was worth it. Because he brought me to this quiet waterfall he told me was called Moinho. It was like the rocks formed a staircase for the water, a pool for bathing below. "We didn't bring suits!" I complained.

He started to undress me. "What makes you think I want them? It's off-season, and the Chapada waterfall gets most of the traffic. Come on!"

We splashed and played in the water, which we had all to ourselves, and then lay on the bank of the waterfall. There is something luxuriously freeing, something magical, about making love in the outdoors. Sunshine poured down on us, and we smelled the earth and leaves, and it was like our bodies were set against a Panavision backdrop. I sat in Graham's lap, him inside me, arms linked around his neck as he fondled my breasts, and we crushed our mouths together.

Shifting positions, I was overwhelmed by the tickle of grass blades crushed in my hands, sun warm on my back, and I wanted to get dirty with him, feel release in loud wails and the grains of sand and mud that pasted onto our legs and backs. I gobbled his cock into my mouth and sucked him, my fingers holding his balls, finding the sweet spot just underneath them, my tongue lapping a spidery vein on his shaft. My fingers playing along his ribs. He was thick in my mouth, hard and twitching as my nail dug into the soft skin behind his testicles. He warned me he was about to come, and I let him shoot in a geyser stream over my breasts and belly.

We washed ourselves, and still we couldn't get enough of each other. We were primitives here, reveling in the theater of the landscape. He took me from behind, palm cupping one of my dangling tits, cock ramming me hard, and I heard myself mewl, fingering my clit as he thrust in and out of me, my knees buckling as I came. He fell on top of me, staying all the way in, and I felt the sensation of my vagina clamping him tight, holding him fast.

"Oh, God," he moaned. Coming.

As I lay on the grass, I felt dizzy, the earth spinning as I experienced a smaller but still powerful orgasm. I shut my eyes and made a low whimper. "Don't you dare move," I told him. Still hard inside me. I smelled the earth and heard the gurgling water, my peripheral vision opening up so that I could see a tree line in the distance. Still hard, ohhhh, feeling him on top of me, the sensation of his hips and his chest on my back, my ass warm under him . . . We were like that together for a long quiet moment. And then we held each other and fell asleep.

◆

A new day, and I was giggling and clapping my hands—no, not over the orgasms, though sometimes I'm tempted to do that, too. This was later. It was over the latest wonder Graham showed me as tour guide.

We had driven out to a town not far away called Tiradentes. It had the feel of a hermetically sealed wing of the Museum of London, with its quaint horse-drawn carriages and its souvenir shops, but he hadn't brought me here for all that.

"Got to buy our tickets," said Graham, knowing I'd be thinking: Tickets for what? Again enjoying his air of mystery. And then we were on a platform to board a train.

A steam train.

We're talking the funny little engine at the front like the Lionel toy locomotives my brother used to play with. (Well, Isaac and our father, who would walk into the living room, fetch a second transformer and engine, and declare in the true spirit of such pleasures, "Let's have a crash!") This thing was life-size with antique passenger cars, and while it only went at twenty kilometers an hour to nearby São João del Rei, it had been operating since 1881. We got on board one of the rust-red painted passenger cars, conspicuous as a couple among tired parents and excited kids.

"I swear this goes faster than the Northern Line," quipped Graham.

We were enjoying ourselves, watching the scenery, me nestled into his chest with his arms wrapped around me. Having a good time right up to the moment when the grim figures took the seats opposite ours and across the aisle.

"*Oi! Tudo bem?*"

Open-necked dress shirts and Polos, designer sunglasses, khaki trousers, and linen jackets. Jackets that had noticeable bulges—guns. Why is it thugs still look like thugs in suits or in casual dress? Ferreira. Andrade. And a set of bookending testosterone cases to keep us well behaved. Too many children close by anyway to start a scene.

Graham sighed as if we weren't in danger, as if we had just been interrupted by a couple of crashing boors.

"I guess it doesn't matter how you found us," he drawled. "But I am curious."

"Haskell," I said, and I surprised even Graham. "You guys keep capacitors in your cell phones so the head office can always find you, right?"

The reason why I ditched my cell in Oxford Street, that day I had sex with Todd in HMV.

Graham nodded, understanding immediately. As a last act of spite, Haskell had sent Graham's GPS coordinates to the gang leader.

Ferreira—large head, broken nose, and the livid knife scar on his neck—was like a bust of a gargoyle under the Minas sunshine. He leered at me and scratched a tuft of white chest hairs through the open V of his shirt. Andrade was equally grotesque, his casual clothes somehow unfitting for the lawyer. He looked like he never relaxed in his life. Weasel.

"We really spoiled your fun, didn't we?" I said to Ferreira. "After all, this whole thing was *your* big scheme. Most people would assume Orpheocon dreamed it up and then recruited you, but you brought the idea to them, didn't you?"

I wasn't sure if Andrade was translating Ferreira's words or voicing his own question. "How did you figure it out?"

"I'd like to know as well," said Graham. God, he was calm. Like there was no doubt at all we'd get out of this fix. It gave me strength.

"Tell me something first," I said, pointing to Ferreira. "When did you decide Luis Antunes had to die? When did you order Marinho to kill him? Marinho must have come to London on some errand to meet with Haskell for you, right? To brief him on the plan's progress, maybe?"

I got a wolfish grin and a nod over this one.

"So Marinho must have thought it would look good to drop in and see Luis in his office in Canary Wharf. A social call paid to the head of Silky Pictures in London. And he found Luis furious. But Luis didn't know that much yet, did he? He was angry over the new documentary division in Brazil, and he was baffled by the idea of Marinho greenlighting a documentary about Islam. I saw them arguing."

Andrade looked to his boss, and they traded more smiles. "His pride was wounded," sneered the lawyer. "Yes, Marinho told us about the argument with Antunes. Pathetic! The man's ego was hurt that he was left out of doing silly little nonfiction films. Mr. Bailey, you will please stop shuffling about."

Graham had sat forward in his seat, trying not to be obvious as he readied himself for any opening. Other passengers were around, yes, but we couldn't just sit there and ride our way quietly to our deaths.

"Just trying to get comfortable," Graham said pleasantly. "You know you're missing a great view?"

Andrade ignored him, looking to me. "As I was saying: No, Antunes didn't have a clue why there was footage of mosques."

"Not then, but he got curious, didn't he?" I said. "He figured it out. This documentary on Muslims didn't make sense. Meanwhile, Luis was getting wise to Duncan with the hard-core nasty films, and then he made his break with Marinho over a poor girl kept as a slave in Richmond. A girl Marinho was happy to suggest he use in porn. He sent an e-mail severing all ties with the parent corporation in Rio. But the idea of the Muslim documentary really annoyed him. Let me guess. Luis, after all, was a *director*. I'll bet Luis realized that the slow pans away from the mosques, all those clever shots, were unnecessary and didn't make sense for a movie—they must be for something else, for reconnaissance footage."

Out of the corner of my eye, I saw Graham shifting his weight again in his seat. I did my best to keep Ferreira and Andrade enthralled by my powers of deduction.

"Luis knew something terrible was about to happen, especially with Marinho involved. Something so big he couldn't count on the Federal Police figuring it out and stopping it in time. So he approached you as Marinho's main rival. It was only when he checked out the Ladrão DVDs that he saw Andrade, and he found out who the yacht belonged to. He realized this whole scheme was yours."

"We had a feeling Antunes would soon figure out everything after he came to us," said Andrade. "And as you discovered, we were correct. He had to die. He knew it was our scheme. Which brings us back to how you realized it."

Whatever Graham was planning, he was poised in his

seat, ready to spring. I tried to keep eye contact with Ferreira, fix him still.

"I read a few items before I came to see you in prison," I replied. "Before your career as a criminal, you were an engineer. Your specialty was hydraulics, and your very first job was at the Itaipu Dam. Who else would have the grand vision for a scheme to get at the Guarani Aquifer?"

All at once, Ferreira's meaty fist shot out and punched Graham in the mouth. I jumped, startled, and before I could react, Andrade whispered: "Don't."

The other thugs snapped to attention, ready to move in. Element of surprise gone. Ferreira's hand shot out and grabbed Graham's wrist, turning it over. He confiscated the small knife Graham had slipped out of some hiding place.

Graham's eyes narrowed, clearly seething inside as he felt his lip, but he kept up his cheerful tone. "Can't blame me for trying."

Ferreira barked in Portuguese at one of his thugs, pointed at Graham, and barked some more at the gangster for failing to pat him down for weapons. Children were giggling loudly and carrying on in other seats. No one had noticed the brief commotion.

Then Ferreira looked to me. "*Por favor, continue. Isso é revelador.*"

" 'Please go on,' " Andrade translated. " 'This is very enlightening.' "

I looked to Graham, lifting my hand to his cheek, but he nodded that he was okay and gave my hand a squeeze. Nothing left to do but keep up this brave, happy chat with Ferreira and Andrade. Graham's eyes told me another chance would come. Somehow.

"You were saying, Miss Knight?" prompted Andrade. "About Mr. Ferreira's grand vision."

"Right . . ."

340 · LISA LAWRENCE

"Please go ahead."

"You were brilliant at anticipating everybody," I said, watching Ferreira. "Nice touch—the angle that the mosque bombing could be interfaith bad blood. You were once contracted to help build a hydroelectric plant—in Syria. Maybe you didn't mix too often with the ordinary people over there, but I'm sure you picked up a couple of insights. After all, you were so good at manipulating the political infighting at MI6. And I'm right, aren't I? That you met Bassam Qabbani there? When he got into the illegal arms trade in Brazil, he was perfect to help you manipulate Beatriz. Hell, you manipulated almost everyone—me, the gangs in Brazil with your phony feud, British intelligence."

Ferreira made a short little bow. The atmosphere on the train was surreal and macabre. We were warmed by the bright sunshine, listening to the anachronistic *chugga-chugga* as children laughed and chattered in the background.

"I'll bet you couldn't stand Haskell personally," I went on. "He's just the type who would take credit for your work with Orpheocon. And of course, I'm sure you were annoyed that he wouldn't let you kill Graham immediately. We know he must have dissuaded you, because Haskell approached him in the street later and made an offer."

Andrade and Ferreira laughed. "We heard you shot him in the knee!"

"Yes, I did," said Graham pleasantly, a shared laugh with the wolves. The knife episode a minute ago dealt with and forgotten.

"He really is—how do you say?" Andrade glanced at Ferreira, looked to us to check the word. "He is an enormous prick!"

"Yes." Graham nodded. "Yes, he is. Now he'll limp for the rest of his life."

"We never like him. We want to thank you for that."

"My pleasure."

The trip to São João del Rei took forty minutes. We were trapped in here, and when we reached the end, we'd be escorted someplace secluded and quiet for our executions. Graham gave my hand a squeeze. *We're all right. We'll be all right.*

"So you're here to kill us mainly because we ruined your masterpiece," I said to Ferreira. "You're here because we hurt your ego. No one will ever know how brilliant you were—and how you were the great brain behind Orpheocon's plan."

Andrade's voice was a singsong. "You should have left Brazil, gringa." He made his little fox grin at Graham. "*Desculpa,* Bailey, I think she is smarter than you."

Graham shrugged. "Yeah, it's one of the reasons why I fell in love with her."

I looked at him. "This is new."

"I was waiting for the right moment. Something memorable."

"Excuse me, the waterfall? Ouro Prêto? What about—"

"No, no, no," said Graham, keeping the banter up as we both tried to think of a way out. "I'm old-fashioned. Scenic waterfalls are fine, but I think a declaration of love needs a collection of gangland homicidal maniacs as witnesses. It's how dear ol' Dad got Mum."

"You're not funny," said Andrade in a clipped, tight voice. "Neither of you is funny."

"Haskell said that too," muttered Graham.

"Right before you shot him in the leg," I put in.

"Well, that part wasn't funny—"

"No—"

"Mr. Bailey, you will come with us now, please."

"Oh, no, thank you, they only serve snacks in the dining car. We've got to wait until we reach São João del Rei to get a decent lunch."

Ferreira growled something in Portuguese. Andrade didn't need to translate, and it prompted Graham to say: "You're right. I really don't know what they're serving in the dining car."

They wanted to split us up because they saw Graham as the greater threat, the one to make another bid to fight back or to escape. I might be escorted off the train quietly when it pulled in, but they couldn't guarantee Graham wouldn't start something again here.

Graham kissed me on the lips as if leaving the house for work. "See you soon, darling."

He stood up to go with three of Ferreira's men. There were still four left to keep me in line, and that didn't even include Andrade and his boss.

Ferreira was saying something. " 'Your bravado makes me want to puke,' " Andrade translated. " 'We take away your knife, and you still act like a big man. Don't lie to your bitch, you fool! Face your death and make an honest good-bye to her.' "

Graham rolled his eyes and looked at me. His expression said: They just don't get it, do they? He *would* be back.

Truth? Even I started to doubt it. I had no idea what they would do to him, but I expected it would involve a muffled shot, probably timed with the whistle blast coming up at the next bend. I was stuck in my seat, unable to do a thing to help him.

15

The engine chugged along as two men led the way out, Graham in the middle, one behind. Tactically smart. If Graham tried to break through the guy behind him, he'd only run into Ferreira's henchmen with me. The two guys in front dissuaded any run forward. Doors slid and rattled, and they were out of the car. I was left in the empty pause with Ferreira and his pet solicitor, while the tourists enjoyed the charming ride.

The train navigated its long, winding bend.

Up ahead, I could see a town. São João del Rei. Must be.

I waited for the whistle.

I strained to hear the crack of a shot, and when it came, I tasted acid rising in my throat, and I shut my eyes for a moment. *No*. Something else had happened. Something else must happen.

Something did. People traded looks because there were, incredibly, footsteps *over our heads,* like the racket of noisy neighbors in the flat above, only this was a moving locomotive, and there wasn't supposed to be a second floor.

The train was curving around, and now Andrade said

something fast in Portuguese to Ferreira. His boss wasn't disturbed at all, making a brutal reply. The essence, I reckoned, was: Can't send more men, we have this gringa to watch. Bailey might get away, but he still has to come back for her.

People strained to look out the windows. Good. You guys look, too. Thank you—

I whipped my elbow into the throat of the creep seated next to me. Served him right for resting his hand on my thigh. The families didn't hear the snap, but they heard the man choking. By then I was up and past him. The guy across the seat got a kick in his belly. That left one thug sitting down with Andrade in his way, and one guy who couldn't reach me in time.

There was no time for them to threaten other passengers to coax me back. I had run out of the train car, didn't stick around to hear any threats. And as I expected, the thugs forgot about the people around them and came after me. They walked—they didn't run. There was really no place I could go, and we both knew I would risk the lives of others if I shouted for help.

The footsteps on the train roof still caused a fuss, and a guy in a uniform went down the aisle, shouting in Portuguese—stay in our seats, or something. He barked at me for my disruptive behavior, this crazy tourist pushing past him in the aisle.

"*Ei, o que você está fazendo correndo no corredor? Volta para o seu lugar!*"

I had five seconds at most, which I wasted completely on trying to look out the window. The eleven coaches were now in a horseshoe on the tracks, and I saw one of Ferreira's men jump off the roof of a car up ahead. Couldn't believe it. He jumped?

His yell sounded less like summoning courage and more like mad panic. The engine noise covered much of it, but the people staring out the windows must have seen him.

And now a second thug leapt off a roof, with more determination. Jeez, I thought in astonishment. Had Graham actually fled by *jumping off the train*? I couldn't see where the men landed—

The train was slowly braking to a stop, and then as if the conductor had changed his mind, the engine started up again. The Portuguese over the PA system sounded indignant and stressed. I imagined the staff guys were radioing ahead. Get a crew to drive back along the tracks and find out what the hell happened.

Ferreira and his thugs came through from the other train car.

No Graham. And nowhere to go.

Ferreira whistled and made an impatient, infuriating gesture, the kind you used to call your dog.

"Now you alone," he laughed.

I didn't answer. I thought: I'm not alone anymore. This case started that way, but that's not the way it will end. My man will be back in a few minutes, you creep.

Outside the windows, the unique roundhouse for servicing the locomotives came into view, and then we pulled into the station.

We're all right, Graham had told me when he held me in his arms. It was after he was freed from Marinho's house. *We're* all right.

Poor Ferreira and Andrade didn't have a clue about the surge of confidence I felt.

"What are you grinning for, woman?"

"You remember what I said, gentlemen?"

"Oh, yes!" laughed Andrade. "You said Ferreira would wish there were still iron bars between you. Your empty threat."

He translated for his boss, who replied: "My men are each going to have their turn with you, and you can threaten all you like with your legs wide open."

346 · LISA LAWRENCE

I am *so* going to kill you, I thought.

Most of the departing passengers made their way towards the railway museum. Ferreira's thugs herded me elsewhere, through the main exit to a street called Hermilio Alves. As we walked, I saw this eighteenth-century stone bridge and thought maybe if I broke into a desperate sprint I could lose myself in the streets before they opened fire. Not a chance.

Then a peculiar man in a cap and a kitchen apron strolled out of a restaurant with a pot in his hand.

"Chivalry time," said Graham. In other words: *Get down.*

I stepped into the road and ducked into a crouch. I heard a horn blast and tires screech as the car swerved past. That was nothing compared to the shock for the gangsters. Here was Graham in an apron, a uniform of another poor black Brazilian, his eyes down with a servile posture right until he flung the pot's contents in a wide splash—

I heard the sizzle.

Not water—kitchen fat. Boils at one hell of a higher temperature. The henchmen screamed. Andrade got the worst, Ferreira the least (damn it).

By the time I turned to look, hearing the thugs in agony, there was the clatter of the stainless steel pan on the pavement and I felt Graham's hand on my shoulder. Even as I pushed off my heels, he had his hand in mine, and we were in a full-out sprint.

Running. The columns of the Theatro Municipal coming into view, and Graham tugged my hand to lead me into a side street. Panting hard now as Ferreira, Andrade, and the others shouted curses in Portuguese behind us. They must have been fueled by pure adrenaline, and I didn't want to look over my shoulder to see how bad the creeps were scarred. I hoped a lot. My mind can't just switch off, and I thought how inane it was to scream at people as if that would make them stop running away. *Crack.* Well, yes, bullets could change things.

This was no good. We were in a small town where help couldn't get to us in time and where the authorities would be hopelessly outgunned. Racing up a little street that was a mix of residential and small businesses, an old Coca-Cola sign the flag for the corner variety store. We would have to make a stand somewhere—

"Here!" said Graham.

He stopped us in front of a colonial building, three stories tall, its slatted shutters looking worse for wear. It was undergoing restoration. We saw tarpaulins and a scaffold through the window, but we could see no workers. No innocents. Graham sent a powerful side-thrust kick into the door to knock it in.

"They'll follow," I said.

"Good," he snapped, not meaning to sound angry with me, but his nerves were frayed as well. He ditched the cap and the apron.

The space was larger inside than it looked from the windows.

"Teresa, up—we've got to go up," said Graham. "Watch yourself."

The staircases were rotting away, and we carefully stepped up a flight, then another. As we checked out the next floor, I spotted wide gaping holes in it. Place was a death trap.

Graham still had my hand, leading the way, stopping briefly when he didn't trust the floorboards. A shallow, creaky balcony of faded brass and steel offered a view of São João del Rei—unfortunately not in the direction we needed at the moment. Were they coming?

I saw bell towers and a whitewashed façade. They belonged to the town's main attraction, São Francisco de

Assisi. But I didn't need the church and coconut trees—I wanted to see Ferreira and his men.

"What do we do?" I asked Graham. "They've got guns, and we don't."

"We have *a* gun," he said, and he handed me a black pistol. "Got it from one of the jokers on the train. Nice one. SIG Sauer."

"I don't keep up with the brands," I said as I checked the magazine. Full. Good. "How on earth did you get away anyway?"

"Hold that thought." I watched him hurry down to check our enemy's approach. In a moment, his footsteps came back up the stairs. He tripped, and I heard a crunch of splintering wood.

"You all right?"

"Yeah, thanks, let's hope they hit the same step. Bastards are almost here."

He came over and put his arm around me, kissed my forehead. "Oh, the train, right. I just lost it at the last minute. I mean, what the hell? Attacked them in one of those areas between the cars. Managed to do an aikido thing—got Fool Number One to shoot himself. Then I dived into a toilet and climbed out the window. They kicked it in and followed me out."

"So then you jumped off the train."

He looked at me wide-eyed. "Are you mad? I wasn't about to jump off a train! It's not like the movies where you see stunt men land and roll in the dirt then pop back up. We were at twenty kilometers an hour! I climbed down the side of a passenger car. Fool Number Two ran up, and I gave him a nice shove and waved bye. Now the last guy—he was *really* stupid. He must have seen too many Westerns. He saw his friend dive into the air and assumed he was jumping after me—so he jumped. I couldn't believe it! Made himself into a smear along the rocks."

"So when we pulled into the station . . ."

"I just got ahead of you and watched your progress," he said. "Ducked into the kitchen of that restaurant, and I wasn't even sure what I could use. If you look like you're supposed to be there, it's amazing how often nobody stops you."

"You're a lucky, lucky man."

"We're both lucky, aren't we?"

Yes, we were.

I jumped, startled, as we heard rapid Portuguese from outside, coming from the front of the building.

"We'll be all right," he whispered.

"Yeah? Well, I'm scared."

"Don't be," said Graham, but still he took the gun from my hands to check the magazine. Our eyes met, and he remembered I'd already checked it. "Don't be scared. Be pissed off like me."

"Uh-huh."

He handed me back the gun. "You're up here, I'm down there."

"Then shouldn't you take the gun?"

He shook his head. "No. They'll probably split up, but in case they don't, I want them to think we're unarmed. When they're finished down there, they'll barge upstairs and come looking for you. They won't expect return fire." He headed for the staircase again.

"Whoa, whoa, what do you mean 'when they're finished down there'?"

I realized why he'd given me the gun. In case he couldn't hold the line.

"Graham!" I whispered.

But he was already at the bottom of the stairs, moving on the floor below.

I heard the crash of the door kicked in. Ferreira needlessly barking at his men: Search everywhere.

I couldn't stand it. I moved as softly, silently as I could to a large hole in the floorboards. I couldn't just hide in a corner, listening to a gun battle. I squeezed through the hole, and after a moment Graham's arms grabbed my legs to lift me down.

"What are you doing?" he whispered crossly. I saw he was arming himself with a few bricks. There were more stacked in a pile by a scaffold.

"This is nuts," I told him. "You and I are used to working alone. Well, this has got to be together, side by side."

He nodded and kissed me. We looked for hiding places.

Two of Ferreira's men came creeping up the first staircase, and we heard a sudden crunch of split wood and then a curse. Yep, guy hadn't looked, and his foot had gone through the same hole in the stairs, only deeper. The two henchmen began bickering, and that was when Graham tapped my shoulder, and we ran forward.

His moves looked ruthlessly, jaw-droppingly violent, executed with an athlete's grace. He threw one brick, then another at the two thugs. One struck the guy on the higher stair with shattering impact, a torrent of blood erupting from his forehead, and he flew back against the plaster wall. The second brick smashed into shrapnel above his head.

The first thug must have been killed instantly, his body falling in a rag-doll pile. The second guy cowered under the hail of brick pieces, and as he tried to move in panic, his leg was still trapped. I fired—a fixed target.

Bang bang bang bang immediately came up through the floor, and I cried out, and Graham muttered *shit,* and we both hit the deck. We thought it was just response, but no, it was cover fire for another guy climbing up a scaffold on the side of the building, just the two of us here and can't cover every direction. I pushed Graham down as I heard a noise through a plastic bubble sheet in the floor's second room. The gun went *crack,* deafening my ears again as the anonymous intruder dropped. Someone else blasting away behind me—

"Stairs," said Graham. I turned, felt the start of his shoulder blades against my back. He kept watch on the room as I took care of the new visitor firing and rushing up to meet us. Couldn't even poke my head over the rail to see and return fire, and I thought *fuck this* and kicked the rail itself. More wood shrapnel to fly down at the enemy.

I looked once over my shoulder and saw Graham swinging a couple of paint cans like twin maces, one smashing into the floor and making a new crater, his other swing pulling him off balance as he hurtled himself at his opponent. Andrade. Holy shit.

Andrade. No more an advocate, now a player with a gun in his hand. One second to see the rage on the lawyer's face, sputtering, inarticulate, half mad with his entire left cheek mottled and vividly red from the grease burn.

As Graham hit him with the paint can, the two of them went through the crater in the floorboards.

"Graham!"

But I had my own problems. A shot too loud, and then a fist that sent me spinning, made me see fireworks of violet and red. Pain exploding with the sock to my left eye, and the gun went skittering away as I fell to the floor. Then there was a pressing bulk on top of me, and I smelled stale onions. Ugh. Disoriented as stubby, sausage fingers squeezed my breasts and ripped open my blouse, yanking down my bra, his right arm pinning my left wrist. Past the pain came a rush of blind, desperate panic as I sent a hammer fist into his head. No good, no good.

He let go of my arm to grab a fistful of my hair, to yank my head up and try to knock it down onto the floor again, smash my head in. Raking him with my nails, and still no effect. Tried to bust the elbow joint on the arm clawing at my trouser buttons, and Come on, come on, get him off me, get him, get him—

"No, you don't, you fucking, no, you don't—"

In absolute terror now as he laughed like the sick gargoyle he was, and instead of pushing his face into mine to kiss me, he bit me through the cotton of my blouse. This psychopath who had raped before was trying now, and I screamed with the bite pain, and it was a bloody ruse, his hands managing to yank my trousers off my buttocks, taking my underwear with them, and don't feel denial, don't feel shock, just kill him, kill this rabid fucking—

I had both hands free. Couldn't get to his eyes or his nose; he was tucking his head down. Hitting his head did nothing with that thick skull. I brought my hands in a clapping motion—two great pendulum sweeps into his ears. *Boom.* One of the oldest tricks in the book. It hurts. A lot.

Ferreira shot backwards and off me, reeling with the pain, both his hands holding his ears like Quasimodo had suddenly lost his deafness. Good, you bastard, I hope it hurts.

I rolled and yanked my trousers up, and as he made a new transformation from pain to outrage, I had one of my own. I put a side-thrust kick into his gut.

The concussive blow dropped him to his hands and knees. I ran up and did a snap kick to his jaw that knocked him off his legs. As he gathered himself up, he found a hammer and threw it at me. Ducked that. If he'd been smart, he would have hung on to it, not that I was going to let him use it.

I could tell the kick to his gut had done some internal damage, but he was a bull of a man, bringing up a last-ditch boxing guard and trying a few feints. That was fine by me.

I broke his leg with the next kick.

"You feel fear now, you son of a bitch?"

I think he understood me. Panting, I went over and

picked up the gun where it had landed. I was on autopilot as I raised the barrel and adjusted the distance, not taking any chances with how many bullets were left in the magazine.

No. I'm lying. I wasn't that coldly efficient. I paused to listen to sibilant pleadings I couldn't understand.

I wish I could be ashamed, but I'm not. I thoroughly enjoyed Ferreira begging for his life before I pulled the trigger. Luis. Matilde. Beatriz . . . Rest in peace, all of you.

I checked my shoulder. His teeth had left marks but hadn't broken the skin. I adjusted my bra, closed the single button left on my blouse, and only now realized how quiet it was. Move, girl.

"Graham!"

He was trying to reach me, almost at the top of the stairs, holding his stomach, a new gun in the other hand.

"Oh, God, you're shot!"

"No, no," he wheezed and plonked down on the top stair. "Kind of a belly flop when we went through that hole."

I didn't need to ask about Andrade. Dead. Graham told me later it had been a furious grapple after they had crashed to the floor, both of them wounded, until Graham got a punch into his windpipe. He looked weakly over at the corpse of Ferreira.

"We should get out of here," he said.

"We've got to get you to a doctor."

He lifted my chin with two fingers. "You, too. That's one hell of a shiner."

I stuck out my bottom lip and made a face like a petulant, sulking child.

"Hey, you're still beautiful," he said.

"No, it's not that. They spoiled my choo-choo ride."

"Don't worry. We need to ride it again."

"We do?"

"Course we do. We left the car back in Tiradentes."

AFTERPLAY

They x-rayed Graham at the hospital and found he had suffered a couple of bruises to his ribs, which was bad enough. I did the driving back to Rio, hiding my eyes behind a pair of black sunglasses so no one assumed I was a battered spouse.

Hodd was surprisingly accommodating—almost bordering on human. He didn't balk when I told him it wasn't good enough to have my bank accounts unfrozen and the flags taken off my legitimate passport. If he had any decency, he'd get my expenses to Paris and to Rio reimbursed, plus a healthy compensation for the ordeal of being a fugitive. Done, done, and done. My tax deals for Helena and myself were also reinstated, but I had my doubts those promises might ever be kept. We would see.

And Helô. I wanted generous compensation for her. As far as I was concerned, Luis had died to keep his wife's country safe. He was a hero in my book. Fine, said Hodd. He would make sure the Brazilian government knew of the sacrifice made by Luis Antunes. Then I learned why Hodd was being so decent.

"Your methodology confuses any standard appraisal of your talents, but one can't argue with the results," he said.

Jeez. Still a trademark insult salting the compliment.

"There could be a place for you with—"

"No, no, no—"

"I wish you would let me finish, Teresa."

Huh. Used my first name. I guess we'd made a breakthrough in rapport.

"I'm well aware you're not the kind of person who could work for us full-time, but we do have freelance positions for outside contractors."

"I'll mull it over," I said. "And I'll get back to you, Des."

Yeah, right. I had got my fill of spy stuff. Not interested in any more for the time being, thank you very much.

Do I have to tell you none of this ever made the papers? Not on your life. There was conspiracy chatter on the Web, of course. I do know from Hodd that Her Majesty's Government gave a sincere if *secret* apology to Brazil for the whole mess and MI6's involvement.

The arms dealer, Bassam Qabbani, was found dead, shot through the back of the skull in a São Paulo hotel room. No one was quite sure if his murder was True Base vengeance, a bit of Hezbollah justice, or the remainders of Ferreira's gang wanting to take out their frustration on somebody.

Through some Byzantine rules to do with immunity and intelligence operations that neither Graham nor I understood, Cameron Haskell couldn't be prosecuted, only sacked. No sooner had Haskell left Brazil with his brand-new limp than he had quickly been accepted as a high-ranking executive at Orpheocon.

It wasn't over. If the board of directors at Orpheocon didn't like me before . . . Oh, boy.

Hodd said he received a brief e-mail from of all people, Simon Highsmith, who in his usual mysterious ways got

SEXILE · 3 5 7

the latest news about me. "He told me the same thing he told you—that Brazil is a kind of test case. I'm not sure I can believe him. It's too incredible."

"Well, test case for what?" I asked.

Hodd was pensive. "He says . . . He *claimed* that Orpheocon is planning something like that coup attempt to take over Equatorial Guinea a few years ago—you remember, the one where Margaret Thatcher's son was involved."

"In Guinea?"

"No, no, not there," said Hodd, and his face turned grim. "Simon said he couldn't name the place on-line, his Net connection wasn't safe, but . . . Orpheocon wants to do it. They actually want to acquire their own country. Somewhere in Africa, they're planning to take over—a coup d'état. But we don't know when or how."

◆

Graham's work was done here in Brazil, and presumably, he would get the order soon to return to his posting in Africa. I know what you're thinking. I've never sacrificed for anyone. You're right. It's always been me first, chasing cases, jetting around on somebody else's tab. And despite the romance and adventure, an admission of love offered to a bunch of thugs (and not really said to me, if you want to get technical) shouldn't be enough to disrupt your whole life. When the words are said properly and in the right moment, they're a promise, and they only become a seal given enough time—you've got to see if they stick. Plus I wasn't sure if I fancied the idea of watching someone else gallivant around while I stayed on the sidelines. Not my style.

On the other hand, despite Hodd patching things up for me, I was quite bitter about the whole terrorist label and being hunted across Europe. Serve 'em right if I stayed in exile and published some defiant account somewhere of what actually happened.

Oh, yeah, and what about Daddy and Isaac? And my other friends, and lazy days at the climbing gym in Sutton and workout nights at the dojo, and laughing over the latest sex scandal with Helena in Richmond—she always got the best dirt.

I had to let Graham go.

Enjoy the time you still have together. That's what you do.

Hodd's cell rang, and as I moved reflexively away to give him privacy, he gestured for me to come back.

"No, no, it's for you. Someone wants to thank you."

"I'm tired, Hodd, and I should go check on Graham—"

"Teresa, I think Graham can wait. How often do you take a call from the Prime Minister?"

◆

Days later, I watched my man sleep, the blackish purple bruises on his ribs fading, his breathing growing easier as he healed. By habit, he slept nude, and since we gave the air-conditioning a break, the sheet was pulled back. He lay there, on innocent display, and I took in the sight of his wide mahogany chest, as smooth as his shaved head, lifting with each quiet breath, hands burrowed under the pillow. I studied his powerful thighs and calf muscles. God, he was gorgeous. My fingers reached out and slid along the curves of his tight ass, rounding to his legs, feeling him like he was a sculpture left here to mark some solemn memory for me. In a way, he did. A terrible time I thought I was alone and wasn't.

I watched him dream, caressing his leg. His penis stirred, and I realized he was becoming aroused dreaming. I felt myself getting wet, seeing him like this, and I slipped off my panties and crept onto the bed so as not to wake him. Gently, ever so gently, my mouth closed over his cock and sucked him in long soft strokes. The head twitched in my mouth, and he got harder, his shaft swelling to its impressive length. I cupped his balls in my hand, and then he was a steel rod between my lips. He groaned, and his eyes opened.

"Sorry," I said, taking my mouth off him. "You just looked so . . . Lie back, baby."

He did. I put him inside me and lay on top of him. We made love as if in slow motion, kissing slowly, everything done slowly, the caress of his hands on my breasts and gripping my buttocks, so that we became hyper-aware of the rustle of the crisp sheets, any shift of weight on the mattress. There was a mirror in the bedroom, and as I glanced across at our reflection, I grew even more aroused by the sight of our bodies profiled in our embrace. The first time we'd made love there had been a mirror too. Back in the nightclub. We looked good together. I laughed and told him how after all this—after my editing porn movies and the charade in the middle of the night with his sex tape—hey, I felt like fetching my digital camera and filming us doing it. What I really want to do is direct, I joked.

We held each other tight, and he barely had to move inside me. An invisible dial turned down the sounds of outside. There was still the heat in this room with the lights off, the heat of two bodies wrapped together, and the infinitesimal progression of his bar of flesh into my pussy, an achingly long retreat only to begin the advance again. Stroking his face and looking into his brown eyes, the pads of his fingers tracing a route down my spine. His teeth nibbled the curve of my neck, and my orgasm snuck up on me like a burglar.

He got on top of me. He moved inside me a little faster but only a little, making it last. In the mirror, in the

360 · LISA LAWRENCE

perfectly directed scene of my mental movie, the African girl opened her mouth wide and gasped as the tall, gorgeous black man, with his beautiful toned build, lifted himself and thrust. And thrust again slowly. A flex of muscles, a subtle glimpse of his thick organ disappearing into her, her fingers splayed on the slope of his dark ass. She gasps. It's beautiful, missionary sex in profile, if you look properly, the feminine curve of a woman's parted legs, her knees up, the posture of the man holding her, or just his arms pressing to lift his weight. Another thrust, and *mmm*, fingers grip his ass tighter. It's so long, this shot with the camera steadily advancing in for a more intimate portrait, because they look good together. They fit. When the African girl comes, she has tears in her eyes again as she lifts her head and bites his neck, overcome with ecstasy.

My burglar orgasm turned into a steady exquisite invasion . . .

◆

I called London the next day.

"Well, you're respectable again," said Helena.

"Was I ever?"

"Trying to be kind, darling. My point is your friend Carl Norton is making the rounds, filling us all in. It's all sorted. Your name never got mentioned, but they were showing your flat every hour on the news, so now there are stories about how it was all a mistake and so on. Charges dropped, and those nasty people decided they had to defrost my assets. Creeps! I'm not sure if I should test that waiver you got me. But at least it's over. Carl says the murderer died in Rio—is that right?"

"Yes, it's true," I answered, feeling numb for an instant. "It's a long, convoluted tale. Porn, terrorism, greed—"

"And sex, please tell me there's sex."

"Oh, yes. Plenty."

"That's my girl!" laughed Helena. "*We* are going to celebrate. I'm having a party in your honor at the house—I'll
make it two days after your flight so the jet lag won't spoil it
for you. Leave all the details to me—thanks to this debacle,
I now have contact numbers for your friend, Jiro, and a
dozen other people you always talk about and I've never
met. You can give us the whole saga when you get home."

Plane ticket sitting on the coffee table. I needed to put it
away in my handbag.

"Helena," I said nervously, not sure how to say what I
needed to tell her.

Graham walked into the room, passing behind the sofa
and idly taking my hand. I kissed his fingers as he leaned in
to nuzzle my neck. Then he went on with what he was doing. Packing. He boasted it took him literally five minutes
to pack, and my counter to that was: Of course, it does,
you're a guy—you don't carry as much as we do.

I got up with the cordless receiver and walked to the balcony, enjoying the view of the bay. I felt strong enough to
say it now, but Helena was my closest friend in Britain, and
it would hurt.

"Teresa?"

It would be even harder when I called Daddy and then
Isaac.

"Helena, I'm not coming home."

Girl's got a right to change her mind.

The ticket on the coffee table was for my seat next to
Graham's—business class to Johannesburg. I was going
with him back to Africa.

ABOUT THE AUTHOR

LISA LAWRENCE lives and works in London as a freelance writer, contributing to newspapers and various women's magazines. She blames an early boyfriend for inspiring her to write fiction after he regularly dragged her into the West End's various bookshops for mysteries, science fiction, and comics. She went looking for erotica all on her own. Her first novel, also featuring Teresa Knight, was *Strip Poker*.